Finding Cl

A Novel

by

Daniel Murphy

Contents

1. Missing

The phone said It was six thirty already. Nick Innocenti looked in the hall mirror, adjusted his shirt collar, looked away, sniffed, rubbed his nose and looked again. What he saw there was an older, male version of his daughter Ruth... bigger too - he was six two and a tidy fourteen stone. But despite the obvious differences, there were many similarities: the same slightly bent nose, the same dark eyes, the same smooth olive skin he'd inherited from his father and Ruth had inherited from him in her turn. He patted his flat stomach, squared his shoulders, adjusted his collar again. He'd be forty next year, but he was still looking OK.

What was there to be anxious about, anyway? It was only Dorothy he was phoning... only Dorothy, his mother-in-law. Well, was she still his mother-in-law, even though it was three years since Clare's death? Whatever... she was still Ruth's grandmother, still part of the family. In fact, since Nick's father was long dead, and his own mother was stuck in late-stage dementia and had long since stopped recognising him, Dorothy was effectively the last member of the older generation. He looked at the photo that came up with her number - her eyes staring straight at him... but it wasn't those sharp eyes that were making him nervous: it was having to say out loud some of what he'd been thinking, having to put into words that he didn't know where Ruth was, to admit that he didn't know why she wasn't home, to accept that he didn't know what had happened to her.

Ok, it had only been a few hours, but that was time enough for his imagination to have been working hard on some of the possibilities... and most of those possibilities were undesirable possibilities. No, they weren't just undesirable. They were extremely undesirable, gut-wrenchingly undesirable: possibilities nobody would ever want to think about... but once those possibilities entered your brain, it was difficult to find room for anything else.

He walked over to the window and pressed 'call'. Dorothy picked up on the third ring.

'Nick,' she said, 'This is a surprise.' She cleared her throat. 'I don't expect calls from you on a wet Friday evening.'

You shouldn't expect calls from me on any evening, he thought. And how did she manage to inflect her words with that tone of matronly disapproval she had perfected, somehow to convey a message, simply by the tone of her voice, that whatever he had done or was doing, it wasn't quite up to the mark?

'Aye...' he replied, attempting an upbeat tone, 'it's wet here too... and... eh... the thing is Dorothy ... the thing is... I was just kind of wondering...'

'Wondering what?' she interrupted.

'Eh... I was just.... eh... kind of wondering...eh... well... whether Ruth is with you.'

'Ruth? With me?' she said, 'Why would she be with me?'

Yes... why would she be with Dorothy? Now that he was asking her, he wished he hadn't. 'Well... ' he stumbled, 'She said she might be late home... and I'm late back from work... and eh...'

'And?'

'Well... she still isn't home, and...eh... her phone goes straight to voicemail. I'm sure it's all fine but just to check, y'know. She's been talking about going over to see you one of these weekends. I kindof thought...'

'Did she say she was going to come over this weekend?'

'Eh... no... I don't think she did.'

'You don't think?'

'Well, eh... perhaps she did, but I just heard her saying she'd be late... I... eh... like I said... eh... that's why I was just... eh... kind of wondering if she was with you.'

'Well she's not.'

Nick looked out the window. The rain was stotting off the paving stones in the front garden, soaking the lawn, battering down the faded nasturtiums that'd carried on flowering so well through autumn. But it was November now. He should have taken them out already. If Ruth was still out in this she'd be soaked through.

'Nick? Are you still there?'

'Yes Dorothy. I'm here.' He took another breath. 'Do you remember that time before – that was a Friday as well, wasn't it? I was worried where she might be, but it turned out she'd taken the train to Queen Street and then walked all the way out to your place?'

'Of course I remember Nick! And it was never going to happen again, was it?... Nick?... Well?... Was it?'

Nick could almost hear the expression on her face.

'So where do you imagine she might be this time?'

'I thought I should try you first.' ...and what was a bad idea that was!... 'Anyway... since she's not with you, I'll need to phone some of her friends.'

'Not good is it? A girl her age. Coming home every day from that school to an empty house...'

Nick bit his lip... took the phone away from his ear while she carried on talking... Dorothy had so many ways of making it clear, not least through the tone of her voice, that she thought she could do a better job of bringing up Ruth than he could. After Clare's death, she'd offered to look after Ruth during the week: 'After all,' she'd said, 'You're always too busy with your work Nick, aren't you? And for a young woman of her age... there are so many things it'd be easier to talk about with another woman...'

Dorothy had provided what she thought were good arguments... had even offered to pay for Ruth to attend Hutchesons Grammar: *'Hutchie,'* she'd said, 'would be *so* much better for Ruth - smaller classes, better teaching, compared to... eh... what's the name of that school you send her to in Stirling?' Just coincidentally, *Hutchie was* also much nearer to

Dorothy's house in South Glasgow. Nick had sometimes risen to the bait before and arguments had ensued, but none of their many previous exchanges on the topic - what she saw as the merits of private schooling for the individuals involved and what he saw as its social costs for the community at large - had ended amicably. Anyway, it wasn't just schooling that they disagreed about... it was always the same with her: behind every question, every suggestion, there was an implication, and within every implication a veiled accusation: how could someone in his position possibly think that they were capable of bringing up a teenage girl? How could he possibly give her all that she needed? And the thing was... well... maybe she was right? After all, here he was at home on a wet Friday evening... and he didn't know where she was... his daughter... his only daughter... didn't know where she was. He breathed out... a long breath... and put the phone back to his ear.

'I'm sorry I got you worried, Dorothy,' he said. 'I'm sure she'll turn up... you know what teenagers are like. I'll phone some other people.'

'You'll keep me posted Nick, won't you?'

'I'll phone you back once I know what's ha... I mean, eh... where she is.'

'As soon as, Nick. As soon as.'

Nick walked through to the kitchen and took a few deep breaths. It'd been hard for him and Dorothy to get on, right from the earliest days - she was old-fashioned South Glasgow perjink: smart tweed suit and pearls; sprightly, sparkly eyes that missed nothing; a tongue like an educated razor. It was bad enough, she made clear in so many subtle and not-so-subtle ways, that Clare had wanted to marry a landscape gardener, and worse, an organic, vegetarian, bean-eating semi-hippy with little apparent ambition, in the conventional sense anyway; but to marry a second generation Scots-Italian-Catholic semi-hippy landscape gardener... could her daughter have chosen any worse?

He put on a kettle and phoned Pam Fraser: maybe she'd know where Ruth was - sometimes Ruth used to come home late on Fridays after attending the school swimming club with the Fraser girls, though she'd not been swimming for a while. But he drew a blank there as well: Pam confirmed that Ruth hadn't been at swimming and no, she didn't know where else Ruth might be, not did the girls.

Next, he called another good friend of Ruth's: Arlene McSorley. Nick thought Arlene was a good influence on Ruth: an old-fashioned sort of girl - studious, quiet, well-mannered. But Arlene had no more information to offer. She told him that after she and Ruth had walked from school to the roundabout at Causewayhead, they'd gone their different ways, just as usual. And no, Ruth hadn't said anything about going on somewhere else. Arlene had assumed she was going home, like every other day.

So why wasn't she home yet?

Nick wanted a drink. A stiff whisky. But he'd maybe have to go out in his pickup and collect her from somewhere, wherever she was. What the hell was she playing at? Life was difficult enough already without this kind of crap on a Friday evening. He wanted to kick something, punch something. Where the hell was she? What would Clare do, if she'd still been around? He could almost hear her voice: *Calm down Nick. Give it a bit of space. Give* her *a bit of space.* So bloody rational, Clare: still trying to keep him calm from beyond the grave.

He walked through to the kitchen. The rain was driving against the window. The trees in the back garden were heaving in the wind. A wild night to be out. His phone rang: Dorothy again.

'I thought you were going to phone me back Nick,' she said, 'I'm worried sick now.'

'No. Sorry. I was just about to,' why was he apologising? It'd only been a few minutes. 'I've been trying some of her friends but no luck so far.'

'How could you not know where she is Nick?'

Nick took the phone away from his ear, looked at Dorothy's photo, counted to three, put the phone back to his ear. He spoke in a measured, deliberate voice. 'She always lets me know where she is. Otherwise, I wouldn't have bothered you... would I?'

'It's no bother. She is my only granddaughter after all.'

'Yes. And she's my only daughter for Christ's sake!' he shouted at Dorothy's photo on the phone, 'My only daughter!', then immediately regretted letting go: Dorothy had only had one daughter too: Clare... his wife... Ruth's mother. And Clare was dead. Oh God! What would he do if Ruth was dead? No. That was a stupid thought. She'd just have met some friends at the shops after she'd left Arlene... hanging out with them... thoughtless. And she was always forgetting to charge her phone. She was just...

'Nick...' Dorothy's voice was softer, hesitant, 'Are you still there?... Nick?'

'Yes Dorothy. Look, I'm sorry... I'm worried... and I'm getting myself into a bit of a state... I'm sure I don't need to.' He sat down on one of the kitchen stools, resting his head on his left hand. 'She's almost fifteen now. We tend to forget that. She can look after herself. It's only been a couple of hours. She'll be fine...' He hesitated, cleared his throat. 'I'm sorry I shouted there, Dorothy. It's just... well I don't like just hanging around. Waiting. Wondering what to do next.'

'I can come over? It's less than an hour in the car?'

That'd be the last thing he wanted.

'No. It's fine. I'll keep you posted. Probably just forgot to charge her phone battery or something.'

'Phone me the minute she comes in Nick.'

'Of course. It'll be fine....' He scratched his head. 'I'm sure she's fine. You know what kids are like.'

But he knew it wasn't fine.

And Ruth wasn't any other kid.

And it hadn't happened before.

* * *

He toured the house again, looking into each room on the ground floor, taking the stairs two at a time before poking his head round the door of each bedroom... again. Back downstairs, he looked in the hall cupboard. Back upstairs, he pulled down the loft ladder, poked his head up. Of course she wasn't anywhere in the house... he knew that... but he had to look somewhere... and if not here, then where else could he look?

He checked his phone again. Had he forgotten something she'd told him before? He looked through previous phone messages again. Checked his e.mail, *Facebook, Whatsapp.*

He checked round the house again, every room, the walk-in cupboards.

He took a walk round the block.

He walked the route to school and back.

Shortly after 8, and after another discussion with Dorothy, he phoned the police.

The call handler took down the details - her description, where she was last seen, what she was wearing. She was calm, reassuring: of course he was bound to be worried, but almost all missing teenagers turned up safe and well; all local patrols would be alerted; meantime he should call back at any time, and especially if he had any more information.

'Is that it?' he asked. 'I just sit and wait?'

'Call again later in the evening, sir,' she said calmly, 'Patrols will be notified. They may well spot her. And you will let us know,' she said, 'If she turns up.'

Let them know? Let them know! He'd more than let her know! He'd be running round town screaming it at the top of his voice, shouting to anyone that wanted to listen. If she came back safe and sound, what would he not do? And what would he not give now to hear the door opening, her voice calling him... 'Dad... I'm home!'?

Good God how could this be happening?!

She was going to get a piece of his mind when she got home!

No! It'd be the opposite! He'd hug her. Hold on to her. Tell her how wonderful she was.

Without a drink to calm him down, Nick was like a coiled spring. He thought about taking a quick drive into town - just the main streets - but he didn't fancy driving slowly around like some kind of kerb crawler, peering at kids on a Friday night... that's if anyone was out on the streets: the November rain was very cold. Maybe he could run round the streets instead of driving? If he was running, he'd soon heat up. And it might calm him down: running had been his refuge since Clare's death. And the kind of running he often did, running punishingly hard, pushed the stress out of his mind and into his body. He put on his wet weather gear, tucked his phone in his pocket and left a note at the door for Ruth asking her to call him as soon as she got in.

As he headed across the narrow pedestrian bridge from Cambuskenneth, over the Forth and on towards the busy centre of Stirling, he could see the floodlit mediaeval castle sitting high on the rock above, commanding the river crossing: that was one place he didn't need to look surely - the castle. What about the river? No, he wasn't going to think about that... definitely was not going to think about that.

In town, he ran past a few half-drunk smokers milling about at a pub door, then carried on down the deserted main shopping street: bereft of shoppers, it looked a bit run down - another newly empty shopfront, a closing-down sale at *Lookers*, naked mannequins in the window. At the crossroads, he took the road up the hill towards the castle, then back down and across the mediaeval footbridge. Once over the river, he ran up through the Cornton housing scheme, the wind driving rain into his face. A crowd of teenagers was sheltering under an awning round the corner from the chip shop. From the look of them, most of them'd still be at school - Ruth's school, Bruce Academy. They stopped talking as he slowed down. Two of the girls looked him up and down.

'Any of you guys seen Ruth Innocenti around?' he asked.

A tall lad at the back of the group shouted out. 'Who's askin likes?'

'I'm her old man. Just wondered where she was hanging out?'

'Somewhere you canny find her,' one of the girls said. The rest of the group laughed.

'OK... thanks... well if you do see her, can you ask her to give me a call?'

'Aye grandad,' one of the boys said, smirking at his pals. 'Sure we will.'

They laughed some more.

He looked at his watch and ran on. Thirty minutes since he'd left the house. No phone call yet. He was worrying himself over nothing. She was probably home by now, recharging the damn phone battery: she'd been complaining at the weekend how she needed a new phone, how her crap battery didn't even last the day at school. 'Not surprising,' he'd said to her, 'seeing as how it's never out your hands. And anyway,' he'd shouted back at her as she headed up the stairs to her room, 'I thought you had to switch it off at school?'

She hadn't answered that question.

This was never going to happen again. He'd make sure of that... the best phone, the longest lasting battery... whatever it took. Anything. Any damn phone. Whatever it took.

There was nothing to see as he ran back down past the University, no-one about on the wet Friday night streets. He picked up speed as he passed the Causewayhead roundabout and kept up a high tempo on the home stretch, down the country road to their mid-terrace cottage in Cambuskenneth, close to the ruins of the mediaeval abbey. It was well after 10. Still no phone call.

Where was she?

Where the hell was she?

* * *

After a hot shower, he put his day clothes back on and poured himself a cold beer – surely no-one would blame him for having one beer, even if he had to drive somewhere to get her? He placed the empty bottle carefully by the sink, walked up the stairs into Ruth's attic bedroom and sat on her bed. There was enough light from the hall for him to make out the dark shapes in the room. It was this room that had sold them on the house. 'It'd make a lovely nursery,' he remembered Clare saying, 'It faces north so we can keep it darker. And when she grows up, it'll be a great bedroom for a teenager.' He remembered the day they'd bought the little sleepeasy cot, the two of them wallpapering the room with stupid cartoon elephants dressed in frilly pink tutus. He couldn't remember if that had been Dorothy's idea but decided to blame her anyway. It certainly wouldn't have been his. The elephants hadn't lasted long once Ruth went to school: she'd never been much of a girl for pink. Or frilly tutus.

This was the house, the house with the little back garden, the house that Clare had loved - near the river, near her friends. Cambuskenneth was more like a country village - farms and fields on three sides, the river on the fourth – but it was only a footbridge away from the town, a short bicycle ride in the other direction to the University where Clare worked. Nick had wanted to move away after she died, the cottage had too many reminders of a life that was gone. The only reason they were still there was because it was what Ruth had wanted: even though she'd been just eleven when her Mum died, she'd already had a persuasive way about her, a way of capturing feelings in words. 'We can't leave here Dad,' she'd said, 'This is where our hearts are.'

He'd not had any better words.

He took another long slug of the beer. Any remaining anger was completely gone now. All that was left was worry... or was it fear?

He checked his phone again. Volume was up full. Battery still had plenty charge... but checking his phone every few minutes wasn't going to make it ring. He texted her again: *Where you at Ruth? Whatever's happened, it'll be fine. Just let me know you're OK. I can come and get you. Anywhere. Just call.*

He put his phone down then picked it up again.

We'll go up to the shops tomorrow morning and get you a new phone.

He put his phone down again, then picked it up again... put it back down, picked it up again. *Any phone you want,* he texted, *The best in the shop.*

He swallowed the last of the beer before heading back down to the kitchen for another. But once there, he put the kettle on instead: no more drink tonight for him... he might need to drive. He paced round the house, waiting for the kettle to boil – how many times had he had he searched for her round the house, when she was just a wee girl, playing hide'n'seek, opening each door, switching on each light, to find her hiding, under the bed, behind the desk, waiting to surprise him... and then he'd chase her, giggling, round the house...?

If only.

He took his cup of tea upstairs into her bedroom. This time he put the light on, took a slug and phoned Greg Bright: Greg's wife Sheila had been one of Clare's closest friends: she worked as a tutor at the University; Clare and she used to walk together round the University Loch at lunchtimes or run together up the hill and round the Cocksburn Reservoir. Greg and Sheila had been very supportive during Clare's illness, and Nick had become friends with Greg as a result: they played squash together, ran together, drank together. Greg worked for the Council - building control and planning. He'd put in a word for Nick and his organic gardening business with some of his contacts. And Sheila's friendship had been good for Ruth after Clare died – a warm female friend who was comfortable with parts of adolescent Ruth that Nick had no chance of reaching.

'I can't get away mate,' Greg said, after Nick had explained the reason for the call. 'Sheila's out... her *wimmen's* book group, so I'm stuck here with the kids. D'you want to come over here while you're waiting?'

'Can't,' Nick said, 'Need to be here. I'll phone you in the morning.'

'Any time,' Greg said, 'And if you want anything meantime, just holler.'

A pair of Ruth's jeans and a heavy cotton check shirt were lying on the floor beside the bed. Nick threw them over towards the door. He'd put a wash on later... with her school clothes... once she came in. He lined up her shoes under the bed in neat pairs. He tucked the chair in under her desk and rustled through the messy papers on top: History and Chemistry homework, some scrunched-up post-its, a Biology revision book. The laptop was lying open - only a couple of years old, her laptop, but it was tatty-looking now. They'd already agreed she'd get a new one at Christmas. He stroked his fingers across the rough white surface that was all that was left of a label she'd stuck on the lid: the label used to say *Keep out unless you're Ruth Innocenti!!!* but it was half torn off now. Life had been so much simpler, so much easier, when she was just a girl... before the teenage years kicked in, before the social challenges of secondary school... and now this crap on a Friday night!

He closed the lid, tidied up the bedclothes and propped Cromarty, her teddy, up against the pillow. Cromarty's arms and legs were worn bare by years of affection. She might be growing up fast, but it was Cromarty that still got her cuddles at night. He flicked through the clothes hanging in her wardrobe. Her blue fleece smelled of smoke. They'd argued about smoking a couple of weeks before.

'I've only done it a couple of times,' she'd huffed, 'And I didn't inhale.'

'Don't do it at all,' he'd said.

He pulled out one of her sweaters and held it to his face. He'd bought it for her last Christmas... or was it the one before? It carried a clean, fresh smell, her favourite perfume – *Linen*. He dropped the sweater on the bed and took his cup back to the kitchen. When he returned to her room, the scent from the sweater was everywhere. It must be good quality, he thought: a present from Dorothy wasn't it? He switched off the light, closed the door, lay on her bed and pulled out his phone. No call. No text. No *whatsapp*. Tried her again. No answer. Opened Radio 3, the previous night's *Late Junction* - a slow saxophone solo. He picked up Cromarty, rested his head on the pillow, stretched out.

Thinking back over the events of the past few years, it was still so hard to believe, all that had happened. Clare had thought she was just being clumsy - dropping glasses, dropping her case at the airport, tripping on the front step. When she'd started having difficulty swallowing, they'd gone to see the GP. The specialist diagnosis had followed.

'How long have I got?' Clare asked.

'It's very hard to say,' he remembered the consultant saying, 'In the worst case, it may only be a few months, but a few people are still living good lives twenty years on or more. These are the extremes. With mobility aids, communication aids, the majority of people with MND can still have a good life for a number of years. And each case is different.'

Though they'd both been determined that she should live at home as long as possible, Clare's symptoms had progressed much more rapidly than had been expected. She lasted only nine months from diagnosis to the final few days in the hospice. And what a fantastic help Ruth was, right from the beginning, especially with her Mum's communication. They'd spent evenings together, trying to understand the mechanics of the illness from websites, online publications. She seemed to take it all in her stride - different forms of medication, their side effects, 'Advance Care Planning' - so many things a child shouldn't have had to learn about.

After her Mum's death, Ruth had rededicated herself to her school work, mapping out her future. 'When I grow up Dad,' she'd said, full of the naïve optimism of a child, 'I'm going to be a doctor, a research doctor. I'm going to work on early preventive interventions for degenerative neurological conditions.' What a mouthful for a wee girl. What a special kid she'd been back then. It was only more recently that teenage Ruth had emerged – less communicative, harder to understand. Well, harder for him to understand anyway – hormones, bleeding, minute features of her appearance that caused emotional storms. It was such a privilege to have this young woman in his life, but he knew he hadn't handled some things well.

He hadn't handled a lot of things well.

He shut down the radio and phoned the police again. 'She still hasn't turned up,' he said, 'Nothing from her phone. My daughter isn't just any kid. She just doesn't "stay out." She's out there somewhere... in trouble.'

The call handler was very reassuring: the same message. Local police patrols would be informed again. They'd phone immediately if she turned up. He could phone in anytime, especially if he had any new information. In any event, they'd phone him in the morning and someone would probably call round... if she hadn't turned up by then. Was there someone who could come over to be with him? Or someone he could go to? One way or another he should try to get some sleep.

'Sleep!' he thought, 'Sleep! How the hell do you expect me to sleep!' But he said nothing.

He texted Dorothy: *Phoned police yet again. Still no word. Try to get some sleep. I'll call you immediately she turns up. I'm sure she will.*

Dorothy texted straight back: *Pray God she does.*

He poured himself another beer now. And with it a whisky – *Laphroaig*, a large one. It burned his throat and that felt good. He drank the beer and poured another. Another whisky too. There was only rubbish on the tellie. He picked up the magazine supplement from the previous weekend's newspaper. On the cover, some minor female celebrity he didn't recognise was lying back on a sofa: *Doing It My Way*, the headline said. What crap! He threw it angrily across the room. He went back upstairs to Ruth's bedroom and lay on her bed, put on his headphones, searched YouTube for Gordon Duncan's *Sleeping Tune,* Duncan Chisholm's gentle violin… on repeat… in his ears… in his head… right inside his brain.

At some point, he must've drifted off to sleep. When he woke at six, his neck stiff, he saw a half-empty mug of tea, an empty whisky glass and Cromarty, sitting on the floor beside him.

'Where is she, Cromarty?' he said. 'Where the hell is she?'

2. Weekend

Saturday wasn't so much a day… more like a year.

He was up before 7, wanted to call the police straight away but thought maybe he should wait… she'd just turn up… kids did this sort of thing… he'd done it himself when he was young… not as young as Ruth right enough, but certainly when he was still at school… no, maybe not… she was going to get some talking to when she got in… no she wasn't…

He decided he needed to keep himself calm, keeping at bay the panic that was threatening to spill out and send his emotions running rampant. He completed his morning exercise routine - stretching, three sets of weights, an extra set of reps with each, a long plank. After his shower he looked at himself in the bedroom mirror, slapped his stomach – no softness there. He pulled back his shoulders and ran his fingers through his hair, a few grey strands among the black now; white t-shirt from the drawer, faded blue jeans from the wardrobe. He turned sideways on to the mirror, put his hands on his rump. 'I like your tight little bum,' Clare used to say when he wore those jeans. Clare was gone. And what if Ruth was gone too? Would he start to date again?

He frowned. How could you think such a thing? But you did, didn't you? It wasn't your fault, you didn't want these thoughts, but no matter how much you were pretending that this was just another day, that Ruth would be safe somewhere, random thoughts, unwelcome thoughts, could pop into your head from nowhere… thoughts that could turn your world upside down.

Yet here he was, and he was still the right way up. Ruth was missing and he was standing in front of a mirror trying to pretend this was just another day… and let's face it, it was absolutely necessary to pretend… cos if he let his mind rip, really let it rip, he had no frigging idea where it might end up.

He shook his head, shouted at the man in the mirror: 'Get a grip, Innocenti! Get a bloody grip!'

And anyway, never mind Ruth. What the hell were the police doing? They should have phoned him by now. What the hell were they doing that they couldn't just give him a quick call? Changing shift maybe, hand-over routines to go through? Yes, that was it. They'd've called already if there was anything to report, anything bad. Yes, that was it. They'd only have called if it was something bad. He had to remain calm, stay in control. Not calling was a good sign. He'd phone them at 8 if they still hadn't called by then. Wasn't that what they'd said?

He went back downstairs, put on the radio. Just a lot of noise. None of it mattered. He switched it off. He gave the kitchen a going over - worktops, sink, floor. When his phone did eventually ring, around 7.50, his nervous fingers fumbled with the screen and he dropped it. Thank God it still kept ringing. He picked it up and could barely focus on the two choices side by side. His hand was trembling. He steadied himself and pressed 'answer'.

It was a new call handler. 'Is your daughter still missing?' she asked.

Yes of course she bloody well was!!!! What the hell did they think? Didn't they know that if she'd come home, he'd have been phoning them, phoning every bloody person in his phonebook, running up and down the street shouting for joy that she was safe, that she was home. Didn't they bloody well know that? He took a calming breath. 'Yes,' he said. 'I would've called you straight away if she'd turned up.'

'Well,' she said, 'The night patrols have called nothing in. In fact,' she said, 'It's been a very quiet Friday night, with it being such horrible weather, drives everyone indoors.' Why would she think he was interested in whether or not it was a quiet night, for God's sake!! 'An officer will call down to see you in person this morning to get more details,' she said, 'Will you still be in?'

He looked out of the window. The rain showed no signs of letting up.

'Yes, I'll be in.'

He phoned Dorothy, told her Ruth still hadn't shown up, that the police hadn't found her. 'I don't know what to think,' she said, 'It's what I expected when you didn't call. They say no news is good news, but it doesn't feel like it.'

'I fell asleep on her bed.' he said, 'With Cromarty,' he added. 'I felt closer to her - him and me together. We were both missing her.'

'Cromarty? She loves that bear, doesn't she?' He could picture her satisfied smile. She'd given Ruth that teddy, named it for the holiday home her family used to have up North. 'So,' she said, 'What do we do now?'

'I'm just sitting here waiting for the police to call round – I guess they'll ask a few more questions, take a few more details, tell us what they're doing, advise us what we should do. What else is there?'

'You could do what I've been doing since I go up before six,' she said, 'Check the Police Scotland website: missing persons. I've been on other 'missing' sites as well. It's mainly middle-aged men seem to go missing, but at the bottom of the page it tells you what to do if you're worried about someone. And there's an organisation called *Missing People*, a charity... there's a helpline as well. You might want to look them up? I would've phoned them, but I didn't want to without asking you first.'

'That sounds like it's for runaways... but Ruth's no runaway, definitely no runaway,' he said, 'Why don't we just wait for the police for now?'

'I suppose you're right... it's just... well... I want to do something. I just feel so powerless.'

'Me too,' he said. He scratched his chin. 'And I'd be going daft if I was just sitting doing nothing. I've found it's better if you're doing something, something physical... I've given the kitchen the best clean it's had in years. If it wasn't raining, I'd get out and wash the pickup, remove every single weed in the garden... '

'Nick, you need people round you,' she said, 'It's not good to be on your own.'

Nick took the phone from his ear and looked at her photo - Dorothy: he'd never been good enough for her. He never would be. Dorothy's opinion of him had never altered from the very first time they met: why had her wonderful, beautiful, intelligent daughter Clare, the latest in a long family line of advocates and doctors, a daughter who could've done anything, been anything... why had she married a man whose life's ambition was organic gardening?

'I'm going to come through,' he heard her say. Away from his ear her voice sounded softer.

'Look Dorothy, just give me time to see the police and work out what's what, then I'll phone you back. I'm expecting them any minute.'

'I've phoned her Auntie Yvonne, just in case... Ruth and Yvonne get on so well.'

'Oh... Yes...' Aunt Yvonne, Dorothy's sister down in Wales: Ruth and Dorothy had visited her a couple of times in the school holidays. 'I never even thought. I mean... Wales? Ruth's never been that kind of distance on her own...'

'There's a lot of things she's never done before.'

Nick stood up and walked over to the window again and punched the wall. A blue Ford was driving past. The rain was bouncing off its roof. 'Yes. I suppose so,' he said.

'So... Nick...' The tone was very much in Dorothy's natural style: strong... directive... in charge. 'You'll phone me straight away, won't you? I can't settle. I'm like the proverbial cat on a hot tin roof. You know what that girl means to me.'

Of course he knew. Her only grandchild. Of course he knew.

But whatever she meant to Dorothy, it wasn't a fraction of what she meant to him.

* * *

Two constables, a man and a woman, arrived not long after. They told him their names, but he forgot them immediately. The woman looked nearer Ruth's age than his. She had a kind reassuring manner - quick, knowledgeable, efficient. Her gangly partner was a good bit older, overweight. He just seemed to hover apologetically, letting her do most of the talking. 'Couldn't find a prostitute in a brothel, that one,' his Uncle Raymondo would've said - Uncle Raymondo: wise, witty man - he'd doted on Ruth. He'd have been the first person Nick would've called... if he'd still been around.

They asked him for the details of what he thought she was wearing – he'd said it all on the phone, but they wanted him to go over it again: no, he didn't know if she had had plans for the previous evening... he'd assumed she would be home, as usual; no, there were no clothes or anything missing from her room; no, there were no particular issues he was aware of at the moment. 'Just the usual teenage stuff,' he said.

'Such as?' the woman PC asked.

'You know, boys... hair.... falling out with friends... falling back in again...'

The questions went on. He answered as fully as he could. Yes, they had their disagreements... Didn't all fathers have disagreements with their teenage daughters?... He didn't know if they had more than usual... Yes of course she missed her mother, but he was trying the best he could... There were other relatives she was close to, especially her Gran in Glasgow – she spent a fair bit of time there - and there was her Aunt Yvonne, her Gran's sister... She was in Wales. His own father was dead, long since... His mother was in care... Dementia... Eastercroft Care Home... Yes, he and Ruth visited his mother once a week.... No, he didn't have a girlfriend at the moment... Yes, Ruth had 'run away' before, but it wasn't really running away - just to her Gran... and only once... a couple of months back actually... They'd had a silly argument.... He couldn't remember what about, but it wasn't important.

'Important enough for her to go to Glasgow on her own,' the woman constable insisted.

'Well, yes,' he said, 'Of course it was important to her obviously or she wouldn't have gone to her Gran like that but it's just...' He'd been going to say, 'it's just it didn't seem important to me,' but stopped himself in time. The tone of the interview wasn't exactly adversarial, but he was becoming aware that it didn't feel supportive either.

The questions carried on.

No, he wasn't aware of any big issues brewing more recently... No, there had been nothing out of the ordinary, at least as far as he was aware... No, they got on very well... well... usually. He'd just been in the house on Friday evening... No, that was wrong... he'd forgotten that he'd gone out for a run, looking for her... Yes, in the rain... Just round the town, up into Bridge of Allan and back... No, he didn't think anyone had seen him... No, he'd said already there were no problems between Ruth and him.... No, he didn't know why she didn't come home... wasn't that the whole point? Wasn't that why he'd phoned them?

There was a pause in the questioning as the woman constable finished writing in her notebook. Her gangly male partner stood up and walked over to the patio doors, looking out into the small back garden. 'Nice houses here,' he said, 'Quiet.'

The woman constable coughed. 'We'll just need a bit more information, sir,' she said.

He gave her Dorothy's details, Ruth's phone number, the numbers of some of Ruth's friends. He described her usual route home from school, confirmed where her friends had last seen her. She briefed him on the next few steps. Officers would follow up with school contacts, particularly those friends she'd been with at the end of the school day. Information would be posted on the Police Scotland website. News agencies would be contacted. They asked him to email in a recent photo. If nothing came from the initial enquiries and she was still missing, they'd start to check mobile phone and internet, look at her online life. Meantime, if he came up with anything – from friends, laptop, diaries – he should let them know. As things developed, they might arrange a search of locations on or near to her route home.

'Will you look at the river?' he asked.

‘We may do,’ the male constable said, ‘But it’s not top of the list at this stage. Unless, of course, there’s a special reason you would think we should look there?’

‘No,’ he said, ‘But what do I know? It was just an ordinary Friday and now I don’t know where my daughter is.’

They advised him not to be on his own, to get one of his family over, or a friend. They promised to keep in touch regularly. And then that was that.

They went away.

They left him alone.

* * *

He emailed two recent photos of Ruth to the email address they’d given him, then spent some time on the internet. The missing persons’ websites didn’t help - stories of missing children, some of them teenage girls, Ruth’s age: troubled girls. Not like her. This was something that happened to other people, somewhere else.

Not here.

Not him.

The phone rang in his pocket, making him jump. It was Greg. ‘We’re going to come over mate: Sheila says you’ve not to be on your own.’

‘I need to get out Greg,’ he said, ‘It’s driving me daft sitting here doing nothing. I think I’m going to explode if I don’t burn off some of the nervous energy that’s boiling up inside me. I’m desperate to get out for a run and if Sheila’s here maybe she can stay while we go out together? We could run up through the Uni... or maybe over to Cambusbarron?’

‘Wait till I see what Sheila says,’ Greg said... A moment later he was back on. ‘Fine,’ he said, ‘We’ll all come over - Sheila and the girls’ll wait at your house and she’ll get some grub ready while you and me get out for a run. Sheila bought a bunch of second-hand DVDs recently... you’ve still got an old player somewhere, haven’t you? I seem to remember you’ve kept all the old technology... like a museum, your place, isn’t it? Anyway, apparently, the girls have been desperate to start Series 3 of *Hannah Montana* – whatever that is.’

‘Tell you what,’ Nick said, ‘Wear your running gear. I’ll run up and meet you on the road that goes up past to the back entrance to the Uni – look out for me on the road... I can hand the key over to Sheila so they can just let themselves into the house... 20 minutes?’

Before Nick set out on the run, he phoned Dorothy again. ‘I don’t think it’s wise to leave the house,’ she said, ‘What if she turns up? What if you can’t get a signal where you’re running and she’s trying the landline?’

‘Dorothy,’ he said, ‘I’ve got it covered.’ Just what the hell did she think he was... some kind of idiot? ‘I’m going quietly mad here. If she calls, I can be back at the house in no time.’

‘I’m coming through Nick. Someone should be there if she comes home.’

'No. I said already. I've taken care of it. I've got Sheila - you know, Clare's friend Sheila - she's coming over with the girls. Ruth likes Sheila... and she loves those little girls.'

'Don't cut me out of this Nick.'

'I'm not cutting you out Dorothy. How many times have I phoned you already? You're first on my list to call if anything comes up. But I just need to get out. OK?'

'Looks like I don't have a choice.'

'Dorothy. Just remember,' he scratched his head vigorously, 'You're first on the list.'

* * *

Greg spotted Nick at the side of the road as he and Sheila drove in from Menstrie. Nick passed the house keys over to Sheila and the two men headed uphill and out onto the Sheriffmuir Road. Greg used to be a triathlete - competed at his age-group level in his native Australia - but he carried a few more pounds now, a good few more, so from time-to-time Nick pushed on, accelerating for a few hundred yards then running back to meet Greg. In this way they kept together after a fashion, but they didn't do much talking as Greg was struggling and Nick was really pushing himself, pushing his body to the edge of its capability, burning up in hard physical exercise the thoughts that he didn't want to have. It took them 90 minutes or so to get up and down. They were wet through when they got back to his house.

Standing in the hot shower afterwards, Nick thought of his mother, how she must have worried about him the times he'd been out of contact as a student, hitching across Canada, camping in France. But that was different then... he'd been in his late teens... no, early twenties... he would've kept in touch with his folks back them, if he'd had social media available, wouldn't he? But he'd never been welcome in whatever social media Ruth and her pals were using. And texting etiquette with Ruth had been so tricky: unintended meanings that might have been read into what was said, or even worse what was unsaid, calls that were made or not made, the absence of an emoticon. And anyway, what teenage girl wanted her dad following her online? Surely one of her friends would have phoned him if there'd been anything bad on Instagram or snapchat or...? He turned up the shower thermostat some more, blasted himself with the hot water till his skin was red, but he came out feeling strangely better - less on edge. There must be something wrong with him. How was it possible to feel better at a time like this?

Nick stepped out the shower and started towelling himself dry.

How he was missing Clare. She was the one who had sorted him out. Before he met her, he'd been living in his own little fantasy world, imagining himself as some kind of latter-day Thoreau, imagining that he might create some kind of 21st Century Walden Pond in Scotland, whereas, in reality, he'd just been a useless procrastinator. If she hadn't come along and swept him up, he'd still be dreaming unattainable dreams... and doing very little to make them a reality. She'd forced him to meet her in the real world. 'If you want to build a better future' she'd said, 'You need to be *in* the world, not running away from it.' She could scold him alright: 'You're too much in your own head Nick. You don't seem to need friends. But relationships are important. People need relationships to keep their lives in balance.' She'd always been able to find words when he couldn't find his own words. 'You're a hard shell with a soft centre, Nick. Too many emotions bouncing around inside. You need to let them out.' No wonder no other woman matched up.

Two years after Clare's death, there might've been a bit of a something with Angie - one of the women in the MND support group. They'd met up a couple of times, but it hadn't felt right. And he hadn't had the right words to explain to Angie what was going on for him, words to stop the competing emotions churning. And he'd probably just imagined there was more to her friendship than there really was... Angie was just a kind, empathetic woman: a kind woman. He could do with someone kind in his life now, someone to share with, someone like Angie. He looked at his face in the mirror as he towelled himself dry. He looked calm. But that didn't mean he wasn't raging.

* * *

There was a smell of home-made soup and bread from downstairs. Alice and Jess were making a noise, playing with Ruth's old Playmobil doll's house. They were just eight and six, the girls. It was good to have people here, people he loved. He joined Sheila in the kitchen: her warm, round face, her big smiles.

As Nick walked in, she took a floppy strand of his wavy hair and tucked it back behind his ear. 'Dear Nick,' she said, 'She'll be OK. You'll see. She's a very sensible girl.'

'What I wouldn't give now...' he said but as his voice faltered, he walked away to the window and looked out at the rain. It was turning into one of those miserable November afternoons. It was so gloomy they had to switch the lights on.

Cold rain was beating loud against the patio doors.

* * *

After lunch, they found some of Ruth's old toys for the girls in the upstairs cupboard and set them off building a small Lego village in front of the log stove in the living room, its flames dancing in wee Jess's eyes. Jess played with the characters in the toy village the whole afternoon, but Alice insisted on getting out more of Ruth's old toys – ones she'd seen in the back of the upstairs cupboard. By mid-afternoon, there were toys everywhere and a small pretend grocery store had been set up on the stairs, with tins and cartons from the kitchen cupboards. When the adults weren't shopping from the girls' stairway store, Nick found a bit of time to bring his friends up to speed - the police, the website, his futile run round the town the previous night. Nick also spent some more time digging about in Ruth's room, but there were no more clues to where she might be.

At least the girls were having fun.

And time was passing.

An officer phoned about 5. There were no further specific leads from speaking to Ruth's classmates, but they were reviewing CCTV footage. A physical search of some areas on her route back from school was being set up - by the river, in the park at Causewayhead that she walked past, in the woods of the Abbey Craig. The heavy rain would make searches more difficult. Physical searches would stop overnight and resume in the morning. There was nothing more for him to do at this stage. They would keep him informed.

Nick put his phone back in his pocket. 'I'm going to Church,' he announced to his friends. 'Might as well give prayer a try. Nothing else seems to be working.'

'But this is Saturday,' Sheila said, a bit surprised: Nick and Church?

'No... there's a vigil Mass up the road at six. We used to go to there, you know, Clare, Ruth and me... well, me only occasionally, to be fair...' Sheila raised an eyebrow. 'I can walk up now and be back by half seven,' he said. 'What else is there anyway?'

Clare was the one who'd been interested in religion, attended church. She'd even persuaded him to go a few times, though he hadn't been back since her funeral. If Clare had still been around, she'd have been praying alright. He could never see the sense in it, but sense had nothing to do with what was going on now. None of what was happening made sense... and there was only a thin line between hope and desperation.

'If you guys want to wait on.' he said, 'I'll get in some pizzas on the way back down. Or is that too late for the girls?'

'Yeah! Pizzas!' Alice shouted. 'I want one all to myself.'

'Me too,' Jess said, 'I want my own pizza.'

'And you'll get one,' he said, and, picking her up under her arms, he flew her round and round the room, her pigtails flying out behind her.

'We'll get the place tidied up again while you're away,' Sheila said, 'Won't we girls?'

Greg followed Nick to the door 'I'll bring the car and pick you up,' he said. 'It's the big red one, up the hill isn't it, the Church?' Nick nodded. 'What time d'you want me there?' Greg asked, 'Half past? .... Quarter past? In fact,' he added, looking out at the rain, 'You're going to get absolutely soaked. Will I not just give you a run up there now?'

'It's fine,' Nick said, 'I want to walk. I'll see you around quarter past seven.'

* * *

Even though it'd been a good while since Nick had been to Church, one or two people recognised him... a couple nodded as he passed them on the way in. His parents had been stalwarts, same seat every week, so he sat near where they used to sit, where he used to sit as a boy. Not much had changed in the building, but he was surprised by the priest, one he hadn't seen before – young, energetic, articulate. The feast was *Christ the King* and the sermon the young priest delivered was refreshingly political – right on, actually. Nye Bevan was quoted: Bevan, the priest said, had argued that in the era of democracy, all citizens shared not just rights, but the responsibilities that in former times had been the sole preserve of kings. We exercised these responsibilities through our votes, our actions, our consumer choices. We had to be informed about the consequences for others of the choices we made, to exercise our power on behalf of all, not just ourselves. Nick was impressed. As an adult, he'd seen organised religion as a power in this world rather than the next, but even so this was unexpectedly direct – it was politics, pure and simple: heady stuff for the grey-haired congregation. He wondered how long the young priest would last.

In the prayers that followed, one was offered for Ruth Innocenti who'd 'gone missing', and for her father, 'who must be very worried'. One or two people looked round... maybe they'd clocked him coming in... but he kept his head down. He wondered who'd asked for the prayer. One of Clare's friends? But how had they found out? Had someone seen the police at the house? No... of course... the police had been speaking to some of her classmates. The word would be out there, right enough. Nobody was better at spreading news than teenage girls.

He left before the end, didn't want to have to speak to anyone – what would he say? He texted Greg: *I need a drink. Meet me in 'The Settle'?*

'Fifteen minutes,' came the instant reply, *'Set one up for me'*

While he was waiting, nursing his first beer at a quiet upstairs table, he googled *Ruth Innocenti Stirling*. She was already up on the Police Scotland missing persons website. One or two media websites had picked her up too.

She looked good in the picture the police had chosen – her jet-black hair, her wide generous smile: so good. Didn't she look so good? You could see the beautiful woman already there, emerging from the little girl she could still often be. He remembered taking that picture: it had been at the top of the Abbey Craig... after they'd run up there together earlier in the year... she was a good little runner, Ruth... a tryer... game... keeping at it... never giving up... even on the steep sections of the hill.

'What a beautiful girl she is,' Dorothy had said when she'd seen that photo, 'Full of the bloom of youth... a real look of Clare about her.'

But Ruth's dark Italian looks were more Nick's than Clare's.

He took in a deep breath. Blew it out. Breathed deeply again. He texted Dorothy about the media interest... and to tell her he'd been praying too. A text came straight back: Dorothy already had every newsfeed lined up on her phone, on her computer.

Remember, he texted back, *You're first on the list if I get any news.*

* * *

When Greg arrived, soaked, Nick was already getting in his second beer.

'It's hellish out there,' Greg said, 'It's pishing down... And I'll have the same as you, thanks.'

They took their beers over to a table by the logburner. Greg had already swallowed most of his pint first gulp before they sat down, so he was soon back at the bar for another two: he liked his beer, Greg.

'The media have picked things up,' Nick told him. 'Ruth Innocenti, missing schoolgirl, last seen leaving school yesterday. And she's on the Police missing persons' website. Some of the people on there have been missing since the 1970s, would you believe? They must be murder victims, surely? It turns out some people really do get away with murder.'

'Don't get carried away.' Greg said, 'No-one's talking about murder for goodness sake. Ruthie'll be alright, you'll see.'

Both took another long slug and then there was a nervous silence.

'So, what's next?' Greg splurted out eventually, 'Just sit and wait?'

'I guess so,' Nick said, 'We just wait.' He took another slug of his beer. 'We just have to sit and wait.'

And what else was there to talk about anyway?

'Well, let's not wait here too long,' Greg said, 'I ordered the pizzas on the way up.'

* * *

Later that evening, after Alice had eaten all her own pizza and Jess only a half of hers, the girls started watching *Despicable Me 2* with Greg, while Sheila started washing up in the kitchen. Nick picked up a dishtowel and started drying.

'What do you think might've happened to her?' he said.

'I've no idea,' Sheila said. 'Ruth is mature for her age. She's a sensible girl.'

'That worries me even more,' he said. 'I know she's sensible... but this isn't sensible behaviour, is it? I've been holding on to the fact that she's been a bit less predictable recently. I know she's been smoking a bit: some of her clothes were stinking of it. And Arlene said she'd been hanging out with some other kids that... well... not the kind of kids she's been friends with before.' Sheila said nothing, just waited while he busied himself with stacking the plates back in the cupboard. 'I can see there's lots of things going on for her,' he said at last, 'Things that her Dad obviously doesn't really get. And she doesn't tell me... she knows I disapprove of all the commercial crap that assaults teenagers, that I'm nervous about all the social media stuff she's into, all the crap that's out there in the virtual world, in the real world too.'

Sheila stopped washing and looked at him. 'Don't give yourself a hard time Nick. Every parent finds it hard to work around the teenage media environment. You can't ban it... but you've got to believe in your own values, trust that they'll come through... sometimes we just have to hang in there and stay part of their lives.'

'I'm not so sure. At one of the parent evenings, one of the teachers was talking to me about all the stuff they're covering in the school personal and social education course – internet safety, online shaming, revenge porn – I couldn't talk to her about that kind of stuff... I'd just get angry.' He piled more dishes into the cupboard. 'Clare would've handled it better.'

Sheila kept talking as she washed. 'Teenagers need to learn how to handle it all for themselves Nick. And it's not just the obvious stuff... remember the discussions the four of us used to have when our girls were just babies, how we were going to give them the tools to handle what they would face as they grew up? Of course, Ruth's going to be influenced by the big bad world out there, but she's also got strong personal values, she can see how you live, the strong values you have... '

'What values do I have?' he thought, 'Never mind strong values...'

Sheila was still talking. '...she'll put all that together in her own way. You could never do it for her. You just have to trust her. She's a very mature girl, very aware...'

Jess ran into the kitchen. 'Mummy,' she shouted, 'This film's good. Are you coming?'

'After I've done the dishes,' Sheila said. 'Go on... I'm fine... and you're missing the film.'

'I should've allowed her to talk to me more,' Nick said, once Jess had run back through to the film, 'I can remember times when I shut conversations down cos I was just getting angry... but recently it's been her that's been shutting down on me. It's like she's not interested in what I think any more. We used to have great conversations about things that mattered but now we only seem to be able to talk about simple stuff – you know... when she'll be home, what we'll have to eat...'

'Nick,' Sheila splashed the plate she was holding into the water, 'For God's sake stop giving yourself a hard time! This isn't your fault. Ruth's just a normal teenage girl, exploring the boundaries a bit, wondering where she fits in, what's right, what's wrong. She's still highly committed to her work – doing well at school, isn't she? She's like all teenagers... she just needs a bit of space sometimes, needs to starting working things out for herself...'

'Yeah,' Nick said... 'I'm sure that's right... but if she's just a normal teenager, then answer me this: where the hell is she?'

Before Sheila could reply, their conversation was interrupted again. This time it was Greg: 'C'mon you two,' he said, 'Get finished and come on through: we're missing you in the front room.'

They did as they were told.

* * *

Later, when the film had finished, Sheila wanted Greg to stay over but Nick wouldn't have it. He insisted they both go home with the girls and promised to call them in the morning.

After they'd left, he poured himself a very large whisky and went to sit in Ruth's bedroom. He picked up Cromarty from the bed and put him on the dresser, looking out the window. 'You'll see her first Cromarty, when she's coming back down the street... be sure to give me a shout.' He sat down on the bed and texted Dorothy: *Nothing at this end. I'm drinking alcohol to help me sleep. Hope you sleep well.*

She replied straight away. *I'm saying all the prayers I can - don't know what else to do. Whatever happens I'm going to come through first thing.*

I'm sure she'll be alright, he texted back, *but it'd be good if you could be here when she turns up. She always likes to see you.* It was true. Ruth was fond of her grandmother... much fonder than he was. Though, strangely, he was realising that his only comfort now was from this contact with Dorothy – it'd be good for him too if she came over in the morning: after all, she was the only one who loved Ruth as much as he did.

Again and again he went over in his head the events of the previous morning when he'd hurried out the door: with heavy rain forecast, he'd wanted to get started early on Mrs Armitage's garden, clearing up for winter. She was one of his regulars. And she paid well. He clearly remembered Ruth shouting after him as he ran out, but he hadn't heard all she'd said. Only that she might be late. Didn't even go back for a wee kiss. What had he been thinking? What did five minutes matter? Clare would never have done that. She'd have made time to hear what Ruth had to say. If only he could have another go, he'd do it right this time. He'd always put her first... be there to listen to her, support her, protect her: every step, every damn step... whatever it took... he'd be there... every damn step of the way.

When he sat down on his bed, he started to shiver, his arms shaking till he forced them to stay still by clasping his hands tight together: the only thoughts now were the worst thoughts. If something had happened to her.... pray to God she hadn't suffered. Dear God pray she didn't suffer, wasn't suffering. Dear God, please...

Eventually, dowsed in the whisky, he drifted off to sleep.

* * *

They arrived early on Sunday morning... very early... while he was doing his morning stretches, his throat still raw from the whisky the night before - plain clothes officers this time, two of them.

They weren't smiling.

The first one was about Nick's age - a thickset balding man with a florid complexion. He held out his warrant card. 'I'm Chief Inspector... '

'... Clousseau,' Nick found himself wanting to say, bizarrely. How could such a frivolous idea come into his head at a time like this? But the man did have a little moustache... and a pompous manner...

'...Philben, Jim Philben,' he said, 'And my colleague here is Detective Constable Jane Beattie.' Nick stood and looked at them. Why were they here?

'Can we come in sir?' Philben asked.

Nick stepped aside and they made their way into his lounge, Philben standing awkwardly, his big frame dominating the room.

'Can I take your coats?' Nick said, 'Sit down please.'

The rain was beginning to ease off, but their coats were still wet. When he went to hang Philben's coat on the hall coat rack, his hands were trembling so much it took him three attempts to place it on the hook.

'Can I get you a cup of tea?' Nick offered.

'I'll do that,' DC Beattie said. Nick watched her standing up, noticed her trim figure, her short blonde hair, blue eyes, round cheeks... a sharp nose. She walked towards the back of the lounge and pushed open the kitchen door. 'Through here, is it?'

Philben called him back to attention. 'Sit down please, sir,' he said.

Nick sat down.

'We've found a body, sir.' Philben said, 'And we think it may be Ruth.' He paused. 'I'm very, very sorry,' he said. 'Very sorry.'

The silence was broken by the clinking of cups in the kitchen as PC Beattie prepared the tea.

'I know,' Nick said, 'I think I knew whenever I saw you at the door.' He swallowed. 'I've known since I don't know when.' He bit the inside of his lip. 'But I prayed it wasn't true.' He stood up. 'Sorry... I need to get out.'

He ran to the patio door and threw it open. He walked out into the garden and kicked over the green plastic watering can. He rushed at the bird table and threw it over, squatted down and turned over the heavy wooden picnic bench. He picked up a piece of wood and tried to break it over his knee. It didn't break. He roared, loud, like an angry bear as he hammered it against the clothes pole, again and again, till it snapped. His head was exploding.

Walking to the bottom of the garden, he concentrated on his breathing, trying to regain control, slowing everything down. A robin sitting on the back fence was looking up at him. A streak of morning sunlight had broken through the clouds and was hitting the greenhouse. Through the open door, he could hear the kettle starting to boil. Things he would remember forever.

Standing at the bottom of the garden he leaned against the fence, took a few deep breaths, then a few more. He wanted to reset the clock twenty-four hours.

But time only runs one way.

He pushed his shoulders back and walked back to the house.

'I'm so sorry sir,' Philben said again, 'So sorry.' After a brief pause, he adopted a brisker, more business-like tone. 'As you probably know, we'll need you to help us with identification. We obviously believe that the girl we've found fits the description you gave us, the photo, the school clothes... but we do need you to confirm it.'

'When? Now?'

'As soon as you feel able, sir. I know it will be difficult, but it's best all round if we're certain.'

'Her grandmother's probably on her way through,' he said, 'I can give her a call, get her to meet us at the identification. She'll want to be there.'

'As you wish, sir... it's not necessary, but if you think that will help.'

'It will,' he said. 'Can you give me the postcode... of the place where we're going...?'

* * *

When Nick called Dorothy, he could hear the noise of traffic in the background. She was already in the car. 'I'm going to send you a postcode,' he said, 'Put it in your satnav and I'll meet you there...'

'What's happened? I'm almost at Stirling.'

'Just put that postcode into your satnav and I'll meet you in the car park. Just wait for me there', he said, as level-voiced as he could manage.

Dorothy must have been close to Stirling when she phoned, for by the time he got there, she was already standing in the hospital mortuary car park and it was clear that she understood why they were there. They reached out to each other and found a surprising comfort in each other's arms. Dorothy was the one person who knew what he was going through. She was going through the same herself.

The identification was a formality, of course: it was Ruth. The contours of her face were paler now, 'deathly pale' – these clichéd words came into his head, but this was no cliché. This was Ruth. And she was dead.

Dorothy and he held hands as they sat together, her sobbing, him shivering. Neither wanted to leave her, so they stayed for a good while. He wanted to say some words to Ruth, but it felt silly, speaking to her dead body... and in any case, he didn't have the right words. There probably were no right words. How long would they be allowed to stay? He wanted to stay forever. What else was there to do? Nothing else mattered now.

Nothing mattered.

At last, Dorothy took her hand away, covered her mouth and coughed. He looked round at her and she raised an eyebrow. He nodded. The chairs scraped on the tiled floor as they stood up. Dorothy leaned over for one last look at Ruth – they'd been warned not to touch her - then walked slowly out of the room. Nick stayed a moment longer.

'Ruth,' he said, 'RuthRuthRuth... Who did this to you Ruthie? Who did this to you?'

* ... * ... *

He agreed to answer some more police questions, back at the house. 'The first few hours of this kind of investigation are crucial for us trying to find out what happened,' Philben had said, 'We don't want to delay that.' He'd also said they would want to look through her things and Nick had agreed to that too, so he wasn't surprised when, shortly after he and Dorothy had returned to the house, Philben was at the door, with a young female officer in support. She made tea and brought it through on a tray. She'd looked out some biscuits, Nick noticed... a new packet... where had she found them?

'DC Beattie here is what we call a Family Liaison Officer... an FLO.' Philben said as the tea was poured, 'She'll be your main point of contact, supporting you right through whatever lies ahead.' Nick turned to look at her and she smiled at him, an open generous smile, a smile that he trusted immediately... trusted completely.

'We're treating this as a suspicious death,' Philben carried on, 'so there has to be a full investigation and I'll just explain about the investigation team: I'm the SIO, that's Senior Investigation Officer, and here in Forth Valley we have our own CSI team – that's Crime Scene Investigation. Everyone's an acronym these days...' he gave a lame smile.

Nick bit his lip again and looked away.

'We're not presuming there has been a crime, but as it's a suspicious death we can't rule it out. And we've already called in the Scottish Police Authority Forensic Services Team,' he smiled to himself, a complacent little smile, 'We have state of the art expertise here in Scotland with that team. If there's anything to find, they'll find it.'

'Where was she found?' Nick interrupted.

'Her body was found in a disused quarry, sir, at the Abbey Craig...'

'So...' Nick thought, 'The Abbey Craig... she hadn't got very far after she'd left her other friends at the Causewayhead roundabout. To here 26.09 13.59

Philben was still talking: '...you probably know that the quarry is towards the north-east of the site. You can get a good view along the Ochils from a clearing above the quarry, but the woods are pretty extensive and the site's mostly overgrown. It's not easy to get to... and it's well away from the main path people use to walk up to the Monument.' He paused, but Nick said nothing. 'Anyway, as I say, that's where we found her: face down in some casual water: that suggests that she maybe drowned, but it's too early to say the cause of death for sure: we'll need to wait for the post-mortem results for confirmation.'

Nick knew the Abbey Craig well enough, used its paths for some of his training runs. He knew there where the quarry was alright, but he'd never had a reason to go into it... why would he? ... it was a dead-end... with high cliffs all around.

'There's a kind of gang-hut in that particular quarry,' Philben was saying, 'Some local yobs seem to have taken over what used to be a workers' shed. From the litter round about, it seems it's been used in the recent past as a kind of drinking den... drugs too, probably. We already know some pupils of Bruce Academy were using that hut a wee while ago when truanting from school. They should have pulled the place down years ago, of course....' He cleared his throat. 'There'll be a forensic examination of course of every inch of the hut... all the surrounding area...'

Nick could see Philben's lips moving, but he was no longer hearing the words. There was a terrible buzzing in his head. He was breathing in rapid shallow breaths. When Philben stopped talking, Jane Beattie touched his elbow. 'We were wondering if we could look at Ruth's room?' she said. 'There might be important clues for us there?'

'Of course,' he said, standing up and leading them up the stairs.

Philben and Beattie nosed around Ruth's room for ten or so minutes, looked through some of the clothes and books that were lying around, opened one or two drawers and closed them again. Afterwards, Philben asked him again about how he got on with Ruth, what her mood had been that day, many more questions. Nick wondered if they might be treating him as a possible suspect, building up lines of enquiry around his relationship with her. Though he knew it was their job, it left him feeling unsettled. He wanted to trust Philben, but felt a need to be on guard. Surely no-one could seriously suspect him?

He was her father for God's sake.

Is this what happened?

Not long after, two uniformed officers arrived and removed a number of items that Philben had laid aside, including Ruth's laptop. DC Beattie gave him a booklet, 'Information for Relatives' – all the things that might happen, what might lie ahead for him. For now, she said, the most important thing was for him to make use of the support that was available to help him through bereavement and counselling services, support groups and, of course, friends and family. There would be a lot of media interest and the police would offer advice on how he should handle that... they'd protect him from it if necessary... he should let them know if he was being bothered... In any event, he would be very wise not to say anything to the media. He should let the police handle that side of things.

Before they left, Beattie arranged to see Nick at home the next morning. She'd been very empathetic. And thoroughly professional. Nothing but supportive. But he felt guarded with her too.

Left on his own now, Nick couldn't sit still. He couldn't bear to be in the house. He had to get out... to run... to punish his body... to clear his head,

* * *

The rain had stopped and a drying wind was coming in behind him as he set off up the road towards the Abbey Craig. A wood covers just about all of the Craig, a post-glacial crag-and-tail hill which runs down and away to the east from its craggy top. On its highest point, over a hundred metres above the surrounding river plain, sits the nineteenth century Wallace Monument, erected in Victorian times, and paid for by public subscription, in memory of Scotland's mediaeval freedom fighter. A metalled road winds up the western side of the Craig, taking visitors up to the Monument from the car park below. Down to the east, through the extensive woods, there are clear marked footpaths running away from the Monument in the opposite direction and on down the hill. Few use those paths, and even fewer venture off them - low tangles of rhododendron, brambles and bracken can make the going difficult, while precipitous crags make it dangerous to stray too far from the track. In behind lies the quarry.

When Nick reached the Alloa Road, below the Monument, he could see a couple of police vans parked down at the lower, eastern entrance to the woods, the nearest entry point to the quarry where she'd been found. Were they looking for clues to what had happened? Could he go in and have a look himself, see where she'd been lying? The thought of her lying there in the cold rain for two days hit him then, caught him in his gut. He stopped and lent on a fence, overcome with grief and loss, deep painful sobs racking his chest. It took him some time to compose himself, wipe his face, wipe his hands on his running shorts. He pressed on at a slower pace and headed away from the police vans, through Causewayhead Park and up the steep steps that would take him over and into the back of the University, one of his favourite routes. But once up the steps, he turned away from that route and started to run up the metalled tourist road, up towards the Monument. The sky had cleared, giving a little more light, while, since scarcely a leaf had been left on the trees after the recent winds and rain, visibility was very good. Nick wondered if he could find the quarry where they'd found her.

Half-way up the hill, as the steep metalled road up to the Monument snakes back on itself, a rough path takes away east and then a little south, towards the entrance where he'd seen the police vans. Nick took off down that path. Some way down, he began to hear voices - from the north of the woods, away from the path and off to the left, from an area he'd never gone to before. He made his way gingerly downhill through the tangled undergrowth beneath the trees, slipping a little on the wet leaves. There was a broken-down fence and a metal sign lying flat on the ground: *Danger. Steep drop.* He pulled aside some branches, inched forward and peered over a cliff edge into a quarry... no, into *the* quarry: the disused quarry where she'd been found. There was casual water in one corner, while thin saplings were crowded together in another corner, competing for light. A large white tent was positioned at the edge of a stretch of muddy water, the front flap pulled back. Nearby, a man and a woman in white protective clothing were kneeling, picking at the ground.

Nick made his way round along the cliff edge, by the old fence, pushing branches aside as he went. Where the slope flattened out, there was 'crime scene' tape running from tree to tree, cordoning off the quarry entrance. He followed it round and saw two police officers in high-viz clothing. They saw him approaching.

'How did you get here sir?' one of them asked.

'Just out for a run,' Nick said, 'I was up on the path and heard voices. Thought I'd have a look. See what was going on.'

'This is a crime scene,' the first one said, 'The whole area, in the quarry there as well,' he pointed vaguely with his right hand. 'You'll have to go back.'

The other policeman stepped closer.

Nick looked down at his shoes.

'You'll be able to pick up the path again through there,' the first one said, pointing through the woods. 'That'll take you out to the Alloa Road.

'Any idea what happened?' Nick asked.

'No. It's too early to say. We need to let the forensic team do their stuff. But one thing I'll say...' the policeman lowered his voice to a conspiratorial whisper, 'That's quite a wee howff kids have made in there: they've put a corrugated iron roof over the top of an old quarry building and made some kind of a den - there's even a brazier, some seating, some used condoms...' He winked at Nick. 'A bit of sex and drugs and rock'n' roll, know what I mean?'

'Who? Who's been using it?' Nick spoke with an aggressive urgency which caused the two officers to look at each other.

'Well, that's for us to find out sir, isn't it?' the first one said, 'And we will....'

The second officer interrupted his colleague. 'Anyway, that's quite enough for now, sir...' he said, '... more than enough... we don't actually *know* anything at the moment... anything my colleague or I might say is pure speculation. And we never presume anything in an investigation. So...?' He raised his eyebrows.

'Thanks,' Nick said, regretting his earlier tone, 'I'd better get on then. Thanks.'

It was a relatively level run from the quarry, round and back to the main path: a few hundred yards at most. Once on the main road, he headed back down to Cambuskenneth, pushing himself as hard as he could.

Dorothy was still in the kitchen when he came in by the back door, wet and muddy, his face red, his chest heaving, loud wheezy gasps sucking air into his lungs.

3. Investigation

At first, the police investigation seemed to be making progress. Jane Beattie gave Nick regular reports, a drip feed summary of information they had found useful: there was CCTV footage of Ruth and a few other pupils, including Arlene, walking along the road outside the school at 4pm, then footage of Ruth passing the Co-op at 4.06pm, on her own, just as she would've if she'd been heading home. They'd interviewed most of these pupils and their stories were fairly consistent: they'd assumed she was going home when she left them at the roundabout... but none had been able to say exactly where Ruth went... or why.

A passing witness had seen an individual entering the wood by the eastern entrance at around six thirty on the Friday evening: the man in question was about thirty years of age, wearing a blue hoodie-style top, jeans and trainers. The police had been able to identify him from earlier CCTV footage taken at the shops as he was known to them for other reasons. In his interview, he'd claimed that he'd simply walked into the woods to relieve himself and he was able to provide a reliable alibi almost immediately after the sighting. They were keeping him on the board, but he'd been released without charge - if anything linked him to Ruth or any physical evidence from the howff might establish a connection, he'd be brought back in. No other useful CCTV footage had yet been obtained, but the police were widening the search area for relevant material.

Jane Beattie told him that they were conducting follow-up interviews with current school pupils and recent former pupils of the school who were in some way associated with the site, or who were willing to come forward with any relevant information. They were also collecting evidence from both the howff and the casual water lying nearby. There was a lot of material, but it would be variable in quality - the exceptionally heavy rains of Friday night and Saturday hadn't helped. There were layers of graffiti on the interior stonework of the wee howff, testimony to the variety of young people who'd used it over the years. Some of the dates and names attached to messages went back as far as the 1990s. But none of the names offered any clues as to who might have been in the howff on that specific night. Every piece of litter was being collected from a wide area on all sides of the den: old fag packets, rusting cans and broken bottles, rizzlas, a crudely made bong, some needles, used condoms, a number of plastic water bottles. Police had also found soiled discarded underwear, a couple of old hoodies, a towel, a dog lead. There was even a dead cat. There was no guarantee that any of this random collection of rubbish could be linked in any way to Ruth, but they had to follow up every possibility. Some other bits and pieces had been recovered from the quarry floor, clothing fibres had been removed from recently broken twigs, near to the howff and to the site of her death. They might be able to use pollen traces, if a suspect was found and matched to them. The autumn leaves and fallen branches in among the thick undergrowth of tufted grass and bracken had made it difficult to collect any worthwhile footprints in the woods, while inside the quarry itself the remains of a path to the ruined building was lined with stones that showed no footprints. Ruth's phone was still missing. Beattie confirmed that they'd not found her underwear either: 'CI Philben...' PC Beattie concluded, '...said that If the underwear has been hidden, or removed from the scene altogether, then it's likely that we are dealing with an incident of foul play.'

As Nick listened to Jane telling him Philben's conclusion, he could hear Uncle Raymondo's voice in his ear: 'Philben. Police Scotland. Specialist subject: the bleeding obvious.'

Then again, though Nick found faults in the police operation, some of them weren't too happy with him either. When the officers Nick spoke to at the crime scene had recognised him from a photo back at the station, Philben had phoned him, furious. 'That's what your FLO is for,' he said, the anger barely contained in his voice, 'We don't want you snooping around the crime scene, mucking up important evidence.'

Later on, when Nick told Greg about Philben's reaction, his friend was horrified. 'You realise they'll have you down as one of the suspects, Nick,' he said, 'Standard practice, isn't it? Even more so now that you've turned up at the crime scene and pretended to know nothing about it. That's very suspicious behaviour in the police book. They'll be keeping all options open, man. If they find evidence that you were in that howff, and you have no alibi, they'll fit you up...'

'Surely, they won't....'

'At least they haven't interviewed you under caution.' Greg made sure Nick was looking at him. 'At least not yet,' he said.

'No. How could they think that?... I mean...'

'Keep well out of it mate,' Greg interrupted, 'I know it's difficult but rule number one is: you don't trust the police. If it's easy to fit you up, they will.'

Nick hadn't thought of that. Didn't want to think of that. Surely he could trust the police. 'I don't think so,' he said... 'I think they'll want to find the truth, same as me.'

Over the next couple of days, it was clear that Ruth's very active online life was giving the police problems – there was so much of it, and so many potential leads. Philben and Jane interviewed Nick several times about areas of interest arising from their screening of her laptop and phone records, but Nick learned more from the interviews than they did from him – it seemed that he knew very little about his daughter and her extensive internet life... the sites he knew about - YouTube, Facebook, Instagram, Twitter, Pinterest – they were just the starting point. And beyond all the websites she had been on, there was also an extensive legacy of texts, e.mails and whatsapps being filtered and worked through. It appeared that Ruth also had strong political interests and was active in many online campaign forums, e.mail campaigns - banning nuclear weapons, banning fracking, Scottish independence, animal cruelty, climate change... many more.

While much of this was new to Nick, he knew about the climate change campaigning alright. 'You can be such a hypocrite, Dad,' she'd said in one of their recent discussions, one of the many that ended in disagreement, 'that diesel truck of yours belching out cancerous particulates while you go on and on about sustainability.'

'Well,' he'd shouted back, his voice rising with frustration, 'Have you worked out the environmental cost of scrapping that car and using a new one, all the manufacturing costs, the cost of mining metal, growing rubber, transporting it, the rare materials in the battery ... have you costed in all of that?'

She'd looked at him as if he as something unpleasant she'd just stood on. 'Go away,' she'd said, then stormed out the room herself.

'Anyway,' he'd shouted after her as she ran upstairs to her room, 'I need it for my work. And...' he shouted louder, after she'd shut the door, 'I offset my carbon footprint.'

He remembered her opening her door and peering down at him from the landing. 'Big deal,' she'd shouted, 'But it'd be much better if you didn't pollute the air I have to breathe in the first place.' She hadn't waited to hear his reply but had slammed the door shut again.

As part of the discussions he had with the police, Jane Beattie had probed him about Ruth's internet search history. Sites recently visited included the usual teenage list of music, fashion, celebrities, but also included the effects of cocaine, ecstasy, alcohol, organic chemistry revision, Luther and Calvin, sex education, porn sites, online diaries of World War One, global warming - an apparently endless, confusing list. 'A typical teenager maybe,' Jane said. 'But what is typical nowadays? We've got so much of her phone's search history through her Chrome login, and the network have been helpful with call history, but there could be more on her phone that is vital to the enquiry. Kids that age can spend six hours a day ...or more... on their phones, you know.'

'Oh I know that alright... every waking hour...'

'Well anyway,' Jane said, 'for all that we've found on her digital media, we can't find anything specific about last Friday night. So, we're nowhere nearer answering the most important questions: why did she go into the Park in the first place and who might she have been meeting?'

Later, CI Philben went over the post-mortem with Nick. It didn't make for easy listening, but Nick made it clear that he wanted every detail... and that meant *every* detail. It seemed that Ruth had imbibed significant quantities of a strong cider shortly before her death. She'd also taken ecstasy. There was a bruise on her cheek which may have been there before the Friday night, and another one on her neck. Had he noticed the bruises before? He couldn't remember. Philben's tone tended to be impersonal, official, sometimes officious, but sometimes there was a sharper, less polite, overlay. It sometimes felt like he didn't believe anything Nick said. If Nick didn't remember a certain detail, Philben seemed to imply, what other details was he getting wrong, what other important information hadn't he told them, what other things was he holding back?

Even so, Philben gave him the courtesy of a very full briefing. The post-mortem reported that the primary cause of Ruth's death was drowning, face down in the shallow pond where she was found. Estimated time of death was between 6 and 9 that evening. Further tests might give a more precise time. She'd had sexual intercourse shortly before death and there were some signs of force being used with bruising on her upper legs and soft tissue damage in her vagina. Signs of force could indicate rape, but it was impossible to be sure until there was other evidence... the soft tissue damage might also, for example, be consistent with her having been a willing, but inexperienced, participant. Swabs had been taken from her body - particularly the fingers, mouth and genital areas, her legs, her fingertips - but the analysis of any DNA traces would take longer, even in a priority case like this, while, since a condom had been used, there were unlikely to be DNA residues that could assist in the identification of the male person involved. Moreover, the amount of rain that weekend might have obscured or washed away some valuable traces.

At present, Nick was told, Philben's main concern was to locate and interview any other persons who'd been present at the time. Several school pupils and ex-pupils had been identified as regular users of the site, but so far all had alibis for that evening. Once the police knew who else had been there, Philben said, they'd have a pathway to guide them through the wide range of potential evidence that was piling up.

In the days and weeks after Nick was given these details of the post-mortem findings, he pictured again and again the various possible scenarios consistent with the evidence available so far: rape and murder were possible but so also were consensual sex, drug use and accidental death.

Had Ruth, intoxicated or dizzy, stumbled through the woods to the pond and somehow fallen into it?

Had she, confused, dehydrated or drunk, passed out while trying to drink from it?

Had some other person made sure that she stayed under the water?

And why the hell had she gone there in the first place? If there'd been some pre-arranged meeting with an individual or a group, it wasn't recorded anywhere on her phone or her computer. Was it a face-to-face arrangement? Someone from school? School friends she'd met during the day were the first port of call for the police, yet those she was seen with in CCTV footage on the way home from school confirmed that, as far as they knew, she intended to go straight home. She'd said that morning that she might be late. Had the arrangement to meet in the park been made on an earlier day, with someone from outside the school, someone she didn't want others to know about?

The police had also told him of a recent increase in ecstasy use in Stirling and of drug-trading in, or near to, the school. They couldn't rule out the possibility that Ruth had been keeping a rendezvous secret because drugs were involved. They were making a particular point of interviewing those of her classmates who were thought to be users. Everything her classmates said in interviews was being cross-checked, but it seemed that she'd been on good terms with many of the large number of young people in her year at school, moving easily between different groups. Particularly in the past couple of months, she'd become more friendly with some of the kids in her year who, as one teacher put it, were "more into chemicals than chemistry... and more into sex than science". But the same teacher called her 'a sensible girl, careful... always seemed to know how to handle herself in the hurly-burly of teenage life...'

Some of the pupils in her year had been involved with the police before, some were said to be users of the little den in the quarry. But there was a lot of 'noise' in evidence, just as there was in her internet record. The stories the police collected from the many pupils they interviewed, all of whom had some kind of opinion on what might have happened, were not mutually reinforcing, nor was there evidentiary support for a lot of what was claimed. 'There's rumours about every other girl in this school,' one girl had said, 'And most of them are just the fantasies of some sad boys, jerking off.'

One thing, however, was sure. Nick realised just how little he knew, even less than he'd thought, about Ruth's life outside the home, particularly her life on the web. Virtual Ruth was a stranger to him.

'Just a typical teenager', right enough.

* * *

The funeral was delayed till the police had finished with the body. 'Evidence has to be captured and kept scrupulously,' Jane Beattie explained on one of her visits, sitting on his front room sofa, her two hands wrapped round a mug of tea, They'd seen a lot of each other, but there was still a formal professional tone, a distance, in her voice. 'Any possibility of contamination at any point can ruin a prosecution case. People don't realise the DNA tests are getting much more accurate and reliable nowadays. Whenever you touch something, anything, you're shedding skin cells. But there's a much higher risk of contamination of DNA evidence on surfaces. It's different with fluids like blood or semen which are much less likely to be contaminated.'

'Why's that?' he'd asked her.

She put down the cup and pushed a few stray hairs behind her ear. 'It's complicated, sir,' she said. 'The person who committed the crime may have touched someone else and then, also by touch, transferred the first person's DNA to a third person. If that third person was the victim, the first person's DNA might be found on them, even if they'd never actually met them. There was a case recently in the States. The defence were able to show that it was possible for a man to have traces of a dead woman's DNA on his skin though he'd never actually touched her, a cross contamination that could've led to an innocent man being convicted... And rain can wash away evidence... and there was so much rain in the hours before Ruth's body was found... Rain can also bring atmospheric pollutants into the scene...'

She had such a pleasant easy face, especially when she smiled - and she smiled a lot - that he realised that he'd been so busy noticing her smile, that he'd missed some of what she'd said. His face flushed... and she was still talking.

"Sorry,' he said, 'I missed that last bit. Can you repeat it?'

'Sure,' she said, and smiled, 'I was saying that, from what we've seen of the drugs howff in the woods on the Abbey Craig, a lot of people have been shedding, and picking up, a lot of DNA there recently, so any surviving traces are unlikely to tell us anything very valuable...'

'So if that's the case,' Nick asked her, 'how can you use any DNA evidence at all?'

'On its own,' she agreed, 'It may be vulnerable to a clever defence lawyer sowing a doubt about its reliability, like in the American case I mentioned. It's much better if we can fit it in with other evidence. Remember the old-school murder mysteries? It's still good to have *means, motive and opportunity* stitched up, before you start putting any value on DNA evidence. Anyway, without a suspect we're not likely to get a DNA match, and one possible conclusion, based on the evidence we have at the moment, is that this was a tragic accident that happened to a girl who'd just got herself too drunk, too spaced out... and the boy she was with panicked and left her there. I know that may be hard for you to take, but that is certainly one of the possibilities that can't be ruled out at this stage.'

'I know that's possible,' he said, 'But I also know my daughter. She liked her life too much to take risks. Something's happened to her, someone has done this.'

'Well if that's the case,' she said, looking him straight in the eye, 'we'll find out.'

He shuffled in his seat. 'Another cup of tea before you go?'

"No, I'd better get back. I'm sorry.' She stood up and smoothed down her skirt, 'I've still a lot to do today before I go out tonight.'

'Where are you going?' he said, then felt his neck redden ... 'Sorry,' he flustered, 'I don't know why I asked that... it's personal. Sorry.'

'Don't worry... it's nothing important anyway. Nothing.'

He followed her to the door, watched her walking to her car, getting in, starting up. As the car pulled away, she gave him a cheery wave... and a smile: she was a real ray of light in the midst of all this crap.

* * *

Nick intentionally kept the funeral a small affair. He wanted the service to be conducted by the young priest he'd seen at the church on the weekend of her disappearance, but it seemed that he'd been sent over to a parish in central Glasgow. The priest who took the service: Father Adebolo, was a young Nigerian. He found out later that he was studying for a Masters degree at the University and was standing in till a new parish priest could be appointed. That somehow seemed appropriate. Everything that was happening was so random, so exceptional.

The service was simple, formal, traditional. No press were there, no-one that wasn't specifically invited. The school had told Nick that a large number of pupils wanted to attend but he'd refused: the only ones he'd invited to the funeral were friends of Ruth that he'd seen round at the house. 'It's not going to make any difference to Ruth,' he said to the teacher who'd phoned him, 'And I'm sorry to say it, but I've seen some of the stuff some of your pupils – ones I've never seen and I've never heard Ruth mention – I've seen some of what they've been posting online... Facebook, Instagram, no doubt lots of other places too ... and I don't want a chapel full of crying teenage girls, getting off on their grief. If there's a big crowd of them there, it'd take over the whole funeral. And the funeral should be about Ruth, not about them.'

For the same reason, he didn't attend the service held in her memory in the school. But he did give them some photos of Ruth that they could project on the wall and her form teacher printed three of them in the little booklet the school prepared for the service - Ruth as a baby, Ruth at primary school with two front teeth missing, and Ruth earlier this year, that curious teenage face looking out at the world. They sent him a copy later, with signatures and messages from hundreds of the school's pupils attached. He kept it out on the hall table, beside the coat hooks. One day, he'd get around to replying.

Nick hadn't even brought his own mother to the funeral. 'Her memory's so shot,' he told Greg and Sheila, 'That it's a new shock to her every time she realises she's a widow. It's as if my Dad had only just died that day. Why add Ruth on to that? It's only going to upset her even more.'

He took photos of Ruth up to the care home when he visited, repeated stories from last year, and the year before, about what she'd been doing at school, in the orchestra, at the drama club, in the Guides - even though it'd been almost a year since she'd given up going to the Guides. His mother had been in the Guides in the 60s: she really liked these made-up stories.

Each time, on leaving, he told his mother that Ruth might be up to see her next time. He was misleading her for kindness' sake, he told himself, and she wouldn't remember what he told her anyway. All the same, it didn't feel right. It just felt less wrong than anything else. It felt as if the very worst thing to do would be to tell her the horrible, upsetting truth, and then, because her dementia would mean that she didn't remember, to retell her again, and again... every time he visited, every time she asked where Ruth was and how she was getting on... telling and retelling her that Ruth was dead... that they didn't yet know how... and they might never know why.

* * *

As December wore on, Nick found it hard not to keep returning to those two most basic questions, the questions to which there was, as yet, no answer: how and why had his daughter died?

Very little else seemed to matter.

He pored over every possible detail of Ruth's case: the teenage subcultures that might've influenced her, taken her into danger; online chat sites where people shared their experiences of drugs; newspaper reports of teenage drug deaths, teenage murders, teenage suicides. He learned more than he'd ever wanted to know about forensics, drug-use patterns in teenagers, the effects of MDMA, its contamination with other substances, its interaction with alcohol, patterns of sexual behaviour among under-16s. It made him feel that he'd lived a very sheltered life. Would he have been any more help to Ruth if he'd been more aware? Could he have prevented her death by being a better-informed father... a better father?

He also read carefully the various support documents for families of crime victims that different people had given him. He signed up with Victim Support Scotland. He even signed up for a session with a 'bereavement counsellor', but that hadn't worked out well. It had felt to him that she was trying to get him to say more than he wanted to say about his whole life, his wife, his feelings about her death, his relationship with his daughter, so much more that he didn't want to have to talk about: Ruth's state of mind since Clare's death, any unusual changes in her behaviour in the months before her death, conflicts he'd had with her, his feelings about having a daughter and not a son... as if his family life was somehow of interest in her death, or relevant at all. Afterwards he'd felt more intensely than before that hadn't been a good enough father, hadn't been understanding enough about the pressures she was under, what she was going through. The counselling session had intensified his feeling that whatever the immediate details of what had happened to her, he was to blame, at least in part, in some general, non-specific, kind of way. There were so many *if only's,* in which he could've been the main actor... and they all pointed to three very big *if only's: if only he'd offered her more, better, support, more, better advice; if only he'd been around more: if only,* in sum, *he'd been a better father.*

He joined the online forum of SAMM - Support After Murder and Manslaughter - and through SAMM he was in contact with other parents whose children had been killed. Most of the people were women. Before he'd arrived at his first meeting, he'd wondered if there might be someone who could support him, someone he could support, someone there who knew what he was going through because she was going through the same thing. But he also knew that he was very picky, that he set an impossibly high bar. One of the woman, a little older than him, did try to get closer. She was probably just being friendly and supportive, but in practice, in the reality of it, her friendliness repelled him. She was pushing into places he wanted to keep private. He recognised the neediness in her. He was needy too. Just not that needy.

He'd developed a little bit of a crush on DC Jane Beattie though. He was attracted by her no-fuss style, the careful way she spoke, her professionalism and yes, he admitted to himself, how she carried herself: there was a simple elegance to her. One Sunday morning when he was out running on the Carse of Lecropt, one of his favourite running routes, he'd seen her 'out of hours'. She was working in the small front garden of a farm cottage, wearing a pair of oversize dungarees and a black Berghaus fleece that also looked about three sizes too big: on her, the effect was quite cute. But then so was her uniform. Damn it, she'd make anything look cute. He stopped running and leaned over the cottage fence.

'Jane Beattie,' he said.

'Mr. Innocenti.'

'Nice to see you off duty,' he said, 'You look great in your civvies.'

'Oh yeah,' she looked sceptical, but put her hand up to her hair all the same, pulled it back off her face. 'Just my gardening gear. I'm trying to get this bit dug up to catch the frost - breaks up this clay soil....' She laughed, '...of course you'd know that. You're a gardener, aren't you?'

'Nice place though,' he said, 'Nice and open... and you're very near the pool over there,' he pointed across a neighbouring field towards the river, 'Down at the Blue Banks... We used to take Ruth there swimming there... on hot summer days.'

'We swam there earlier in the year,' she said, 'But no way would I go swimming in the river in December.' She shifted the rake she was holding from one hand to the other. 'Anyway we might not be here next year. We're saving for a house, me and Brian. We're only renting here till we can afford the deposit on our own place.'

So... Brian was it? That was fine. It was just good to know there was a Brian. He'd let himself get too interested in Jane, had somehow opened himself up a bit to her, though she couldn't possibly have known it. He felt very stupid, as if he was a nervous teenager again. Running back to the house he gave himself a hard time, but there had been reasons he'd let his defences down. She was comfortable to be with, compassionate, caring. And she knew about Ruth. With her, he didn't have to explain. But at least he'd not said anything. And anyway, he'd known she'd never entertain an approach from him while she was involved in the case. It had been an impossible ideal, unreal, unattainable, all in his own head. But that was the point of a crush, wasn't it? All he'd wanted was the idea. It was all he could cope with.

For now.

* * *

He went over to Dorothy's in South Glasgow late on Christmas morning, after he'd visited his Mum in the care home. It was more of a duty than a pleasure to visit his Mum now: she didn't recognise him; she didn't seem interested in anything. On the other hand, rather surprisingly, Christmas with Dorothy went well. They pooled their photos and videos of Ruth – as a baby, as a toddler, as a little schoolgirl and then, more recently, as a teenager, a young woman, with her own secrets. It was an emotional binge-out. They talked, laughed, cried as they turned the album pages, as they projected digital photos onto Dorothy's widescreen smart TV and played little snatches of home video.

'It was so much easier when she was little,' Nick said, after they'd watched a short clip Dorothy had taken in the garden on Ruth's fifth birthday. 'Recently I didn't know how to say the right things, do the right things.' Dorothy let the comment hang, waiting for more. He walked over to the window. 'When I went up to the end of year concert at school straight from work last year, she wouldn't speak to me at the interval. "Look at you Dad," she said, "You're an embarrassment."' He blew out a long breath and turned round to Dorothy opening out his arms. 'I looked at myself through her eyes, still wearing my muddy dungarees, my mucky work boots, and I realised she was right. Recently I always seemed to be doing something wrong, saying something wrong. Clare would've got it right. Would've known better what to say.'

'Don't be so hard on yourself Nick,' Dorothy said, 'I found Clare difficult when she was that age. I tried, to make her into the girl I'd wanted to be, to push her into the same things I'd done at her age. Then I learned that for her the family tradition was a dead weight: all those family portraits of important men, and they were all men, hanging on the walls. I wanted her to be the woman who would match up to those men, would overtake them, replace them. It took me a long time to realise that I'd probably wanted it as much for me as for her, maybe more, that all she wanted was to be her own beautiful... beautiful...' Dorothy wasn't able to get the next word out.

Later, Dorothy opened a special bottle of wine... and then another one. They laughed and cried and said stupid things. The strains in their relationship over the years dissolved in the backwash of an alcohol-induced nostalgia. Nick stayed over in Dorothy's commodious spare room. In the morning, though they returned to their familiar polite distance, there was a new softer undertow. And Nick no longer felt Dorothy was blaming him for Ruth's death.

Back home, reinvigorated by how comparatively well his time with Dorothy had gone, Nick wondered about clearing out Ruth's room, but once he was standing there, in the room, he realised he couldn't: not now, maybe never. Tidying up her room - or worse, removing some of her things – would feel like getting rid of the evidence that Ruth had ever lived there: it felt t like the first step in sending her away on a journey into the past. And he definitely wasn't going to do that. It was like she'd said: her heart was still there. And Cromarty was still sitting on the bed, his back against the pillow, keeping watch, waiting for her to come back through the door.

* * *

In the weeks after Christmas, Nick tried to find some meaning by going back to God, whoever she or he was... back to the religion of his childhood: after all it had worked for Clare... maybe it would work for him. He started and ended each day with prayer, hoping to embrace the images and poetry of that older language that he'd found so wanting during his undergraduate philosophy studies, when the religious teachings of his childhood had been shredded by the intellectual razors of Hume, Marx and Nietzsche.

But it was the aesthetic side of the church, its poetry and symbolism, that Clare had valued, not its rational philosophy. After she'd died, the words of hope and redemption, the comforts of eternity, had seemed even more of a sham to him. He hadn't found the 'grace to bear his burdens' that his grandmother used to pray for, but he was trying to find that grace now. A Church energised by the young priest he'd seen in November might have kindled something, but the young priest wasn't there any longer. An older priest, Father Ratherly, an angry man ill-suited to his vocation, had taken charge of the parish after Christmas. Ratherly was a bitter commentator on the world in which he was growing old, a world which neither recognised his authority to make moral pronouncements nor valued sufficiently the sacrifices he felt he'd made in becoming a priest. If there was 'grace' to be found in the congregation, or in this angry old man, it was hard for Nick to see it. But without faith, he knew he'd never see it anyway: that was what Clare used to say to him. 'First you have to believe,' she'd say, 'And then once you believe, everything flows from that.'

Religion isn't science, Nick,' he remembered her saying on another occasion, 'It's not trying to establish facts. It's the art of understanding how to live, understanding our human lives and how to live them well.'

He'd tried to find what Clare had found in prayer, but his prayers just felt like words: empty, meaningless, useless words. Yes, he did believe in something... some things: he believed in Clare; he believed in Ruth; he believed in caring for the planet; he believed in caring for the body. After all, Clare used to say that valuing the body was prayerful, that the body was 'God's gift'. But, for him, it didn't matter where his body came from... it was the physical activity of the body that was good: above all, pushing his body hard brought him a kind of calm. As a self-employed gardener, he got plenty exercise at work in the summer, but his kind of work was harder to come by in mid-winter. And it was in winter, with more leisure time, that he worked on aerobic and muscular fitness – running, working out in the gym. He had Greg to share some of his running sessions. They shared some hard drinking sessions too.

New Year's Day would've been Ruth's 15th birthday: always so easy to remember her birthday. He took his mother out for lunch. When they got back to the care home, he spent the afternoon with her, looking through her many photo albums, full of pictures of Ruth: as a baby, as a young girl, as a teenager. Another year was starting, but there was still no convincing lead as to who'd been in the drinking den with her that fateful November night.

* * *

In January, Nick landed a short-term winter contract at 'Glassingall', a country estate near the Trossachs, while the permanent gardener was recovering from an operation. It involved cleaning out the greenhouses and preparing the walled garden for spring planting. The work was well paid, and it gave him a welcome daytime routine to fill the day. Out of the house before 8, he was usually back home around 6.

It seemed that just about everyone he knew had told him not to sit on his own at home – that he should spend time with other people - so he filled the long January evenings and weekends with a blizzard of commitments. He booked a regular gym class, ran twice a week with Greg, joined the University community choir, two evening rehearsals a week – it was an ex-colleague of Clare's who'd suggested that. The choir was preparing for an Easter performance of Handel's *Messiah*. On Saturdays, he first took his mother out for lunch and a hurl in the park in her wheelchair, then went on through to Glasgow for supper with Dorothy. He joined a Sunday climbing group that was learning about winter climbing on some of the easier *Munros* - Scottish mountains over 3000 feet, so called after Sir Hugh Munro, who catalogued them at the end of the 19th century. The days were filled. He was beginning to sleep better at night - and the more strenuous the day, the better he slept.

Meantime, PC Jane Beattie continued to give him an occasional edited version of all the information the police were collecting and processing. He was quite happy to accept what she told him at face value: she had an earnest, sincere manner. Philben's strategy, she said, was a good one; all that could be done was still being done; the investigating team had given it, were giving it, would continue to give it everything they could. She gave him regular short précis of all the gigabytes of information they were gathering. All of it - stories about the 'howff' in the Abbey Craig woods, scene of the crime forensics, interviews with classmates - was pumped into the data management software. So many people in the town had been anxious to help that the police had been working on a great many potential lines of enquiry, lots of stories, many of them crossing over each other, more and more checking and cross-checking needed. But despite all the people who'd been keen to help, the reams and reams, hours and hours, of evidence... there were no clear patterns emerging. The one story the police really needed to be able to tell was there somewhere, she had said, but there was still no definite lead to tie a specific person, or people, to that drinking den at that specific time on that specific, fateful, November day. And so it wasn't a real surprise when, starting in January, the meetings with Jane Beattie, that'd been frequent at the start, began to tail off. It seemed that none of the leads they'd followed up had so far appeared to lead anywhere useful.

Near the end of that month, however, she told him that Philben wanted his permission to feature Ruth's case on *Crime Helpline*, a popular television show that was broadcast from London... that Philben thought this was just the kind of case where TV exposure might lead to a breakthrough. Nick wasn't too keen – he'd always thought the programme was more a bit of commercial voyeurism than a genuine contribution to police investigations - but Jane Beattie was persuasive. It was amazing, she said, what had been turned up in some other cases. Even if no quality information came forward, it was good for the profile of any case to get it on to UK television. Why not give it a try? When she'd put it like that, he couldn't help but agree. The following week, a BBC production assistant called him from the London studio to explain what would happen.

4. Re-enactment

Greg invited Nick over to watch the programme when it aired in early February. Sheila had headed out to her choir practice and Greg was still putting the girls to bed when he arrived.

'I've been keeping back a bottle of *Smoky Black Grouse*,' Greg told him, 'It's in the cabinet in the lounge. Why don't you pour us a couple while I get the girls settled?'

Nick poured two long measures, added a little water, and settled into a chair. He brought the glass up to his nose. Sipped. Rolled it around his tongue.

'Well? How is it?' Greg said when he came back down and saw Nick nosing the whisky.

'It's good,' Nick said, 'If I hadn't seen the bottle, I couldn't't've told you it was a blend. Mind you, all whisky tastes good to me.'

'You said it,' Greg said.

By the time the show's familiar theme music started up, they'd managed to drink another whisky... and a couple of beers.

Watching Bill Oates and Sam Hill, the show's presenters, on Greg's wide screen telly, Nick remembered how slick and professional he'd found them when he'd met them briefly on Zoom earlier in the week. Of course, they were good with people - good listeners, empathetic, respectful - but it was more than that. They came over not just as good *with* people, but as good people themselves. Good people.

He wanted all Stirling to be watching, to remember what they'd been doing, what they'd seen on that wet Friday evening, to phone in those little bits of information that might build together with other little bits... to build a picture that would help the police establish what had happened to Ruth. But when Sam started the programme by telling viewers about progress with crimes featured in previous episodes of the show, Nick's head was buzzing so much that he couldn't take in what she was saying. There were so many suppressed emotions, the whisky, Sam Hill....

Greg saw his attention fading and shook his arm. 'C'mon mate. Pay attention. You'll miss out.'

'Sorry Greg,' he mumbled, 'It all feels a bit too much.'

'Well, I tell you man, that Sam Hill, she's certainly a bit too much. Look at her!' Greg pointed his empty tumbler at the screen, 'I wouldn't mind giving her one, mate. I bet you she's a goer alright. Just one look at her and you want to... well... you know...'

Nick rolled his glass across his cheek. 'You've got a one-track mind, Bright. One-track mind.'

'A woman like that has so much power, so much power.' Greg said. There was something mean, resentful, in his tone. 'She could have any man she wants. And she knows it.'

'C'mon mate,' Nick said, 'Lighten up. Let's just watch the programme.'

He wasn't going to tell Greg that he'd been thinking about Sam Hill too, thinking about her a lot. In odd moments around the house, out running, late at night. Of course, she was a special woman... you wouldn't get into that kind of job unless you had special qualities of compassion, intelligence... matched with the right technical and interpersonal skills. Now, watching her on TV, he was reminded that she'd had a powerful physical effect on him too. She wasn't beautiful in a classic sense, whatever that was: her chin was a bit too noticeable; her face not perfectly symmetrical; a few blemishes in her skin... but there was something about the way she carried herself, her confidence in herself, the strength and humanity in those big green eyes: once they caught you, you couldn't get away from them. And though she looked great on the TV screen, it didn't do her justice: it didn't show up the soft smudging of freckles across her nose that Nick knew were there; didn't quite catch the rusty colour of the hair that tumbled down and over her shoulders; didn't show how every man in the room looked at her.

So OK... yes.. she looked great... but it wasn't just how she looked: it was the effect she had on others. She'd had that effect on him too... made him feel good about himself, made him feel as if he was someone worth knowing, as if she'd really taken to him. Of course, that's why she'd got to where she was. Made everyone feel better about themselves, in the way she treated them, the respect she showed them. People wanted to be with her. Wasn't that what 'attractive' really meant? Yes, she looked great, but it was her whole person that was attractive, not just the gloss on the surface.

She kept herself in good shape: walking, cycling, running. She'd told him she came up to Scotland a few times a year to walk with her media pal Katy Calman: they were 'bagging Munros', well over a hundred already, but it was difficult fitting trips north into her busy diary. When they'd first met, she'd put him at his ease by getting him to talk first not about Ruth, but by asking him to talk about himself, some of the hills he'd climbed. 'I might see you one of these days,' she'd said to Nick when they parted, 'On one of those high mountain tops.' Of course, that wasn't going to happen, but it was kind of her to be friendly. And now there she was, on national television, talking about his daughter. Another fine woman he could put on a pedestal, whom he could admire from a distance. There was no harm in it, sure there wasn't.

Sam introduced the re-enactment, but Bill did the voiceover: *Sometimes,* he said, *Ruth would walk home at about 4pm with some of her school friends.* A drone camera view was following the route as Bill talked. *It's only a few hundred yards or so from the school, starting on a busy street, passing a major roundabout junction with shops and a busy cafe, then alongside Causewayhead Park and the Abbey Craig and from there down through a country road to the village.* The screen cut back to Bill in the studio, talking earnestly: *on this particular day in November, she was with a group of friends till the roundabout... then she set off for alone as usual for her home in the village of Cambuskenneth. She was seen between 4 and 4.10 walking along the road at Causewayhead Park. A school friend remembers waving to her from the bus.* On screen, on cue, the actress waved from a bus window, then the film cut to 'Ruth', beside the park. The actress was wearing a school jacket, looking a bit too young, Nick thought. Ruth would've done something to make her look older than she was. He thought of the way she used to stand in front of the hall mirror, checking little details before she'd go out – tying her scarf a certain way, pushing her tie slightly askew, a shiny belt. Try as he might though, he couldn't picture her that last morning when he'd run out the house thinking it was just another day, that they'd meet up again that evening.

We don't know why she deviated from her normal route, the TV voice was saying, *but it seems she never made it home.* The drone camera soared up several hundred feet to give a birdseye view of the entire Abbey Craig before the commentary resumed. *The Abbey Craig is a small crag-and-tail hill in Stirling, topped by The Wallace Monument. The wooded slopes of the tail drift down over half a mile or so to the level of the surrounding countryside. Although there are some well-made paths through the woods, there are also some parts that are difficult to access, some are even dangerous. At the north-east corner* (the camera drone was flying in that direction) *is one of three disused quarries – the hard whinstone quarried in the Craig was used in the construction of the monument and later was used to make millstones.* The drone descended towards the back end of the wood and into an open, quarried space, littered with cut stones. *It was here, in one of these quarries, that Ruth's body was found.*

The screen cut back to the studio and Bill was standing in front of a large screen projection of the Craig. *There are only two ways,* he said, *that she can have gone to the quarry. She could've either climbed up the steps at the back of Causewayhead Park... here,* he pointed to the photo, *and then onto a path from which she could have worked her way down to the far end of the Craig... or...*Bill repositioned himself to point at a different part of the photo, *she could have walked along the main road for a few hundred yards and entered at the little used Craigmill entrance here, at the bottom end of the woods... But whichever route she took, there is no clear path into the old quarry where she was found...* he paused to add emphasis... a*nd it's not signposted.*

Bill left the photo and walked over to his desk where he and Sam exchanged glances. She picked up the story then, looking earnestly into the camera and, it seemed to Nick, out of the screen and straight at him.

It was a murky twilight, she said, *with a strong wind blowing in from the East, heavy rain on its tail. So far, the police have been unable to speak to anyone who witnessed her enter the woods... nor to anyone who might have been there with her... nor to anyone who saw her walking in the woods. Nor can anyone explain why she would deviate from her usual route home to go in there in the first place. Can you help? Maybe you saw something?*

Nice touch, Nick thought, as the point of view changed again and a blurry 'Ruth' could be seen at the gate into the park through a wet bus window.

Were you on a bus, or in a car, on the stretch of road from Causewayhead down to Craigmill between 4 and 4-30 that wet November evening? Can you remember seeing Ruth on the pavement, in the park or at the Craigmill entrance? Can you remember seeing her or anyone else enter the Park, or the woods, on that afternoon? Perhaps someone she knew called her over, or perhaps she'd arranged to meet someone there. Perhaps there was a cry for help, and she responded. Police are anxious to speak to anyone who saw or heard anything on that evening, or who spoke to Ruth about where she was going, and why. If you were in the vicinity, or if you might know why Ruth was going into the woods that evening, you may be able to provide vital information.

As Sam carried on with the commentary, her soft voice was becoming a bit harder, a bit more theatrical, a bit more urgent, while the view on the screen was now from a hand-held camera, bobbing up and down, taking 'Ruth's' viewpoint, crashing through the undergrowth, sweeping branches aside... heading for the quarry.

To get to the disused quarry you have to leave the path and strike out through the woods. A heavy covering of wet leaves and pine needles made it difficult to find clear evidence of Ruth's exact movements, while the forensic evidence from the site where her body was found was of poor quality – there was so much heavy rain that weekend... The camera was beginning to sway about, with a heavy, panicky, panting soundtrack, with overhanging branches being pushed to the side. Greg looked round at Nick who was sitting forward now, his jaw clenched, his hands tight round his glass, while onscreen the shot cut back to Sam... *We can't show you what happened in this quarry. We just don't know. But Ruth Innocenti ended up face down in casual water in this quarry, drowned.* The screen cut back to the camera shot, now in the quarry, circling the little howff with its corrugated iron roof. *Near where she was found, there is a kind of improvised gang hut used by local youths. The hut is based on a ruined quarry building, but there is evidence that local youths have been using this hut for drinking and drug-taking sessions.*

Nick's head was pounding, but Sam's voice was slowing down now: the worst was over. *Police have been working on forensic evidence from this site – what they now need is to link the different pieces of evidence they have to a person or persons. Your information could make that connection. If you were one of the people who was in the quarry that afternoon, the police would like you to come forward. If you are someone who has used this hut recently, even if you were somewhere else on the night Ruth died, the police would like you to come forward. If you have heard someone talking about this hut, please come forward, or if you may have seen Ruth that Friday twilight from a passing car or bus, please come forward. Here's a reminder of...*

Nick snatched up the remote and switched the TV off. He stood up, flushed, breathing fast. The drink had loosened his usual inhibitions and something true was desperate to get out. 'Christ's sake,' he shouted, 'Why haven't they found the bastard?'

Greg stood up and took the remote from Nick. 'It'll be alright, buddy,' he said, 'It'll be alright. They'll catch whoever it is... and they'll put them away for a long, long time, don't you worry about that.'

Nick grabbed his friend's arms and stared at him. ''Put him away,' he said, and then again, louder, 'Put him fucking away?' He blinked and shook his head. 'See if they find him Greg,' he said more slowly, quietly, 'They'll have to be fucking lucky if they want to put him away cos they'll have to stop me getting to him first. I'll fucking kill him. And before I kill him, he's going to suffer. I'll rip his fucking cock off and stuff it down his fucking throat.'

'Let go mate,' Greg said, 'You're hurting me.'

Nick let go and collapsed back onto his chair, his breathing heavy, an angry flush spreading from his neck onto his face.

'Don't worry,' Greg said, 'They'll find him. They'll find him.'

Nick jumped up again, walked over to the window. He was still on the boil. It wasn't just anger, though there was a lot of that. It was fear too. What if there was no-one else to blame? What if Ruth, his teenage Ruth... if she was just a victim of her own recklessness, a disregard for her own safety? What if she'd gone there willingly, had sex willingly and then just stumbled and fallen, drunk, into the water? And what if the finger then was pointed at him - not someone else's finger, but his own finger? What if it was really him that was to blame? - the Dad who didn't want her to grow up, who pushed away the teenage Ruth who was replacing the wee girl he'd loved, the teenage Ruth who'd been moving away from the trusting, enclosed world of the loving child into the confused, dangerous world of the young adult. What if he was to blame? - the Dad who was too busy with his own work to notice those warning signs that were so easy to see now? When she wouldn't always tell him who she'd been with. When she'd started giving up her sport. When she'd stopped going to the orchestra. When she'd spent so much time on her phone, in forums he knew nothing about, with people he instinctively mistrusted. What if he was to blame? The Dad who didn't know who her new friends were, who didn't know what she was getting into online, what she was doing when she'd been... how had Sheila put it... 'exploring the boundaries'? What if the real culprit was the Dad she'd stopped talking to, sharing with? The Dad she couldn't trust? The Dad who'd let his daughter down? The Dad who'd not been such a good Dad... after all?

* * *

The following week, Jane Beattie told him there had been 100 plus calls since the broadcast, many concerning the little howff. That was a good return for this kind of exposure, she'd said. Of course, the police had to follow up each one. Even discounting attention seekers, there'd still be many individual interviews so it would all take time. But she reassured him that with so many calls they would surely make some progress, that something would come of it.

And things did seem better for Nick, at least for a while. The hope of finding out what had happened, or at least trying to, was like some kind of displacement activity. As long as there was action, investigation, new leads, new information, there was something to look forward to, some possibility of a breakthrough. Of course, it didn't really matter - it could never, after all, bring Ruth back - but finding the killer, if there was one, and bringing him to justice was something worth doing. It was, at the very least, something that could be done in her name.

But though Nick remained interested in the police investigations, he believed it would probably come to nothing, that the exact circumstances of her death might remain a mystery.... and that whether progress was being made in the enquiry... or not... at some point everything around him, everybody around him – in the national media, the local press, in Bruce Academy, Cambuskenneth, Stirling – everybody would go back to 'normal'... in fact, that process was already begun, was almost complete: the waters had to a large extent closed over: the ripples set in motion by her death were no longer rippling.

'Life,' people might say... even people close to him... 'has to go on.'

'It's so hard for Nick to find some closure. We understand that,' they'd say. 'But still... there comes a point... all things being equal... when life... has to go on.'

But people around him learned pretty quickly not to use the word 'closure' in his hearing. He hated that word. He hated the whole concept. It was ridiculous to even think it. Closure was like a kind of betrayal of Ruth, a forgetting, so that you were somehow supposed to get on with a life that now wasn't worth very much, a life that didn't mean anything now that she was gone and there was still no reason why.

The whole concept of 'closure', it seemed to Nick, was a pretence, disguised as some kind of solution: it spoke of some future, inevitable outcome that he would eventually, reluctantly of course, have to accept. But he... Nick... Ruth's father... he knew different. He knew that when your daughter has been raped and killed... and when you know where and when but you still don't know who or why... there never could be, and so there never would be, 'closure'.

5. Witness

The week after *Crime Helpline* aired, Nick was working up near Callander, on the Glassingall Estate. He'd been tasked to do a bit of tidying work and was working down near the pebbly shore of Loch Venachar. The sun was low in the sky and cast the kind of clean, stark light on the tops of the mountains to the North that you can only see in January or February. This was a part of the world he loved. When Clare was first expecting Ruth, and before they'd settled for the cottage in Cambuskenneth, he'd suggested they look for somewhere to live, up by one of the lochs. They'd been walking up Ben Ledi, on one of those muggy late summer days that sticks in the memory, plagued by midges on their way up, but resting on the summit, in the fresh, clear breeze that swept across the top of the mountain.

'Think of what a great childhood she could have if we found somewhere to live up here,' he remembered saying to Clare, 'Big sky, tumbling water, clean air.'

'Sounds good in theory,' Clare had said, 'But if I'm stuck at home with a new baby, I want to be somewhere where I've got friends nearby - shops, shows, trains - you know? ... civilisation? Somewhere you're not trapped if you don't have a car.'

Maybe once all this was over, he'd move somewhere like this, somewhere in the countryside, away from the city, away from people: a new life. And maybe he'd find someone to make a new life with? Could he imagine that?

His phone rang. It was Jane Beattie. He pressed *answer* and walked down to the water's edge.

'Hello Jane,' he said, 'What can I do for you?'

'Mr Innocenti... ' she hesitated, 'The thing is...eh... I need to see you. There's been a development.' Nick felt a breath of cool air shiver up the back of his neck. 'Don't worry. It's positive: nothing to worry about... but I've got a bit of time at the desk later today. If you can come into the station at Randolphfield?'

'Sure. I can just pack up now. I should be with you within an hour.'

'Make it two hours. Just come to the front desk and ask for me. I'm not going anywhere.'

His pulse was hot and loud in his ear. The Menteith Hills on the opposite shore were in shadow now, Sitka Spruce and Scots Pine covering them with a dark green blanket. A small log was bobbing up and down in the water, thirty or so yards offshore. She'd never asked him to come in at short notice before; it'd always been pre-arranged appointments or telephone updates. He walked down to the water's edge and started throwing little stones at the log.

The first stone plopped into water - well short.

It was three months since Ruth's death. It'd been two weeks since *Crime Helpline*. After the initial flurry of excitement when the programme aired, it'd begun to look like nothing useful was going to come from it. But now, this phone call.

His second stone was bigger, heavier. It made a splash a bit beyond the log. The ripples it made pushed the log off to the right.

Jane hadn't been in touch for over a week... and she'd never asked him to go in to Randolphfield before. Please God not another disappointment.

The next stone missed on the left, its splash pushing the log further to the right again. He picked up a few more stones and walked towards a small rocky promontory that jutted out into the water amid some green rushes: maybe he could hit the damn thing from there.

As he walked round, a heron started out of the rushes. Easy beats of its wings took it down the shore away from him. When it landed it looked back at him – 'try catching me now,' it seemed to be saying, then it took off again and, hugging the shore, disappeared round a stand of trees, The words of the song 'Follow the Heron' ran through his head in Karine Polwart's clear voice:

In darkness we cradled our sorrow
And stoked all our fires with fear
Now these bones that lie empty and hollow
Are ready for gladness to cheer...

He dropped the remaining stones and wiped his hands on his overalls. He still wasn't yet ready for gladness. And he certainly wasn't ready for cheer. But he was ready for whatever Jane Beattie had to tell him.

* * *

After reporting to the reception desk, he had to wait a while till she came out to greet him, conducting him into an interview room, pulling back a chair for him to sit down.

'Can I get you a tea or a coffee, sir?' she asked.

Sir? - he thought - still so formal?

'Tea would be good...' he laughed nervously, cleared his throat as she left, looked around at the walls - painted breeze blocks, high windows tight shut, storage heaters that had been kicked in more than once. Was this where they took people for an interrogation? She was taking her time. Why had he asked for tea? He hadn't wanted tea. He just wanted her to tell him what was going on. Where was she?

There were various initials carved into the desk, words scratched into the wood then sanded over, but he could still trace the edges out with his fingers: P.. O.. L.. I.. S. he moved to the next line A.. R.. E.. S.. C.. 'Polis are scum!' he said to himself, just as she came in, two mugs of tea wobbling against each other in one hand while she closed the door with the other. They both heard someone shouting in an adjacent room.

He pointed to the words. 'Whoever tried to erase this graffiti didn't make too good a job of it, did they?'

She frowned but said nothing, put the two mugs down on the table and sat down gingerly, as if testing to make sure the chair didn't collapse under her.

'I'm sorry,' he said, 'I'm just nervous. I know this must be something big or you wouldn't have called me in.'

'Look, Mr. Innocenti, the thing is...' she spoke quietly and shuffled a little in her seat, '...we've been able to locate someone who was in the howff on the night of Ruth's death... and she has named another person.'

He took a deep breath, then another. Closed his eyes. She was still talking but he hadn't heard.

'Sorry,' he said, 'Can you repeat?'

'I was saying,' she said, 'There's a girl has come into the station this morning. She claims she was there, in the howff that night, and she's given us another name... and before you ask, I can't give you the name. She and the person she's named are both under 16. The other people that came forward after the TV, all those phone calls... as you know there was very little helpful information from them. But this girl knows things, things that check out with what we know of the scene. We've got a few more things to clear up, but Iif what she says stacks up, it could give us the key we've been looking for and the story may start to fall into place.'

'How come she's only just come forward?' he said.

'She's been away, in England somewhere... way south. Went the day before Ruth was found. Mother says it was all planned long before but that'll have to be checked. Anyway, this girl wasn't even on the radar, never been involved with the police before. But if the other one she's named was there? Well...' she arched an eyebrow, 'He is well known to police in Stirling.'

'So... what does *he* say?'

'He's not been questioned yet. And she was only in the station this morning, with her mother, and, like I say, there are still details to be checked out. But I... I mean we... wanted to let you know this is happening. We'll bring this lad in soon and, depending on how things go, the press may have it tonight, or tomorrow, if something comes of it. It's harder to control information these days, so the team wanted me to let you know in person, before you hear from another source.'

'Thanks.' Nick drained the mug of tea. 'So... what happens now?'

'Well, we're going to question the boy she's named obviously, see if we can tie any of the physical evidence we have to this witness statement, and to whatever he says. Because he's under 16, there's a different set of procedures... you know... the law has to treat him as a child... the Fiscal has to have a look at the evidence we come up with and decide what, if any, charges should be laid. If it's a serious charge it goes over to Edinburgh, to the Lord Advocate's office, for a decision. It's a complicated process, can be quite lengthy, but you'll get a full briefing as and if a charge is laid. There may be no charges of course... the likeliest outcome of the investigation is that Ruth's death was accidental... I told you that before... And if there's anything you want to know, if there's anything that comes up on the media that throws you... you've still got me... for now... then again, you'll probably lose me soon, if it does go forward.'

'How d'you mean?'

'Well if it's going to go further, to the courts, you'll have a VIA - Victim Information and Advice officer. They take over... provide support for anyone in your kind of situation... once things get to court.' She checked her watch. 'You can still contact me obviously if you want to, but once a VIA is assigned, they'll be your main contact... and I won't have the up to date information on the court side of things...' He wanted to speak but she talked over him, keen to get all the information out. He noticed a red flush spreading up her neck. '... and I want you to listen very carefully to what I'm going to say now. This next bit is about your behaviour... what we expect from you.' She paused, settled him with her eyes, then carried on.

'Once the media get hold of this, and bearing in mind that this has been, and still will be, a very high profile case from their point of view... well... I just need to advise you... that it can be very difficult to retain control of what gets said out there.' She paused. 'Also, there can be unhelpful journalistic speculation going on... and you're going to have to think very carefully about how you're going to handle yourself. You'd be well advised to keep right away from the media... there's a risk anything you say to them could contaminate any case that we might want to bring, or you could even get yourself into more trouble – any story with *you* in it, rather than the crime, might make you the focus of media attention, not the case...' she took a deep breath and looked straight at him, 'So...you're going to have to let us do our job, keep a low profile... not get involved. Do you understand?' It was a professional question - not unfriendly, but insistent, impersonal, like a teacher making clear to a child where the boundaries lay - what was allowed... and what was not.

Nick nodded.

'Good,' Jane said. 'And there's more.' She stood up and pushed the chair in. 'We may need to ask you some more questions if these interviews lead to new evidence, new lines of enquiry. It depends how the PF wants to play it. The VIA - they can advise and support you on all of that if things go further. One of the VIAs will be in here later. I can get them to come in and see you if they've time, just for a preliminary chat, explain their role, what might happen kind of thing. If you want that, it may take a wee bit of time to set it up, but if It can be done soon, you could just hang on for a bit, or go for a walk and come back.' She smoothed down her skirt, her neck and cheeks still flushed. 'I don't feel very happy about just leaving you like this in the meantime, but...I've got to get on I'm afraid. There's going to be a lot of work here... and there's new cases on my desk also need attention.' Her tone felt a bit curt. Or maybe just professional. She had a job to do.

'Sorry,' he scraped his chair clumsily as he got up, 'No worries, ay?' He fumbled in his pocket for his keys. 'I'll see this... what was it?... VIA?... person... at home. Not here. I'll go mad if I stay here, waiting... Get them to phone me before they come to the house. I might be out for a long run.'

'Are you sure you're OK?' she said.

'Absolutely sure,' he said.

She picked up the mugs. As he followed her out and into the reception area, he noticed the slight sway of her hips, the fall of her hair. And it felt good, what she'd told him, that things were moving on. Was this the start of the endgame now? And was there another life waiting for him out the other end? She punched the release button on the outer door of the station and stepped aside for him to go out.

As he passed her, he took hold of her elbow and turned her towards him. 'Your support has been the best bit of all this for me. I just want to thank you.'

'Just my job,' she said, stepping back slightly and taking her arm away, 'Take care.' And with that the door was shut and he was out in the car park.

On his own.

* * *

Nick poured himself a very large whisky that night. He was pouring a lot of whiskies these days, and most of them were large ones, very large ones. He went back over what Jane Beattie had said, trying to remember every word, wishing he'd recorded it. Was there any hidden meaning he hadn't picked up?

Jane Beattie: she was a big part of the story, had been with him on the journey, sitting by his side. Now she was cutting herself out of it, cutting him off... well that's how it was. It was just another job for her, after all, why should it be any different? Just cut him off. That easy.

And Sam Hill too. There was another one... he put his glass down on the table and replaced the cap on the whisky bottle... another one that'd held his hand a little on the road, then left him. On his own. And here he was, getting drunk. Also on his own. He rubbed his hands all over his face, scratched his head, under his chin, then took the cap off the bottle again and poured himself another one, just a little one this time. Couldn't do any harm.

He didn't even know Sam Hill, had only met her once. Now he was watching her on *Crime Helpline* every week, like some introverted wee teenager with a first crush. You couldn't call it a crush, could you? Not at his age. What would you call it then? Was there something creepy going on? Jane Beattie... Sam Hill... were they too young for him? He didn't think so. What age were they? Late twenties?.... no. Early thirties at least, maybe mid-thirties? Yes. Probably mid-thirties. They still looked quite young to him but definitely not too young. And why had he fallen for them, why did he want them still in his life? They were both attractive women, no doubt about that, but it wasn't that. It wasn't just how they looked: it was how they were. There was a kindness to them, a kindness, an openness, that had helped him to feel that life might possible, easier, again.

But was he making that up, just cos they were women? Making them into some kind of mother-figure or maybe, given their age, more of a sister figure... how a sister would've been, if he'd ever had a sister? Eyes, smiles, warmth, compassion – it was all their goddam goodness – that was what had opened him up, got through his protective shell: their goddam female goodness.

He shook his head, stood up, wobbled a little to find his balance, walked over to the window. He was a fool. Letting himself think this way was going to get him into trouble. It was all a lot of crap, sentimental crap, all in his own head. It was drink talking, messing with his brain. He needed to give himself a shake. They were good women, no doubt, but they were just doing their job, and doing it well. This was much more to do with him than them. He was a lonely man. A man alone. On his own. They'd walked with him on the journey for a while then they were bound to move on: there were other cases, other people. But he wasn't going to move on. Couldn't. There was no other case to move on to, no other life to take up, no other daughters waiting in the wings.

And he was vulnerable too - emotionally vulnerable – his whole life was very near the surface now, had been since.... And that had made him needy, needy for something, somebody, to believe in. These women gave him hope - their little kindnesses, their sympathetic words, their welcoming smiles - hope that somewhere down the road life might get better. He'd put them on a pedestal, held them up high there, untouchable, untarnished, out of reach. Looking at them up there, it had been almost possible to believe that life would be worth living. OK, maybe not now, but... he took a sip of the whisky and rolled it around his mouth... that was a very good question, wasn't it? A very good question. Was life worth living? His life? What was his life for... what exactly was he for? Now?

It wasn't the first time he'd asked that question of himself. It was the question that had taken him into philosophy, the course he'd pursued at University. What exactly was the point of his miserable existence? And the answer he'd ended up with then - after all the reading, all the arguments in tutorial sessions, in late night discussions round the kitchen table of the flat he shared with a medic and a vet, in the essays he'd had to write... his answer to that question hadn't been in the abstract thought of philosophers, or in politics or in religion... or in any words at all: words were just that - words. They meant nothing if they didn't stand for something real, in the real physical world of touch and smell and sound. Meaning wasn't intellectual. It was physical. The daily miracles of life were in the body, in the soil, in the plants he helped germinate and grow, not in the empty words of philosophy books. In the physical world around him, in the real people he loved, the flesh and blood people, the people who lived and breathed, not the people in books. Meaning was in the people that mattered to him. In Clare. In Ruth. He finished his glass. He wasn't going to drink any more. He had to get real. That was then. And this was now. No more whisky. A cup of tea would do better. He needed to drink less whisky and more tea.

As he stepped back into the hall, he saw the anasphone on the wall blinking red again, another thing to add to all the problems that were building up around him – unanswered work calls on his mobile and his anasphone, unanswered e.mails in his website enquiry box, unanswered texts, unanswered letters, unpaid invoices, reminders stacking up on the desk. This was his business, his gardening business that he'd been so proud of - *One Man and His Labour*: *organic, renewable* - more than a business really, more like an identity. It had seemed so important before – but when it came down to it, what did it matter?

He carried the empty glass through to the kitchen and splashed his face with cold water.

'Get a grip, Nick,' he said to his reflection in the dark kitchen window, 'You're not some angsty teenager. You're a man, in charge of your own destiny. This is your life. You have to take control of it. Only you can make it how you want it. Get a fucking grip!'

He poured a cupful of water into the kettle and stood waiting for it to boil, his legs twitching. But was this life he had worth anything? No-one in his family had understood him, what he'd wanted for his life. 'You're moving fast,' Uncle Raymondo had said to him affectionately after his first year in his eco-gardening business, 'Unfortunately, it's in the wrong direction... backwards!' He could see Uncle Raymondo's point now. His work, his whole manufactured identity, was a sham. Ruth had seen that. Calling him out for pretending to be green while driving a monster diesel truck.

He poured his cup of tea and took it through to his bedroom.

'Just keep putting one foot in front of the other, getting through one day, then the next.' That's what Greg had said to him after Ruth's funeral. 'Day to day mate,' he said, 'Just day to day.'

'Thoreau was right enough Greg,' Nick had said back.

'What did Thoreau have to say when he was at home?'

'If we're to believe Thoreau, I'm in good company Greg. There was a great quote somewhere in Thoreau that I always remember ... well, I may not remember it exactly, but it was something like *Most men live lives of quiet desperation*. Quiet desperation, Greg ... quiet fucking desperation! That's me exactly. Quiet. And desperate. That's exactly me.'

'I don't see Thoreau anywhere around here,' Greg had said, 'But I'm here... and I'm your mate... and I'm not despairing.'

6. Prosecution

Things did begin to move more quickly the following week, with Jane Beattie keeping Nick updated about what was likely to happen. Several possible charges were being considered by the Procurator Fiscal. The case might go to Edinburgh for a final decision.

'What are the likely charges then? What are the Fiscal's choices?' Nick asked her.

'That's above my pay grade,' she said.

'Could the charge be murder?'

'It's possible.'

'Rape?'

'Yes, that's possible too. As I told you before,' that teacherly tone was back again in her voice, 'It all depends on the evidence. The evidence required to support a charge of murder is high bar to aim for. There're many other possible charges – culpable homicide, for example, and the drugs charges as well... like I've said before, there's no point speculating really. It's all down to the evidence. Fiscals go where the evidence leads. The police don't get to call it. Our job is to collect and present all the available evidence and our job stops when we hand that evidence over. That's why I'm handing you over to VIA... remember?... the Victim Information and Advice officer?'

'And do I have a say about that? What's to happen?'

'Of course! What you think, what you feel... all of us involved in detection and prosecution understand that it's important to hear your voice. We all want to know what you're thinking. But the charge to be brought, the legal processes – that's all for the professionals.'

* * *

Over the next couple of weeks Nick tried to shrink his horizons down to the routine of daily living, trying to notice the little things, to find a peace in the everyday. His life was going on, and he was going to have to live it, even if it didn't feel much like living. And wouldn't Ruth, Clare, wouldn't they want him to live his life in full?

Not long after, he was called into a 'handover meeting' with Philben and Jane. Emily Derwent, a young lawyer from the Procurator Fiscal's office, was there. Nick thought she looked about 15. Andy Marshall, the VIA officer who'd been assigned to his case, was there too. Andy was heavily overweight: the mere act of walking seemed to cause him enormous effort, given the heavy breathing that accompanied every movement. He had a sad, resigned kind of manner. A dark, sweaty, stubbly shadow covered his double chin; hair sprouted from his nose and his ears, dandruff speckled the shoulders of his worn suit jacket. Andy was definitely no Jane Beattie, but he'd been around the block a few times and seemed to know what he was talking about. As details of the case were discussed, and possible next steps outlined, it all sounded quite technical, professional. Nick felt that the case was in good hands. The police and the prosecution service were doing their job. They were doing it well.

* * *

Nick had also been working on his relationship with Dorothy. Since their Christmas meal, they'd had been meeting every second week or so at the Blythswood Square Hotel in Glasgow for Saturday lunch. Each time they met, he'd given her a brief edited version of what Jane had told him about the police investigation, but now, with lawyers involved and the possibility of a trial looming, he was dreading having to tell her more details of what might have happened that night in the drinking den and of the legal process that was attempting to deal with it... the inadequate legal process, as far as Nick was concerned. When all was said and done, the best the legal process could do was to try to prevent those who committed this from committing any future crimes, to try to discourage others from similar crimes, and thus, somehow, to mitigate the potential impact of this crime on society more widely. But there was no 'after the fact' process that could ever mitigate the *real* impact of the crime on the *real* people who had *really* suffered: Ruth was dead. And she wasn't coming back. Ever.

Nonetheless, Nick felt he should be upbeat with Dorothy. After they'd ordered their lunch and exchanged a bit of meaningless small talk, he briefed her on some of the less challenging developments – the new set of professionals who were dealing with the case now that it seemed likely to go to court, what the procedures were, where things were likely to go next, how long it might take. 'I gained an impression that all the people involved are quite competent,' he said as they sipped their coffees after lunch. 'And a lot of this stuff is in that booklet they gave us way back... remember? It was called *Information for bereaved families,* or something like that anyway...'

'You'd think I'd know a lot about the courts since my father was an advocate,' Dorothy said, 'But I don't. It'll be hard to keep track of all these people and what they do. The SIO, the VIA, the FLO. Why can't people say the proper words these days? It'd be so much easier if I had pictures, so I could see their faces. I just hope they do their job properly.'

'You know,' he said, 'how I told you they can't give us the names of the kids who were in the 'howff'? - you can't with under 16s apparently.'

'Yes, you told me that,' she said.

'Well... when... that is... if... the case goes to a pre-trial hearing I'll be able to attend, see them in person. You too if you want.' Nick looked around the room. 'So... it's probably better if I tell you the kind of things that might be said, so it won't come as a surprise to you. Some of it's not very pleasant, so just tell me if you want me to stop. And once I tell you, you'll have to be careful about what you say, even to close friends. None of this can come out in public. The police warned me that anything we say in public could prejudice any trial, if a trial takes place at all that is.'

'Of course.'

'Well... what I'm going to give you is a summary of what they've told me of the evidence this girl provided, the one who turned up after the TV programme? The first thing is that... well... I don't quite know how to say it.'

'Just spit it out, Nick, for goodness sake. I'm seventy four years old.'

'Well... so...apparently.... Anyway... '

'Get on with it, Nick, for goodness sake!'

'OK. Sorry. You see... what it is... is... that this girl says that Ruth was interested in a boy and asked her, the girl that is, to set up a meeting with him.'

'What boy?'

'Just 'a boy' that she apparently wanted to meet, or so this girl says...'

'So, there was a meeting. What then?'

'Well... the meeting was to take place after school in the 'den', the one where Ruth was found. Ruth was told to be there, told to keep it a secret. No other people were to turn up – it'd just be the two of them and this boy. In the version this girl told it was all meant to be "a bit of a laugh". Only things got out of hand.'

'Was she a friend of Ruth's, this girl?'

'Not sure if you could say 'friend' as such, not one who's ever been round the house, as far as I know, but then I don't know who the girl is. But Ruth had been getting involved with a different crowd after she started back in fourth year. And there were lots of things she didn't tell me about.'

'Go on.'

'The boy brought along some cider, very strong cider apparently, and some ecstasy. *Eccies*, they call them, apparently... the ecstasy tablets. They hadn't been mentioned before, but the girl says Ruth was up for it: "wild" was the word she used. According to her, Ruth had drunk an awful lot of cider, much too quickly.'

Dorothy slammed her hand on the table so hard that the cutlery jumped up in the air. 'The girl's a liar,' she growled. 'What you should say... Nick...' she fixed him with her eyes, '... is that they forced Ruth to drink more than she wanted. It's quite obvious to me that this girl is nothing more than a little strumpet. If anyone was "wild", you can bet your life it was her, the little tart!'

'Well.' Nick paused, swallowed, took a quick look round. Dorothy was going to like the next bit even less. 'Whether she was pushed into it or not, Ruth seems to have got drunk very quickly. According to this girl, Ruth said she wanted to try the drugs too, laughed about it. The girl says she told the boy not to give Ruth any, cos she'd never taken them before, had drunk too much alcohol, but Ruth insisted, so she says, so it ended up they were all, as the girl says, *loved up* – I think that means the drugs made them feel kind of well... you know...'

'For goodness sake Nick, I'm not an idiot! I've got the idea. And the boy?'

'I don't know about the boy. They only advised me what the girl might say. Apparently, ecstasy can make you feel, well... kind of lovey-dovey, but not necessarily sexy ... in some cases, men can lose their erection.'

A waitress came over to ask if they wanted anything else, but Dorothy waved her away impatiently.

'Go on Nick,' she said, 'Don't spare me. I need to hear the whole thing.'

'Well. It seems the boy showed the girls some porn on his phone.' Dorothy winced as if she'd just sipped a bitter drink. Nick took another look round the room – all around, south-side and west-end ladies, with money to spend on their shoes and their outfits, were at lunch, sipping their tea, sharing their confidences. He didn't think any of them could've heard anything he'd been saying. Anyway, hadn't one of the Sunday papers done an investigation into 'porn in the suburbs'... maybe they were all at it, more than he'd ever been... He carried on.

'So... According to this girl, there was a lot of dirty talk and the three of them were,' he leaned in and whispered, 'The word that was quoted to me was...' he hesitated again... *'horny...'*

'For goodness' sake Nick!' Dorothy scolded, 'Don't be ridiculous! There's no need to be squeamish with me. I know the meaning of the word *horny*. You'd obviously be surprised just how much I know. A damn sight more than you I expect. So just spit it out! Get it over with!'

'OK.' Nick looked round the room again. 'So... It seems that, according to this girl anyway, both the girls had condoms. She says that they got them from a drop-in clinic at the school.'

'What have we come to?' Dorothy asked. 'When did children stop being children? What on earth have we come to? Condoms being given out to school children? And I'll tell you this Nick: I don't believe a word this girl says. She's a liar start to finish. I hope you don't believe all this either.'

'I'm just telling you what's might be said in evidence at the hearing. I don't know what to believe.'

'Of course... I know that... Sorry... Just carry on.'

'The girl says that she had sex with the boy. She says Ruth just watched, could hardly move...said she was *wasted*, apparently...' Nick hesitated but Dorothy waved her hand for him to carry on. 'So... the girl says that she fell asleep then... and didn't wake up till after Ruth was gone. Quite convenient I know, but that's her story... more or less... as I understand it from the police.'

'Very convenient. More than convenient. It's absolute rubbish. It's so obviously just absolute rubbish.' Dorothy twisted the napkin in her hands, 'Absolute... bloody... unbelievable... rubbish.' She took a deep breath, put down the napkin, squared her shoulders. 'So. What did she say happened to Ruth? That's the whole point, isn't it?'

'She claims she didn't see anything after that. The last thing she remembers before she passed out was Ruth complaining about being dizzy, too hot. When she woke up later, Ruth wasn't there. She assumed that Ruth had gone home.' Nick paused.

'Go on with it,' Dorothy said, motioning to him to carry on.

'The next morning, she went down to stay with her aunt in the South of England – she used to stay down there apparently, but that's where I think her story doesn't add up Dorothy.' Nick's tone picked up, more assertive. 'She must've known something wasn't right, else why did she run away to the south of England? That was before it even was in the papers or anything. Her story is that she knew nothing about Ruth's death till she saw the TV programme, but it's obvious that the police wouldn't believe that. Teenagers are constantly on their phones. It would've gone round her social media world like wildfire. She'd have found out right away whatever part of the country she was in.' A group at a nearby table had just finished paying their bill. Nick stopped talking while they made their way slowly past and out towards the exit. 'All the same,' he went on, 'Whatever her reason for going away, it seems that she decided she had to say something after she'd seen the *Crime Helpline* broadcast.'

'Well as far as I'm concerned, it's a pack of lies,' Dorothy said, 'A downright pack of lies. Ruth would never have... in a place like that... And didn't the post-mortem show that she'd been raped? They must have forced her, and that girl was part of it, I'm sure. Trying to cover up her part in it. A little hussy, she is, for sure. I wouldn't believe a word a girl like that says. A bare-faced liar...'

Dorothy suddenly started sobbing, loud retching sobs. One or two of the ladies at nearby tables looked over. Nick thought he should get up and put his arm round her but, while he hesitated, she pulled herself together, bristled a little, cleared her throat, returned to her usual commanding manner. 'What charges are going to be laid against this girl, this boy?'

'I don't know. The police are obviously comparing what she said to the forensic and witness evidence they already have. Nothing's off the table. There may be charges of culpable homicide and rape against the boy, but they keep telling me that the final charges "all depend on the evidence". There may be less than they want, maybe even less than they need.'

'What else do they need?'

'Well, for example, I believe the police did find used condoms in and around the scene, but none that could be linked to this boy. Of course, after what happened he could have removed it, disposed of it somewhere else. He's had quite a lot of time to cover his tracks.'

'So. The girl?' she said in a short peremptory voice, 'Why isn't she being charged?'

'She's apparently quite a vulnerable girl. A bit of a victim herself. Her safety seems to be more of a concern than anything she might do to anyone else. She's already under some kind of supervision. The police will probably want the Children's Panel to find the best way forward for her.'

'I'll bet you there's more to it than that. Vulnerable indeed. Girls like that can get boys to do whatever they want. She's at the bottom of this, mark my words.'

'The girl says she didn't expect there to be alcohol or the drugs when they got to the howff – the police have been able to establish that the boy did buy alcohol around about that time, but not the ecstasy. On the other hand, she says that it was the girls that brought the condoms. It wasn't Ruth who obtained them though. That was the other girl. She says Ruth was in on it... but didn't want to ask.' He caught the expression on Dorothy's face and put his hands up. 'I know, I know!' he said, 'I'm just telling you what I've been told. The police view seems to be that at the very least the boy may have some kind of responsibility for Ruth's death by recklessly – that's an important word apparently - supplying the drugs and the alcohol. If that's what he did, then the charge will probably be culpable homicide... you know that's the Scottish equivalent of manslaughter, don't you?'

Dorothy gave Nick an imperious look, a disdainful look. It wasn't necessary to answer the question.

'It's a terrible thing to say Nick,' she said, 'but I really wish I hadn't lived long enough to see this happen. What a world we live in. Ruth would never...' Dorothy looked as if she might lose it again but swallowed and recovered. Her face only showed anger now. 'All I can say is I hope I live to see justice done. I wish she'd never gone to that damn school.'

'Dorothy,' Nick said. 'Let's not fall out over that again. Many perfectly good kids go to that school, from all kinds of backgrounds. Ruth was a good kid. It's a good school.'

Dorothy tucked her head in a little but said no more.

Nick had had more experience of drugs than Dorothy. He'd gone to a few raves in his final year at school in the 90s, smoked a few joints in those days too, and a few more in his student days at Glasgow University... lost it a few times. He knew people who'd taken ecstasy back then, but he never had himself. A guy from his school had died at one event. He'd been careful after that. And he'd been so much older that Ruth when he had his little experiments with drugs - and with sex – nearer 20, he'd been. She wasn't yet 15, desperate to be all grown up, but still a child in so many ways.

Nick offered to accompany Dorothy home, but she refused. She was keeping up her routines. There was an afternoon meeting at her Church. She wasn't going to miss it. There was nothing else to do, she said, but carry on with life.

On the Stirling train back home, Nick went back over time and again all that Andy had told him was likely to happen. The boy involved had already appeared at a private court hearing 'on petition', based on the evidence the police had provided. Since he already had some sort of a record for violence, he'd been remanded in custody, while the Crown Office checked every bit of evidence and looked for any further evidence that might strengthen their case. They'd be working out their case strategy and anticipating ways in which a defence lawyer might challenge the evidence. The first public step in the case was a 'preliminary hearing,' where the charge would be laid and the defendant would have to plead: it was a kind of preparation for trial, clarifying technical details.

Andy told Nick he'd have to give a signed statement – what he knew, or didn't know about Ruth's habitual behaviour, her friendships, her intentions on that day. Nick wondered what he would say. He was only too aware now of how many things he hadn't known about Ruth. If the case went to trial, Andy explained to Nick, the hearing would just be the beginning, but the Crown Office might prefer the boy to plead guilty to a lesser charge, with a lighter sentence. Plea bargains were a good way to avoid the inevitable expense, media exposure and delay of a trial: this involved a defendant pleading guilty to a lesser charge and receiving a lighter sentence. Where the evidence was very strong, no fiscal would go for a plea bargain, but if the evidence was weaker there was a risk that a jury might return a 'not guilty', or even a 'not proven' verdict. Nick listened and took it all in, but he had very little to say about it. After all, it was all out of his hands anyway.

When he got back to the house, Nick collected the framed photos of Ruth that were round the house - on the walls, in the front room, on the tallboy in his bedroom - and placed them all together on the kitchen table. He poured himself a large whisky and kept the bottle to hand. Ruth as a baby. Ruth as a talkative three-year-old. Ruth in her primary school uniform. Ruth on her first two-wheeler. Ruth with Clare on their Welsh holiday. The three of them at Dorothy's 65th birthday party. He poured another whisky, drank it, then poured another. And then he poured another...

* * *

Spring was on the way and Nick's work commitments were building up again. Many of his regular customers had gardens that needed preparation work done - shrubs that needed pruning, borders that needed prepared, seedlings that needed pricking out and bringing on in the greenhouse. Sometimes, when he got involved in his work, he found that, if only for a short time, he'd not been thinking about Ruth, the trial, what was still to come.

And he still had his running, his singing on Tuesdays, his mother and Dorothy at the weekend, running with Greg once or twice a week, pints afterwards. He even fitted in a couple of Munros. Nothing felt very worthwhile, but he was keeping busy... and days were following other days... and those other days were turning into weeks... and soon the spring flowers would be ready to show their faces. Was this what people meant by 'moving on', he wondered? If it was, he didn't want it. He didn't want to 'move on'.

How could he... how could anyone... 'move on' from their daughter's death?

* * *

Andy's briefing about the possibility of charges other than murder proved prescient. Two weeks later, on the day before the hearing was due, he phoned Nick to inform him that the charge of rape had been dropped: the evidence supported just one charge - culpable homicide, based on the reckless supply of alcohol and a controlled drug to a 14-year-old girl resulting in her death. Nick took the call while he was planting seed potatoes in his allotment, scrabbling at his phone with his dirty fingers.

'So that's it then, is it?' he said, 'Rape doesn't count?'

Andy hesitated before answering, careful with his words. 'The lad maintains that any sexual activity was consensual, as it clearly was with the other girl. And there are no other witnesses to say otherwise. The other girl's testimony works against Ruth – she says Ruth did agree to go there, and there was evidence that she was interested in the boy, and the girls did obtain the condoms from the school clinic – Ruth wasn't there when the other girl asked for them, but the teacher remembers her waiting at the door. It might be difficult to convince a jury *beyond reasonable doubt*.'

'I thought there was bruising,' Nick shouted down the phone, 'Tissue damage.'

'Nick,' Andy said, 'I'm really sorry. They just don't feel the evidence is strong enough. Virginity makes tissue damage more likely... and rough sex can still be consensual. In fact the PF thought it would be very difficult to make any charge of rape or sexual assault stick. The defence can use evidence that shows Ruth was interested in sex.'

'And I suppose it's the same story with homicide, is it?' Nick took a deep breath. 'Evidence not strong enough for murder, is it?'

'Yes, that's right. There was no forensic evidence to tie the boy to the site where she drowned. And both he and the girl tell the same story, Nick. Ruth told them she was going home... maybe she felt remorse or shame or just was frightened by what'd happened. They didn't see her drown.'

'*Remorse*? Is that the word they used Andy? *Remorse*? Sounds like just the sort of word kids would use, doesn't it?'

'Nick, I know you're upset...'

Nick took the phone away from his ear. Tears were streaming down his face. He fell to his knees and sat back on his heels. Andy was still talking. He put the phone back to his ear.

'...so once this additional evidence was looked at, together with the forensic evidence, it just didn't stack up as murder. The best the Crown can go for is culpable homicide on the grounds of recklessly supplying the drugs... I'm really sorry.'

Nick felt an uncontrollable rage building. 'So better to fucking kill your rape victim than let them live cos you can always cop a plea to a lesser offence... is that it? What kind of fucking justice is that? What kind of lesson does that give to other rapists eh?'

'Nick,' Andy said, 'Nick, Nick... the defence can argue it was consensual. There was evidence on her laptop that Ruth had been looking at porn sites...'

'Yeah... to find out what kind of stuff was out there... what kind of perverts she might meet... what the boys in her class were watching... not for her own interest surely, for God's sake.'

'... and it wasn't just the girl's evidence that showed she'd been interested in the boy. There was some internet chat, enough to support an alternative story the defence could put to a jury that Ruth went there of her own volition, wanted to take part in what was on offer, that what happened afterwards was no-one's fault. That the whole thing was just a terrible, tragic accident.'

'So... the innocent online chat of a wee girl, just getting into something she didn't fully understand. So that's now to be used against her.'

'Until we had the names, Ruth's chat room chatter was just all part of the background noise. There were so many bits, so many different people. But this lad's name, the one she was supposed to be interested in, he was in there... he was in there....' Nick waited for Andy to say some more. '... and you have to say it looks a lot less like rape, doesn't it, if it's the girls who carried the condoms?'

'I just don't believe it,' Nick said, 'I just don't believe it. It must've been the other girl that was carrying condoms... Ruth may not even have known that she was doing that....'

'You're her father Nick. Of course, you don't believe it. And just so you're clear, I personally don't believe it either. But it doesn't matter what we think. The Crown has to prove it to a jury, and a judgment has been made by the people who know about these things that there isn't the evidence to prove it.'

'Fine then. Fine. I can see where this is going. Don't think I won't fight it. I will. I bloody will.' Nick took two or three deep breaths. 'If he's found guilty, what kind of a sentence will he get? Ten years? Out in five? Slap on the wrist.'

'That'll be up to the judge Nick. The defence can make a statement in mitigation – for all we know there may be factors in the boy's family life, abuse the boy has experienced at home, that sort of thing... but you can make a victim statement as well. I can help you with that. And of course the ages matter. Children under 16 don't always go to a Children's Panel you know... for more serious offences, they can end up in court... but they may still be treated differently, even in a court setting.'

The breathing had helped Nick to calm down. He watched a robin digging about in the soil he had recently dug over. It was a beautiful world and a hellish world, all at the same time.

He put the phone back to his ear. 'I can see,' he said, 'why it's better not to go to a trial. But I'm going to do my darndest to make sure they've considered every possible angle, every scrap of evidence. If the prosecution put a foot wrong, I'll be on their case.'

'As I said before, you have the chance to make a victim statement. I'm going to send you the form,' Andy said, 'You're still on the same gmail as before, are you?'

'Yes.'

'That's me sending it now...'

'Fine. And what about Ruth's grandmother. I assume she can make a statement too.'

'Of course.'

'I'll print out the form for her. It may be easier for her to write it by hand.'

'I can send you a printed copy for her if that's easier.'

'It's going to be a while before any trial, isn't it? And there'll be social work reports, all that kind of stuff... our little statements won't really count for much, will they?'

'Yes. But the victim statement is very important. Don't belittle it. The judges take it very seriously.'

'Do they Andy? Do they really?'

Nick ended the call and stood for some time watching the robin darting in and out of the rich earth. His teeth were clenched so tight that his jaw was hurting. Already he could imagine the plea in mitigation, drafted by a clever defence lawyer: *he'd had a difficult childhood; he had every reason to believe Ruth was a willing participant; he was really sorry he hadn't looked out for her after giving her the cider and the drugs; he knew they should have followed her when she ran off; he'd never do that again; it really wasn't his fault and he'd certainly learned his lesson.* Christ, he might even be found not guilty.

Even thinking about it was painful. He'd told Andy he'd be on top of every detail of the case, but in a tiny part of his brain a thought was growing: in a trial, the defence would be sure to drag Ruth's name through the mud. If the evidence didn't stack up, wouldn't it be better for the Procurator Fiscal just to say 'enough' rather than put her memory through all that? After all nothing was going to bring her back.

Andy phoned Nick again a few minutes later. 'Hi Nick,' he said, 'I've been thinking about what you said. I want you to know I can really understand where you're coming from. There can't be anything worse can happen to a parent than what's happened to you...'

Nick said nothing.

'Thing is, I wonder if you've thought of getting some help. You know. Counselling. I talked to you about it before...'

Nick said nothing.

'I've worked with other people… not exactly in your situation but victims nonetheless. For some of them it really helped. You know? To have someone they could speak to, an experienced person who could help them come to terms with what's happened?' He waited longer for a response this, but still none came. 'Nick? Are you still there? Nick?'

'I'm still here.'

'So will you take what I've said on board. It only comes from my experience.'

'I'll give it some thought, but at the moment, Andy, the idea of "coming to terms" seems a bit ridiculous, frankly. Who would want to come to terms with the death of their daughter? Don't you think that's ridiculous? Andy? The death of your daughter is something you're never going to come to terms with, is it? It's a life-changing event, like people say. What that means, Andy, when people say "life-changing" is that life is changed, that life will never be the same again. And I can tell you from where I am now that that is exactly what is happening to me. My life is never going to be the same. How do you "come to terms" with that, Andy?'

'Of course… I understand… Things are pretty raw just now. But if not now, or next week, month…?' Nick said nothing in reply, so Andy carried on. 'Maybe in time you might come back to it Nick? And I can help put you in touch with the right people. Victim Support are good at this sort of thing.'

'Thanks Andy.' Nick said, then switched off his phone.

He was angry, confused, upset, sad, torn. But above all he was angry. And that was good, right? What kind of a person would he be if he didn't have these feelings? These feelings weren't just inevitable, they were right. There was no way he was going to be 'counseled' out of them.

* * *

Nick and Dorothy agreed to attend the Preliminary Hearing together and met outside the High Court in Glasgow at 9.30.

'I don't like this dark sky,' Dorothy said, 'It's a bad omen don't you think?'

Nick was tense. 'It's just a natural phenomenon,' he said rudely, 'It can't be good or bad.' They walked in together, but neither of them spoke again.

Court 7 of the High Court in Glasgow, where the hearing was to take place, is in the basement of the old building, downstairs and along a narrow corridor. There were several hearings booked for that morning and it seemed that there weren't enough seats in the public gallery for all those who wanted to attend the morning session, so those whose cases had not yet been called were having to wait in the corridor, a crowd of relatives and friends of both accused and victims, mingling together, waiting for their cases to be called: The court professionals - advocates, their gowns hanging off the shoulders, solicitors in smart suits, court interpreters – swept confidently through the crowd and on into court, keying in the door entry code.

Announcements were being made on the tannoy system but with the buzz of loud conversation in the narrow, crowded corridor it was impossible to hear what was said. The atmosphere was hot. People were on edge. Andy had said he would meet them at court but there was no sign of him. There had been several policemen at the main entrance, but Nick thought it would have been much more sensible to have them down here.

'Fuckin' ridiculous this is,' a woman said, to no-one in particular, 'Fuckin ridiculous. They just treat us like animals, ay? Came through early from Stirling and couldnae even get to see my son. An now we're stuck here.'

She'd come over from Stirling. Was this the mother of the boy who'd killed Ruth?'

Nick turned away. He wasn't wanting conversation, but the woman had seen the expression on Dorothy's face. 'An you neednae put that face oan missus. How'd you feel if it was your laddie?

One of the other women with her turned towards Nick and Dorothy, 'Never mind Michelle,' she said, 'She's upset. Her son's up this morning.'

'I'm very sorry for her,' Nick said, 'But seeing as how it's my daughter that was murdered,' he paused, then shouted, 'I think you should shut the fuck up!' In his head Nick wanted to carry on... to grab the woman by the neck and throw her against the opposite wall... but instead, taking a visibly shaken Dorothy by the elbow, he steered her up the stairs to the cooler hallway above. Andy had just arrived and was out of puff. He apologized profusely for being late.

'It's crowded down there,' Nick said to him, 'They're only letting people into the court for their own case so all the people for our case are standing around waiting. I could easily have got into a fight with the family of the boy who's appearing.'

'Yes... it's a bit of a nightmare Court 7. And you're quite right to have got out of there. I've seen a fight break out in that corridor before.'

Just at that, as if on cue, a crowd of people came up the stairway arguing. At the top of the stairs, a young man and woman broke away and pushed Dorothy aside as they ran towards the main door.

'Come back here you wee shites!' a voice called out and a massive woman, tattooed on her shoulders and forearms, pushed through the crowd, waddling after the two runners at a surprising speed.

A man in the following crowd winked at Nick. 'She's a right bam that one,' he said, 'Her man just got put away. Ten years.'

The crowd dispersed quickly. The next case was being called.

'This is us now,' Andy said. 'We need to get down there sharpish.'

* * *

Inside the court, a glass screen separated the lawyers and defendants from the two rows of public seats. An older couple Nick hadn't seen before were sitting in the corner, but most of the seats seemed to be taken by the woman called Michelle and her group. They looked Nick, Dorothy and Andy up and down when they first walked in, but nothing was said.

Three burly security guards brought in the accused from the side. The boy looked a lot older than fifteen. He was tall, athletic looking, with a muscular physique, broad square shoulders, an intimidating shaved head. The woman who'd objected to the expression on Dorothy's face stood up, ran forward and pressed herself against the glass. 'Jimmy! Jimmy!' she cried. The policeman came forward and gestured her to move back to her seat. The boy turned to look at her and his face twisted into something halfway between a smile and a sneer. Dorothy was clearly very uncomfortable, but Nick was finding himself somehow fascinated in a strange way by the human drama of it.

The robed judge came in and all had to stand. Although there were mikes all around the court, the judge seemed to mumble, his head away from the mike, so it was very difficult to make out what he was saying. Nick felt like shouting 'speak up!'

Emily Derwent, the young lawyer from the Procurator Fiscal's office, was sitting at the table beside the Crown Advocate. Nick wanted to catch her eye, but she didn't once look behind her to the public seats. Opposite her were lawyers and advocates whom he assumed were for the defence. Nick strained to hear what was said. The defendant was called James Stevens. Because he was under sixteen when the crime was committed, the judge explained that he'd be subject to a different set of trial rules to those for adults. A plea of not guilty was entered. There was some discussion about dates and reports. And then it was over. Andy, Nick and Dorothy stumbled out and up the stairs and back up to the entrance hall, without a word. As they stopped there, the other group, led by the woman he assumed to be James Stevens' mother, swept past. No words were exchanged but Nick held Dorothy's hand as they walked together out of the court and into a taxi.

7. Trial and Sentence

The trial was scheduled to start on May 15th. Andy helped both Dorothy and Nick to craft their victim statements. These might assist the prosecution in making the case and the judge in deciding sentence. Nick and Dorothy compared versions, drafted and redrafted bits of the story... Clare's death, how well Ruth had responded to life without her mother, Ruth's career ambitions, the quality of her schoolwork, the loss of her potential to the wider community, the sharp painful grief of her death. The statements they ended up with weren't poetic, but they were worthy. And there was a surprisingly therapeutic aspect to the process. Meantime, they read again the many tributes that had been posted up online by Ruth's schoolfriends: lots of positive words - words like 'honest', 'fun', 'bright', 'optimistic' - words that made Nick feel proud of his daughter. Andy said he would print out these internet tributes and attach them as appendices, along with her school reports.

And all the while the days were lengthening, there was more heat in the sun, spring flowers were blossoming and soon it would be time to start to harden off outside the plants that had been nurtured in the greenhouse. Nick had also been spending more of his time at rehearsals for the Easter performance of Handel's *Messiah*. The choir was one place in Stirling where he wasn't known as the father of 'that girl who was found dead in the Abbey Craig woods' - at least not yet. Though Nick hadn't been back to a church since his brief flirtation at Christmas, in these rehearsals he found something different... his voice was just one among many, lost among a hundred others.

On Easter night, the air in the Holy Rude Church was theatrical. The building itself exerted a strange power... how many stories had those old stones seen and heard? There was a buzz of heated conversations as the congregation awaited the start of the service, their faces shining like so many bright moons in the pale candlelight. The beeswax candles, the emotional heat of the choir, the nervous twittering of the sopranos... every part of it ran in and around the soloists' voices as they soared on up and out, beyond the vaulted roof and up towards the heavens. It was a heady, sensual experience. When those first beautiful words - *Comfort ye, comfort ye my people* – had rung out in the clear bright tenor of the guest soloist, Nick had to wipe away the tears that ran down his cheeks, for Ruth, for all the victims who'd gone before - killed, murdered, raped - for those who mourned them, who missed them, for the resonance of those words, the beauty and power of that clear tenor voice. He could almost see Ruth in the audience, feel her beside him in the choir, recognise her in the haunting beauty of the words of the King James Bible, here in the very Church where King James himself had been christened, then later crowned King of Scotland, centuries before. And Ruth was still with him in every single thing that he did. She always would be.

Next to Nick in the back row with the other basses was Simon Davies, a retired University professor. During rehearsals they'd chatted about singing, the music, Simon's family - but though Nick had told Simon about his work, he'd been guarded about his situation, said nothing about Ruth or the trial. At the end of the performance, Simon held him back. 'Join us for a celebratory drink Nick? I'm meeting up with a few friends and family.' Nick was about to demur, but Simon took him by the elbow. 'Come on,' he said, 'I want you to meet my wife Pam. She's been asking me about you.'

Simon's crowd was gathered at the top of Broad Street, fifteen or so, old and young together. Pam was a silver-haired little elf, not quite five feet tall, all sharp features and bright eyes. As they walked together down to *The Settle Inn*, she took Nick's arm. 'You're the quiet one Simon's been telling me about,' she said.' Nick let himself be led. 'So, did you enjoy the performance? Simon's been singing in the choir for so many years I can't remember. But I thought tonight was one of the best…' She let go Nick's arm, 'Just a minute,' she said, changing tone, 'I want to introduce you to my daughter, Phoebe.' Pam's quick, clacky steps echoed on the cobbled street as she caught up with a young woman. They waited for Nick by the Mercat Cross.

'Nick, meet Phoebe,' Pam said, 'Phoebe, this is Nick.'

'Yes,' Phoebe said, holding him with eyes as bright as her mother's. 'Nick,' she said, and shook his hand, 'I saw you singing. Your tears. It's such a beautiful piece.' It was hard to tell how old she was, early thirties perhaps. None of the people walking past seemed to be taking much notice of her, but her smell, her smile, her tousled black hair, the warmth of her face, was overpowering him. As they turned out of Broad Street and down towards *The Settle*, mother and daughter chattering away at his side, Nick was swept along in their enthusiastic embrace, their happy chatter: Phoebe had never heard *The Messiah* performed at Easter. It was often performed at Christmas, Pam agreed, but it really suited Easter with its redemptive theme. She added that the first performance was at Easter, and in Dublin, also in a church. Handel had composed it in about three weeks – new information for Nick. Pam tried to remember a quote from Beethoven, praising the work, but they'd reached the pub and the conversation was lost as their noisy group sprawled inside, surprised to find it almost empty.

'This is my treat,' Simon shouted out, 'Order what you want at the bar… I'm paying.'

'Let's sit by the fire,' Phoebe said to Nick after they'd seen their drinks order noted down by the barman. 'Have you done much of this kind of singing?' she asked as they sat down.

'No, not really,' he said. It was hot and noisy, and he was flustered. Everything was crowding in. His senses were shot - sight, sound, smell - too many things were going on, including Phoebe. Sitting tight against the wall, it was a struggle for him to get his coat off. He could feel himself tensing up, across his shoulders, the back of his neck. He felt he must look a bit stupid, struggling with his coat. She was speaking, but he hadn't picked up what she was saying. The key ring in his pocket was jabbing into his leg. He took it out and laid it on the table. Phoebe picked it up and looked at the pictures of Clare and Ruth.

'This must be your daughter,' she said, 'She's lovely. Looks like you. And your wife? They didn't come to see you tonight?'

'No,' he said abruptly, then, 'I can't do this.' He stood up and looked around him, as if for some kind of help. 'Sorry,' he said, grabbed his keys and his coat and pushed his way through the crowd towards the door. Simon called after him, but he pretended not to hear.

Walking down the road, he tried to work out what had happened. The table they'd been sitting at was the same table where he and Greg sat the night before Ruth's body was found. That was unsettling for sure. But it was more than that. There was the heated atmosphere of the pub, the awkwardness of trying to get his coat off in a confined, hot space while he was sitting on it, the loud conversations of people he didn't know. And Phoebe. She'd been perfectly friendly but his reaction to her had just added to his emotional confusion. It was Jane Beattie and Sam Hill all over again. Since Clare's death he'd been careful with himself, guarded in the company of women. So what was it about these particular women that left him feeling so... so what? What was it he felt? They'd picked his lock, opened him right up, drawn out emotions that he kept suppressed. Without invitation, without even trying, just by being in his company and being who they were, they'd breached his defences, exposed his vulnerability. It left him confused. It felt wonderful, exciting, but also scary, even threatening. Could they sense how vulnerable he was? How needy? Were there little below-the-radar signs of vulnerability, neediness, that he was giving off and that they were picking up... the man whose daughter was killed. Yet their potential to sooth, to heal... that too was frightening. He wasn't ready to be healed, wasn't ready to be soothed... it wouldn't be right, would it... to get on and enjoy life when Ruth had none? But is that not what she would've wanted for him?

He stopped on the narrow bridge over to Cambuskenneth. There'd been a lot of rain up in the mountains and on the ebb tide the river was high, gurgling and rushing around the stone piers. This business wasn't finished. Jimmy Stevens was to face trial, but Nick felt like he was the one who'd been imprisoned, trapped, by this horrible crime, unable to move on into any kind of a life beyond Ruth's death. What words could make sense of what he was going through? Would he ever be free from it?

* * *

The spring weather was dry and warm that year. Working days were long. And so May 15th came soon enough.

The trial was to be held in front of the same judge in one of the larger courts of the Glasgow High Court. A jury had been empaneled. The lawyers were ready. Dorothy decided not to attend - she'd found the preliminary hearing too stressful - but Greg took the day off work to be with Nick when the trial opened: it wasn't, he said, something to do alone. When they got to the court, Andy met them at the entrance.

'They've set aside a few days for the trial,' he said, 'But I don't think there's going to be a lot of evidence led.' Andy put out his hand to Greg. 'I'm Andy by the way.'

Greg took his hand. 'Greg,' he said, 'Nick and me go back quite a way. Wouldn't have seen him come here on his own. Not today.'

'If I can, I try to come along to support where I've been involved in a case like this, even if it's just at the start.' Andy said to Greg, 'For people who've not been to court before it can be quiet disorientating, the procedure, the formality. Especially given that, for most people, the emotions are raging.' He turned to Nick. 'Speaking of which, how are you feeling?'

Nick's face registered no emotion. It was blank rather than calm. He cracked his fingers. 'I'm not expecting anything,' he said, 'That way I'm not going to be disappointed.' He squared his shoulders. 'I'm quite sure the law will take its course. And anyway,' he paused, swallowed. 'The worst that can happen has already happened. Anything else is unimportant. Whatever happens here can't be worse than what's already happened, can it? I'm only here for Ruth.'

'Why don't we just go in now?' Andy said, 'Get yourselves settled. I'll stay with you for the first little bit, then maybe for lunch depending on the timings. After that you'll be on your own, but you know where I am if you have any questions. Any time,' he added, catching Nick's eye as he said it.

Nick felt intimidated by the whole thing – the courtroom, the pressure of what was about to happen – Andy had warned him that the defence might want to blacken Ruth's character a little, to throw responsibility away from the defendant. They were likely to lead evidence that Ruth had drunk strong cider before as a way of showing that she was a willing participant, that any 'recklessness' on that fatal evening had been hers, not his. On the positive side, in view of the ages of the victim, the judge had imposed reporting restrictions. That would make things easier for Nick now, but they might be lifted at a later stage depending on what happened in the trial. Shortly after Greg, Nick and Andy had sat down in the public gallery, Jimmy Stevens' family crowded into the public benches around them. It was a very uncomfortable situation. No words were necessary: looks said everything.

The trial opened with technical conversations between the judge and the jurors, then between him and the lawyers. The judge had a habit of speaking away from the microphone so that most of the words were lost. Around them, Stevens' family fidgeted. In the dock, Stevens himself looked calm. More than calm. Almost arrogant. As if the whole thing was beneath him. As time passed, Nick became more and more agitated. He couldn't imagine putting up with this for a whole day, never mind a week. After an hour or so of conversation between the prosecution and defence counsel and the judge, the trial was adjourned till the afternoon.

Nick's head was buzzing, a loud pulsing in his ears. He couldn't hear anything that was being said to him. After the court rose, Greg and Andy almost had to pull him physically from his chair and guide him into the corridor outside. Andy filled them in. It seemed the judge was unhappy with some of the evidence that the prosecution was intending to lead. He'd asked to meet with both sets of lawyers in his chambers.

'But we'll get onto the real trial, the witnesses, all that sort of stuff in the afternoon, won't we?' Greg said.

'I hope so,' Andy said, 'I'd really like to hang around for that, but I've got other appointments, so if it's alright... I'm really sorry... They always want me to do too many things.'

'That's fine,' Greg said, 'We'll call you if there's anything we want help with.'

'Please do. Phone me any time.'

'Sure,' Greg said, 'We know where to find you.' He took Nick by the arm. 'C'mon,' he said, 'We're going to get a coffee, or maybe something a bit stronger. And then we're going back in.'

Outside the court, Jimmy's mother was standing in a huddle with her family and friends, lighting up. As Nick and Greg walked down the steps, they fell silent. A small man about Nick's age pointed at him. 'Your daughter was a wee slut,' he said, 'Whored herself out for drugs and roped our boy into it. I hope she rots in hell.' Greg's fist tightened, but he thought better of it, taking his cue from Nick who didn't react at all, didn't even appear to have heard what was said, walked past them as if they weren't there, his gaze fixed on some point in the distance, and then on down towards the river.

Someone shouted after them. 'That's an innocent boy facing prison cos of your whore of a daughter.'

'Shut the fuck up!' Greg shouted, facing round to the crowd. He was raging. 'You didn't even know her!'... but Nick was walking on towards the river as if he hadn't heard. Greg had to turn and run after him. The shouts that followed them died away.

'Jesus truly wept man,' Greg said, as they walked along the riverside towards the city centre. 'What is that all about... I mean... that Jimmy boy's a born gangster. Guilt written all over his face. Did you see the snidey little smirk on his face? Did you bloody well see it?'

Nick had seen it alright, but it was something else that was on his mind. 'Could that be right Greg?' he said, 'What that guy said? That Ruth gave sex for drugs?'

'God's sake man, no way! No way. Just get your head straight. Believe me. If Ruth'd been into that sort of thing, there'd've been all sorts of mad stuff going on in your house. All the time man. I lived with a druggie when I was at Uni in Oz. If she'd been into drugs, you'd know about it alright.'

'But she had been a bit different since school started in August. Dropped her swimming. I didn't see so much of her friends. She was maybe keeping different company. The other girl that was there that night - I don't even know her. She never brought her back to the house.'

'Sure. All teenagers have their ups and downs, but sex for drugs? Ruth? Put it right out of your mind. No way. No fucking way, mate.'

When they got to the old suspension bridge over the Clyde, Nick stopped. 'I need a few minutes quiet Greg,' he said, 'I'm just going up here.' He walked out onto the bridge, stopped half-way and looked down into the dirty water below. Greg fell silent too but followed him onto the bridge, kept close: he didn't want Nick doing anything silly.

It had begun to rain, gentle rain. They stood there for five, maybe ten, minutes, letting the rain soak into their hair, watching its sprinkly patterns as it fell on the river. At last, Nick raised his head. 'Well Greg old pal,' he patted him on the back, 'Thanks for being with me. I don't know what it all means, but I think we should go and get hammered. Let's head for the *Pot Still*. I used to drink there when I was a student – they have a great selection of whiskies.' He pointed vaguely in the direction of the city. 'It's all too much, the trial, those people. I'm not going back in there or I'll be the one that's up for murder. I'll kill someone... starting with that little shite outside the court, what he said about Ruth... In fact, if I see them again, and if one of them says anything, I'm going to go for them. I don't care what happens after that.'

'So we're definitely not going back then?'

'Definitely. I mean what I said. I'm standing here trying to control it. My anger. You know what I was imagining when I was standing here looking down at the water? I was wondering where I could get a sub-machine gun. Whether I would have to practise using it before coming back later this afternoon and mowing that whole family down right outside the court. I could seriously do it Greg. And they'd deserve it. But it'd be wrong, wouldn't it? We're not supposed to do that sort of thing nowadays, are we? And I'd probably cock it up anyway. I'm not very good at violence. But,' he looked round at Greg and there was a mad gleam in his eyes, 'It'd be so good, wouldn't it? Mow the fuckers down. Kill every single one of those worthless shits who killed my daughter... cos they all share a bit of guilt, don't they? It was maybe the boy who killed Ruth, but the mother, the rest of them... they must have some responsibility for what a little shit he is... and then I'd maybe go for the TV companies, the people that sell illusions to kids instead of educating them... Christ... I'd take a fucking machine gun to the lot of them... any society that can nurture little shits like that... but it's not just them, is it? It's us too. We're all responsible aren't we? Any society that nurtures these people... it deserves a bazooka up its arse, don't you think so?... if it doesn't know how to bring up its children... all its children? What a horrible world we live in.'

'I don't get all this stuff about society mate, but if you decide that's what you're going to do that wee shit Stevens, get in the queue behind me, cos I want to have a go at him first.'

'I know it's just a fantasy though, isn't it? I'm not a crazy mass killer, am I? But if you don't do something you're left wondering, aren't you? Wondering if this is it. That you just have to take it. Do nothing. Just take it. Just accept that this world is irrational, unfair, that nobody really cares, except that they're glad it didn't happen to them. What do they say I need to do... just *let the law take its course*. Just *find closure*. But how can you find closure, mate, when your daughter is dead?'

As they walked up past Central Station, Nick phoned Dorothy.

'This'll have to be quick,' he said, 'Hold on a minute.' He stopped at the kerb as a taxi came whizzing round the corner and into the drop zone on Gordon Street. He shifted the phone to his other ear and crossed over. 'Are you still there Dorothy? Sorry about that. Just crossing the road... Yes... Anyway.... Look... I'm not going to stay for the trial so I won't be phoning you tonight to tell you what happened... I can't bear it... I know... You were right... It's too upsetting... Look Dorothy... I know... yes, I know all that... of course... I know.... look I'm sorry... but I can't do this... have this conversation just now... I'm sorry,' he stopped at another crossing, stepped back into a doorway. Dorothy was speaking again but he shouted over her. 'I don't know what to think either Dorothy, I'm in a total dwam,' he said, 'I'm walking through Glasgow with my pal Greg and we're going to drink whisky... No, I don't think that's going to give me the answer but I'll feel a helluva lot better than if I sit in that court one more minute...' He listened for a moment, then started up again, forcefully. 'Look. I'm sorry. I know. All of that is true. We'll have a good talk about it all next time we get together. Maybe the trial will be finished and it'll all make more sense then, though I doubt it. Nothing we say or do looks like it's going to make a difference anyway. I'm really sorry.' They were at the pub door now. 'I'm really sorry. Bye... Bye... Yes... Bye... Yes... Yes... I'll get in touch soon. We'll talk then.'

Nick switched his phone off. Once inside and he and Greg sitting with their double measures of Glen Garioch, half pints to chase them down, Nick couldn't settle, his right leg twitching as if keeping time to some demented music playing in his head. He emptied the whisky down his throat too quickly and started coughing, painful racking coughs. People at nearby tables stopped talking and looked over. Greg thumped him on the back a few times. The barman brought over a glass of water and Nick sipped it slowly. Conversations started up again around the pub. Nick drank some of his beer.

'Must've gone down the wrong way.' Greg said,

'Yeah. Sorry. Stupid.'

Nick looked around him and took a couple of deep measured breaths. 'This is the wrong pub for us,' he said, 'It's a good pub for a quiet chat, but I've got nothing to say. I'm numb. I can't do this stuff anymore. I don't want to talk about it, think about it. Let's go somewhere else, somewhere we don't have to talk, somewhere we don't have to think.'

'We can go to Malone's,' Greg said, 'There's always some sport on there – on the big screen.'

* * *

Malones was crowded but they managed to get a seat near the bar. There was a football game on the massive screen. Real Madrid were playing a team Nick didn't recognize. It was measured, deliberate, distant, like an elaborate formal dance routine, a chess game - very continental. No-one on the pitch seemed very excited, until a goal was scored. The game, the big screen and the drink occupied Nick's senses. Another game came on. They watched that too, ordered some food. Greg tried to get Nick to talk, or to go home, but he wanted this place.

When they left the pub, quite drunk, it was dark. They ambled along to Queen Street station for a late train. Greg shared his thoughts on the Madrid game, their overpaid stars. A two-carriage train to Alloa was sitting at the platform, but since the previous Dunblane train had been cancelled, all those going North past Stirling would take the Alloa train, then catch the train from Edinburgh to Dunblane at Stirling... and the Alloa train was already standing room only... and they weren't the only ones on board to have spent some time in the pub. Three scruffy kids were standing by the door, no more than 16 or 17 years old, but drunk as skunks, making a nuisance of themselves almost as soon as the train left the station. Only they knew why they were chanting, to the tune of *Go West*, 'We're shite and we know we are, We're shite and we know we are, We're shite and we know we are...'

'This is going to be a long journey buddy,' Greg said as the train inched its way through the tunnel. Nick turned away and looked at his feet, his jaw set. As the singing died away, an elderly man who was sitting near the door stood up.

'Would you boys mind toning it down?' he said, 'My wife doesn't like that kind of language.'

One of the boys louped over, eyes popping, and shouted in his face. 'S'at right you auld shitebag? I bet she likes it when you talk dirty but, y'auld prick.'

Things happened very quickly after that.

Nick sprang over to the boy who was doing the talking, picked him up under his chin and slammed him against the carriage door. 'If you don't shut up,' he said, up in the boy's face, 'I'm going to stop this train with that little emergency hammer up there, you and me will get out, and only one of us will be having breakfast tomorrow morning.'

The boy's two friends were too stunned to move at first, then made to go for Nick, but Greg stepped towards them. 'Take one step more,' he said, 'And you'll regret it.' They sized Greg up, looked at Nick, then at each other and stayed where they were.

'Well, what's it to be?' Nick said, 'Are you going to shut up?'

'Aye,' the boy said, 'Dinny go aw radge on us. It's only a wee laugh mister ay? Nae offence like.'

'No,' Nick said, 'There was offence. A lot of offence.'

The train was slowing down for its first stop at Bishopbriggs. Nick pulled the boy over to the other side of the carriage, away from the exit. The man and his wife hurried down to another door before getting off the train without looking back, without saying a word. One of two other passengers getting off gave Nick a little nod. A young couple mimed applause as they walked past.

'Mister,' one of the other boys said to Greg, 'We need to get off here.'

'Well off you get then,' Nick said, 'He's staying.'

'Naw... that's no right,' the taller one said, and was about to move towards Nick again but Greg's bulk propelled him off the train onto the platform. 'Now stay off,' Greg said, and half pushed, half threw the other boy out to join his pal on the platform. Greg stayed at the door till the train pulled away. Nick still had the first one pinned. His flailing arms were making no impression on Nick's strong grip. 'Now you're going to apologise to the rest of the carriage for your bad behavior,' he said, 'Or you won't be getting off at Lenzie either. You'll be coming back to Stirling with me.' He was right in the boy's face, noses almost touching.

'Let go of us mister,' the boy said, his voice panicky now, 'You're choking us. I can hardly breathe. This is a kidnap. I'm just a boy ay? I'm underage, ay? You're molestin me. You're fuckin molestin me. You're an abuser, a fuckin nonce. Get tae fuck.'

Nick shifted his grip to the boys' hair. He pulled his head back, exposing his neck, tight, white. 'Shut the fuck up,' he said quietly in the boy's face, 'Or I'll break this fuckin window with your head and shove you through it. Fancy your chances when you land on the track at seventy miles an hour?'

The boy shut up.

'Now you're going to apologise to these people,' he said.

'Sorry,' the boy said.

'Louder,' Nick said, 'They can't hear you.'

'Sorry,' the boy shouted.

'That's better. Now the other end...' And the two of them walked to the far end of the carriage and the boy repeated the apology.

As the train slowed down coming into Lenzie, Nick held the boy at the door and whispered in his ear. 'I'm on this train often,' he said, 'And see if I ever hear of you behaving like this again, I'll find you and I'll do things to you that'll make you wish you were dead.' He took the boy's phone from his pocket. 'I'm going to hand this in later. You can pick it up from Scotrail,' he said. 'I'm sure you can find your way home without it. It's only a couple of miles down the road. Just a wee lesson for you to behave yourself on the train.'

When the train doors opened, the boy jumped onto the platform and ran a few yards before turning round and starting to shout back at Nick... 'You're a maddo, a fuckin auld maddo fuckin nonce poofter thievin bastard!' Nick stood at the door and watched. The boy danced around throwing V-signs in his direction. Just as the carriage door closed, Nick threw the boy's phone out onto the platform.

'What was all that about, Nick?' Greg asked. 'Man, you were possessed.'

Nick was breathing slowly, calming himself down. 'I just let myself go,' he said, 'And it felt good. It felt very, very good.' He paused for a minute, watching their reflections in the window of the brightly lit carriage. 'I've never hit anyone in my life except on a rugby field,' he said, 'and that was legal. But I could easily have killed him, Greg. Snapped his scrawny little back like a twig, the little shite.'

'That's the drink talking man. Just stow it.'

The carriage emptied some more after Croy. They were able to sit. 'That wasn't like you, man,' Greg said, 'You're gonna have to watch yourself you know. The boy there was obnoxious, but you can't hurt Jimmy Stevens by taking it out on someone else. In fact, if Stevens heard that you were getting done for assault that'd probably make him happy.'

'Maybe,' Nick agreed, an ironic smile playing about his lips, 'Maybe he's happy already. What's the most he'll get if he's found guilty? Five years? Reduced for good behaviour? That'll make sure he never does anything bad again, innit Greg, innit? When he comes out, he'll be ready to play a positive role in society, innit?' Each successive 'innit' was louder, more insistent than the one before, as was the bastardised London accent Nick was putting on. 'It'll be all over then, innit? It'll be fuckin closure mate, innit? Fuckin closure mate?' He moved closer to Greg and spoke slowly into his face, angrily, as if Greg was the problem. 'Closure bruv, innit? Fucking closure.'

Greg moved away from Nick's beery breath and no more was said. Later he tried to get a conversation going about the football match, but Nick wasn't interested. Before they'd arrived at Stirling, Greg'd phoned Sheila to come and pick them up, but she'd refused. 'I can't leave the girls just cos you're drunk,' she said. 'Get a taxi.'

But there were no taxis in the rank when they came out of the station at Stirling, though there was only one other person, an older woman, waiting. They stood in silence and watched as a taxi pulled up and she put her shopping bags in the boot and got in.

'I'm not going back to the trial, Greg,' Nick said, after the taxi had pulled away. 'I can't bear it. I'm going to switch off the TV, internet, phone. Look at me on the train. What it did to me. It's turning me into someone else. I'm a pacifist for God's sake. You can let me know when the verdict is announced if you want. I'll text Andy. Tell him I'm not going to attend. That he's to keep you informed as things move forward. I'm out of it. It's too much.'

'What are you going to do then? This week?'

'I don't know. There's a guy up north was pestering me to do some work for his mother a week or two ago, said I can stay up there in his caravan. I'll maybe see if he still wants me. I can put in long shifts up there, keep out of mischief. I just can't do this trial thing anymore. I can't do anything anymore.'

Greg was silent for a few moments. 'I can see what you're saying. I think it's quite wise to stay away from it all. Today was just a mess. And like you say, the worst has already happened, and it can't be undone. But going away? All on your own? Is that wise? You need to be around friends. If you bottle it up inside yourself, things are only going to get worse.'

Another taxi pulled up. 'Get in,' Nick said, 'I'll be fine once I'm up north, working.' He pushed Greg towards the taxi. 'Go on. Get in. I'll send you a postcard,' he shouted, 'If anyone still sells them these days.'

* * *

Nick didn't send a postcard, but he did whatsapp Greg a couple of beautiful photos of the spring sun on the northwest coast. Greg whatsapp'd Nick more often - a couple of times a day, every day. He told him about the weather, football results, the book he was listening to on his i-phone – David Attenborough's *Memoirs*: 'he's had some career, that guy.' Early on Thursday, Greg texted that the final summings-up were to take place that morning and it was likely that the jury would deliver their verdict that day. On Thursday afternoon, he texted again: the jury had asked for more time and were going to carry on overnight. The result would come on Friday. He asked Nick if he wanted him to phone or text the result.

'No,' was Nick's answer, 'I'm coming back on Friday afternoon anyway. Meet me in *The Settle* at 6.'

* * *

Friday evening after 6, *The Settle* was unusually quiet. The after-work drinkers had left to get food, the Friday evening drinkers had not yet arrived. Greg was already in a corner seat when Nick arrived after dumping the pickup back in Cambuskenneth. He bought Greg a second pint.

'So. How was the work?' Greg asked, 'D'you get it finished?'

'Kind of.'

'How kind of?'

'Well. Turns it out it wasn't a job for a man with a spade and a few days to spare, but I did get a fair bit done. You can get in a 13 or 14 hour day now, with the sun up so early.'

'And did you? Get in a 14 hour day.'

'Well not on Monday. I was here on Monday. And not on Tuesday, cos I was driving up in the morning. And not today...

'Cos you were driving back down. I get the picture.'

'Overall. Yeah. I did a good job. All the drains are in. The topsoil is ready for cultivation. There's stuff she won't be able to grow up there... it's so wet... even with the drains... but she has friends down the road a way who've been experimenting. They know what'll work in her micro-climate. There's still all the paving and the fencing to do.'

'Where was it again?'

'Ullapool. Well not exactly. But nearby.'

'So. Bloody hell Nick. You're so bloody cool. D'you want me to tell you the outcome of the trial or not or are we gonna spend the whole fuckin evening exchanging pleasantries about the fuckin weather in Ullapool for chrissake?'

Nick took a slow pull of his beer. Wiped his lips. Sat back in his seat and took a deep breath. 'Ok then,' he said, 'Tell me.'

'The jury found the case "Not Guilty". There was a story in one of the papers that the jury had obviously not been able to agree on what verdict to bring in... that's why it took so long... there'd been quite a bit of toing and froing.'

Nick's face didn't change. He said nothing.

'D'you want to know any more? Or are you going to play zenmaster for the entire evening?'

'I don't know what I want. But I know what I don't want. I'm not going to be poring over every detail, spotting all the flaws in the Procurator Fiscal's presentation, getting angry with the defence lawyers. Fifteen good men and women have listened to the case in detail and found that he was not guilty. That's has to be good enough for me.'

'You must want to know more. What evidence there was that he did it, that he was the main culprit, it was him who plied Ruth with the drink and drugs.'

'What'd be the point of that? I'd just start going over it all in even more detail. What am I going to do about it? Suppose it was him who was the main cause of her death, what was the phrase, "recklessly supplied her with drink and drugs"? The evidence wasn't there. It can't be proved. Isn't that it?'

'Well, kind of, I suppose.'

'We're going to have to be satisfied with that. Nothing in life is perfect. I've been preparing myself all week. I'm going to have to live with it. There's lots of people have to live with worse things. People that have lived through war, people that have...' Nick stopped talking.

'You don't have to be so bloody philosophical,' Greg said, 'It's alright to be angry, to let it all out.'

'You're wrong Greg.' Nick picked up a beer mat and started methodically tearing into pieces, halves, then quarters, then eighths. 'You saw me on that train, with that obnoxious kid. I wanted him to kill him, I really did. I could've killed him as if he was an ant, or a fly, or... I don't know. But one thing I do know. I'm not letting that beast out in the open again. I realised that I've got something inside me that could do terrible things. For a few minutes I just didn't care. I could've thrown him off the train and not thought about it again.'

'But you didn't. You wouldn't. You're too decent.'

'Am I Greg? You don't know what's going inside me.'

'Fair enough. All I'm saying is that you can share what you're really thinking with me. Christ, I'm not going to judge you.'

'What I'm really thinking.' Nick looked intently at the stained ceiling, as if the answer was written up there. 'What I'm really thinking is that this whole thing is a mess, that life is a joke, that nothing means anything anymore, that we're all trapped by circumstances, you, me, Jimmy Stevens, my daughter Ruth…' He took a tissue from his pocket, blew his nose, wiped his eyes, but his voice was clear. 'What I'm thinking is that I don't know how to live with what has happened. What I'm thinking is that I wish Ruth had had a chance to tell her side of the story. I know she was no angel… she was a teenager, trying things out… I know that. But she was a careful girl, controlled, not reckless. It's so unfair that everyone else, even people who never even met her, get to tell their version of events, but the most important person in the whole thing is left voiceless, defenceless, so that anyone can traduce her and she has no right of reply. You heard that wee guy outside the court that day - "whored herself out for drugs". I should have torn his tongue out, tied him up, raped his wife, castrated his children and then torn him limb from limb. And that still wouldn't be enough! I could do it, you know… I've thought about it. And it felt good. Real, proper revenge, like they used to do in the old days, before so-called civilisation took over. But something prevents me. What's stopping me? I don't know. It's not conscience… my conscience isn't clear when I'm doing nothing, so it's not going to be any worse if I take my revenge, is it? Lethargy? Maybe that's in there somewhere…. though what an accusation that would be - that I was too lazy to avenge my own daughter? That I couldn't care enough. What a terrible indictment that would be of me and of all that I believe. Couldn't care enough? Is that what I'm reduced to, that kind of man? A man who's too scared to do anything, or doesn't even care enough? That'd be even worse.'

Greg blew the air out of his lungs, but there were no words. He took a slug of his beer and waited. Nick picked up another beer mat and began to half then quarter it in the same methodical way. Greg finished his drink and picked up Nick's glass. 'Do you want another one?'

'No. Let's get something to eat. Are you due home?'

'Sheila told me to take however long you wanted.'

'Well let's eat then. Then let's get ourselves out for a run. I was running in the dark every night, up there. Helped me sleep.'

'I don't know. I've had a couple of pints.'

'By the time we've eaten… and walked down the road… you'll be fine.'

'I don't think so.'

'Well let's wait and decide after food.'

'And what about tomorrow? What are your plans?' Greg asked.

'I've got a few tools to get while I'm home and then I'm going back up North. There's another local boy agreed to help me with the two-man jobs. There'll be a completely rebuilt garden ready for planting out by Wednesday.'

'Who'll do the planting?'

'I'll leave that to her... she seems to know what she wants after I've done the heavy lifting.'

'It's going to be in the papers you know. The judge lifted the restrictions on reporting once the verdict was in. And it's already caused a little twitter storm.'

'Vultures,' Nick said. 'Vultures. What's the point? What is the goddam point of it all? None of it's going to bring Ruth back. None of it's going to make this world a better place to be. The only control we have in all this is over how we deal with it ourselves.'

'Like I said,' Greg said, 'Zenmaster. You've got so much going on inside, but looking at you know, who'd know it?'

8. Coping

In that first summer without Ruth, Nick's long days outdoors were filled working for old clients who valued his organic, nature-friendly approach - some new ones had come on board too. If he found himself going over the whole sad story in his mind, he'd throw himself into physical activity, taking pleasure in his strength and endurance at work. Long Sunday morning training runs took over his weekends. He was in the shape of his life: lean, fit, muscular. He kept the little collection of photos of Ruth on the bedroom tallboy, making time for a little chat, or just even a little look, little memories... every day.

He was keeping a tight control of his private life too. The garden, even the house, were conspicuously tidy, 'OCD tidy' Greg said. For much of July and August most of his food came from his early harvests from the greenhouse, the cold frames at the allotment - organic fruit, organic veg. Two or three times a month he was out at the Bright's for a meal, or to babysit, or both. On Wednesdays Greg and he ran together then shared a few drinks. In company he seemed relaxed, as long as the conversation kept away from anything personal. Routines ate up the hours.

But there was little joy. And any occasional seeds that sprouted, seeds of planning for the future, seeds of hope, weren't nourished for long. Simon was in touch about the choir's next Christmas performance - Bach's Christmas Oratorio – it'd be exciting, he said, but would stretch them, so rehearsals would be starting a bit early. Nick wasn't that keen, but Simon's enthusiasm won him over. He agreed to go along.

He was careful with himself. With women too. Not that he saw any in his current way of living. And he wasn't bothered by that. Even those random thoughts that might spark the possibilities of a relationship were stamped on. Everything was tight, controlled, every minute filled. He didn't want to talk about the trial, the verdict, Ruth, Clare. He didn't want someone to try to get him to 'share', to 'open up', to 'heal'. This was his life now. It wasn't great. But it was better when his days were active.

* * *

One sunny Saturday in August, when Dorothy was away at her sister in Wales, Greg and Nick walked from Elie to Kingsbarns among the summer flowers, the sounds and smells of the open beckoning sea, seabirds riding thermals above them in the blue blue sky.

'If I was to live somewhere else,' Nick said, as they sat looking over Crail watching two little boats heading out into the North Sea, 'I think it would be here. A person could make a new life somewhere like this,' he added, 'Somewhere beautiful like this.'

'It's good to hear you talking about a new life,' Greg said.

When Nick's mother died the week after, it wasn't unexpected. She'd been steadily worsening, scarcely able to walk, losing weight. But all through, he thought he'd been able to see some little part of her that was still there... glimpses of recognition that disappeared as soon as they came, sudden bursts of memory, an occasional smile to hold onto. Only a small number attended the funeral service - most of her friends had already 'gone before her', as she would've said. He laid her to rest beside his father, and not far from Uncle Raymondo, in St Peter's Cemetery. Since the house had been cleared when she moved into care, there was very little left - just the family photos she kept on the windowsill of the care home room. But looking at them every day reminded him how empty his life was and so he put them away in a drawer. The three women he had loved the most, the three most important women in his life, were all gone.

Maybe he should go somewhere different now - make a new start? But where?

* * *

In September, Nick entered the Loch Ness marathon, aiming to match the 2 hours 45 he'd done in his 20s, but it didn't turn out as he'd hoped – he blew up at about 16 miles and took well over four hours. At Greg's suggestion, he agreed to go back north the following weekend, walking this time, 'sociable, not solitary' as Greg had put it to him. They booked Saturday night in the Esk Arms, an old-fashioned country hotel in Edzell, with the idea of walking both days in the Angus glens, but when Greg got held up at home, they didn't get away till noon. Arriving at Edzell, they found the cloud cover low, the weather higher up wet and windy, so they salvaged the day by heading down to the Montrose shore for a bracing walk on the long beach, circling back round by the basin that lies behind the town. There they found geese and eiders, lapwings and dunlins, redshanks and oystercatchers. A grey heron, standing on the water's edge like a tall prehistoric sentinel, following them with his eyes as they walked by. Nick remembered the heron he'd seen on the shores of Loch Venachar, Karine Polwart's voice haunting him as he drove south to meet Jane Beattie. How much his life had changed since that phone call.

There was a noisy big wedding back at the hotel, so after drying out and eating, they took whiskies into the empty billiards room and played a couple of leisurely games of snooker. There was something reverential about the game, the hush of the room, the quiet kiss of white rolling into red on the soft green baize, the satisfying clunk as ball settled into pocket. Few words were spoken. They set up for a third game, a decider, but Greg put his cue to the side and picked up his empty glass.

'Let's just sit for a minute or two,' he said, 'I'll get in another couple of whiskies: large ones.' A few minutes later, they were sat down together in two tall leather-backed chairs.

'You don't even need to drink this Lagavulin,' Greg said, 'Just the aroma man. Just smell it.'

Nick grunted. Greg shuffled in his chair a little, then stood up, walked over to the empty fireplace and turned to face the room as if warming his back at an imaginary fire. He took a sip.

'You know we're all still tip-toeing around you mate, don't you?' he said.

'You don't need to.'

'Oh we do alright. We know the topics that are off limits alright.'

Nick looked down at his glass.

'Sheila says to me the other day that she'd love to see you find someone else,' Greg went on, 'So?' He waited till Nick looked up. 'How d'you think you might do that? Online dating now. There's the thing. Try before you buy. I've had a look... if I wasn't married, I can tell you I'd be getting right in there. There's some great looking women out there, looking for men. And some of them are just looking for a bit of fun, no strings, no consequences. We could have a laugh, the two of us. No harm in just looking. Then you could let me know how you get on...'

Nick rubbed his chin and blew out a long breathy sigh. 'Whatever,' he said.

'Remember what you said about that media girl who covered Ruth's story... Sam Hill was it? Or that wee policewoman you fancied? What was her name? Jane something, wasn't it?'

'Jane Beattie,' Nick snapped back, 'And I didn't fancy her. I admired her.'

'If you like,' Greg said, 'But I bet you'd have given her one if you got the chance.'

Nick didn't respond, didn't even look at Greg, fixing a stare on some point of interest on the carpet a few feet in front of him.

'All I'm saying is... well, Sheila and me both.... you'd be better off with someone in your life... and it's not going to happen unless you go out and do something about it. You go around the place like a coiled spring... there's so much tension inside you. I look at you sometimes and see how tight your jaw is clenched. You're still holding on to it all, aren't you? You've not moved on. I know I'm not supposed to use the word "closure", but truly mate, and I'm speaking to you as a friend, it'd be better if you let it all out, and then put it behind you. You need to get it out. At some point, and I know you won't want to hear me say this, you'll need to move on...' Greg waited for a reaction but there was none, '... and you can't do that till you get it out from inside you, bury it *outside* you, leave it behind.' Greg didn't push for a response... just waited... and it took a minute or two.

'Look Greg,' Nick said at last, looking up at him, 'thanks for the homespun advice... and I'm sure you guys care for me, mean well in what you say... but like you said to me before, it's just one day at a time for me.' He stood up and stretched, shutting the conversation down. 'Anyway, cut all the life advice. I think you're just playing for time cos you know I'm going to hammer you, now I've got my eye in.'

Greg won the next frame, but Nick insisted they play 'best of five' which Greg won 3-2. Although more Lagavulin was drunk that evening, quite a lot more, nothing more was said about Nick's state of mind.

Sunday brought a fine morning, bright and windy with high wispy clouds above the Angus glens. They drove up to the head of Glen Clova. From the car park they strolled through the ageing trees, their leaves yellowing in the autumn sun, up and into the Corrie Fee nature reserve. As they emerged at the top of the woods, they stopped for a few minutes to take in the dramatic rounded bowl of the corrie, scooped out by the ice thousands of years before, the high crags and the open sky above.

'God,' Nick said, 'Scotland is such a beautiful country.'

'Everywhere man,' Greg said, 'Anywhere you go.'

'That young man who was with Ruth that night? Do you think he's ever been anywhere like this?'

'Don't know mate. Not something I've ever thought about.'

Nick started walking towards the waterfall tumbling down over the crags. 'I think about it all the time,' he said, 'I think about him all the time. What was in his mind? What was important to him? What did Ruth see in him, if she saw anything at all that is.'

'He was a good-looking boy,' Greg said, 'That kind of tall muscular type some women go for, square shoulders, square jaw...'

'Square head,' Nick said... and they both laughed.

They walked on for a bit more.

'I mean, d'you think he ever had the chance to do something like this, in the open air, experienced for real the wonder of this planet we live in? I think of him stuck in his life, skiving off school, scavenging money for drugs, wanking off to porn, manipulating girlfriends. Then again maybe that's all in my head. Maybe if he had other choices, he'd still be the same little shit. But maybe I know nothing, maybe I've made all this up. Maybe he works on a farm at the weekends. Maybe he's a poacher. Maybe he does charity work. I don't know. I try to put it all behind me, but I just go over and over it.'

'He's not the only one wanking off to porn,' Greg said.

They carried on walking.

'And punishment?' Nick asked, 'I've been thinking a lot about punishment. I mean in general. Not just this guy. What's the point of it? Locking people up.'

'Protecting the public? Keeping them out of harm's way?' Greg said.

'But then they're just going to come back out, aren't they? Just the same as they went in, only maybe worse?'

A couple of golden eagles were circling above the crags. They stopped again for a few minutes to watch them, their easy way. Nick took some photos.

'For me,' Greg said, 'I'd string that bugger up by his goolies. I mean, it just doesn't seem right. He fills two young girls with cider and ecstasy, fucks one of them, rapes the other one and then when...' he hesitated, stole a glance at Nick, '...when she ends up drowned nearby, he gets off with it! I've got a better idea.' he chuckled. 'They should cut his goolies off, so he can't ever father any more little bastards like him.'

'Only natural, isn't it? To want revenge.' Nick said the word in a deep dramatic voice. 'I think about it: revenge. I think about it a lot. But it's no real answer is it? *An eye for eye ends up making the whole world blind.*'

Greg said nothing.

'Know who said that?' Nick asked.

'Nope.'

'Gandhi.'

They were climbing up the steep path beside the waterfall now, up to the top of the craggy corrie. Greg was breathing heavily so Nick forged on ahead. He didn't stop till he reached the grassy slope above the crag. Back the way they'd come he could see the river meandering across the bowl-shaped plain below, just as it had for centuries before, and today, this very day, it was his special moment to be here, to be part of it all. A skylark was singing somewhere behind him, its voice carried on the breeze. Against expectation, the sun had broken through the clouds, warm on Nick's face. Ruth was present to him then, beside him, wanting him to enjoy this moment. He lay down in the sun. In a little while, Greg came over the brow of the corrie, red-faced and panting and threw himself onto the grass beside Nick.

'I thought I'd have to stop there, mate. That was some steep climb. I'm totally done in.'

Nick took a couple of little easy peelers out of his rucksack and threw one over.

'He called it *ahimsa*,' Nick said, as he peeled, 'Gandhi's philosophy. Fight violence with more violence and everyone loses. He's one of the reasons I decided I was never going to enter the fast lane when I left Uni, why I took up my gardening, him and Thoreau. Finding a place of harmony with the world. *Leave no permanent footprints* – that was my motto in those days. *Leave the planet at least as good as you found it.* How come I ended up living a suburban life with a big diesel-guzzler? I like the way I used to be back then. Maybe I'll go back to it.'

'I didn't see you practising non-violence that night on the train.'

Nick laughed.

'And, if I remember rightly, you told me afterwards that it felt good. In fact, I think you said it felt very good.'

'Just cos it felt good, doesn't make it right,' Nick said, 'Like I said to you already, it felt dangerously good. I could've done anything.'

They finished the fruit then lay back and looked up at the sky.

'It was Clare that brought me into this world we live in, the world of too many things,' Nick said, 'When I was younger, I didn't want any of it: conspicuous consumption...

greed… people permanently dissatisfied, wanting more, faster, better… till eventually humanity's going to use it all up, the whole damn planet, fucked. And now I want out again. I don't want to be part of it. A simple life'll do me. No hard choices. Grow food, pick it, eat it. Live with the earth, the sky, the rain, the sun. I'm not interested in conflict, fighting, competition, all the anger and struggle… what's it for? None of it's important… I want to walk away from it… that's why I walked away from the trial… all the details…'

Greg snorted. Nick turned and saw that his eyes were closed. He started snoring. Nick pushed him roughly. 'Don't go to sleep on me, you lazy bugger,' he said. Greg opened his right eye, shielded it from the glare.

'If I hadn't met Clare,' Nick went on, 'I think I'd be living out in some croft, or in a self-sufficient commune maybe, if I could find one. You know what I mean. The retreat from society.' Nick settled back down on to his elbows, 'But I can't imagine being completely alone. There'd have to be other people. Or at least one other person,' he added, 'I'm better when I have to be with people. I know that. Maybe not with you, obviously, if I had a choice.'

'Ha bloody Ha.' Greg sat up, 'I don't know what I'd do if anything happened to my girls,' he said. 'I get mad if I even think about it.' He drank a little from his water bottle.

'It's hard for me to admit it,' Nick said, 'But I don't think we'll ever be completely sure what happened in Ruth's final hours, will we? Maybe he didn't have much to do with it, Stevens is a victim in his own way. The jury reckoned he wasn't to know Ruth would die. Maybe all there is to it.'

'You're starting to talk sense mate. Maybe you can put this behind you.'

'Maybe,' Nick said. He pulled at the seed head on a long grass stalk, flicked the seeds out with his thumb. 'Maybe. But the thing is… I maybe don't want to put it behind me. Maybe I can't leave Ruth behind as long as no-one's heard her voice. I've thought of going to a medium, you know, see if there's a message for me from her, from the other side. What she wants me to do, wants me to say on her behalf. Hers was the only voice that wasn't heard at the trial and I've often imagined what her testimony might have been, from beyond the grave…. Maybe she went along so far and then wanted to stop, maybe she tried to resist him, maybe there was a struggle… after all there were marks on her body…'

'She wouldn't want you going all over this again and again, man. She'd want you to have a new life man, that's what little Ruthie would want. Clare too, I'm sure.' Greg said, 'I've told you that before.'

'Maybe.'

When they stopped talking there was only the rustle of wind in the grass.

'It's good for me to be here,' Nick said, 'This place, these ancient hills, the open space all around … when you're up somewhere like this you really understand how puny our little lives are, our three score and ten on the planet. We're just little blips, aren't we? Meaningless little blips.'

'Speak for yourself mate,' Greg said. He patted his paunch. 'I'm no blip.' He licked his lips then rolled them together for a moment. 'And my life means a lot to me. It's all I've got.'

They both heard the skylark again, right above them now. They squinted into the sun to see it.

'Listen to that,' Greg said, 'Is that not the most beautiful thing you've ever heard.'

They lay and listened some more. Both of them dozed off this time.

When Nick woke up with a stiff neck, he shook Greg. 'Wake up man. We're missing the best of the day.'

Greg stretched his arms out. Sat up and rotated his shoulders. Yawned. Took a sip of his water while Nick opened the map. 'It's not far to the top of Mayar,' Nick said, 'It'd be a shame not to go up since we're this close. On a day like today we'll get a view across the mountains to the North and West.' They stood up and Nick double checked the way forward on his compass. It didn't take long to get to the top and the fabulous panorama of the east of Scotland it offered. Jock's Road lay below them, heading over to Braemar, Lochnagar dominating the view to the north. They were near enough to the top of Dreish, another of the Angus Munros – and since they could see what looked like the route, and checked it on Nick's phone from the *walkhighlands* website, they decided to take it on. It made for a long day on the hill, a long but very satisfying day.

Driving back down the road to Stirling, Nick was still in reflective mood. 'At some point, I'm going to have to move away from Stirling,' he said.

'Where to?'

'I want away from civilization. I want out in the open air, the open sky. Today reminded me how much I love it up in the mountains. And the sea: I love the sea, out by the East Neuk... next stop Holland... but the housing there is too expensive for me... and it's too busy... I'm sure I could get into some kind of environmental job, up north or west maybe... maybe when this is all over.'

'You mean it's not over?'

'Not yet, for me anyway. I just couldn't cope with a move now. I've thought about it a bit, but I can't face it. Not yet.' Nick said. 'Research, planning, selling up, saying goodbye to familiar clients. It would mean giving up routines, worse, it'd mean giving up the house, Ruth's bedroom. It feels like too definite a step. It'd mean, in that horrible phrase I hate so much... it'd mean...' Nick made exaggerated commas with his fingers, "...finding closure...". And I don't think I'm ready to do that yet. I'm way off being ready. Way way off.'

But time was moving, however slowly. Weeks were turning into months and before long, it would be November again - a year since Ruth's death.

* * *

Nick and Dorothy met up at her house on the morning of the anniversary. They'd agreed to spend some time together with their memories, as they had the Christmas before. The thoughts were all there anyway, all the time. It was indulgent but might also be cathartic.

Dorothy brought out her albums of photos from Clare's childhood as well as her photos of Ruth. When Nick looked at Dorothy's photos of Clare as a child, Clare before he knew her, he wondered what was going on behind those eyes gazing out at him from the past. What would she have thought if she'd known what life had in store for her? Would she have made different decisions? What would she say to him now? Would she be proud of him, how he was coping? At least today surely, she'd be pleased with him, spending time with her mother. They had lunch at Sherbrooke Castle, near to Dorothy's flat.

'I'm thinking of moving to Wales, Nick,' Dorothy said as they drank their coffee, 'I've been thinking about it for some time, but wanted to be sure before I spoke to you. I mean... I have my life here, but the people I see at bridge, the Hutchie former pupils' club, the Church... the life I have... it feels tired now. These aren't the people I want to grow old with. Well,' she corrected herself, 'I should say older, shouldn't I?'

Nick nodded encouragement.

'Yvonne recently told me about a bungalow near her, a small two-bedroom place, all on one level. I miss being near her. We were very close when we were girls you know, and it feels like our lives will bring us back together again as we get older. Maybe I can be a help to her as well. Bill isn't keeping so well these days, you know. And it's a nice part of the world.'

Nick sipped his coffee.

'I'm trying to look forward, she said, 'I'm not getting any younger. And I have no family here. I mean I appreciate us keeping in touch just now. But I'm not depending on you. And there'll come a time when you need to move on too, Nick.'

'Have you moved on then? Is that what this move to Wales is about?'

Dorothy pursed her lips. 'Nick,' she said, 'When you put it like that, then the answer must be no. Maybe 'move on' isn't the right phrase. Let's face it. Neither of us will ever really move on, will we? How could we? They'll still be with us whatever happens... our two lovely girls.' her voice trembled, 'But we've got to make the most of it. They wouldn't want us living in the past. I'm quite sure of it.'

'What do you think about that lad now?' he asked, 'You know. The one that was on trial.'

'I try not to. It upsets me too much.'

A waitress hovered a little, but Dorothy gave her a look and she went to clear another table.

'I try not to as well, but there isn't a day goes by I don't think of him.' Nick said, 'There isn't a day I don't have to push him back out of my mind, yet he always creeps back in. Hardly seems like justice, does it? He as good as killed Ruth... and now he's killing me slowly, taking over my brain. But I get confused too. I don't know whether to be angry or just sad. Was it all deliberate? I'll tell you this though... if I knew for sure that he'd killed Ruth, it'd all be so much easier. Every day I go into Stirling town centre, I worry that I might see him, with his mates, standing on a street corner, laughing, that sneer on his face, the sneer I saw at the hearing. And when I see that...'

'I hope you can bend that back,' Dorothy smiled at him. Nick had bent the soup spoon he was holding into a u-shape. He tried to get it back to its original shape, but only succeeded in putting another bend into the spoon. When he held it up for Dorothy to see, they both laughed.

'Nick,' Dorothy chided him, 'Oh Nick. You're so full of tension, regret, anger, remorse. Don't give yourself a hard time about it. I'm not in the least surprised how you feel. You're right to be angry, vengeful. Ruth was raped and he got away with it. It wasn't even on the charge sheet. No. And as far as I'm concerned, she was killed, murdered.' Dorothy took a moment. 'Murdered by that hooligan and by the culture that spawned him.' She squirmed.

'That's where we differ Dorothy,' Nick said, 'We always have. If it's to do with the culture, like you said, then how can we blame one person, especially not someone who's still really just a kid? Some kids just have a much better start than others. We all share a responsibility, don't we? For how fair our society is, for who feels left out? And the more money we have, the more responsibility goes with it. That's down to all of us. Do you really think that kid had a decent start in life?'

Dorothy shook her head and tutted. He threw it back to her.

'So, what's your answer then, Dorothy?'

'Never mind society. We're each responsible for what we do before God,' she said, 'He did it, that boy. I'm sure.' It was said in a flat matter-of-fact voice, 'And I know it's wrong to,' she added, more in sadness than anger, 'But I think his life should be ruined too. Can that be so wrong? Why should he have a full life when Ruth never had that chance? If I was forty years younger, and if I was a man, I wouldn't let him get away with it, scot-free. He'd pay for it alright.'

'I've had some of those thoughts too,' he said, 'Revenge fantasies, where I end up taking him on, making him suffer, like Ruth suffered.'

'No-one could blame you if you did,' Dorothy said, 'No could blame you.'

They were both subdued as Nick walked Dorothy home. A year on, remembering what had been, and thinking about what might have been, Ruth's death was still casting the same grey shadow over their lives, present and future.

* * *

Christmas Concert preparations seemed to be going well, though for Nick the Bach didn't have the same emotional impact as the Messiah: it felt more clinical whereas the

Handel had felt joyful, joy he badly needed. During rehearsals, in the many pauses and interruptions, he put on a brave enough face with the other choristers. And he enjoyed the company, particularly Simon, who had such a positive temperament. He'd opened up to Simon about his situation, asked him to apologise to Phoebe on his behalf, felt he had to offer some sort of explanation after running out on her at Easter.

Simon loved the choir, was always bringing up points from previous performances all of which had been 'magnificent', 'fabulous', 'so musical'. Though he was retired, he was still heavily involved in the teaching and research life of the University – 'Just the admin I've given up Nick,' he said with his hearty polished laugh, 'That's the bit they had to pay me to do.' He was active everywhere – on the board of a local foodbank charity, chair of a social enterprise café training people who had been long-term unemployed in catering skills, volunteering with a food delivery scheme that involved shopping for local people who were too elderly or housebound to shop for themselves. And he loved talking about his four grandchildren, showing them off in little *WhatsApp* videos. The week before the performance, Simon was telling Nick what he'd planned for Christmas. 'They'll all be back you know,' he said, beaming, 'Full house! You met Pam didn't you? There's Pam's mother, resident baby-sitter, then there's the three boys and their wives, the four children, Phoebe of course. She's the only one not hitched yet. We always have such a grand evening after the concert.' Simon chuckled, 'Maybe you won't run out on us this time?'

When Simon repeated his invitation after the concert was over, Nick did stay on for a drink, and then for a couple more. The chatter was mainly about the performance, what they should take on for Easter. He waited till he saw Phoebe standing on her own – she looked as good as he'd remembered her, a long woolen coat, navy coloured, her black hair tousled down over her shoulders. Might there be something there? Was he ready to start that journey?

'Hi,' he said, 'I have to apologise to you. At Easter, you know, when I stomped out. I was just a bit raw.'

She shrugged. 'Don't worry. I found out later what a good reason you had to be uptight. You had a lot to handle.'

He took a slug of his beer.

'I was watching you again tonight,' she said, 'You didn't seem so involved in your singing. Was that just the Bach? More restrained?'

'Yeah, could be,' he said, and then his tone freshened, 'Anyway what about you? You're a bit of a glutton for punishment, aren't you? Coming back for more?'

'I like to get my time off to coincide with my old man's concerts,' she told him, 'It keeps him happy… and it keeps me happy too.'

Simon had told Nick a bit about Phoebe. She was a doctor with *Medecins sans Frontières*, working in Cambodia, back in Scotland on Christmas leave.

'How long are you back for?' he asked.

'I'll head back just after New Year. I've been working on malaria prevention... there's strains there that are resistant to artemisinin. And there's so much uncontrolled use of the drug in the wider Mekong area that the resistant strains are spreading. WHO has launched a major containment programme.' She was speaking urgently, passionately. 'If we don't contain this resistant parasite there's a real danger of it spreading to other areas and with no new anti-malarials on the immediate horizon that could be disastrous. There's another project starting next year on Hep C. I'll be involved in that too. It's exciting.' Her words, her world, were like an unstoppable avalanche of energy and enthusiasm. Nick asked questions and Phoebe kept piling on information – statistics, scientific details, Cambodia's crazy politics...

'Why do you want to go back?' he asked, 'Sounds like a nightmare.'

'It's crazy. It's corrupt. It's too wet and it's too hot and we're fighting on too many fronts but it's a frontier Nick,' she said, 'A human frontier where real people, wonderful people – beautiful, wonderful people - are needing something I can give. Of course, if it was only medicine that would be much easier, but there's education, and good governance, and political controls. I don't think I could come back here to work. There isn't the buzz, the need. It feeds me.'

'It must be great to have something like that, something you believe in,' he said. 'Maybe I should do something like that. Only I've no skills to offer.'

'It can help, being valuable to others, being needed,' she said, 'One of my colleagues came out after the break-up of a relationship, threw herself into the work, found a new purpose.'

'I guess that's what I'm trying to do too,' he said, 'I've no special skills to offer like you. I make my living from organic gardening, contract work, round and about. I throw myself into it. I like the physicality, just me and hard physical work. It keeps me "grounded".' He'd put air quotes round the word and laughed apologetically. 'Sorry about that.'

'But,' she wouldn't be put off as easily as her father, 'Is it getting easier? Is your life any better?'

'Not really,' he said, 'I don't know if I'll ever be able to move on. The young man that supplied the drink and the drugs that contributed to my daughter's death? He was charged with culpable homicide – that's the Scottish version of manslaughter. The trial wasn't long after that Easter concert where we met?' She tilted her head a little, raised an eyebrow. 'Well, anyway...' he hesitated... was he really going to get into this, put it into words? '... the way it all ended, it made it look as if it was everyone's fault, that Ruth was partially to blame for her own death. I was told the defence had virtually made out that she was a wee slut, into everything, drunk, drugged up,' his voice was getting louder now, 'That's what bugs me the most, that she was denied her voice at the trial, while everyone else gets to say whatever the hell they like about her. That's the bit I can't cope with.'

She waited for him to go on.

'You don't need to listen to me.' he said, toning it down again, 'You don't need to be polite.'

She put her hand on his shoulder. 'I'm interested,' she said. 'But I don't want to intrude either.' She swirled the beer round her glass and looked over at her father. Simon was in the middle of a group at the bar, contented, a wide smile on his face. They sipped their drinks.

'Bit of a conversation killer, isn't it?' he said.

'Yes, it is a bit. But for what it's worth, I understand. Terrible things happen in the world. Some of the people I'm working with in Cambodia, they went through the 'killing fields' time, lost parents, partners, brothers and sisters. There was a process through 'extraordinary courts' to bring some of the killers to justice, but most of them weren't brought before the courts, only a few of the leaders. Many of the victims never had their story told. Many of those who loved them have to live with the knowledge that no-one has been held to account, no-one knows the real story. Some of the killers were still walking among them... could've passed them in the street every day. They're mostly dead now, but it's still hard for the survivors, even fifty years on.'

It didn't feel appropriate to say anything trite or banal, or just anything at all really. After a minute or so, Phoebe took out her phone. 'Look,' she said, more brightly, 'It's busy in here and I need to say hello to a few people. I'm around for the next few days. Why don't we meet up, take a walk round the castle or up Dumyat one morning? I'll phone you once I know what else is on. What's your number?'

'A walk sounds good,' he said, then watched while she punched the number into her phone.

* * *

When she called the next morning, they agreed to meet up later in the week and walk through to Dunblane on the Darn Walk. 'Just so we're both clear,' she said when they met, 'This isn't a date or anything like that. I'm kind of hooked up with another MSF doctor at the moment. He's still in Cambodia. It's just, well, I like you. I think we could be good friends.'

Nick hadn't seen it that way. He'd thought there was a little spark, a connection, allowed himself to hope there might be something more. He'd let his defences down a little. All the same, they did meet up and walk to Dunblane later that week. He enjoyed her company, hearing more about the work she was so passionate about. They exchanged e.mails and promised to keep in touch.

'Can a man and a woman ever be "just friends"?' he asked Greg later. 'I mean you're bound to think of more than just friendship when it's a woman you really like.'

'Is she good looking?'

'Yes. Whatever that is.'

'So. There's your answer. You're bound to think of… well you know. Haha. I mean if the girl's halfway decent looking, you're always thinking, aren't you, I mean like, thinking, "would I? if I got the chance?" Aren't you?'

'Chrissake Greg… You're like a wee kid sometimes.'

'Don't tell me you're not thinking the same thing.' Greg said, suddenly angry, 'And don't be such a bloody prig, such a stuck-up, bloody prig. You know that's what you've become. A tight-arsed, stuck-up prig, so bloody *holier than thou*. You're no fun to be with anymore, I mean, Christ knows you've got good reason, but where's the anger man? Where's the emotion? Where's the spirit?'

Nick didn't answer.

'Look at you,' Greg said, 'Mister bloody miserable.'

'There are lots of great women in the world,' Nick said, 'And the three of them I was closest too are all gone. What are the chances?'

'Look mate,' Greg said, 'Don't take any offence but I'm talking to you straight. As a mate. Don't wallow in it. If you want to, you can get back on the pitch, back in the game, any time. And Clare, and Ruth, they'd want you to do that too. You're needing to start asking what are your future chances? That's a better question. Start looking forwards, not back.'

* * *

The start of the following year was no easier for Nick, but it was no worse. Dorothy didn't set in motion the process of selling her house till January - 'a well-maintained stone built upper flat conversion in the desirable Strathbungo area of South Glasgow' as the estate agent described it. She had several bids well over the asking price in the first week and settled in a fortnight. He spent more time with her then, helping her clear out, pack her furniture, books, objects, photos, a lifetime of memories. In February, Nick drove down and spent the weekend to help her settle in. It was clear to him that she was moving on, though she didn't use those exact words again. She wanted him to take some of her books and furniture, but he only took one photo of Clare. It was one that had been hanging in the hallway, a black and white portrait photo taken when she was a leggy teenager, a little puppy fat still round her face. It showed her more like Ruth than any other.

9. Meeting

There were no more long Saturday lunches after Dorothy moved. To keep his weekends fully occupied, Nick searched out running events in different parts of the country. Not that he was competing with others… just competing with himself, trying in every event to run better time than before. There were long drives to parts of Scotland and England he didn't know, listening to his podcasts, his audiobooks, his music. It passed the time. He still didn't feel a lot of joy in his life. He still wasn't sure what his life was for. But he was keeping busy. At Easter, he drove up north for the 'half Ben Nevis run', a two thousand foot climb up the Ben, Scotland's most iconic mountain, a mountain he'd never yet climbed.

The clear blue skies on the drive up to Fort William showed Scotland at its best, even in the queues of traffic across Rannoch Moor, stuck behind the ubiquitous caravans and motorhomes. Only when he got to the Ben did he discover he'd entered the date wrongly in his phone diary. He was a month early. After walking around Fort William in the late morning, looking for something to eat before heading back, he was taken with the notion to climb the Ben anyway, and picked up some fruit to eat on the climb. It was already close to twelve, so he went into one of the mountain gear shops to confirm his route. A rangy-looking young shop assistant spotted Nick fingering through a guide to the Ben Nevis range and started up a conversation with him.

'Looking to go up the Ben?' the guy said.

'I actually came up to do the half Ben Nevis run, but got dates mixed up in my diary. It's such a great day though. Thought I'd go up… since I'm here.'

'Next month, isn't it, your run?' the guy said.

Nick nodded.

'Been up the Ben before?'

'No. Well, a bit. I started out on the Arrete… a good few years back now right enough… but had to turn back.'

'Why was that?'

'I met the worst sleet I've ever been in at just over a thousand feet up.'

'There's a lot of days like that up there,' the guy said, a kind of misty-eyed enthusiasm overtaking him. 'It's the most beautiful and at the same time the most savage mountain on the mainland of the UK … it often lives up to its name… you know what Ben Nevis means, don't you?'

Nick pursed his lips and shrugged.

'It means 'venomous mountain'… and it can be really venomous… but it can be really glorious. Taking the ascent by the Arrete, for example… it does give you a more interesting ascent. You really see the Ben at its majestic best from that side. But if you're going to try it today, you're a bit late starting out and if you're coming down in the dark… well you don't want to be on the Arrete in the dark. I wouldn't do it.'

'Go on,' Nick said, 'Tell me more. You obviously know the hill.'

'Don't get me wrong,' the young guy said, 'The tourist route has its challenges too. Even if there's good visibility, and that's not often, there's cloud hangs about on the summit plateau most days, you're still going to need compass and map at the top to avoid the gullies, going up and coming back down.' He pulled Nick over to a large aerial display photograph of the summit of the Ben, one of several display photos in the shop, and pointed to the steep cliffs of the fearsome North face. 'Two experienced young climbers already went down earlier this year,' he said, 'OK that was in February... in an avalanche. But last year, about this time, or maybe a bit earlier, two guys died on the Five Finger side, walking straight out onto pure unmarked snow with nothing beneath it. There's still a fair bit of snow up there – it can sit there well into summer, or so-called summer,' the guy chuckled. 'If you fancy that route, check it out on *You Tube*. There's loads of climbers have posted videos of their climb. But watch out for the snow cornices... there's still some up there even this late in the year, and they're lethal.'

'I fancy trying the Arrete,' Nick said, 'And I'm thinking about my time. If I crack on, I reckon I can get up and down today. What do you think?'

'Yeah... probably. You look fit enough.' the guy said, 'You'll need to do a bit of scrambling though. I hope you've got a good head for heights.'

'So far,' Nick said, 'I'm going to give it a go.'

The climb didn't disappoint. On the early stages, on this clearest of West Highland days, he had a great view of the outrageous North face cliffs. Though his binoculars he could see a group of four climbers, roped together, picking their way up near the top of one of the buttresses. Once onto the Arrete, he navigated his way along it briskly, then pushed on up the boulder strewn Eastern slope, He was closing up on another lone figure a little up ahead, late on the mountain like him - a woman he thought, from the billowing red hair. As he got closer, up at the snow line, he recognised her and that gave him time to prepare his lines.

'Sam Hill,' he shouted as he came up fast behind her, and then, when she stopped and he came alongside her, he slipped into a cod American accent, *'Of all the mountains in all the world, you had to climb onto mine.'*

She squinted at him into the sun. 'Do I know you?' she said.

'Aye. Sure you do.' Nick held out his hand and smiled. 'Sorry about the corny line. I'm Nick Innocenti? You covered my wee girl's murder?... well, they didn't find a murder verdict. The guy that caused her death got off with it. There wasn't the evidence to convict... Anyway...'

She was peering at him more closely then. 'I do remember now. Somewhere up here. Well not here exactly... in Scotland I mean.'

'Stirling,' he said, 'You did a good job. I don't know if you find out what happens in the cases you feature, but it was a breakthrough. After your programme, a witness came forward. But she hadn't seen the important elements of the story. In some ways her testimony made a conviction less likely.'

'Yes,' she mused, 'It's coming back now. We do a catch-up for viewers on what's happened in cases we feature. Ruth, wasn't it? Ruth...'

'Innocenti,' he said.

'Yes. Terrible, what happened to your daughter. It was a terrible loss.' She paused, as if she had something else to say, and then removed her sunglasses, shook out her hair. She looked him up and down, taking him in. There was something vulpine in that look.

'Anyway,' she said, changing her tone, 'It's good to be out here, today, isn't it? Just look at that view.' She stretched out our arms and pirouetted round, surveying the scene. 'Such an immense space. Those mountains, row upon row. Puts us in our place, doesn't it? `

'It's more than a year ago now,' he said, standing up beside her. 'The trial. And the boy that did it, he's on the streets. I could run into him any day. In the pub. At the bus stop.'

'I'm sorry,' she said, 'That must make it harder.'

'Yes,' he said, 'But it's also true that on days like today I can almost forget. I just take each day at a time.'

'Come on then,' she said, 'We can get to the top together, if you like. It's not far to go now.'

As they pushed on up the slope, Sam was panting heavily. She had to stop again a few hundred feet from the top. 'I'm a bit out of puff,' she said, 'Not done... so much walking this year... I used to be up in Scotland... once a month... at least... and it's harder walking here... I didn't expect this snow.'

'I remember you as a hillwaker... we talked about your walks when we met.'

'Did we?' She looked surprised. 'Well I'm too busy... too bloody busy, my life.'

'You told me you walked with Katy Calman.,' he said. 'You were "doing the Munros" together.'

'Yes that's right. Well remembered.' - how could I forget?, he was thinking. She sat down, pulled a water bottle from her backpack and took a long slug. He couldn't take his eyes off her. 'Katy backed out of this weekend at the last minute. Some man thing. God knows. Anyway I needed this, so I decided to go for it on my own – she did Ben Nevis years ago. I only have thirty two more to do. I'm going to finish on the *In Pinn* on Skye, next year, you know... the *Inaccessible Pinnacle?*' He nodded. 'At least that's my ambition... We're planning to do the last few together.' She sat down on a boulder and brushed her hair back off her face. 'And you? What are you doing up here?'

'Me?' he blew out a long breath, 'I'm into running more than hills these days. I came up here for a running event and found I'd got the wrong weekend. It was such a fine day I decided to climb the Ben. I've tried before but was driven back by low cloud and horrible driving sleet. And there aren't that many days when it's as clear as this, so I reckoned this was my day. Then I met you and I knew it must be.'

She didn't respond, but he wished he hadn't said it. He'd meant it, but once it was out, it just sounded corny. Mind you, she probably heard every corny line in the book several times a day... and more.

'I've been up here many times and never managed the Ben,' she said, pointing. 'I've climbed all of the Mamores over there, and both Aonach Mor and Aonach Beg,' she pointed vaguely in the direction of the two mountains, 'Those two were among the first Katy and I climbed.' She named other mountains they could see, to the north, to the east. It was as if the whole of the Highlands were laid out before them. 'I've avoided the Ben till now, cos it's always so busy... but I had to get it in, and since Katy wasn't available this weekend, and the weather suited... Well... just look at it!' She took in the view once again, 'People disparage Ben Nevis, because it's popular I suppose. I felt a bit the same, before today. Look around you! What a magnificent mountain. Especially this route.'

'You should know,' he said, 'You seem to know more about Scottish mountains than me... a lot more.'

Sam stretched her neck and smiled. 'I do know a lot,' she said in a self-satisfied kind of way. 'Anyway, we need to press on, get up to the summit and back down. I don't want to be up here when it's getting dark.' He offered her his hand and when she took it, he pulled her to her feet.

'Oh,' she said, 'Strong hands.' And there was something in the way she said it, the way she looked at him. If he hadn't known better, he'd have thought she was flirting, teasing him perhaps. Or was it just that he was a jumping, nervous bundle of energy, all his senses on full throttle? Or that she was used to handling men? God, he was no use at reading women.

They pressed on towards the summit.

'Fancy joining me for a meal afterwards,' she said, the next time they stopped to take I in the fabulous view. 'I've had a shitty week and could do with some good company.' Her lip seemed to tremble just a little as she spoke. She looked vulnerable, for a second or two, the breeze tugging at her hair. 'I'm staying at the Inverlochy. We can just eat there when we get down... if it suits you that is?'

It suited him. He'd assumed he'd be driving back down the road, made no arrangements for staying over, but this was an invitation he couldn't refuse, even it meant sleeping over in the pickup, at the side of a road.

Not many had climbed the Ben that day, though those that did wanted to linger on the summit - the late afternoon sky was so clear, the views so good. Sam and Nick spent an hour up there on the top, finishing their snacks, taking photos, talking about mountains they could see. She signed a couple of autographs. When clouds began to gather, they thought it wise to start on their route down... not by the Arrete but back down the safer 'tourist route'. He let her navigate them across the west side of the long summit plateau, changing the bearing *en route* to find the safe line between the gullies, gullies that had claimed amateur walkers before, and would probably do so again. After the half-way lochan, they took the Allt a'Mhuillin path. Nick was really tired, and his knees had taken a pounding from the long steep descent, but Sam seemed to have a second wind and pushed on. By the time they got to Torlundy, the sun was on its way down. They stood at the gatehouse in the gloaming for a minute or two and looked back to the Ben, looming indistinctly above them.

'Let's get a couple of beers in before we eat,' she said, 'There's a great selection here.'

Halfway through the second beer Nick realized how much less on edge he'd been, how relaxed. It felt as if some kind of internal switch had been reset. She asked him about the trial, but he didn't get into feelings, keeping his reply vague, general. She asked him how he was feeling right now and so forced him into finding words: it was like Ruth and he had been on a road together, he said, but though he was on his own now, Ruth was somehow still there, wouldn't let him go. And anyway, he didn't want her to: Ruth's voice - the one voice that should've been the most important voice at the trial - was the one voice that hadn't been heard. 'I think she wants me to know what actually happened and to speak for her.' he said, 'But she can't tell me what it is I have to say.'

'That's a lovely idea,' she said, 'That the one who is dead, killed, murdered... that they are the only one who doesn't have a voice at the trial... Can I use that in the programme? I'll mention it's from you... if you want?'

'Use it if you want,' he said, 'only don't mention me.'

Sam did most of the talking. But it was no hardship listening to her. He loved the almost musical variation in her voice, the rise and fall of emotion on her face, the energy of her. And her voice was enthusiastic, encouraging: his business sounded fabulous; she'd love to be doing something like that; she'd always had some kind of fantasy of settling down, living the good life, the organic life, the 'leave-no-footprints' life he talked about. She confessed that though she was fed up with her lifestyle, she was addicted to it: wanted to get out but didn't know how.

They ordered club sandwiches and shared some french fries with a bottle of Malbec. At some point late in the evening, Sam laid her hand on Nick's, leaned over and kissed him full on the lips.

'There,' she said, 'I've been wanting to do that all evening.'

Nick pulled back a little and rubbed his chin. 'Wow,' he said.

She laughed. 'I like you,' she said, 'There's something honest about you, I'd say naive but that's not quite the right word.' She tapped his nose with her index finger, 'Innocent by nature as well as by name, eh?'

Nick felt a bit patronized, but he didn't mind. She could say anything and he wouldn't mind.

'I want a bit more of what you've got,' she said, 'Media life is so up itself. All knowing-ness, in-people and out-people, meta-narratives, super-sophisticated self-indulgence, new therapies, first world problems... I don't know... I'm a hypocrite too. Actually. You know what?' she said, speaking more to herself now, or maybe she was always speaking to herself, and he was just there to listen. 'I like my life,' she said, assertively, 'I like it too much. I just fantasize about giving it up. I probably never will.'

He carried on listening...

'It's like.... well,' she laughed again and rolled her tongue round her lips, 'Like I said. I wish I had something of your rootedness. It's like you couldn't give a shit about the kind of stuff that's important in my world. I like that.'

He scratched his chin. He didn't give a shit about very much at all, but he was giving a shit about her. She swilled the remaining wine round in her glass and finished it off. 'We should carry on this conversation somewhere quieter,' she said, 'Come on up to my room. It's rather nice.'

They took another bottle of wine up. Once inside, the conversation turned physical. He came almost as soon she touched him. He might've been embarrassed but she was kind. They dallied a while, drank some more wine, then she got him up again. This time they took it slower. She told him what she wanted and he was able to oblige, more than able, and they found pleasure in letting it all out. Collapsing beside her, he wept uncontrollably, so much pent-up emotion pouring out of him. She comforted him as if he was a baby. It was as if they were old familiar lovers, as if they'd known each other for years.

'I like you Nick Innocenti,' she said, cradling his head to her breast.

'You might not say that if you knew me better,' he said.

'I already know you... more than you think, anyway.' she said, 'I'm pretty good at reading men, well most of the time anyway. I get a lot of practice with the people in my business. I wouldn't give most of them the time of day, outside of work.' She got out of bed and made some tea. He sat up and drank in every inch of her, her slender fingers, her thick rusty hair, the delicate way she plopped the tea bags into the bin. Every damn thing about her was so fine.

'I love your freckles,' he said, 'It was the first thing I noticed about you when we met... you know when you were interviewing me for the programme. Remember? And you were so... it's not "charming" – that suggests some kind of veneer, superficial, not genuine. I mean you obviously had all the manners, all the skills, I could see that, but I don't know...' He'd run out of words. She started laughing and he joined in. It was good to be able to laugh. He imagined Ruth watching him from wherever she was. She'd be laughing too.

The mattress was deep and wide, somehow neither too soft nor too firm, 'a Goldilocks mattress,' he called it. Sam was quickly asleep, snuggling into him. Nick too began to drift away, his legs twined with hers, but he didn't want to sleep, he wanted to squeeze every moment of pleasure and enjoyment from this unexpected evening. How can we be so intimate so quickly? he thought, I feel like we've known each other for years. If this is a dream, he thought, I don't want to wake up.

* * *

Sam had vaguely thought of climbing in Glen Etive on the Sunday, but when they woke first thing and saw the heavy rain, they stayed in bed and made love again. Over a late brunch they talked about everything and nothing. She wanted a refill of her coffee and he watched as she walked over to the bar, the way she moved, the way her hair hung to the side when she leaned her head over. Everything about her was perfect, including the fact that she wasn't perfect: she was no cute little princess trapped by her own self-image as he imagined other celebrities to be. So what the hell was she doing with him? When she turned round, he smiled a lopsided smile, an apologetic smile.

'What?' she said.

'Nothing. Just feeling good.'

'Good,' she said, 'Now what about today? I don't need a flight till the evening, but it must be tonight. I've a meeting at noon tomorrow I can't miss, and I need to prepare. There are things back at my place I need to read over.'

'Where are you flying from?'

'Glasgow.'

'Why don't we head into the city? I can show you some of my Glasgow. I was a student there... a few years ago right enough.'

'Fine,' she said, 'I don't really know Glasgow so well. I always just want to get up north to the mountains.'

She followed Nick in her hire car, down the Loch Lomondside route, along the Dumbarton Road. After they'd parked in Kelvin Way, they walked by the river and he pointed out the University Buildings, the Art Gallery and Museum. She wanted to see the Cathedral, so they took her car - along the Broomielaw and up the High Street - but there was some kind of media event so they couldn't get into the old church.

"Let's go up to the Necropolis,' he said, 'There are some great views of the city from up there, if you don't mind walking among the gravestones.'

As they strolled through, reading the occasional stone, Nick gave an enthusiastic commentary on what he knew of the bits of Glasgow they could see. Parts of him that had been dead were coming back to life. 'It's such a brilliant city,' he said, 'It's got its own individual identity, but it's also very cosmopolitan. Not the refined effete cosmopolitanism of some rich European city with two thousand years of history – sure there's high culture here, but there's also an earthy internationalism, a mixing of people on the margins, refugees, asylum seekers, Asian entrepreneurs, the old working class, many of whom don't work any more, or if they do it's certainly not in the old industries, the heavy industries of Glasgow's past. You'll need to come back and I'll show you more.'

'More of Glasgow or more of Scotland?'

'Both.'

'Or more of yourself?' She pulled him towards her by his jacket collar and kissed him briefly. 'I've enjoyed our time, but all good things must come to an end. I'll call you during the week. You know there must have been more than coincidence to us meeting again on the mountain. I don't believe these things just happen. But my life is in a bit of a mess at the moment. I've just broken up with someone and I don't really know what's going on. This weekend was just what I needed. You were just what I needed. But I'm not sure what happens next.'

He felt a catch in his throat. 'OK,' he said, 'I don't have any commitments to break. Just give me a call. I'd like to see you again. I can be where you want. Anytime.'

She dropped him at his pickup on her way out to the airport. The glow that Nick had captured and held on to since he met her on the Ben carried him home that evening. He imagined what Ruth would've said if she'd been there when he got home, standing in the kitchen, boiling up a kettle for him: 'You're going out with Sam Hill, Dad? Cool.' Sam was in a different league, a different world. He had no idea where it might be going, or if was going to go at all. Of course, it wouldn't last, couldn't last.

But as long as it did, he'd be there when she called.

* * *

Greg picked up his change of mood when they were out running, midweek.

'What's up mate?' he said, 'We're running along and you've got this silly grin on your face?'

Nick told him about the weekend.

'You lucky dog!" Greg shouted, "Fucking lucky dog! I bet she's got a sweet little fanny that one.'

Nick stopped running. 'Shut the fuck up Greg,' he shouted, 'Just shut the fuck up. God. Sometimes I just don't get you.'

'What man? I'm only joking, ay? Don't get your arse on fire. I know. She's a sweet girl alright. Just a bit of talk. You know what I'm like.'

'OK,' Nick said, 'Just... it's not like that. It's, well, it's... I don't know. It's disrespectful.' They ran on for a bit and Nick was getting angrier. 'Just don't talk about her that way,' he said, 'What is it with you anyway Greg? You're like some kind of old Ozzie lecher. It doesn't suit you.'

'Don't pretend you're not in the same game,' it was Greg that was starting to get angry now, 'You can't blame me for thinking. That's all I get to do these days. Bloody thinking. Stuck with the same woman. And what if she's not keen? Which is most of the fucking time by the way. It's bloody difficult.'

'Relationships are hard.' Nick said, 'But you don't say everything you think.'

'Don't be such a fucking prude,' Greg said, 'So fucking honourable. You're the one got your fucking end away. With Sam fucking Hill.'

They were coming back into Riverside then. Not far to go till they got back to Nick's place. Nick pushed on and left Greg behind. Once he was back in the little front garden, he started his stretching routine.

'OK. Look mate,' Greg said when he arrived back at the house a little later, 'I'm sorry. Shouldn't have said what I did about Sam. I was just joshing. No offence intended. The thing is, I wish it was me.' Greg turned in on himself then. 'Me and Sheila aren't doing too well. That's probably my fault more than hers. I know I'm being a cunt, but I can't help it.'

'You're lucky to have Sheila,' Nick said, 'Lucky, man.'

'So everyone keeps telling me but let me tell you, Sheila's hard to live with. Knows what she wants and what she doesn't want... lets me know all about it too. There's a lot of things men are to blame for, in her book, and as the nearest man, I'm the one that hears about it most often.'

'Appreciate what you've got Greg. Look at what happened to me.'

Later on, over a pint, Sam came up in the conversation again and Greg gave Nick some advice in return. 'Be careful Nick,' he said, 'No one man can do it all for a bird like that. She'll move on to someone else, nothing surer. In fact. she may well have several at the same time.'

'I know the score Greg,' Nick sighed, 'I wasn't born yesterday. I'll take it as it comes and enjoy it while I can. It feels like,' he hesitated, trying to find the exact word, 'It feels like, well, she might be helping me to start to come back to life.'

* * *

For Nick life with Sam in it, and she was definitely in it, was amazingly busy. Spring became a whirlwind of activity, fun, pleasure. The arrangements for finding time to meet were necessarily complicated. For a start there was a 400-mile gap to cross. Then there was her schedule. A hectic mixture of TV, promotional work and endless meetings he had to fit around. One week she came up Thursday and Friday and went back for the weekend. The next time it was an extended weekend into Monday. He took whatever time was needed to be there whenever she could make it. She seemed to like the taste of this other life in Scotland, with a guy who paid her a kind of perfect attention she hadn't had much of recently. They went to the Cairngorms together so she could get up Ben Macdui, one of the Munros she was still missing. They went to Mull to walk up Ben More but were rained off on the Saturday. They stayed over at the Pennyghael Hotel. Nick knew the area from his childhood when the family took annual holidays further down the peninsula, near Bunessan. 'If it's still raining tomorrow, we can maybe do a low-level walk,' he said, 'There's a great walk I did with my Dad as a kid, out on the north of the loch, past Tiroran and out to the fossil tree. The whole area out there is called *The Wilderness.* It fascinated me as a kid.'

'*The Wilderness*?' she said, 'What an amazing name for a place. Who would ever want to go there?'

'Exactly,' he said, 'But isn't that the attraction of it too? And it has an astonishing geology... basalt columns, same as on the island of Staffa... you know, Staffa? Fingal's Cave...?' She nodded for him to carry on, 'And trapped in the basalt there's an old fossil tree... It's like the end of the world.'

As it turned out the weather on Sunday was even worse, so they headed back to the mainland early. As they got to know each other better over the next couple of months, and as Nick became more confident, their lovemaking became more relaxed. She liked his naive physical ardour, his vulnerability. He responded to her open appetites, her experience, her sexual exuberance. It was a good time for them both.

They talked all the time. She helped him find words, words that gave a shape to the holes in his life. Sam for her part talked mainly about her work: the cynical and the supercilious and the shallow of her world, affecting so many people, but not always in the ways that she wanted. Nick was a good listener, supportive and analytical.

She didn't talk about Alan, the partner she'd just broken up with, but Nick had looked him up on Wikipedia - some kind of big noise producer in TV and the Arts - a whizz-kid entrepreneur in his youth, he'd now turned fifty, specialised in making money out of high culture - 'the commercial doesn't need to be crass,' was his famous catchphrase, apparently: made his first million in his twenties, and since then had made a few more. Sam and Alan, it seemed, had been in and out each other's pockets for years. They'd had other relationships but, somehow, they kept going back to each other. Nick disliked everything about Alan. And he disliked everything about the world of Alan. Whenever he pictured them together, he got a wrenching feeling in his gut. But more often than before he was finding himself smiling. In odd places. In the shower, driving his pickup, in his allotment.

Smiling.

Sam didn't invite him into her life in London. It was never an issue: he had no desire to be part of her Knightsbridge flat, expensive watering holes with people he didn't know, polite conversations, with him the object of polite, fleeting interest. And he didn't invite her to Stirling. His functional little cottage would only emphasise the differences between them. Meeting on neutral ground gave them the freedom to be with each other without too much of the daily baggage, to share things that were new to both, and therefore special just to them. Nick didn't ask her any awkward questions about where things might go next. He didn't ask them of himself. But, of course, it couldn't go on forever.

To do Sam credit it could all have been done on the phone, but she did come North to see Nick on a late August weekend when they'd planned to head up to Loch Maree to climb Slioch – the plan had been for him to pick her up at the airport in Inverness. Nick guessed there was something wrong whenever she told him she'd changed her flight from Inverness to Glasgow. She asked him to meet her with the pickup in the short stay carpark, not to come into the airport. And when she got into the pickup there was no overnight bag, no climbing gear.

'Let's go somewhere for a walk,' she said.

It was a dreich miserable day, a soft warm smirr settling on Glasgow as it so often does. Nick cut back through the Clyde Tunnel and parked at the Transport Museum. There was a break in the rain as they walked along the Clyde, towards the city. 'It's going to have to end,' she said. 'It's been great but I can't do it anymore: hold these different bits of my life together. It's too much.'

The relationship had started by walking, and now it was finishing that way.

'Why must it end?' He spoke slowly, desperate not to sound desperate.

'I owe you more of an explanation, I suppose,' she said, 'but you won't like it. For a start, there's Alan. He's moved back in with me this week. For just now anyway. This is what we do. We get too close, and I need a break, but he's just too much part of my life. And there's you. I can't give you more. It's been good but I've got a busy summer schedule coming up. I'm in the States next month. Then I have a big assignment in Australia that he can help me with. You need something else, some*one* else, someone who'll be around more...' She waited for him to say something, but he had no words. 'We just have to move on Nick,' she said.

'We could make it work.' He drew the words out, conscious that his bottom lip was wobbling a little, trying not to sound pathetic, 'I'm not looking for anything more. I'm not looking for anything different to what we have just now. Can we not just carry on, like we have been? I can help you get those last Munros. I can come with you to Australia, instead of him.' He could hear the slightly self-pitying tone in his voice but couldn't get rid of it. When he turned to look at her face, he could see it was set: he knew she didn't want him in Australia. They walked on. A few leaves were drifting down onto the wet path.

'There's so many things. You've no idea,' she said, 'how difficult it's been for me to organise my weeks to get up here; turning things down, shifting things around. Before I could come North or not as I wanted, on a whim. At first, with you, it all felt fresh, new. It's begun to feel compulsory.'

'You don't need to come up so often,' he said.

'The strain's been telling on me. I need to join up my emotional life and my working life. With Alan back it's possible. He can support me during the week, advise me about what to do next...'

She looked round at him then. Tears were coursing down his cheeks. They stopped walking.

She put her hand to his face then ran her finger round his chin. 'You're a lovely man Nick. I've enjoyed being with you but I'm not the woman you need. I can't give you what you need, but I've given you what I can. You need to go on now, maybe make that new start you've talked about to me, go up the west coast, sell your house, travel, do something new.

You can respect your old life, the life that's gone, you can still hold on to it without letting it block your new one. It's time to go and find that new life.'

He blew his nose and collected himself. 'I suppose I knew this is how things would end, but I don't regret it. Not for one single minute.' She tilted her head and her red hair fell to the side. 'And,' he said, aware that he was sounding a bit pathetic, 'if you ever get fed up with your life down there, you'll give me a call again won't you, give me another chance?'

Sam cleared her throat and spoke quite directly then, assertive and clear. 'Nick I'm going to go now, before this gets too... well, you know what I'm like. I can't stand it when things get too maudlin. Don't keep flying a flag for me. I'm really not worth it. I should've told you before, but, you see, Alan came up with me – he's waiting at the airport to make sure I go back with him.' They were near the Crowne Plaza Hotel. There was a queue of taxis at the door. 'So,' she said, 'I'm going to get a taxi now, back to the airport.' She put a hand up to his cheek. 'Take care of yourself, Nick. You'll make some woman very happy. Not me. But I'll always remember you.' She kissed him on the cheek and ran off. After a few yards, she stopped, turned round, waved and ran over to the taxi stand, her phone in her hand already, off into her busy life where there were so many people to see, arrangements to make, events to attend, taxis to hire. Nick watched her go, every last glimpse of her, down to the view of her head in the back window of the taxi, swaying to the side as the driver jerked into second gear. And then he couldn't see her anymore. There was a hollow ache in his throat. An emptiness in his gut. It was beginning to rain again as he stood watching the taxi shoot on up the road.

Sam was gone and she wasn't coming back.

He headed back towards the Transport Museum where he'd left the pickup. Where would she be now? Would she just have gone through the tunnel? Was she on the motorway yet? Was she already at the airport? With Alan? He visualized her on the plane, looking down at Glasgow as it turned south. Would she still be thinking of him?

He drove home on autopilot. It didn't feel so bad, just numb. He'd known it was coming, from that very first day on Ben Nevis. But as the evening progressed his mood darkened. He sat on Clare's Habitat sofa, staring round his familiar, tired-looking little room, seeing it through her eyes. How could he ever have imagined that she would be interested in him? The hungry hollow ache in his stomach wouldn't go away. It was a real physical pain now. No-one had died. Just the little bit of hope that had been growing inside him. The amazing thing was that it had ever happened at all.

Late in the evening he went for a long run up the steps at the back of Causewayhead Park, up through the woods at the back of the University, out onto the Sheriffmuir road then back round through Bridge of Allan. The podcast he was listening to was *In Our Time*. Melvin Bragg and his guests were discussing 'punishment' – what is it for? when is it just? does it work? what are the alternatives? - questions Nick had been asking himself for the past year. Melvin and his guests couldn't agree with each other. But that really wasn't surprising. After all Nick couldn't even agree with himself. There were so many possible answers, and all of them had merit.

10. Howff

Over the next few days, the thoughts that had shifted so easily into the background when Sam had been in the foreground came back, but redoubled in their intensity, as if they'd just been resting, gathering their strength for a renewed attack: Ruth, the police investigation, the look on Jimmy Stevens' face when he was found not guilty. There really wasn't anything else worth thinking about.

Would Nick recognise Stevens now? He'd be 18 now maybe. As much a man as a boy. Nick imagined what he might do, what he might say if he ran to him by chance in the Stirling shopping centre. He imagined them getting into a tussle, saw himself sitting astride Stevens, mad and angry, his hands round his throat. In November, it would be two years since Ruth's death, but it still felt raw, an open wound, unfinished business. And Ruth wasn't letting him go. Maybe she never would. And maybe that was right. Maybe she wanted him to get to the end of the story, to tie up the loose ends. Maybe he should.

When Greg and Sheila asked him out for dinner one Sunday in late September, it was the first time he'd been out to their place for a while. The house sat up the back of Menstrie, a stone-built semi set against the steep braes of the Ochils. Two mature copper beeches dominated the back garden. It'd been one of those warm autumn days and they were able to eat outside in their shade. The conversation seemed supremely unimportant to Nick, an easy place for him to be - work the Brights had had done on their roof, how the girls were getting on at school, whether and why they were going to stop shopping at Tescos.

It began to cool in the early evening, but the girls carried on playing in the garden after the adults retreated indoors. The sun was shining through the bay window of the front room, casting a rectangular light onto the carefully restored wooden fire surround. Nick was sitting in an armchair, a glass of red wine in his hand, watching motes of dust moving lazily around in the sunlight. Greg had been standing with his back to the window. He had a glass in one hand and the paper in another, absently checking out local house prices and giving a running commentary on what he'd found. Sheila was sitting on the huge, contoured sofa that faced the fireplace, a glass of red wine in her hand, black jeans, a silk waistcoat over her plain white blouse, her warm open face, her feet curled under. Did Greg really understand what a lucky man he was?

'It's really annoying that I still haven't been able to get my holidays sorted out for next year,' Greg way saying, 'All of us in my work team have kids at school. We all want the same time off. And I missed out last year.'

'What about you Nick?' Sheila asked. 'Any holidays planned?' Nick shrugged. She pressed on. 'Are you going back into the choir for the Christmas concert? You missed Easter, didn't you?'

'I'm not sure what I'm going to do now,' he said. 'Since Sam dumped me, I've tried to think about the future, but to be honest I just keep going back to where I was. What's the point going on to something new, when I don't want something new? I know everyone wants me to move on, but there's unfinished business... we still don't know exactly what happened... and when I lie in bed at night, unable to sleep, I think about it again and again, over and over and over...'

Greg put down his paper and sat down beside Sheila. 'Go on then,' he said, 'We can both see you're wound up. Just let it all out.'

'I contacted Andy - you remember him, Greg? the guy you met at the court?'

'Victim Liaison or Support or something wasn't he?'

'That's right. He showed me how I could access the court proceedings. I've read that judgement so many times now, looking for answers that aren't there. What we do know is that only three people can say what happened in that wee druggie howff. We heard plenty of what two of them had to say, but no-one got to hear Ruth's story. The only thing there is, the *only* thing, is that somebody's got to believe in her, that she wouldn't have put herself in that situation, and who's going to do that, for God's sake, if it's not me, her Dad?' Nick looked at Greg, then at Sheila, 'The law may be satisfied that justice has been done, but the only thing they actually knew in that court room is that they didn't know what really happened. And how can you have justice if you don't have the correct story. It's the true story that matters to me, matters even more now than it did at the time of the trial. I couldn't give a monkey's for the verdict, the sentence, someone else can deal with that. It's not revenge I'm after. After all, nothing that could be done to him... other than maybe cutting off his balls and stuffing them down his throat...' He smiled then, whether at the thought of it, or because it was intended as some kind of weird joke. 'No. imprisonment wouldn't make me feel any better either, though I accept that it might make the streets around here a bit safer for other young women.' He paused. 'The thing I really care about... is to know what really happened... and for other people to know it too. But the only person who knows is him, her killer. So how can we know? He's already traduced her with his lies. He could do it again. He's the only one who knows what happened, and he's also the one least likely to tell the true story.'

He poured himself some more wine.

'So,' Sheila said, 'how could you find out what the police couldn't?'

'Well, it's not as if they actually found out anything worth knowing. They mainly found out what they didn't know... that their "best guess" couldn't be proved. I couldn't have done any worse.'

'Sure, but...'

'So,' Nick interrupted, 'The girl that was supposed to be there? Her account conveniently missed out all the important details. They all seem to have happened after she zonked out. It's obvious she was telling a pack of lies, covering her own back. That was Dorothy's angle. She told me that the girl must've lured Ruth into it, knew a lot more than she let on. The trial lawyers, they let her off the hook completely. She was seen as a victim not a criminal.' Nick paused briefly as he caught Sheila and Greg looking at each other. Never mind. He was fed up holding all this in. They'd asked him and they were going to get both barrels. 'Even if Ruth...' he paused as if mulling over which words to use, 'Even if she knew the other girl was taking condoms along, like the girl said, I can never believe she wanted to have sex in a park – why would she want to have her first sexual experience like that? Ruth was nobody's pushover. It's just unbelievable. That girl, she's said something. Set it up. Told that boy one thing and told Ruth another. And Ruth wanted to be her pal, so she's gone along thinking one thing, whereas something else had been planned all along.'

Nick's right knee was twitching. He took another slug of his wine. Greg and Sheila exchanged glances again.

'You know what,' Nick pointed his glass at them, 'Very convenient, her so-called falling asleep. That means the one that killed her gets to tell the story. Whatever lie he wanted to tell, that became the story. He just said whatever he thought would get him off.' He put on a sour face. *'She was the one that wanted it. We were all loved up. Mutual consent."* What a load of crap! So, according to him, she's supposed to be fine and dandy after all that, says bye bye and trips away home skipping! And he's supposed to have said 'aye on you go', even though it's obvious she wasn't in a fit state to look after herself.' He stood up and started pacing round the room, the glass still in his hand, waving it about above their heads. 'I mean... the whole thing is ridiculous. How could anyone, never mind a jury, believe that Ruth would beg anybody for anything, never mind beg for drugs? Ruth? Beg for something? Really?' He stopped walking, scratched his head and carried on speaking in a quieter voice. 'But I'll tell you this for nothing: that boy Jimmy... he's guilty for sure. It must've been rape. And it was probably murder. The police didn't find out, so the court didn't know and the jury wasn't convinced. But that's not good enough for me. Ruth's not had justice. What if he killed her? Got clean away with it? And by the way, just as an afterthought for you,' he screwed up his face before speaking again, 'That wouldn't be very good for him either. How...' and he changed tone, putting on a cod BBC accent, 'How, as one of my old professors used to say, can the moral life of a person be improved if he or she doesn't recognize the true nature of what they've done, if they don't understand the consequences? Don't even understand the part they played.' Nick's knuckles were white round the glass. 'And isn't our moral life, as human beings, the only life worth living?' he asked, 'If we have no moral life, what are our lives for? Aren't they just as *nasty, brutish and short* as Hobbes said they were? And if that's the way it is, why should I bother my arse, or anybody else's for that matter... why should I want to be good, want to do good? Why don't we all just do whatever the fuck we want and not give a shit about ...?' Nick turned to the window. 'Oh fuck it!,' he shouted, 'Fuck it, fuck it, fuck it!' He took a couple of deep breaths and turned back to face them. 'I'm sorry,' he said, 'But you can see what's going on inside my head.'

'I thought he'd get some time at least,' Greg said. 'Should have.'

Nick sat back down. 'So did I.' he said, 'But what difference would it have made? As soon as they told me they weren't following up rape and murder, I knew this wasn't about the truth. It was about the law... what's manageable, what's acceptable. What's driving me mad now is the thought that he could be walking about in Stirling, just as if nothing had ever happened. Right now. Out with his mates. He could be doing the same to some other girl. That's what really gets me.' He stood up again and started pacing the room. 'And I might run into him in town in a shop, in a pub... that snidey look on his face.' He put his glass down, his voice calmer. 'Maybe there should be some kind of exile, don't you think? Like in the old days. Send people like him to Australia. Never to come back.'

'Don't send them to Australia,' Greg said, trying to lighten the mood, 'we've got enough crazies over there.'

No-one laughed.

They sat quiet for a minute. Sheila spoke up then, calmer, more measured. 'Do you know that the number of rapes and of other sexual assaults has been increasing over the past few years? One of my students has been doing a study of sexual assault patterns in Scotland. In fact,' she carried on, sitting forward on her seat, 'Sexual crimes in Scotland were recently at their highest level since records began in 1971. Our society is saturated with sex – it's not just young people...' she looked over at Greg, 'it's older people too. People used to think that sexual freedom would reduce the problems, but now everyone thinks they're entitled to whatever they see on the internet porn sites. We've become a society where if you want it, you grab it. It's such an awful crime, rape. A violation of your whole being, your body and your spirit....' She left it hanging, looking for agreement, but neither of them spoke, so she carried on, 'And, of course, the real number of rapes is much more than those reported. Ruth's is a particularly tragic case, a terrible case, but it's part of a pattern. I'd love to see the person responsible brought to justice, but I'd also love to see society change, improve... to live in a society where this kind of thing couldn't, wouldn't, happen.'

'I'm much more bothered about Ruth than I am about society,' Nick said. 'He didn't only rape her. He denied her her voice. That's the worst thing of all.'

'We're not going to disagree with you about that,' Sheila said, 'But it hurts us to see you so tangled up, to see you so twisted with your grief. And Ruth wouldn't want it. This boy has done the worst he could do to Ruth. Don't let him do the same to you... take your life away from you, not by killing you, but by twisting you up inside, killing your spirit.'

Nick looked away. He was breathing deeply as if he'd just come in from a training run rather than sitting with his friends, a glass of wine in his hand.

'I understand how strongly you feel,' Sheila said, 'Goodness knows you have reason enough. But I hope you're going to let me challenge you, Nick. I hope you realise that it's not cos I don't sympathise or understand, cos I do. I share your feelings about the justice system, and about Ruth. But it's been close on two years now, and Greg and me, we both saw how the Sam Hill thing lifted you. You didn't let go of Ruth but you were beginning to enjoy your life again. Ruth would want that for you – you know she would.' She could see that Nick was digging his nails into his palms, his jaw tight. 'Ruth wouldn't want her death to ruin your life. I know this maybe sounds harsh Nick, but Ruth wouldn't want this. She'd know that even without her in it, your life has value, has meaning.'

'I'm not seeing it.'

'What I'm going to say now maybe sounds a bit too pushy, but I hope that we're good enough friends that I can say it and you'll listen and know that it comes from a place of care, of concern.'

'I'm listening,' Nick said, deadpan, 'That's why I'm still here, isn't it?'

'OK. So, you may not think any of this has relevance just now. And of course, that's for you to judge. But I'm saying it now, cos we're having quite an open conversation, and if this isn't the right time, just park this advice and come back to it another time. You see... how can I put this... I think you need to start having more of a social life again. It seems that Dorothy was the only family member you kept in touch with, and now she's away, who else have you got? We seem to be just about the only friends you have... '

'Not the only friends,' he said, 'Just the only important friends.'

'Well,' Sheila looked at Greg before carrying on, 'If that's the case, like I said, we're maybe the only ones that are able to speak frankly to you, without being scared that you're going to take it the wrong way.'

'Go on then.' he smiled, 'I don't doubt that you both care for me. You're my friends. So, go on. Give it your best shot.'

'Greg and I have talked about this before but didn't feel able to say it, but hearing you tonight, it seems like as good a time as any to offer you another bit of advice. You've been through a tragic loss, Nick, the kind of traumatic stress that people end up suffering from, a form of PTSD if you like. And we both think you should consider getting some professional help, don't we Greg?' Greg caught Nick's eye with the briefest of nods, not an enthusiastic nod, more of a *no-matter-what-you-think-she'll-beat you-down-with-her-common-sense-till-you-realise-that-she's-right* kind of nod. 'I'm not talking about drugs,' she said, 'I don't believe it's good for people to have some kind of chemical lobotomy, you know that, but proper professional clinical therapy can help. Or if not therapy, then at the very least some skilled non-directive counselling. There are some great people out there who could really help you. There's nothing wrong with getting help to deal with what you've been though, are still going through. There's no shame in it. You're a victim. A different kind of victim to Ruth. And above all... and you know this by the way, you really know this don't you? You know it, Nick. You know it,' she insisted. 'You know that she wouldn't want what happened to her to ruin the rest of your life, would she?'

Nick closed his eyes and rolled his lips together, again and again. He ran his hands through his hair. They waited for him to speak.

'OK,' he said. 'What you said is actually quite helpful. As I was listening to you, I was clarifying what I think. And now I can put it into words. Cos here's the thing. I don't want to leave Ruth behind... and I'm not going to try to make it alright for me, because it's not alright for her. It's never going to be alright for her. It's never going to be alright. Ever. And I *want* my feelings - I don't want counseled out of them. They're true feelings. They're honest feelings. There are some things in life that are absolute, that you can't walk away from, you can't just close them off as if they never happened. You just can't. And if ever there was such a thing, then this, my good friends, this is it.'

Greg nodded. 'Fine mate, fine. Let's leave it at that.' He looked over at Sheila. 'We've said our bit on the matter. Maybe, like Sheila said, you'll give it some thought down the road. Maybe there'll be a time, but this isn't it.' Greg leaned over and started to refill Nick's glass when Alice and Jess burst in.

'Mummy, mummy, mummy,' Alice shouted. 'We're coming in. It's getting cold out there now.'

'It's cold,' Jess shouted.

Alice was ten now, and Jess almost eight. Growing up so fast. Seeing them full of life made Nick think of Ruth when she was that age. It was a great age, proper childhood, before the hormones took over. Wouldn't it be good, he was thinking, if kids could just stay at that age, spend the years of puberty in some kind of pupa from, say, 11 to 18 and emerge, mutated, as full-grown adults? He thought about himself at 18... maybe it should have to be later... 20, 25?

'Time for bed now,' Greg said, 'I'll give you a start then I'm going to chase you up the stairs. You've got till three. One...', he shouted.

'No Daddy, no, no Daddy,' the girls squealed.

'Two...' he shouted louder.

They both ran out of the room screaming and on up the stairs.

'Three... I'm coming to get you...' and Greg raced out the door. They heard him chasing the girls into their room, the door slamming, squeals and giggles.

'So,' Sheila said, 'What next?'

'I don't know,' Nick said, 'I've been thinking about moving away. Somewhere new. Maybe that'd help me make a fresh start. Somewhere near the sea I think... up north, west, north west...'

'We'd miss you Nick... miss you a lot.'

'That's kind,' he said, 'But if I stayed somewhere nice, maybe you'd come and visit me. Up the west coast, I could maybe get some land, maybe have a dairy cow or two, or goats, some chickens, do odd jobs for people, look after some holiday homes... I know someone does that for an agency... they could maybe give me a contact... get me started. I've been looking at prices. I might be able to do it.'

'I can imagine you somewhere like that,' she said, 'It could be the right move.'

In a little while, Jess and Alice came back downstairs to say goodnight. Jess wanted Nick to read her bedtime story – *Anne of Green Gables*. It was an illustrated version, abridged for younger readers. He took her back upstairs and sat on the bed beside her as she snuggled in under the covers. 'There's a bookmark Uncle Nick,' she said, 'That's where we left off last night. And you've got to do the voices.'

Nick wasn't quite sure what a Prince Edward Island voice would sound like, but it seemed that, whatever he did, it was good enough for Jess. The chapter was one Nick remembered. Gilbert Blythe called Anne 'carrots' on account of her red hair and she broke a slate over his head in retaliation. The teacher inflicted a number of humiliating punishments on Anne.

'I don't think it was fair,' Jess said, 'Anne being punished when it was Gilbert Blythe who called her "carrots". He should be the one that got punished. He was just a bully and she was right to hit him. I'd've done the same thing.'

'You don't think she should have told the teacher?'

'That teacher's a wimp,' she said, 'He's a rubbish teacher. He wouldn't have done anything.'

'But if we all took the law into our own hands, people would be fighting all the time.'

'But he got away with it,' she said, unpersuaded, 'And that's just not fair.'

He tucked her in and heard her prayer, just as he'd heard Ruth's prayers at that age, the prayers Clare had taught her. As she listed the people she was praying for, he wondered what or who he would pray for, if he believed in prayer. 'Never underestimate the power of prayer,' his mother used to say. But how could it work if you didn't believe it. What did he believe in anyway? He looked at Jess, eyes closed, coming to the end of her list. He believed in this little girl, her future. He believed in caring for the planet, respecting its complex interdependent systems. He believed if humanity was clever enough... and disciplined enough – admittedly two very big 'ifs' - there might even be a human future through the other end of the climate crisis that was already upon us. He believed that his life had effectively ended, or at best been put on hold, when the police had come to his door. But Jess had been right too. It seemed that in fiction, as in the real world, life just wasn't fair.

They said 'Amen' together when she finished.

'That was a lovely prayer Jess,' he said, 'Now you get a good night's sleep.'

When he got back downstairs, Greg had opened another bottle of wine. 'You can stay here tonight,' he said, 'Don't want you going back to that little house on your own.' But the mood had changed. What else was there to say? Greg put on one of his spotify playlists and tried to coax Nick into playing a game... recognizing the tracks that came up from the first few notes... but Nick wasn't interested so Greg just let the music play on. It wasn't long before the bottle of wine was finished. Nick staggered to his feet.

'No more wine,' he said, 'I need to get home. I'm going to walk. Where's my coat?'

Sheila tried to persuade him out of it. 'It's after half ten,' she said, 'We can easily get you a taxi. You've had a lot to drink.'

'It's only a few miles,' he said, 'A bit over an hour. I can cycle back over and collect the pickup in the morning. Look out there for God's sake! Look at that moon! Come on. Look at it. It's a brilliant full moon!'

He started dancing round the room, as if an invisible partner was on his arm. He grabbed hold of Greg. Both of them then waltzed round the room, like drunk men acting up: they *were* drunk men acting up. Greg shouted up to the vaulted hall roof, 'Look at the moon! The full moon!'

'Quiet Greg!' Sheila hissed, 'You'll waken the girls.'

'I've got to go,' Nick said, 'Thanks for everything, but I need to go.

Sheila handed Nick his coat and took his face in her hands. 'Don't do anything silly, you,' she said. 'Things are going to get better, I know it. It's going to work out. I liked the sound of your idea, moving up the west coast. You can take Ruth with you. She'll always be with you.' She kissed him lightly on his cheek. 'And we'll be there to help you if you need it,' she added as she opened the door.

* * *

Nick took the path that runs along behind the Hillfoots villages. There were rustles from the hedgerow, the sound of the occasional car from the main road below. Cold sweat was sticking his shirt to his skin in the late evening breeze. The Ochils sat to his right, a steep silvery grey in the moonlight. Passing houses, he heard dogs barking, echoing back from the hill slopes. The drink was keeping him in the present, a world of sensations - the lights of Blairlogie up ahead, the feel of the breeze cold on his face, the steady hum of the village as he passed behind it and on towards the shadows cast by the trees - Chestnut and Oak, Beech and Lime. In the moonlight he stopped to stare at them and saw them as earlier generations had seen them, before streetlamps, before electricity, waving and rustling in the breeze, sometimes friendly, sometimes sinister. He walked on, down and along the path that rejoined the road at the back end of the Abbey Craig. In this light the wood on the Craig looked dark and untamed, like the wild wood of children's stories. A stiff gust suddenly sent a shiver through him and set the trees roaring. Across the field, he could see a light flickering in the wood, then it disappeared and reappeared again as he walked. What were people doing there, at this time of night? There it was again. It looked like it might be coming from the quarry, that quarry, yes that very quarry, that terrible dread quarry.

The drink was still in him. He climbed over the fence and set out across the field, across a style and he was into the wood. It was difficult going underfoot, wet from the week's rainfall. Everywhere there was bracken, a full season's growth of it. Clouds had broken up and bright moonlight cast an eerie light, through the trees, enough for him to see his way. Once in the wood, he realized that he'd entered too far to the west. He was going to have to climb above the quarry and tack round and down to get to the entrance.

He edged round the cliffs as he did that first weekend when he met the police guarding the site, but this time he made sure he wasn't heard or seen as he crept down into the quarry. The moon shone on little open patches of bracken, its swirls and eddies made more mysterious by the shadows cast by the tall trees. He heard voices before he saw the flickering light again and, hearing them, he stopped silent. The voices were very low, whistling sibilants and guttural Scottish vowels. He sneaked up closer to make out the words and stopped dead when he saw a hanging torch and the backs of two heads through the open door. There was a sweet smell of ganja on the air.

'Mind o that time wee Goagsy goat rat-arsed up here an he went hyper man...?'

'Aye Jimmy thon was a laugh ay?'

Jimmy? Nick couldn't see the faces. Was this Jimmy Stevens?

'He was a radgy bastard thon boy, the same boy. D'you hear about him and that lassie wi the tattoo on her neck?'

'What lassie was that?"

'Ken her wi the tattoo...she's fae up St Ninian's like. She ustae hang about in the town at the seats an that?... ustae wear thon wee check skirt an the big boots, ken.'

'Aye I've got her now. Big tits. Wee heid. Big nose.'

'So, she's up the poakie and he's gonnie move in, that's whit they're sayin. Wee Goagsy a faither. Sno real. Fuck. Whit's happenin tae us? Can you imagine wee Goagsy's bairn, man? Wi those ears o his an her big conk? Like Dumbo the fuckin elephant man.' They both laughed.

The one called Jimmy took a deep draw on his spliff and blew it out slowly. 'It's good to be back out though, ay man? Fuckin barry.'

'Brand new, man.'

'Back in the scene o our many fuckin triumphs.'

Nick pulled back and circled round to try to see a bit more of their faces. A twig snapped under his foot.

'Is some cunt out there?' the one called Jimmy shouted, squinting into the trees, 'If you're out there, c'mon in an get yoursell a blaw'

Nick kept deathly still. He could see the face now. It was him, his Jimmy, Jimmy Stevens - there, right in front of him. All three of them waited then, silent. The wind was sounding in the trees above them, a long low moan.

'Must've been something else,' the smaller one said after a minute or so, 'Fuckin great though now you're back an aw, big man. Fuckin brand new man. Just like the old days ay?'

'Too fuckin right Craigsy ma boy. Fuckin England ya radge? I'm glad to be back. Fuckin delighted. It's aw cunts doon there. Made some good connections but. An ken what that means, Craigsy ma boy? I've goat some wicked fuckin blaw comin next week, an I'm wantin you to help run it for me.'

'Where are you gonnae keep it. Your uncle choried the last stash. 'member?'

'Course I fuckin remember. I've goat it worked out. Keep the stash up here. It's near enough the flat. Five minutes an we can get whit we need when we need it.'

'There's cunts comin up here aw the time. Dogs and aw.'

'No worries wee man. I'll have it sorted. The dogs won't be able to smell nothin, trust me. I've seen how you can dae it.' Jimmy took another long drag on his spliff. 'We had some good fuckin times up here wee man though, did we no?' he said, 'Wee Sadie ay? The wee grass. If it hadnae been for her there wouldnae've even been a trial.' He took another long drag. 'But no hard feelings ay? She had a sweet wee cunt man, Sadie... sweet as fuck. Long as you didnae have tae look at her ugly puss when you were ridin her. I wouldnae mind giein her another ride the now.'

'She eyewis fancied you Jimmy.'

'I've no seen her since I goat back. Have you seen her around?'

'Nut. No me. Someone telt us she wis away hersel, Devon or someplace. Hightailed it, didn't she, eftir the trial? Or was it away in Spain? I canny mind. Naebody's seen her anyway.'

'She wis awright Sadie. Even though she grassed us up, she never telt what really happened that night, ken. See if she'd seen aw that happened, and she'd telt what she saw, I'd have swung for it, man. She'd've been in bother too, mind. It was her that got the lassie to come up here to start wi.'

'Whit did happen like?'

'Fuck off Craigsy. I never telt the polis, so I'm' no gonnae tell you am I? Like was said at ma trial Craigsy boy, nae cunt knows. No even me. I wiz blitzed. Not guilty, ay? They couldnae prove a fuckin thing.'

They took one last draw, a long one, then let it out, slow and easy.

'Never mind Craigsy boy,' Jimmy said, 'Look tae the future. We're eighteen an we're fuckin free, free as the fuckin birds. There's plenty more cunts out there tae fuck, an I want tae fuck them aw.'

'Nae worries. Fucking freedom,' Craig said, taking great care with his pronunciation, 'Free as the fuckin birds.' He stood up and started waving his arms as if flying then fell back down with a bump. They both started giggling again. Giggling uncontrollably.

'Fuck's sake man. Don't make me laugh,' Craig said. 'I'm fuckin wettin masell.'

'It winny be the first time you wee cunt... s'long as you dinny shit yoursell an aw.'

Then there was more laughter. And the laughter turned again to giggling, hysterical uncontrolled giggling. 'Fuckin free,' Jimmy spat out, before the giggles took him over again.

Nick wasn't laughing though. Nick wasn't giggling. Jimmy Stevens, right there in front of him, smoking weed, more or less admitting that he'd been guilty, would have *swung for it....*

Nick's head was pounding. The wind was getting up and the sighing in the trees was louder again. What the hell was going on? This was madness. Was he the one that had been taking drugs, trapped in some kind of terrible hallucinatory dream? What was he going to do now? What should he do? What would Ruth want him to do? Dive in and start a fight? Then what? It was all too sudden, too overpowering.

Nick inched his way back, away from the little howff. He stumbled through the undergrowth and after a few minutes picked up one of the paths to the main Alloa Road. His trousers were torn on the brambles, his shoes thick with mud, bits of vegetation were sticking to his coat, his hair. When he stumbled out onto the pavement under a streetlight, passengers in a passing car rubber-necked him. He bolted across the main road and on down towards Cambuskenneth. He didn't stop running till he got home.

* * *

Back in his bed, he tried to sleep but his pulse was racing. His thoughts wouldn't let him be. At one o'clock he got up and pulled out all the paperwork he had from the case, the information for victims' families, the support services. He went online and looked at court procedure, previous cases, decisions. He found one for supplying drugs which led to the victim's death – that guy got eight years. Why only eight? But why didn't Jimmy get eight years then, at least eight years? That girl. Sadie. She was the one who'd made the jury believe his story, that Ruth was somehow in on it, wanted it, played an equal part in the whole thing, was in some way responsible for her own death. He was angry. Angry with Sadie, wherever she was. Angry with Jimmy Stevens. Angry with the court.

But he was angry with himself most of all: he'd gone along with it. His own daughter: and he'd given up on her like everyone else, like they were telling him to, had just accepted that she must have played some part, that she wanted to be there, that she was an equal participant. Why had he accepted it so easily? Why had he been so bloody passive? He'd known she would never have willingly got involved with those kinds of risks. Known it. Of course he'd known it. But he just allowed himself to do what was expected, suck it up, let her go, let her share the blame, get on with life, 'find closure'. Never mind, he was going to make sure the case was re-opened. He'd start with the police.

He fell asleep on his front room sofa sometime after four, then woke with a crick in his neck at eight. He called the police HQ at Randolphfield, wanted to speak to Jane Beattie. He had to wait till she came back on at 9. He phoned again. Made an appointment to see her on Tuesday first thing.

It was a long twenty four hours.

* * *

Jane came out to meet him in the reception area. She looked tired, and a little harassed. 'I can't stay long,' she said, 'Other cases piling up.'

'What would you say,' he launched right into it, 'If I told you that I'd heard Jimmy Stevens... heard him more or less admitting that he'd raped and killed my daughter.'

'Whoa whoa whoa there sir,' she said, 'Let's go back a bit. You say you heard him saying things.' He nodded. 'Where was this?' she asked.

'It was in the woods of the Abbey Craig, near where Ruth died. He said he was just back up in Stirling, from England. I was walking home.'

'In the woods?'

'No. I was walking back from my friends in Menstrie..'

'Walking from Menstrie?' She sounded sceptical.

'Yes.'

'What time was this?'

'It was late. After 10 anyway Maybe after 11 by the time I got to the woods.'

'And why were you walking so late.'

'I'd had a drink. Didn't want to risk driving. And it was a great night, a full moon. I wanted to be out in it.'

'You'd had a drink?' He could see what she was thinking in her face. 'How many?'

'Just a social drink, at friends, but perhaps enough to put me just over the limit. And it was a beautiful night... the moon...' he hesitated.

'Go on then...' Her tone was even more sceptical.

'I saw a light and I was curious. Every time I pass those woods. I wonder who's in there, what they're doing. I've got a damn good reason to be curious about what goes on there. You would too.'

Jane looked at her watch.

'Should you not be writing this down?' he said.

'This isn't a formal interview sir. I've just come out to see you cos, well, cos I know you've been through a lot. If we get to a formal statement, you'll need to go through the process. Someone else will probably interview you.'

He got tetchy then. 'I see. OK. Well is there any point in me carrying on.'

'I'm listening.'

He told her what he'd heard in the woods. 'So that's it,' he said, summing up, 'The way he was talking, it was obvious it was rape and murder. And... '

'OK,' she said, 'This needs to go somewhere else... maybe to the Crown Office? You know there was a new 'double jeopardy' Act went through the Scottish Parliament a few years back, after the Andrew Sinclair case – it is possible to retry certain cases, but only if some strict conditions are met. I'm not sure about a new charge of murder. I suppose it might be possible to prosecute for rape... the police don't make these decisions, you know... that's the Fiscal's job. He needs to hear what you've got to say. I could give your VIA officer a call - Andy Marshall wasn't it?' She looked at her watch again. 'D'you want me to call him?'

'That sounds fine,' he said. 'I'll wait to hear from him.'

'I hope something gets sorted out,' she said, stood up and shook his hand. 'Thanks for coming in.' And that was it.

Andy called Nick in a couple of days later and took a statement. 'Leave it with us,' Andy said, 'We'll see what the Fiscal has to say.'

The old wounds were fully reopened now. Nick was right back to where he'd been after Ruth's death. His friends had supported him through so much, and now here was another nightmare. He didn't think they'd support him this time. They'd be thinking like Sam - that he needed to put it behind him, that he should give up this obsession, that he should 'move on'. That sounded like good advice in some sensible alternative life. But this was his life. And he couldn't give it up. He wouldn't give it up. He wasn't going to move on.

He thought about phoning Dorothy – at least she would listen to him - but it wasn't something for a phone call. And even if she listened, so what? She didn't have any answers, any more than he did. So. What was the point of going all the way to Wales to leave her with the problem that was giving him sleepless nights? But although there were sleepless nights, and although the old wounds were just as raw, he was enjoying it in a strange way. He wasn't having to suppress his emotion, or his imagination. He was giving it free rain.

He made up a full-scale A1 mind map of all the issues and posted it on the wall of Ruth's bedroom. He pored over the double jeopardy act and associated online discussions. He paid a local lawyer a few hundred pounds for a short consultation which told him no more than he already knew - his witness account of hearing a confession, in the absence of corroborating forensic evidence, would be insufficient, particularly given his interest in the case. Any such 'confession' could simply be denied. And it was quite possible that the forensic evidence collected from the scene of the crime had been disposed of. It was really up to the Crown Office to decide whether his new information could lead to any new prosecution. They'd take a view based on the evidence.

Emily Derwent called him in to see her a few days later. Andy came along to support.

'I'm so sorry,' she said. 'We've looked at your statement. We've re-interviewed Stevens again under caution. He denied rape just as he did before, denied everything. Stuck to his original story, very consistent. If we had anything new on the forensic side, we might be able to put on a bit more pressure, but the evidence collected at the time was inconclusive and since the case ended with a 'not guilty' verdict, it's been destroyed. There is no prospect of collecting any new forensic evidence in relation to rape. And we've not been able to trace Sadie McHugh. Her relatives in Devon thought she was in Marbella, waitressing, but had no address... we can't trace her at all. She might become a person of interest again if we had reason to reopen the case, but my senior took the case up the chain, just to make sure and the same answer came back: there is no chance of a successful prosecution, given what we have. Justice has taken its course. I know you'll be disappointed. I'm really, really sorry.'

'So that's it then,' he said. 'that's it.'

'I'm sorry,' she said again, stood up and shook his hand. 'Very sorry.'

He couldn't feel angry with Jane Beattie, Emily, Andy. They were just doing their job. What was the point in getting angry with them? He was just sad. Sad and tired of the whole thing.

When would it let him go? First the press had moved on. Then the police. Then the courts. Even Dorothy had moved on. Why couldn't he?

But he knew the answer, and it was a convincing answer: because moving on would mean leaving Ruth stranded, unjustly dealt with in death as in life, with Jimmy Stevens' lies as her epitaph. But what was he to do? What could he do?

11. Crossroads

In the days that followed, Nick wanted no slack time, no brooding time. Work was his therapy during the days. In the evenings, he was on the allotment. When he could fit it in, he was in the gym or running with Greg. Two weekends after he'd met Emily Derwent, Sheila took him over a casserole and found a stack of empty wine bottles in his recycling bin. He told her he was working his way through a pile of second-hand DVDs he'd picked up at the Oxfam shop, a bottle of wine, sometimes more, each night, 'to help me sleep,' he said.

'You don't see anyone all day,' she scolded him, 'Working on your own, listening to your podcasts – you probably don't even hear people speaking to you, then you come home and eat on your own and then sit in on your own watching tellie. And how much wine are you drinking? You're going to have to be careful Nick. Ruth wouldn't want this for you. It's not a healthy lifestyle. And it can't be happy.'

'Yahdiyahdiyah,' he said, grinning now, 'I'm fine... I've got my running, my work. What else do I need... except time?' he said, 'I just need time.'

'You're not fine Nick. I agree about time... but it has to be spent doing the right things. I know I'm going to sound like your mother, but you're drinking too much and that's not going to help.'

'I'll come out of it,' he said, with no great enthusiasm. 'I know things have been drifting a bit. Simon's been on at me about going back to the choir when they start rehearsals for Christmas. I might get up the energy to go. But maybe not. I might be in Wales at the end of October. It's not a busy time for me, workwise. Dorothy's going to the Canaries for a few weeks then, with Bill and Yvonne. She suggested I take a holiday in her cottage. She says there's great sea walks where she is, near the Pembroke Coast. I might do that.'

Sheila didn't look convinced. 'More time on your own?' she said.

'I've got a mate in London I've not seen in a while, goes back to when I was at Uni. I might see if he's free – we used to see each other every year. It'd be good to catch up.' He avoided her eyes. 'I'm still just "taking each day as it comes" ... just like it was at the start. And work helps. It's a busy time. I'm earning enough to save a fair bit. That might go some way towards buying that property up the west coast I've been thinking about.' He ran his hands through his hair several times and scratched the back of his neck, as a dog would with a flea. 'I've got through it before,' he said, 'I'll get through it again.'

'Alcohol is not your friend,' she said, 'It could be a slippery slope.'

'I know. But it helps me get to sleep.'

'Don't shut your friends out,' Sheila said.

* * *

Early the following week, Nick pulled out a DVD called *In the Bedroom* from the Oxfam pile: the cover photo was of Sissy Spacek. She looked a bit like Sam Hill, similar colouring, freckles, wide mouth, but a flatter nose, a rounder face. *Starts deceptively calmly,* the blurb on the cover read, *but builds to a climax of shattering desolation.* That sounded like him, only in his story there was no climax. Just the desolation.

The film was slow-paced, intense... and it held Nick captive right from the start, when a young man is killed by his girlfriend's ex-husband, the focus then moves to the dead man's parents - played by Sissy Spacek and Tom Wilkinson - their reaction to his death, to the killer. What kind of coincidence was it that he was watching this film, now, after what'd happened to him? The parallels were too close. Surely this was meant? As the film finished with Tom Wilkinson driving his big 4x4 back over the railroad tracks, Nick was nowhere near sleep though it was close to one in the morning, another empty bottle of claret on the bedroom floor. He was burning with anxious nervous energy. He strode from room to room, opened and shut the doors, as if he might find an answer lurking somewhere in the house. He took the stairs to Ruth's bedroom in threes and stared at Cromarty, then ran downstairs again.

He had to calm down. Sure it was similar but not the same. He didn't have a friend who might help him for a start, or rather none he would ask. He didn't have a plot of vacant land where a body could be buried. Clare, unlike the Sissy Spacek character in the film, would never have sanctioned a killing - but then again there were lots of other differences with the film: Clare had never had a son, had never met her child's killer in the supermarket as the Sissy character did. What was he thinking? It was only a film for God's sake. He got off to sleep eventually, a couple of whiskies later.

In the morning he had a hangover headache, drank water and went for a long run, not pushing himself too hard, his Van Morrison playlist on extra loud. But however loud Van shouted in his ears, Nick's thoughts kept returning to the film. Standing in the shower afterwards, he went back over the film's plotline in his head. It wasn't 'revenge' Tom and Sissy were after. It was something different. It was justice for their son, whose killer had walked free. Just like Ruth: Ruth had never had justice either. And no-one else cared about that, then or now, no-one except him. She'd been killed, her name had been trashed. The least she deserved was to have her name cleared of the lies that Stevens had told, not the selective version that the prosecution in the trial had gone for, but the full story of what had happened to her. As far as the jury knew, the most that Stevens might have been guilty of was 'reckless endangerment' with no intent to kill. That was the case the prosecution had led, the evidence they'd been given. And the evidence hadn't even convinced them of that. He'd tried all legal means, gone to the Procurator Fiscal, the police, the jury. He'd trusted them, let them do their job. And Ruth's killer still walked free. None of them had heard Jimmy Stevens speaking in the wee howff. But he'd heard Jimmy... heard him make a confession that couldn't, shouldn't, be ignored: *If she'd telt whit really happened that night, ken, I'd have swung for it.*

Ruth hadn't 'whored herself for drugs'. It was hard enough even to believe that she'd gone there of her own accord. Terrible enough that she'd been raped and murdered... but that was compounded by the story that was told afterwards - that she'd "got herself drugged up, drunk, lost control and drowned". Talk about blaming the victim! She needed him to tell the real story of what happened. And who else would do it, if not him?

That evening, he looked out another bottle of wine and settled down to watch the film a second time. The closing credits said the film was based on a story by Andre Dubus. He looked up Andre Dubus. The story was called *Killings.* It was published in a book of short stories. He downloaded the book from Kindle Cloud and read through the story, looking for a further message: Matt Fowler and his wife Ruth, their son Frank, his lover Mary-Ann, her estranged husband Richard – what were they saying to him? He read it a second and then a third time, even though he'd already known what it was telling him: it just took him a while to admit it.

He'd been wasting time. Spending time with Sam had created an illusion that he might have another future, but it had only been an illusion. There would be no future, till he'd dealt with the past. He'd run away from its challenge the night in the woods when he'd seen Stevens with his wee pal Craigsy, but now he knew it for what it was. Even Clare would have seen it, if she'd been here. Even Clare would have seen it now.

* * *

Nick had a lot of work planned for the next week, but he phoned round and cancelled all the clients he'd booked in: he assured them that he'd make sure he caught up with everything when he came back. On the following Monday, he met up with an officer from Stirling Council Land and Property section, Edith Constable: the two of them headed out west in his pickup to look at a property he'd seen advertised for sale on the Council's website.

As they drove, Edith briefed him on the property. 'Central Regional Council,' she said, 'acquired the bunker and the surrounding land from the Ministry of Defence away back and Stirling Council inherited it after the break-up in 96. But it's just been lying empty and nothing's been done in it, or to it, since the Army had it back in the 70s. It comes with around 1.3 acres, and at present that's just scrub woodland. There is the possibility of residual contamination of course – that's probably why there've been no buyers yet. And that would be your responsibility as the new owner. I think the Council wanted the Army to clean it up and there were ongoing disputes... unresolved disputes... I think they were going on for so long that it seems everyone's just given up on it. The Council was never quite sure what the Army were doing here: you could do anything in that concrete bunker... and no-one would see it... or hear it.'

She signed for him to turn off before Kippen and they drove up through mixed broadleaved and coniferous woodland and onto an unmetalled estate road, up into the trees on the lower slopes of the Gargunnock Hills. Edith told him to stop the car by a rusting metal fence, overgrown with brush and saplings. There was a weather-worn Council 'For Sale' notice tangled round with briar and an even older notice on the ground, signalling that this had been 'Ministry of Defence Property: Keep Out'. She opened a padlocked gate and they walked along an overgrown gravel road for twenty or more yards before coming on a squat concrete shed. It was set down into the ground, its rusty steel doors held shut by a bar and padlock.

'This is the place,' she said, 'There's a little burn down the back. I think it's quite muddy down there: it floods the bottom area in winter and spring. The whole property's just been lying neglected as you can see. We can walk the curtilage if you like, as much as is possible anyway. There will definitely be no planning permission for any housing development here. I don't think you have a chance of changing it to a dwelling – I think I said that on the phone - I know some of the planning team wouldn't allow it. But since you're looking for workshop space, with land around, it could be ideal, as long as you can deal with any contamination issues. I can't promise, but it sounds like something they might let through.'

'What did the MoD do here?' he asked.

'We're not really sure. Some kind of store maybe? There were a lot of exercises used to take place up in the hills, back in the day.'

Nick took a walk round, snapped a few photos. 'Can we take a look inside?' he asked.

'Sure.'

Although the key turned smoothly enough, the doors only swung back slowly, with a creepy, rusty creech. Inside the hut, it was dark and damp. Edith's torch beam searched round. In one corner were a couple of metal chair frames. The canvas had rotted. In the centre was a large two-piece metal locker. Nick opened one of the locker doors and something scurried past him and out through the door. Edith was too slow with the torch for to see what it was, but there must be access somewhere if it was a small mammal that'd got in. There were no windows, but Nick had a look at the low-level metal ventilation grills. One or two were blocked but air was circulating from the other two. The concrete walls, although wet, were still solid. A wooden beam ran the full length of the building at head height.

'Can you shine the torch on the beam,' he asked. There were signs of woodworm. He wrapped his arms around the beam then pulled his body up off the floor. It still seemed to be able to bear his weight easily enough. There were two or three large hooks fixed to the beam at intervals.

'These look handy,' he said, 'Do you think they were there for lifting?'

'I don't know,' she said. 'Could be. Do you need to see any more? This place gives me the shivers.'

'Yes, it's creepy, isn't it?'

She shivered again. 'Have you seen enough?'

'Well,' Nick said, 'It does have potential for a workshop. But there's a lot done. The asking price seems steep to me.

'Well the valuation will be based on similar properties... it's not just a made up figure... and you know there's no planning permission for a house. 'You'll have to offer what you think is a fair price,' she said, 'It'll be someone well above me who decides whether your offer is good enough.'

'I'm certainly interested,' Nick said, as she replaced the padlock on the door. 'I'll need to arrange a survey, and a contamination specialist will be needed too, I guess. Will I be able to get access at the weekend if I need to, for the specialist?'

'I would think so. You can have the key any Friday afternoon if you want access over the weekend. It's not as if there's been a rush of interested buyers.'

'I'll do that. Maybe even this Friday.'

* * *

That evening, Nick approached a group of young guys hanging about outside the Thistle Centre, Stirling's concrete shopping mall.

'Any of you guys know where I can catch Jimmy Stevens?' he asked.

'Jimmy?' one of the boys said, then looked round at the others before turning back to Nick. 'Who's askin likes?'

'I heard he was doing deals,' Nick said. 'And I can pay well for good stuff.'

'Oh aye?'

'Here's my number,' Nick handed over a piece of paper. 'Get him to text me. There'll be something in it for him.'

A couple of hours later he got the text. 'Heard you were looking for me. Meet opposite The Cowane pub, 5pm, Tuesday, beside the pillarboxes. Send photo. J.'

The location was perfect as far as Nick was concerned. He searched Google for a suitable photo. He chose one that looked a bit like him – age, hair colour, shape of face - then spent the day on a tidy up at his allotment. Lorraine, who kept the neighbouring plot, invited him over for a mid-afternoon cup of tea. She'd been in for an operation on her hip earlier in the year and Nick'd done a bit of digging and planting for her. 'I think I'm going to put bushes in next year,' she told him, 'In that other half I'm going to put rasps and blackcurrants for jam seeing as how I can't manage a full plot of veg anymore.' Just a normal afternoon at the allotment.

Nick left at four and headed home to change, a tingle of nervous anticipation speeding up his walk back to the house. He arrived at the pillar boxes just before five. There was no sign of Jimmy, so he walked past the pillar boxes and on towards the town where he bought a newspaper, before strolling back. Still no Jimmy. He walked into the *Old Post Office* pub and took a bottle of Peroni over to a table by the window, then thought he might be too visible. He pulled back and stood further in, at the bar, from where he could still see out, but it would be difficult for anyone to see him. Still no Jimmy. Then he noticed a movement in the window of *Willie's Bar* on the other side of the street: it was Jimmy, standing at the window, up to the same game, looking to see who was coming and going, who would be waiting at the pillar box. Nick took out a pen and pretended to do the crossword. At quarter past five, Jimmy left *Willie's* and headed at speed up Friar Street, talking on his mobile. Nick left his drink and followed him at a discreet distance, head down, looking at his phone. At the top of the street, Jimmy paused and looked back. Nick carried on walking, playing about with his phone, as if texting. Jimmy walked into the *Cross Peels* bar. Nick slunk into a doorway and changed his reversible jacket from yellow to a neutral blue. He took a black beanie from his pocket and pulled it down over his ears, then followed Jimmy into the pub. Jimmy had bought a drink and was standing at the bar looking at the entrance, but looked right past Nick as he walked in. Nick walked to the other end of the bar, ordered another Peroni and took it over to a table by the window. Jimmy sat down at a table, talking to two of the guys there, then finished his beer and stood up to leave.

Nick hadn't had a specific plan. He'd thought he might follow Jimmy home, follow his movements, work out a plan from there. When Jimmy left the pub, he tried to follow him, but as he left the pub all he could see of Jimmy was one leg... the rest of him was already inside a red Astra with blacked-out windows and a noisy stainless steel exhaust pipe. The car roared off down the road.

What now?

Later that evening Nick got a text from Jimmy.

'You never turned up. I need to see you if we're going to do business.'

'Sorry. Got held up. I'm working for a rich client. He's very famous. It's got to be superconfidential.' Nick texted back, 'He'll pay top price if it's good. How about a sample?'

'Sure. The junk I've got's not your regular Indica Sativa – it's a new one. *Potent Dreams* they call it. Wicked. Quarter ounce sample £150. £300 ounce. £500 if you want two. It's top grade.'

'Start with an ounce. If it's good he'll want more. Will text on Friday at 6 to confirm handover.'

'An ounce is OK. If he wants a lot more, I'll need to order it.'

'Fine. Keep it confidential. You don't mess with this guy.'

'Stirling's never seen weed this good. If your man smokes this shit he'll get fuckin ripped.'

Nick went back to work the next day. Friday couldn't come soon enough.

* * *

Later in the week, Dorothy phoned Nick. 'I'm just checking up on you,' she said, 'You sounded very depressed the last time we talked. I was quite worried for you.'

'Thanks,' he said, 'But I'm fine. I feel this week that I've turned some kind of corner.'

'Well that's good news. What brought this on?'

'Oh several things. Nothing in particular. I just realised that I'm going to have to look forwards, not back. And I'm going to work on something I can look forward to.'

'We neither of us will ever move on completely, Nick,' she said in a kind, motherly tone, 'We said that before. Life will never be the same, will never be as good.' She paused. 'But life can be OK. Look at me. I've got some different interests now and it's been good for me. I've joined the bridge club down here. Yvonne's a bowler, ten-pin and lawn bowls, so I've joined in with that too. And it's a very nice Church community here, Anglican - I never was much interested in the doctrinal side of things but they have lots of activities, clubs, the guild. I'm sure you could be doing that sort of thing too.'

Nick said nothing.

'Are you going to get back into your choir? You enjoyed that didn't you?'

'I will go back. I missed Easter this year. But I will go back. And I'm going to start walking again.'

'Good. Remember you're welcome down here any time. There's plenty of good walking in the Welsh mountains.'

'Thanks. I've been thinking about your offer of staying at your place if you're away on one of your jaunts. We can try for a weekend, maybe, early next year? I've got a good friend in London and we've talked about getting a walking weekend in Wales sorted maybe in the autumn, but realistically it's probably into spring now.'

'Why that's great,' she said, 'I'm really pleased. You're welcome any time. Don't even need to tell me when – there's space for you both. If I'm away, I keep a key under the grey stone that sits to the right of the garage, away from the door. And there's an alarm. The switch is inside the cupboard as you come in. There's a six digit code you need to enter but it'll be easy for you to remember... Ruth's birthday.'

'Thanks Dorothy. Can you text me all that, or e.mail? I've got to go,' he said, 'I'll phone though, if I want to stay.' He finished the call, resisting a sudden urge to tell Dorothy what he was planning. She might be the only person on the planet who'd understand, might even approve.

Later he phoned Edith Constable to tell her he'd engaged a ground contamination consultant to identify potential on-costs from any chemical or other spillages on the site.

The only time the consultant could come was at the weekend. Could he pick up the key on Friday?

'I'm sure that'll be fine,' she said. 'It's not as if you can do any damage to the property. If you come over just before 5, I'll sign it out to you. I won't need it back till Tuesday morning. Bring it back any time on Monday.'

* * *

Nick finished early on Friday and picked up the key on his way back from work. Once home, he went up into the floored attic of the cottage and cut up the old pink carpet he'd laid up there when they first moved in. He put an eight foot square in the flatbed of the pickup on top of some of his garden tools then fitted the hardtop canopy over the back. He patted the tailgate door affectionately after he'd slammed it shut. The pickup was a bit of an environmental disaster, but it was very useful for lots of jobs, even a very unusual one like this. He made a mental note that, if everything worked out, he'd add some more into his carbon offsetting payments at year end – pay the pickup's dues not just for the carbon she was spewing out currently, but for all that she'd breathed out in past years. The remnants of the carpet went into a couple of black bags to be disposed of later. He raked around in the garden shed for some rope and found an old washing line. He threw it, some tape and a couple of water bottles in under the carpet. Only another half hour to kill, so he made himself a cup of tea and sat, practising his calming breathing in the narrow back garden, watching the breeze shift and rustle through the few remaining leaves of his cherry tree.

He'd been running through the arguments again during the week, building up a balance sheet in his head. The police and the courts hadn't delivered justice. They couldn't. They'd not been able to find out what happened, so they'd based the case on the only part they could establish beyond doubt. As a result, the only story out there attributed at least some of the blame to Ruth and worse, had trashed her name, her reputation, her memory, in public. That was unjust. It was unfair. What he had in mind might not be right, but it was no more wrong than what had happened before and it was, in a certain sense, inevitable: it had to be done. He could see that now and that inevitability made it easier: if the true story was ever to be told, then he was the only one who could do it. And he was the one who needed to do it. Then maybe there could be talk of 'closure'.

At 6 he texted Jimmy. 'We're on. But he wants ten ounces, just as a starter. I've got money in cash. If it's good, if he likes it, he'll want more. Lots more. There could be much bigger money involved for you if you've got a reliable source of the same quality.'

'That's OK. I've sourced a new supply. Where and when?'

'I'll tell you when you confirm you have it.'

'Give me an hour and I'll confirm.'

After texting Jimmy, Nick parked offroad, out of sight, in a Network Rail worksite near the eastern entrance to the Abbey Craig woods, near where he'd seen the police vans parked that awful morning two years before. He opened up the back, and slung the length of line over his shoulder, slipped a torch, the tape and a flick knife into his pocket. At the last minute, he'd thrown in his old cricket bat. He took it out and whipped it round a couple of times to feel the weight of it, the whooshing sound it made as it flashed through the air. He locked up and waited till there were no cars from which he might be observed, then sneaked over the road and into the woods.

Once inside he stopped and took his puls: one hundred and fifty - that was all nerves. He knelt on a bed of pine needles and used his breathing to slow it down. Calmer now, he picked his way through the trees, keeping close to the boundary of the woods, till he came to the quarry entrance then beat up the side of the cliff to a viewpoint from where he could see the little howff below, the howff where it had all happened. He heard a crow cackling in the tree canopy above him and then there was completely silence save for the occasional lorry on the road. Ten minutes, half an hour went by. Hadn't he heard Jimmy say that his stash was near the howff? But maybe there were several stashes. In different places. What a fool. And the longer his wait went on, the more fool he felt he was.

And then he caught a glimpse of a red jacket in among the young trees below. He checked his watch. It was eight thirty.

12. Softly, Softly

Nick stayed still, super still... even when his stomach made a funny gurgling sound, nobody but he could've heard it. A big wind passed through the trees above and set every branch soughing, an arboreal lament. He picked up the cricket bat and made his way down to the entrance to the quarry. His heart was racing, his ears pricked for any sound. There was a rustle, very close. Jimmy must have clocked him first and was on top of Nick before he even knew it, caught him in the midriff before Nick could respond. 'Ya cunt,' Jimmy shouted.

They fell together with Jimmy on top, his forearm pressing into Nick's throat. Jimmy was strong. It was all Nick could do to push him up enough to take the pressure off his throat. It turned into an arm wrestle, a test of upper body strength. Nick was able to hold him up but just couldn't throw him off, then he changed tactic. Without any warning, instead of pushing up he pulled Jimmy down fast, but to the side. Jimmy lost control and Nick was able to push him over and scramble to his feet. He felt the cricket bat under his foot and in one swift motion, picked it up and clouted Jimmy on his neck. Jimmy fell but pulled himself together, shook his head, like an angry bull thwarted on its first charge, and drove for Nick again, but Nick squatted low to the ground, dodged to the left and, with a two-handed grip, brought the bat round at speed, clacking hard on to one of Jimmy's shins. Jimmy shouted out in pain and collapsed to the ground. 'Holy fuck,' he screamed, writhing around. He tried to get up but couldn't. 'You've broke ma leg, ya cunt,' he shouted, 'I'll fuckin kill you.'

'I don't think so,' Nick said. He stood over Jimmy and raised the bat over him. 'Turn over.'

Jimmy reached for Nick's legs and tried to pull him down, but he couldn't get any purchase or leverage. Nick brought the bat down on his wrists. He fell back. 'Turn over,' Nick said again. Jimmy didn't move.

'Right. I'm going to have to do this the hard way,' Nick said.

Jimmy made a grab for Nick's ankles again, but there was no strength in his grip. The fight had been knocked out of him by the bat.

Nick knelt down and grabbed hold of Jimmy's feet, placed one over the other and, lifting his legs a little, flipped him over onto his front and sat on him. He took the rope from his pocket and tied his hands behind his back, ankles together too. He taped up his mouth, picked him up and placed him over his back in a fireman's lift. He was heavy. There would inevitably be a trail through the woods that any investigator might follow, but it was going to be hard enough to carry his dead weight without giving himself the extra hassle of cleaning up the mess he was leaving behind. What the hell. Nobody knew they'd been here, knew who he was. When he got near to the road, he laid Jimmy down, waited till the road was empty then went back up to where he'd left the pickup, drove down to the entrance and reversed in. He rolled Jimmy up inside the carpet square, kicking and struggling but unable to make a sound, lowered the tailgate of the pickup, and laid him inside.

He shut the tailgate then, remembering about the mobile phone, opened it again. It was easy to find it in Jimmy's back pocket, a Sony. Nick removed the batteries and slipped phone and batteries into his pocket. Another one of Jimmy's pockets had the weed that Nick had offered to buy. Nick emptied it out into the gutter. Jimmy looked very uncomfortable. Maybe a gag inside the rolled-up carpet wasn't such a good idea, but he had to keep him quiet: they might be stopped at traffic lights, anywhere on the road where shouts from the back of the pickup would arouse suspicion. Nick pulled the security cover over the top of his captive.

As he jumped in behind the wheel, Nick took several deep breaths: he wondered what Ruth would think, imagined her looking down at him from some other place, wherever she was now. What would she be thinking about what he was doing? He hoped she'd approve, approve even more of what was to come. He put the pickup into gear and drove off round the town and onto the Dumbarton Road. Part one of his plan was complete without too much of a hitch. He'd backed himself against Stevens and come out on top. That gave him confidence for part two.

* * *

The drive out to the Gargunnock Hills was uneventful. When Nick reached the gate that led up to the concrete bunker, he parked so that his headlamps shone down the path. He took out an old Tilly Lamp he'd kept from camping expeditions years before, pumped it up and lit it. The bunker door opened easily now. He hung the lamp from the wooden beam. It cast quite a good light round the space, a sharp kind of light, harsh and unforgiving. His rational mind was trying to break through, peppering him with doubts from the edge of his conscious self, but he suppressed the doubts. He couldn't go back now. He'd done this for good reasons and now he had to carry it through. Reason, with its cautious pessimism, had no place. He walked back to the pickup. Jimmy was awake but wasn't wasting energy on a useless struggle. Only his eyes showed that he was very much alert and aware of what was going on.

Once he'd got him inside the bunker, Nick loosened the ties round Jimmy's ankles while sitting on his legs to keep him still. He wanted Jimmy shackled but with enough leeway that he'd be able to move his legs a little, keep the circulation going. With the remainder of the rope he tied Jimmy to the wooden beam. He passed it under his arms and round his chest, so he could take a bit of weight off his legs if he chose, then removed the tape from Jimmy's mouth.

'Shout all you want in here son,' he said, 'No-one can hear you.'

Jimmy was alert now. He was using the extra bit of freedom to try to move his legs about, almost dancing on the spot, testing out the strength of his bonds, testing out his legs. It looked like the blows Nick had inflicted had not had any permanent effect. Nick repositioned the lamp well away from his feet. He looked around at the scene, the enormity of it. What would anyone think if they saw it now, before he'd had an opportunity to establish what actually happened to Ruth? But what else could he have done? Just leave those questions that were burning away at him, hollowing him out, leave them unanswered?

He felt a sudden involuntary spasm in his gullet. He was going to be sick. He ran out of the bunker and threw up in a bush outside. Long deep retches emptied his stomach and left his throat sore and his body exhausted. He felt like he'd run a marathon. He took a couple of deep breaths then poked his head back in the door to check on his captive.

'What's aw this about mister?' Jimmy said, 'It's aw been some big fuckin mistake. I've never done nothin.'

'Stay where you are,' Nick said, 'I'll be coming back for you later.' He moved to shut the door.

'Mister, come back!' Jimmy shouted. 'Come back you fucker! Dinnae leave me!'

Once the door was fully closed, Nick, on the outside now, could hear nothing more. He walked round the building, feeling his way. At the back wall were the low-level ventilators. There was a faint glow of light from inside the bunker. If he put his ear close to them, he could hear Jimmy, still swearing, but once he stood up, he couldn't hear it at all. Nick walked back to the pickup. It was still open. He rolled up the carpet – he'd need to dump it somewhere. He put one or two other items in a bag - water, chocolate, grapes, the mobile phone - and started back to the bunker, then retraced his steps. He didn't want to leave the pickup next to the gate. He turned, a five point turn was needed, and drove it back down a few hundred yards to a point where there was a wide verge, just before the main road. He parked on the verge, locked the pickup and walked slowly back up to the bunker.

13. Interrogation

Nick shut the door of the bunker carefully and walked over to Jimmy. Jimmy was quiet, but his eyes were burning.

'I want you to know,' Nick starting pacing back and forward, 'that I am not mad. I want you to recognize what you have done, what you have destroyed, the consequences of your actions. And It'll be good for you. to be a captive, to be have to listen to me, to understand what you've done and its consequences. But first you'll have to own it - what you did - to say it out loud. You see, if you deny it even to yourself, you can never learn anything.' He stopped pacing, catching Jimmy's eye in the light of the Tilly lamp. 'You also need to know that for once you've met someone who is harder than you, someone who is not restrained by the law, someone who can do whatever.... the hell.... he likes.' He turned away and resumed his pacing, like a schoolteacher scolding a pupil at the end of the class. 'All your life,' he said, 'You've been dealing with adults with their hands tied behind their backs. Well, you're an adult now and you're the one with your hands tied behind your back. So you're playing with the big boys now, more specifically, this big boy.' Nick stopped and caught Jimmy's eyes again. 'And I'm quite prepared to do whatever... let me empahasize that word... *whatever*... I need to do to get the right story, what really happened. I want you, now, to imagine the worst thing that could happen to you... what can you think of? Having your balls cut off?... having your tongue cut out?... having every one of your fingers broken? I've imagined doing those things to you, and I'm quite happy to do them, one by one or altogether...if I need to. I think I'd quite enjoy it. If you want me to do it, all you have to do is say nothing... But just in case you think you can say anything that comes into your head, I need to warn you: you better not tell me lies, cos I'll know: you need to believe me, I'll know if you're telling me lies.' Nick had thought he was in control, but a different voice forced its way up and roared out his mouth like an erupting volcano of rage, 'And I'll do whatever I need to get the truth.'

Jimmy held his stare and returned it. It was Nick that moved away. It'd been silly to let rip with his voice. He felt as if someone had punched out all his wind, had sandpapered his throat till it was raw. First the vomiting, now a tender throat. Jimmy was tied up, but who was really the weaker one here?

'I dunno who you are mister,' Jimmy said, 'But you're a fuckin radge bastard. You've got the wrong cunt tied up. I've never done nothin.'

Nick tried to clear his throat, counted to ten and carried on, but his voice was still damaged. 'I know you killed my daughter Ruth,' he croaked, 'but I don't know how it happened. That's all I want. The whole story, straight from your mouth.' His self-control and was returning as he spoke. He cleared his throat and spoke more easily. 'I want no lies, no deception, no pretence. You just need to give me the facts and I'll be happy. You may not think it, but things could get a lot worse for you, so why not just tell me now what I want to hear?'

The hint of a smile crossed Jimmy's face. He took some time to reply. 'Ruth's faither ay?' he said, 'Fuckin hell! I had you aw wrong. I thought you were workin for they Romanian cunts that're meant to be shifting crack. Didnae know what I'd done to deserve the attention like. Small fry, me. Wondered if I'd made some mistake.' He appraised Nick afresh, taking in his height, the breadth of his shoulders. He almost sounded relieved. 'Ruth's faither ay? Fuckin hell man... Ruth's faither.'

'Come on then. Just tell me. Make me happy.' Nick said, 'What really happened? That's all I want. What happened that night?'

'Wee Ruthie's fuckin faither, ay?' That little smirk that had so annoyed Nick at the hearing appeared briefly on Jimmy's face. 'You've goat it aw wrong but. It was just like they said in the court. I never killed Ruth. Straight up. They tried to say I should've looked out for her. But it wasnae anyone's fault like. Aw three of us wiz drunk as skunks that night. An she was the worst.'

'No. I won't buy that. You see I heard you. Just last week. You were smokin some kind of weed, in your wee howff in the park. You as good as admitted you'd killed her. I heard you say it. You told your wee mate – Craigsy, wasn't it? – you said that *if Sadie had told the full story of what happened, you would've swung for it.*'

'Naw man. You must've heard it wrong. Why would I say somethin I never done?' Jimmy cricked his neck, first one side, then the other. 'Naw man: it wis just a fuckin laugh ay? Smokin that shit, you just talk shit. Gives you the fuckin giggles man. Say any fuckin thing, ay?'

'No. I heard you.'

'Naw you didnae.' Jimmy spoke clearly, confidently, 'An it's no me that's in deep shit man. It's you. What wid you cry this, what you've done? Kidnapping at the least... that must be a life sentence anyway, when they catch you, like.'

'That's not what I want to hear,' Nick said. He walked over to the bag, took out the roll of tape and gagged Jimmy. Jimmy thrust his chin forward and nodded, a knowing nod. He might be gagged, he seemed to be saying, he might be tied up, but he didn't care. He was still the man, still in charge.

Nick walked back out of the bunker for a breather, stood there for a moment or two: no point in being squeamish now; he was going to have to go through with it. He was psyching himself up by remembering Ruth's dead body, the post-mortem, the trial, what Jimmy had said. He walked back in and picked up Jimmy's phone. Using Jimmy's finger, he opened it up using touch i/d and changed the security settings, a numerical code, Ruth birthday. 'You're off to London,' he said as he put the phone away in his bag, 'or at least that's where your phone's going...' He put his hand under Jimmy's chin and pulled him forward so he had to balance on his toes, '...and let me tell you something,' he said, 'You're probably thinking I should treat you better than you treated my daughter. You probably imagine that people like me will always obey the laws, only do what they should do. You expect me to treat you with the fairness you've denied to others...' Nick was recovering his anger now, as if unwinding a coil inside his gut. He could feel the veins standing out on his forehead, a pulse pounding in his temple, the familiar trickle of cold sweat under his arms. 'But you are so wrong.' He put his hand on Jimmy's face and pushed him back. As Jimmy swung back towards him, he punched him hard in the stomach. Jimmy fell forward and spluttered as the rope round his chest took his weight. Nick lifted him up by the chin, supporting his weight on his outstretched right arm and looked him in the face again.

'You got yourself out of control, didn't you? Don't think you can use it as an excuse. You chose to get into that state, knowing you might lose control. But you knew! You knew what you were doing alright. But you didn't care, didn't care about anything except your self.' He let Jimmy take his own weight again then slapped him hard across the cheek with the back of his hand, 'You knew the agony you were causing an innocent person. You're the one that killed her. But she was the only witness to what happened, wasn't she?, so she had to go. You drowned her in case she could tell on you. That's how it was, wasn't it?'

Jimmy just stared back at him.

'Well? Wasn't it?"

Didn't even blink. Just stared.

'Bugger!' Nick said to himself. Jimmy wasn't anywhere near to being softened up yet. Well, he'd half expected that. So he needed to get going with the next part of his plan. 'I'm leaving you to sweat in here on your own,' Nick said, 'And while I'm away I want you to remember what really happened... work out how you're going to phrase your confession. And if it's not ready when I get back, your confession that is, I'm going to start to work on you... do you know what I mean by that? Do you remember those things I talked about? ... or maybe some others... in fact here's a few more for you to think about, some more things I might do, some more things I'm mad enough to do if you don't tell me the whole story of how Ruth died.... I could start with the fingernails, rip them off .... or maybe the nipples, what pain I could give you there!!... in fact there are a lot of places where I can inflict pain: which place would you prefer? Maybe tonight? Maybe tomorrow? You see I've got to go now, but I'll be back. And while I'm away I want you to remember... like I said... so you can tell me what I want to know. You can shout all you want in here while I'm away and no-one will hear you. No-one's coming to save you.' Nick pressed his face close in to Jimmy's. 'You see... the next person you see will be... me.'

Nick shut the door behind him and pushed home the padlock with a satisfying click.

14. London

When Nick arrived at the pickup, he stopped and took a few long calming breaths. The clock said it was only 11.14, but so much had already happened. He drove home fast, adrenaline pumping through his system, no cars in front to slow him down. One bend came up too fast and the pickup's inner front wheel bumped up onto the verge as he overcompensated on the steering. He stopped. Took another deep breath. Calm.... Calm.... No room for error now.

Back in Cambuskenneth, he parked outside his cottage, grabbed the overnight bag he'd left in the hallway and checked his train ticket – the overnight train to London Euston from Inverness, leaving Stirling just after 12, arriving Euston just after 7. His ticket was for the unbooked seated accommodation – anonymous, easy, cheap. The seats were wide but it was difficult to get comfortable. As he tried to doze, visions of his young captive, trussed up in the concrete bunker, flitted across his mind. As his plans had developed, he'd cast himself as a on the right side of this story, stacked up the arguments in his favour. But now, as the night wore on and the train bumped and rumbled towards London, the word 'kidnapped' that Jimmy had used stuck in his brain. In the official record, Ruth's death was just an accident, a drugs night gone wrong, a young girl caught up where she shouldn't have been and exposing herself to risks. A sad, tragic event, not a crime. If others had been more sensible it wouldn't have happened, but they couldn't be blamed. It was still an accident. But what he was doing now? That was no accident. It was planned. Premeditated. In cold blood, as the saying had it. His tired brain was going into overdrive. He was going to London just so he could send a diversionary text from Jimmy's phone, buying some time in case he was reported missing. How crazy was that? What if Jimmy was found while Nick was away... and it was all traced to him. What a risk! It had seemed like a good plan when it was just a plan, but now, in the middle of the night, it felt absolutely crazy. Why had he thought it would work? What would happen if Jimmy was found? He'd be the criminal, the kidnapper. What else had Jimmy called him? The child abuser. Well. He was eighteen. He wasn't a child. Not like Ruth.

During the night of fitful sleep, as the train rumbled south, the flaws in Nick's plan kept rising to the surface. Not surprising really. This wasn't his kind of game after all and the more he went over what had happened, the more flaws he saw. He'd left a trail. His vomit littered the vegetation outside the door of the bunker. There must be DNA in vomit surely. Or was there? His body had rejected it after all – it was material his body didn't want. His pickup tyres - they could be covered in soil or pollen or other traces that could link him to the bunker, couldn't they? Anyway, never mind that! He'd been given a tour, signed for the key for God's sake – no other clue was needed! The trail he'd left was a mile wide. And why hadn't he put some kind of camera in the bunker, one he could check from his phone while he was away... to see what Jimmy was doing... why was he only thinking of this now? He really was an amateur.

Did it matter though? If things didn't end well, did it matter? He'd been over this already. From that first night when she hadn't come home from school, nothing was ever going to end well again. There were no good endings. Did it matter if it was him who ended up in court? Wasn't that what he wanted: 'to have his day in court', to speak up for Ruth? And here he was now, with his best shot. It had all been inevitable really. One thing led to another, as if the story was already written, and here he was going to London to send a fake whatsapp... but what if Jimmy didn't use whatsapp... another flaw in his plan, another thing he hadn't thought of till now. How many other things hadn't he thought of? But Jimmy surely had some form of social media, surely? And one thing was for sure. The bunker key had to be back with the Council on Monday morning, so whatever was going to happen wasn't going to take long.

He drifted off again, the rhythm of the train taking him under, his head lolling and jerking back up before settling down again. He snapped awake at Preston, wiped the saliva dribbling from his mouth, then went under again as the train pulled away. He was vaguely aware of stopping at Crewe, the platform lights, and then it was 5.30 and he woke again with a jolt, his neck sore, his mouth dry. The train had stopped abruptly at a signal and began to crawl through Milton Keynes station. Commuters were lining the platform. He looked at them and they looked at him. Just another guy on the overnight train. He stood up and stretched. Over an hour still to go. He took out his phone. No messages, no whatsapps, nothing. He opened the music player, put in his earbuds, and as the Bedfordshire countryside rolled past he listened to the Beethoven string quartets. Was he a psychopath? Wasn't this how someone like Hannibal Lecter would have behaved - quietly, calmly, listening to Beethoven, while his kidnapped captive was trussed up in an evil-smelling ex-army bunker?

The music calmed him down: he went over again the arguments that had let him to take action: he'd sat on his grief, sat on his disappointment, sat on his anger that Ruth's reputation had been traduced, that in killing her, her killer had gained the right to tell the story of what happened that night. He'd played the sensible victim, neutered, powerless, emasculated, while the authorities dealt with his daughter's death. But now he was doing something. And it felt good, really good. Things had got all distorted in the night, that was always the way of it. But he'd heard Jimmy admit that he'd killed Ruth: that was no distortion, that was the beginning and end of it. And by the time he got back to the bunker, Jimmy would be softened up for Round Two of the interrogation - after a few hours without food or drink his hard nut would be cracked, his soft inside exposed. OK. Mistakes had been made already, but he didn't care... the point wasn't to get away with it... what would be the point of that? The whole point was to get Jimmy Stevens to tell the real story of what happened and then to publicise it. As long as he got his day in court, the same way as Jimmy had, that day in court would allow him to tell Ruth's side of the story.

The shave and hot shower in Euston station were reviving. He bought a flat white and a chocolate croissant from one of the stalls. There was still some time to kill before he sent the message. On a visit to London when Ruth was still a baby, the three of them had stayed near the British Museum, walked up through the Regent's Park to the canal and back round by St Pancras. He had a quick look at the route on his phone. 4 miles give or take. Just over an hour. It was 8.30. A very pleasant day. He could send messages from Jimmy's phone from the park. Train from Euston or King's Cross at 10-ish? Maybe 10.30? Back in Stirling by 5? He headed out of the station, his bag over his shoulder.

London was busy. When is it not? The main drag in Regent's Park was full of so many different people... men in suits, women with prams, joggers, children on their way to school, people going places, not like Jimmy. Mind you, he'd be trying to escape, for sure. Could he escape? He worked back over all the details, the rope, the knots he'd tied, the positioning. There was no way out. Was there?

He reached the canal quicker than he expected. It was good to be beside the canal, something soothing about its gentle movements. There were coots and moorhens, ducks aplenty, two elegant swans dipping their long necks to the water. An older gentleman, a *Telegraph* under his arm, who looked as if he might've stepped out of a Trevor Howard film with his double-breasted suit, paisley tie and black felt fedora, greeted Nick enthusiastically. 'What a glorious day,' he said, in pitch perfect BBC English. Behind him, a group of Muslim girls were laughing and chattering, clowning about with each other, hijabs fluttering in the breeze. An older woman sitting on the bank, who looked as if she'd slept out, clutched her bag and turned away. Two teenage boys, their deep black skins beautiful against the white collars of their school uniforms, were engaged in friendly argument. Something to do with the Battle of the Somme. History homework? If this all worked out, maybe he could find a new life, down here in London, where no-one would know his name, where he could walk along this canal each morning and no-ne would give him a second glance. There must be plenty people down here would like to have an organic garden, people who would pay well.

At Camden Lock, Nick popped into a café and ordered a cappuccino. He opened up Jimmy's phone and pressed the *whatsapp* icon. He found a stream from Jimmy to his mother and read a few to catch the tone, Jimmy's habitual mid-spellings. In the cold light of a London morning, the supposition on which he was basing all of this - that his mother wouldn't be keen to report him missing if she thought he was involved in some deal – seemed pretty fragile. But he was here now. Whatever his doubts, he had to go through with this plan.

In London, he typed on Jimmy's phone, *Chance to make big money. Back Monday.* He read it over three times then pressed 'send'. Seconds later, the phone rang. Jimmy's mother's picture came up on the screen. Maybe Nick's message was so unusual as to have the opposite effect to the one he intended, alerting her that something was wrong. Maybe Jimmy never told her where he was, where he was going. He switched the phone off. He really was an amateur, wasn't he? Maybe there was someone else Jimmy had planned to meet today. Getting past the first level of security had given him access to everything on Jimmy's phone. He checked through some of the other whatsapp streams now, Instagram, Facebook, Snapchat... there were flags on all of them but nothing that he could see of any importance to him, nothing else planned for the weekend. Then again Jimmy probably used some secure software for his deals... or maybe a different phone. He turned the phone off to save battery and headed back down onto the Canal. Even if he didn't get Jimmy taken in for Ruth's murder, there'd be enough evidence on the phone to get him done for drug dealing at least, surely? But would the evidence be admissible given how it was obtained? Such a bloody amateur. He was blundering about in a world he didn't understand. What kind of a crazy scheme... he was out of his depth... how had he ever thought this was going to work?

He still had time to kill before the direct Stirling train at 12. He headed back towards the station. The only other time he'd been north of Kings Cross was back when he was a student. The post-industrial wasteland he remembered had been turned into a buzzing commercial area - restaurants, hotels, smart new apartment buildings. And King's Cross station, restored to its original condition, looked superb in the morning sun, thousands criss-crossing on the open forecourt. He leaned against a railing on the corner of Euston Road and checked his phone. It was 9.25. No messages. Here he was. An anonymous nobody with no friends in the heart of the big city. No online profile to speak of. No family. Well, Dorothy. She was family. But she wouldn't mind, wouldn't even notice. He could just melt away now, change his name, disappear, never go back to Scotland, take out his money, transfer to a new account, new identity. Leave Jimmy to rot. Could he do that?

'Nick,' someone shrieked. A woman. He turned to look. 'This way you idiot!' He turned again. A taxi had stopped right on the corner. 'Can't stop here,' she shouted, 'Get in... hurry!'

It was Sam Hill.

He looked to right and left. A queue of cars was building up behind the taxi. One of them was blasting its horn angrily, then another. 'Hurry up,' she shouted again, 'Get in you fool!' He leapt over the railing and got in.

They looked at each other.

'Of all the taxis in all the world...' he started. She laughed.

'No gin, I'm afraid,' she said.

'Fine, it's not noon yet, at least I hope not.'

'Sorry,' she said, 'I just hijacked you. I'm heading for the Royal Opera House and then I saw you standing at the corner. Couldn't go past. What the fuck are you doing down here?'

'Oh,' he flustered, 'It's an old friend.'

'You never mentioned friends in London...'

'No... he came over from Canada,' he improvised, 'Visiting his parents. Thought I'd come down and catch up. Caught the overnight train.'

'So,' she screwed up her face, 'I'm probably taking you in the wrong direction?'

'No, it's fine. We're not meeting up till the afternoon, well 12 on the dot actually, back at King's Cross. He runs a tight schedule, but I've got the morning to kill.' What was he saying? He didn't have the morning to kill. She still absolutely had a hex on him, everything about her. Close together in the back seat of the cab, it was her smell, that hair, those eyes... and still those freckles, those bloody gorgeous freckles, right across her nose. Every damn thing about her. He could feel the blood pumping in his ears. Their knees bumped against each other as the cab swung round another corner and that little touch started an erection. He swallowed, looked out of the window, put his hand up to his neck and dug his fingernails in... the erection began to die away. She'd been talking away and he hadn't heard a word she was saying.

'...so my meeting shouldn't last much more than 40 or 50 minutes,' she was saying, 'why don't you wait in Covent Garden and we can get a coffee after I've finished. You'll still have time to meet up with your friend. I'd like to hear how you're getting on.'

'Sure,' he said, 'That'd be good. And you? How are you? You're looking great. Better than great. You're looking fabulous. Absolutely fucking fabulous.'

'That's kind Nick. You always were kind,' she said, 'A kind man.'

If only you knew, he thought.

'And yes I'm good,' she said it in a stiff-upper-lip kind of way. 'You probably saw me and Alan are no longer an item.'

'Oh?' He hadn't seen that, had stopped following her, her busy online life, after that day in the Park, in Glasgow. 'I didn't know.'

'Never mind. Not worth talking about,' she said, then carried on, 'He's such a rat. Turns out he had her all set up in a private mews cottage for God's sake. How could I not know? Blind, that was me.' She tugged on his shirt collar. 'You'd never do something like that, would you Nick? Much too kind. Too good. That's you.'

No, I'd do something much worse, he was thinking. A picture appeared in his head of the squalid little ex-army bunker, the kidnap, his young captive - what he'd done, what he might do. Thinking about it in her presence made him feel sordid, ashamed.

'No,' he said, 'I wouldn't.' She was looking in her handbag, pulling out her phone. 'Anyway,' he said, 'That's fine, what you suggested... I'll just go into Covent Garden and nosey about. Text me when you're finished. Do you still have the number?'

'Sure,' she said, 'Just give me a moment... I need to have a look back over my notes for this meeting... the key points are here in a mnemonic.' She opened her phone and pressed the screen a few times. The taxi was stuck at a red light. Nick looked out of the window. It was raining and the colour had drained out of the city. London didn't look so attractive now. People with pinched faces were scurrying past each other, cyclists dicing with death on the slippery roads, everywhere there were people and the things they wanted to consume... consumption, consumption and more consumption. When they arrived at the Opera House, she paid, gave him a quick peck on the cheek and ran off. 'Won't be long!' she shouted, 'Then we can have a good catch up!'

He looked at the market but wasn't in the mood for it. There was a Church outside. The plaque at the door said, 'Welcome to St Paul's, the Actor's Church'. He walked in. Despite the high windows, it was gloomy, but quiet. On another day he might have taken an interest in 'the actors' - who were they and why did they have a church? - but not today. His mood had become sombre. It was worse than sombre. It was black. He was overcome with tiredness and grief. Black grief. He took a seat near the back of the Church, opened his phone and found Enaudi on his music player, put in his earbuds and shut his eyes. He wasn't sure how much later when he was woken abruptly by a man shaking him. 'Can't sleep in here mate. Not allowed,' the man was saying, 'Your snoring's echoing round the church. Never heard anyone snore so loud!'

'Sorry,' Nick said, 'Sorry.'

He stumbled out into bright sunshine. It was still only 10.25. No word from Sam. He noticed the gardens to the side of the church and walked in. A place of peace in the middle of the city. He sat down on one of the wooden benches and texted her. *I'm in the garden at the side of the Actors Church*. It was a quarter to 11 before she arrived.

'Sorry I got held up,' she said, 'You know how it is.' He didn't know, but he nodded. 'Have you still got time for a catch up?'

'Sure,' he said, 'I've texted my pal and put him off till later,' he lied.

'Well what d'you fancy? Coffee or what? You look tired now. How about something stronger? *Lamb and Flag's* just round the corner.'

She only took a soda and lime. He downed his first pint and was on to a second one within five minutes. It hadn't been that long since she'd said goodbye to him in Glasgow. There really wasn't very much for him to tell... except, of course, that he'd kidnapped the boy who'd killed his daughter and had him tied up in an old military bunker near Stirling. She was so easy to talk to, so easy to trust, that this, the only thing that he couldn't tell her, was exactly what he found himself wanting to tell her.

He kept on the front foot by asking her the questions - this was how their relationship had worked before, with Sam doing most of the talking, and him doing the listening. And she was good at it, talking. And so good to look at, to be with. And that soft clear voice of hers. There were so many good words for her, the sound of her and the sight of her, the lines that creased around her eyes when she smiled, her hair hanging to the side. He realised she'd stopped talking... it'd been something about a bust-up at work. It was his turn. 'So how are you feeling about it all now?' he improvised.

'Like I just said,' she said, 'There's no way I'm going to the States. If it comes off at all now, it can't be before the middle of next year at the earliest. You never know,' she said, 'I'll maybe get up to Scotland to finish off those Munros after all.'

He nodded. There was no chance of her coming back to him in Scotland. Not now. Not now that he was a kidnapper.

'Anyway, what about you? Have you moved on?' she asked, 'You know?'

'I'll never move on,' he said, 'I can't. Could you?'

She seemed to bristle a bit. That put a bit of distance back in. 'I don't know,' she said. Her phone vibrated. 'Excuse me a minute. This may be important.' The way she said it, it was like a bucket of cold water, as if he wasn't important, not as important as her call. He watched her walking over to the window to get a little more privacy for the call. How had he been so stupid? How had he allowed himself to be intoxicated again so easily? She was a narcissist, only interested in him because she knew he wanted her, cared for her, found her beautiful. She didn't want him. She wanted the affirmation. And now she knew he'd been here, she could tell police how it was possible that Jimmy's phone had been in London. Mind you, that was only the latest of many problems with his scheme. It'd never been going to work, had it? It wasn't the perfect crime... it was a comedy of errors. But it would be worth it... it would all be worth it... as long as the true story of what happened to Ruth came out, one way or the other.

'Well,' she said, when she returned to the table to pick up her handbag, 'I need to get on.'

'I'm not coping very well,' he blurted out, without really intending to, as if impelled to say it.

'Nick,' she said, a bit defensively, 'Nick, Nick, Nick.' She paused. 'I'm not sure I can be much help to you. You know what I'm like. I'm sorry.' She put her hand on his and held it there as a parting gesture, against his reflex to draw away.

'Sometimes I feel so violent, so vengeful,' he said, 'I feel that I have the right of revenge, to avenge my daughter's rape and murder, to kill the bastard. To draw it out. To make him suffer like he made her suffer.' His voice assumed a driving tone, unstoppable, the gates were open and words were flooding out. '

She blew out a long breath and sat down again.

'It's like some sick fantasy, but it might be the only way to make him realise what he did... I didn't feel like this at first: I wanted nothing to do with it... but It's eaten away at me, day after day, week after week, so now I want to know exactly what happened. And I want him to repent, to realise, to really realise what he's done. It's like my life has become the story line of a second-rate movie and I'm the man in the middle. I can't let go of it. What else is there in my life?' He finished his beer, wanted another, but couldn't stop his words. 'You know the Old Testament verse *a time for every purpose*? Well... ' he tried to drink from the glass again - he'd forgotten it was empty, '... there's lots of times for different things in that chapter, but what people don't realise, and I always remember thinking this from when I was a kid, is that it also says there's *a time for hating*. People like me, we always turn the other cheek, don't we? It's expected. But it turns out the Bible was right enough... there is 'a time for hating'. Maybe everyone should do a bit more hating.'

They both could hear the sounds of the street. Heavy rain had started up and was driving against the window behind them.

'I don't want to live in a world where,' he swallowed and composed himself, 'Where my daughter's killer walks free. Where he goes on to live a new life, hurts other people, wreaks carnage in other lives he touches.' He was speaking now in a controlled logical way, as if this was an abstract philosophical question. 'Jimmy Stevens. You've not seen him, but to me he's just like what Nietzsche had in mind when he talked about the 'blond beasts' ... the rest of us are his weaklings, his pawns: as far as he's concerned, we're here to satisfy his needs, his desires. We think we live in some imaginary world, a better world that doesn't actually exist, a world where people like him should be treated the same as everyone else, when what we should be doing is taking action now, here, in this world, to stop them doing harm. They just don't care, you see, the blond beasts. They don't care. So someone needs to put a stop to him, stop him doing any more harm... call him to account for the harm he's done already. More than that... stop him doing it again... stop him for good.'

'I don't know about Nietzsche,' she said, 'But if you're talking about some kind of revenge, you know it can never be right to 'serve it cold', as the old saying has it. I mean you can empathise where there's hot emotion, the spur of the moment, but if it's planned, cold-blooded, it becomes something else: sinister. Inhuman. That's not you Nick, not the Nick I know. If you're having these kinds of thoughts, you should think about getting some help. Anyone would find it difficult to cope with what you've been through. And I've said it to you before. You're too inclined to bottle things up. Then eventually they're all going to come out, but under enormous pressure there's a good chance they'll come out the wrong way,.'

Nick wiped his lips.

'Anyway, you just have to accept that you may never know how Ruth died - you may have to face that fact. I know it's very difficult, but you may have to accept it, if you're going to move on. Lots of people have to make a life through the other side of tragedy.'

'I know how she died,' he said. 'And I think other people should know too. That's what's bugging me even more than him walking about as if nothing had happened. The fact that it's his version of events that people know. Ruth wasn't just killed. She's been denied her voice.'

She sat forward a little in her seat. 'What do you mean, *you know how she died.*'

'I saw him, Stevens, with a wee mate of his. I heard them talking. In those woods, the wee hut where it all happened. Heard him admit what he'd done. I heard it with my own ears. That he'd have *swung for it*, he said, if the other girl who was there with them had told the full story.'

She gave him a moment.

'The police', he sounded bitter, 'They more or less told me to get lost. They're not interested any more. My word against his. No other evidence to support it. Case over. So if Ruth is to have justice, maybe it's me that has to deliver it. What the hell? There's nothing left in my life that's worth very much anyway.'

'This is silly talk Nick. You know that, don't you?'

'Don't get me wrong Sam,' he backed off, 'I just think about it,' - lying was so easy - 'It drives me round and round and round. It drives me mad.'

'Nick,' she said and put her hand on his again, 'No amount of punishment will bring Ruth back. The courts have done their best. C'mon,' she said, brightening up, 'I'm going to get us a coffee and put my next meeting off for half an hour.'

As she walked up to the bar, Nick watched her, that neat little bum that he had caressed not so long ago... had that really happened? And he thought about Jimmy Stevens, dirty and cold, in the dark, dank bunker. Sitting here in a London pub it all seemed a very long way away. Some other person might just leave him there to rot, to die, starving, steeped in his own shit. But he couldn't. Wouldn't. He was going to have to go back. And anyway, there was the key to return... as if that mattered. He jumped up and headed for the toilet, signalling to Sam as she carried back the coffees. He held his head under the cold tap for a count of 50. He pushed his hair back and blew hot air on his face with the dryer. There was a fixed grimace on the face that was looking back out at him from the mirror. No way back. He'd gone too far already to turn back. He was going to have to carry on. Back in his seat, he felt composed again and was able to speak clearly and directly.

'Sam,' he said, 'I'm really sorry. I think that beer must've been stronger than I thought – went straight to my head. I was just driveling on. And you still have a hex on me. Seeing you, it's like bits of me, I don't know... without even trying, you can just open me up, like I've no defences.' He bit the inside of his lip to stop it trembling and reached for his coffee, spooned in some sugar and stirred it. 'I know you're right,' he said, 'I will get there. Life will seem worth living again. And maybe I will get some help... when I'm ready to accept it. I know I can be a stubborn bugger. Too stubborn.' He had to take another moment. The coffee was lukewarm. He drank it down in one slug. 'I'm glad you shouted on me from the taxi, Sam. We were meant to meet up again, like on that day on the mountain. I've really missed you.' She tried to interrupt but he pushed on, 'Look I need to go soon... and so do you. And don't worry that I'm harbouring any illusions. I know what you said to me by the river that day was right. You know what I think about you. You're fabulous, wonderful, unique, loving... everything, just everything about you... a special human being... but don't worry... I know it's just like you said before. There's no way forward for us. I understand that. Your life is too different to mine.' He stood up and walked round to where she sat and kissed her forehead. 'I'm going to get out of your life now. I'll let you know how things go, ay? Send you an e.mail once I've calmed down, next week, next month, sometime,' he said.

'Dear Nick,' she said, 'Nick...' But he was already walking out without looking back. He was glad he'd been able to say these things to her.

Once outside, he caught a taxi to Kings Cross. The 12 o'clock train had left already, but there were plenty of other trains north on the East Coast line. He dozed on and off most of the way after Peterborough, had to wait 20 minutes in Edinburgh for a connecting train, but still was back in Stirling just after 6. He trudged back down the road and over the pedestrian bridge to Cambuskenneth. It was hard to believe it was less than 24 hours since he'd walked up the road to catch the overnight London train. As he came to the cottage, he saw his next door neighbours, Pat and Val Steerman, at their front gate.

'Hi Nick,' Pat said, 'How are things?'

'Fine thanks, just a bit tired.' He tried to keep his voice light.

'We're wondering what's happened to Ollie. He's usually back for his food by now but you know what cats are like?' Val attempted a little laugh, 'Maybe better send out the search party?'

He joined in the polite laughter and made the door. 'Hope he turns up soon,' he said.

And as he pulled the door to, he heard Val say, rather too loudly, 'He looks as though he's seen a ghost.'

Nick dumped his bag in the kitchen, poured himself a whisky, then had a reviving shower. What would happen if he couldn't get any more out of Jimmy? And could he trust anything he did get out of him? The truth seemed as far away as ever. It was just a mess, a bigger mess now that he'd poured his mess onto the mess that was there already. So what to do? Hand himself in and hope for sympathy from a jury of his peers? No chance. Run for it, but where? These were options that left Jimmy Stevens as a sympathetic victim. Then again, all possible options were bad options. Once your daughter is raped and murdered there are no good options. The least bad one was the one where the real story came out. And he was in the endgame now. An endgame with only two players in it. But getting the the real story out of Jimmy, was that the end? Maybe it wouldn't be. Couldn't be. Wouldn't it just be the beginning of another stage.

Was Jimmy going to die? Would that be the end? He hadn't intended it, didn't intend it. And if it came to it, he wouldn't be able to do it in cold blood. Just taking a knife to him, slitting his throat. He'd been able to punch him, sure, slap his face, of course, but he wouldn't be able to kill him, cold. But in a fight maybe? If he was attacked maybe? And what would he do afterwards? Take his own life? But then no-one would know what he'd been thinking. What his motivation had been. That didn't seem right either. It wouldn't do anything for Ruth. People needed to know the real story. Wasn't that the whole point? Ruth had to be given her proper place in the tragedy... had to be given her voice... so Jimmy couldn't die.. Jimmy had to tell the truth. Nick toweled himself dry and put on a fresh pair of jeans, a clean shirt. It was after 7. Whatever happened, he was going to get the real story out there, record it somehow, make it available, as widely available as the false narrative that had come out of the trial.

He phoned the pizza parlour near the station and ordered two large pizzas but when he turned up to collect them fifteen minutes later, they'd forgotten his order. He'd have to wait another fifteen minutes. 'I'll walk round the block,' he said irritably, 'Get some cash.'

He went to the cash machine beside the Old Post Office pub. One of the smokers hovering outside the pub door came over to him. 'Mr. Nick,' the man said. He loped an arm round Nick's shoulder breathing a potent mix of beer and whisky in his face. 'It's funny seeing you. I've been thinking about you recently, since my retirement.'

Nick recognised him. 'You're a policeman, aren't you?' he said, 'You were at the house that first day when she was missing.'

'Aye... but I wasnae involved in the investigation after that.'

What's your name?'

'Davie... Davie Henshaw.'

'Davie Henshaw... yes, I remember,' Nick said, and put out his hand, 'Nice to meet you again. So how are you doing?'

'55 last year, me. Got out soon as I could. Thirty odd years in the police but nobody's interested now, ay? I got a wee job working down at Tesco's. Just have to stand around at the doors. Kid's stuff really. But never mind me,' Henshaw said, 'How are you? Don't know how I'd have gone through what happened to you. Terrible.' He seemed to disappear into his own space for a moment. 'And I'll tell you something else,' he slurred, 'We missed out you know, the police, your case. In the old days, I'd have got more on that wee shite Stevens. One hand tied behind your back now. Both hands...' Henshaw began to ramble. 'Right little shite. Always has been. I know these people. I was born here. His father was a shite too.'

'So what? You think he killed Ruth?'

The question made Henshaw look at Nick as if he'd just become aware that he was there. 'Oh don't get me wrong Mr. Nick. We had nothing to go on. It's probably just that I hate the wee bugger. And the mother. She was just as bad. Colluded with him. You know what we should have done,' he said, poking Nick on his shoulder, 'We should have cut his balls off and hung them over the Auld Brig as a warning - that would've had more effect on crime in Stirling than any posse of social workers.'

Henshaw coughed. And coughed again. He brought a hankie out of his pocket and waggled it around his mouth and nose. 'Tragedy. Tragedy,' he said, staggering a little to the side then catching Nick's arm and regaining his balance. 'You know what really pisses me off?' he said, 'We have the most sophisticated investigation machine anywhere, all the technology, the protocols, the top brass, meetings, forms, complaints processes, people crawling over you... and yet we canny even tell how a young Stirling girl died on an everyday Friday in Stirling, in our own town. Shocking.'

Henshaw pulled out his cigarette packet then put it away again. 'Look. Can't stand out here all night. Can I get you a drink?'

'No,' Nick said, 'I've got to get on. But thanks.' He put a hand on Henshaw's shoulder. 'Thanks,' he said, 'You've been a real help. Just what you said there... it made me feel better.' Nick turned away and walked briskly back to collect the pizzas, two of them, a bag of chips, a litre of water, a litre Irn Bru. He didn't relish what lay ahead of him, but there was nothing else now. He was just going to have to get on and make it work.

He ate most of his pizza on the way out to the bunker, washed it down with some water. As he pulled the pickup in beside the bunker gate, he once more had the strange feeling that this was not really him. He tried to locate the feeling more precisely. It was like he was acting in some bizarre film, or that he was dreaming this life - that he was inside someone else's head, as an observer. This couldn't really be him, yet he knew it was. It was him. Locking the pickup door and walking the short distance down the track in the dark, turning the key in the lock, opening the bunker door to meet his captive, his prisoner, his daughter's killer.

15. Bunker

The smell was the first thing that hit him. It was a fetid damp smell. It made Nick think of the monkey house at the zoo in Edinburgh, a favourite visit before Ruth had started giving him grief about animal liberation. How strange it is, he thought, that memory for smells is so good… very particular smells taking you right back to a particular place, a particular time. He'd always remember this smell, and with it this place, this time, but he could hear nothing, not even breathing. It was completely dark. He stepped inside and switched on his torch. It stabbed into the black and picked out Jimmy, squirming away from the light as if it had been thrown in his face. Jimmy started yelling: 'Took your time, cunt! I'm just about deid here. Fuckin torture, that's what this is. Fuckin torture. You're fuckin mad man, a fuckin mad torturing fuckin maddo bastard.'

Nick ignored him and shone the torch onto the rope ties. They seemed secure enough. He pumped up and lit the Tilly Lamp then closed the door. A wet patch on Jimmy's trousers had spread down to his knees. Nick walked over to him. Jimmy tried to spit it into Nick's face. Nick slapped Jimmy hard across the cheek.

'You should be glad you're able to feel so angry son. You get that chance cos you're still alive. You maybe didn't like the last few hours, but at least you had a few hours, ay? A few hours to feel angry. Ruth'll never be able to feel angry again, will she? Cos she's dead. But you knew that didn't you, seeing it was you that killed her. Tell you what Jimmy Stevens. I'll tell you what. I like you being upset. Why should you get to be alive and to enjoy your life? If you are still to have a life, isn't it fair that you should suffer a wee bit. Is that not fair? I think it's really good. The more I see you suffering the happier I am.'

Jimmy said nothing.

'And what's that stink?' Nick lifted the lamp higher. 'Have you been a dirty boy? Couldn't wait to go to the toilet?'

'I'm gonnae kill you, you bastard,' Jimmy hissed. 'You're a fuckin radge bastard.'

'I'm going to loosen your bonds a little,' Nick said, 'Get some circulation back in your limbs. I don't want you dying on me, well not just yet anyway.' He knelt down to adjust the rope tying Jimmy's ankles. Jimmy tried to kick out at him, catching him on the wrist. But there was no strength in the kick. Nick ignored it, loosened the rope a little then did the same to the one that was looped round the beam and tied behind his back.

'I'm gonnae kill you when I get out of here. Fuckin tear you into wee fuckin pieces.'

There was something almost admirable about Jimmy's strength of will, still challenging, still hurling abuse. If I let him, Nick thought, he'll walk all over me. 'Here's something you'll understand,' he said, slapping Jimmy across the cheek once, twice, three times. 'Now I want you to be a good boy,' he said, 'Cos I'm giving you something to eat.'

Nick laid an opened pizza box on the ground beside Jimmy together with the opened bottle of Irn Bru. 'You should be able to move about a bit better now, be able to kneel down,' he said, 'You might need to lie down to eat. But I can't loosen your wrists. They have to stay tight behind your back. So I'm leaving all this for you as a wee test. And as a help I suggest that you try to get the bottle in between your knees, for drinking, that is. See. You're going to have to work for your food and drink. In the dark. Just be glad I don't make you sing as well. Build a fire under your feet.'

'I'm no eatin that shite,' Jimmy said.

'Fair enough,' Nick said. 'So let's forget the food and just get to it. What this is all about. You killed my daughter didn't you? You raped her and you killed her, didn't you?'

'Sure I fucked her,' Jimmy said, 'You ken that frae the trial. But it wisnae rape. She wanted it.' He gave that snidey little grin to himself that Nick had seen at the trial. 'An I shouldnae've bothered. She was a rubbish fuck anyway. Tight wee cunt. Couldnae even get ma cock right in.'

Nick jumped up and hit him on the side of his head, then kicked at his ribs when he fell back. The glancing blows didn't catch Jimmy cleanly and he was able to work himself back up to a sitting position. 'Fuck's sake man,' he said, 'You wanted the right story... but see if that's what happens when I gives you it, I'm no tellin you any mair.'

'Ok,' Nick said, blowing heavily, 'You're right. I shouldn't have lost control... but you were baiting me. And I'm warning you, if you say anything insulting about Ruth again, I'll make you pay, God, I'll make you pay... I'll do things to you that you didn't even know existed. You see, I know you killed her. I heard you say it, in the hut, with your wee pal. Maybe you were out of it... I don't know. But whatever you tell me, remember I've been all over the trial record. Every word. I can spot any inconsistency, any lie.'

'I can tell you one thing for nothing,' Jimmy's tone was deadpan, 'I've never raped any girl, me. Don't need to. I can get it when I want it.' He nodded his head and a little smile was playing around his lips. 'An I'll tell you something else for nothing. I never killed nae cunt.'

Nick clacked Jimmy round the chin with a cuff which knocked him backwards. 'I can kill you, you know,' Nick said, 'Unless I get the truth. And what you've told me this far isn't true at all.' Nick cuffed Jimmy again, drawing blood from his nose. 'I'll know it when I hear it, and when I do, maybe, just maybe, I'll allow you to survive so that you can face the consequences and Ruth's name can be cleared.'

It was hard for Jimmy to keep his balance with his ankles loosely shackled but he faced up to Nick. He snorted in the back of his nose, coughing up a mix of snot and blood into his mouth – once - twice – and then, deliberately, and precisely, he spat again into Nick's face, a mixture of blood and spittle. Nick jumped back. It seemed that the harder he pushed, the harder Jimmy Stevens became. It was as if fighting gave Jimmy strength.

Nick went back to the pickup and brought the cricket bat back into the bunker. He walked over to where Jimmy stood and played with it a little, as if practising hits, whooshing it right and left of Jimmy's head, forcing him to duck.

'Thing is,' Jimmy said, ignoring the bat, 'I could tell you whatever shit you want. Could just say it. But how'd you know it was right? How'd you know I wisnae jist sayin it? That's your problem, ay? You'll niver know if what I say is the right story or no. You're gonnae huvtae trust me. But you canny trust me, ay no?'

Nick walked back over to the door, out of the circle of light cast by the lamp. He squatted down. The way things were turning out, it seemed that Jimmy was right. It turned out that Jimmy was smarter at this kind of thing than Nick was. How would he know if what Jimmy said was true? His only test was those words Jimmy had said under no duress, in the howff: that if the girl had seen what happened, he'd have 'swung for it'. That's what gave Nick certainty, the line from then back to now, the line that would set Ruth free from the web of lies Jimmy had built around her death, had publicised at the trial. He'd made the jury doubt Ruth, even though they'd never met her, never seen her, knew nothing about her... even though she didn't have the chance to speak in her defence. He stood up, started talking, walking round the room with the bat in his hand. Jimmy was no therapist, but he was listening. He had no choice.

'She used to be quite musical you know,' Nick said, 'She played the flute, well till you killed her anyway, but you probably know that. If she felt fed up, or upset about something, music picked her up. She was strong. Inside herself. Know what I mean? Helped me through her mother's death. Made me want to look ahead.' Nick started wandering through Ruth's childhood, picking out memories, but as he talked, he saw Jimmy opening and shutting his fists, raising and lowering his knees, stretching his toes; he saw Jimmy's eyes darting around the space, looking for possible weapons, weighing up options.

Nick gently positioned Jimmy's chin back so they faced each other close in. 'You're not listening to me, are you?' he said, 'Well. I don't need to say any more. I'm sure you get the picture. Its's a shame that you just have no idea what you missed by not taking the time to know her.'

Jimmy shifted around. 'Ma legs are killing me, man. It's like they've gone to sleep. Goan take these ropes off of us ay? I canny do much wi ma wrists still tied behind my fuckin back can I?'

'OK,' Nick said. 'I'll do it in a minute.'

Jimmy was struggling to keep his balance. 'Now,' he said, then suddenly screamed, 'Oh my back,' and doubled forwards. Instinctively Nick moved towards him to hold him up and Jimmy pushed into him, his head banging upwards on Nick's chin. As Nick staggered backwards, Jimmy kicked the Tilly lamp, smashing the glass and plunging the bunker into darkness. Jimmy attempted a kick at Nick. Nick sensed it missing him by the rush of air to the right of his head, then heard Jimmy swearing as he was jolted back by the rope behind his back.

On hands and knees, in the pitch blackness, with Jimmy's heavy breathing behind him, Nick felt his way back towards the door. He still had the bat in his hand. He pushed the door ajar and a strip of moonlight shone over to where Jimmy was struggling to regain his footing. Nick walked round the perimeter to come at him from behind, in the dark. He steadied himself and aimed a blow at his calves. It caught Jimmy hard. He groaned as all his weight came back onto his arms.

'Naw. Fuckin naw.' he gasped. 'I'm fuckin done man. Nae mair fightin, ay? That wis ma last chance. I've given it ma best shot,' he gasped for breath again, 'But I'm done. I'm fuckin done.' There was another longer pause while Jimmy recovered his breath. 'Just let us off this fuckin beam, mister, ay? Ma arms are comin ootae their fuckin sockets. Please. Just let us off this fuckin beam?'

Nick was exhilarated. He scrabbled about to find the torch and shone it on Jimmy's face.

'I could go further,' Nick said. 'What are the chances I could knock you out, kill you even, with one blow from this bat to your skull? But I don't want to kill you, do I?' He walked In a circle round Jimmy. 'But I will if I have to. If you don't fancy having your skull cracked open, you're going to have to be a very well-behaved young man from now on.' He held Jimmy's chin up with the handle of the bat. 'Understand.'

Jimmy didn't respond. Nick jerked his chin up some more.

'Understand?' he said again.

'Aye.'

Nick checked his watch. It was near to midnight. He was emotionally and physically exhausted. 'You're still pretty hard aren't you Jimmy? A hard man. Still fighting. I respect that. You know I don't believe you though, don't you? I think you're playing for time. I think you think you can still escape, that I'll make some mistake, that you'll be able to get to me, mentally, or physically. And I get it. Your hard man game is impressive, very impressive even. But it's not wise. I can assure you of that. Not wise. Not at all. All it means is that I've decided that you more you resist, the more softening up you'll need. And you know something Jimmy? Everyone has a limit, everyone, no matter how hard they are, and I now know just how hard you are. Very hard. A right hard man, all round. But the harder you are, the harder I have to work to break you. Electrodes on your balls and nipples maybe? Tear lumps of hair out of your head? A flat blade screwdriver up your bum, or even better, a chisel. How would you like that Jimmy. A chisel up your bum? The list is endless.' Nick started pacing again, pacing back and forward in front of Jimmy. 'And the thing is Jimmy,' he said, 'Everyone, even the hardest of hard men, they all have a breaking point. So, I'm going to leave you for another night... on your own... wondering all night about what punishment I've got lined up for you. Am I going to bring in a transformer, and some wires, attach them to your balls, and gradually turn up the voltage? Am I going to bring in a broom handle, that'd be better than a chisel, wouldn't it... fuck you up the arse with it. How would you like that, Jimmy? The garden broom handle... you should see how thick my garden broom is, thick as a man's arm, so thick it could stretch your arse good and wide. How does that sound Jimmy? Fucked up the arse with a broom handle. How does that fucking sound? It sounds good to me. It would be justice, don't you think? Rough justice, but justice all the same. Give you the same treatment you gave Ruth. Remember what you said about Ruth? 'Tight wee cunt,' you said. I didn't like that Jimmy, I didn't like that at all. So I'm going to make sure I say the same to your mother, only it'll be the other way round. I'll tell her that you had a tight arse, that I couldn't even get the broom handle right in it, ay? You can be thinking about that while I'm gone Jimmy, about that big fat broom handle forcing its way up your arse... again and again... all through the night, Jimmy. Think about it.' Nick picked up a stick and placed it in between the cheeks of Jimmy's backside and Jimmy jumped forward, letting out an involuntary yelp of fear.

Nick threw the stick to the side, loosened the rope at Jimmy's back a little more, lengthening it so that he could stand easy, take a few steps if he wanted. 'And by the way,' he whispered again up close behind Jimmy's ear, 'I tested this place. No-one can hear a thing from outside. It's soundproof. It's bombproof. And no-one's coming to save you. Tell you what Jimmy... tell you what.... no-one... even... knows... you're... here.'

16. Sunday morning

Back home, Nick had no trouble getting to sleep after a warmed whisky nightcap, a large one. After that, he slept through till 6, untroubled. Standing in a reviving hot shower, he went over the events of the night before again and again. People would see what he'd done as wrong, find him guilty. If Jimmy died, they'd maybe see him as a murderer. But they had to look at the case, the individual case. Wasn't that what ethics was all about? Yes, it was wrong, what he was doing, but not doing something was wrong too – letting a false story be told, one that damaged Ruth and her memory, validating the lying version of events that had been told by the very guy who had already raped and killed her – that was wrong too. You couldn't look at what he was doing to Jimmy in isolation. It was more complex than that. You had to look at the whole story: it was what Jimmy had done to Ruth that started it... not what he was doing. The only way for individuals to find their way through the moral complexity of a situation was not by following rules, but by using their moral compass. How many people would condemn a man who'd gone after the person who'd raped and murdered his daughter? And it wasn't as if he was motivated by some primitive emotional overdrive for revenge. If that had been the case, he'd just have killed Jimmy, like Matt Fowler in that film *In The Bedroom*. No. His mission was harder. He had to get Jimmy to say what had really happened. And he was going to have to use any means to do it... and some of those means might be terrible, as bad, in their way, as what had happened to Ruth. But though they might be terrible, they might also be necessary.

For how else could people learn from this story? What they'd learned so far was that his daughter had died and no-one was responsible. But there was a story to be told about where the boundaries were, who should take responsibility, to help people to see 'this is what happens if you kill innocent young women', and 'this is what happens if the law delivers an unjust verdict'. And he had to replace Jimmy's version of events with the correct story because he was the only one who could do it... And it wasn't his fault that he was reduced to these horrible methods: that was Jimmy's faulty too. It really was Jimmy's fault. It was Jimmy who'd started the whole thing... and it was Jimmy who was making the ending unnecessarily bleak, unnecessarily difficult. If Jimmy had co-operated earlier, then it needn't have got so nasty. If he co-operated now, it wouldn't get any nastier. And whatever happened, Jimmy was going to get off easy. He wasn't going to end up dead, dying alone, away from all those he loved... if there was anyone he loved, that is, or anyone that loved him.

Moral responsibility could be found more widely too: it wasn't just about Jimmy. Other people were culpable in smaller part. If the police had done their job right in the first place, assembled the right evidence, if the Fiscal had been more interested in getting the true story than in getting the easiest conviction, maybe then he wouldn't have had to do what he did. Maybe if Ruth hadn't gone with the other girl that day. What had made her go with her? What had the other girl said? Maybe she was partly responsible... not just Jimmy. Maybe if there was less porn on the internet where kids could look at it on their phones, then maybe boys of 14 wouldn't be tossing themselves off while watching rape scenes and worse. If you thought about it long enough, all the stuff that was out there, you could argue that the whole society was fucked, going down a plughole of self-indulgence... the self, the self and only the self. Everyone was to blame.

But if everyone was to blame, then no-one was to blame. And whatever anyone else might have done or said that created a world in which such crimes were possible, only one person had killed Ruth. So, in the end, it all came back to Jimmy. He was the one who killed her. And Jimmy must understand the true nature of what he did, to own it, to regret it, not just because the consequences would be long and painful, but because it was wrong.

Maybe others, if they heard the story, would learn from it too, would learn that what Jimmy did was wrong... and that people who were tempted to do that sort of thing would worry they might get caught, and that if they were caught, it would be very unpleasant for them: that was what would make this whole sorry, tragic, awful mess worthwhile. Remembering what had happened to Jimmy might make them pause, think twice. Some people, he thought, might see these arguments of his as flimsy, self-serving. But they were all he had. And as he'd thought last night, so this morning – to turn back would be even worse than going forward.

And not everyone would think he'd done wrong, would they? Suppose he'd offered his own life for that of his daughter? If only he'd had that chance, he'd have taken it, like a shot. Suppose he'd been there when Ruth was killed and he'd intervened, in an attempt to save her, but died himself, or killed Jimmy in the process. What would people say then? He'd have got a lot of sympathy then. He'd have been 'heroic', 'noble', 'brave'. So what was different about sacrificing his life this way, doing things he would never have done had it not been for these very worthy motives: to do her justice, to make people think, to shove this issue into their faces so they couldn't ignore it, couldn't kick it into the long grass, couldn't stuff it into the lumber room of issues they didn't want to deal with. He was saving her honour by sacrificing his own, wasn't he?

Suppose this was a film – it would have to be Liam Neeson playing him, who else? - what would people feel then? They'd be cheering him on, wouldn't they? Cheering him on. What was the name of that Liam Neeson film? He looked it up: *Taken.* And there were more revenge flicks. It had become a cult. Who knew? But why was it a thing? Because people liked violence? No. It was because people hated injustice, hated killers getting away with it. That's why revenge felt right and why it was allowed, in many societies, all over the world because it didn't only feel right. It was right. But what was 'right', after all? Was there such a thing at all? But there must be, cos there was certainly wrong, wasn't there? Wrong was the opposite of right... and wrong was what Jimmy had done to Ruth.

Thinking like this was helping Nick get himself worked up, stoking his anger.

What kind of society would allow Ruth's death to go unpunished, her killer walking about freely, unchanged, or maybe even coarser, less sensitive, because he'd got away with it, able and ready for the same again, not even understanding how evil it'd been... and everywhere, even here in Stirling where it happened, people were getting on with their lives as if that was alright, as if it didn't matter? They walked past. They turned their heads. 'The law had taken its course. Done its best,' they'd said. Even his own friends, his own friends for God's sake, justifying their disinterest. Someone else's problem.

Well, it wasn't alright.

It did matter. It was their problem. And it was his problem too.

Above all, it was his problem.

* * *

Nick turned off the shower. His pulse had been racing. He slowed down, long deep breaths, towelled himself dry, dressed for the day. Once they found out what he'd done, people were going to sit up and take notice of Ruth's case, the principles behind it, ask the kinds of questions he was asking. That was what would make his sacrifice worth it. For that, he now realized, was what he was doing, sacrificing himself. He didn't know the details of how it would end, but whatever those details were, he knew they weren't going to be good for him. That thought came suddenly, and it came as a kind of liberation. No point in struggling. This was the endgame and it didn't matter what happened afterwards. The life he'd known was definitely over. But it'd been over pretty much since Ruth died anyway. There had never been any way out of this mess and back into his old life. His old life was gone. And he didn't care all that much for any hypothetical new life yet to happen. The next steps weren't going to be about him though. They were all going to be about Jimmy. It has all been about him from the start really. He was the one that had no boundaries. He was a person who could kill without thinking about it, could kill and then go home and eat his breakfast. And now he'd turned Nick into someone who might do that too.

Over toast and coffee, he searched through Police Scotland's 'missing persons' page for Jimmy's name. But there was no listing for him. Yet. He googled 'Missing People Scotland' and searched there. Nothing. Maybe the London *whatsapp* to Jimmy's mother had worked? Maybe he was going to get the couple of days grace he wanted.

The clothes Nick had worn the previous night were in a black bag, ready for dumping in a supermarket bin. His pickup would need cleaned at some point. He took a quick run round the little cottage, tidying up. But this was only a cursory covering of his tracks. He wasn't going back to his old life, was he? He found Cromarty sitting on the bed in Ruth's room. 'What do you think Cromarty?' he asked. 'I did hear him. I didn't just make it up, did I? He did say that he should've "swung for it", didn't he?' Cromarty didn't answer. He picked

Cromarty up and brought him downstairs, sat him in on the hall table, looking at the front door. 'You look after the place for me,' he said, 'I don't know when I'll be back.'

He locked the door, got into the pickup, the big engine throbbing through his body as he started it up. Would Jimmy crack today? Violence and threats hadn't worked so far. It seemed that whenever he was pushed, Jimmy came back stronger. And he wasn't going to kill him in cold blood. Couldn't do it. Jimmy knew that too. Jimmy knew that the best thing he could do was to hold on to what he knew. So, what did that mean? It meant that the interrogation would have to take a new tack, he'd have to come at it from a different angle: maybe he could give Jimmy a fair chance? Free him for some kind of duel to the death? He could imagine killing him then. He'd enjoyed the combat they'd had, when he'd had to arm wrestle with him. He'd come out on top then. It would be fairer to give Jimmy a chance. But it would be risky. Nick was taller, heavier, stronger, but he wasn't a fighter. And Jimmy was a big strong lad, just coming into his prime, adept in all the arts of the street. And if he overpowered Nick, he wouldn't hesitate to kill him, with the perfect excuse. He'd been kidnapped, held captive. He pictured Jimmy on the television, being interviewed. "It was him or me. I thought he was going to kill me. He was mad, man. It was him or me." Jimmy might even end up the hero. This could end up as his story. Who would there be then to tell the world the real story, to explain what had really happened?

He slapped the steering wheel, turned the engine off and reversed back to the house. If the real point was to change the story, give Ruth back her dignity, to make people sit up and take notice, examine their own thinking, then he'd have to leave some kind of record that maybe Greg or someone else could follow up, make available to the press, put out on social media. Make sure that his side of the story, Ruth's side of the story, got out there, even if something went wrong and he wasn't there to tell the tale himself.

It was about injustice. And it was about getting the right story for Ruth. That was what Dorothy had said, on the first anniversary of Ruth's death. Nick pictured her sitting that day at the window table in the Sherbrooke. 'The least we can do is defend Ruth's honour,' she'd said. 'She was raped and he got away with it. As far as I'm concerned, she was killed too, murdered.' He'd thought of what she'd said so many times before and done nothing about it, forgotten it, brushed over it. How could he have forgotten her saying that? What else had he forgotten?

He got out of the pickup and went back into the house. He phoned Greg and got Sheila.

'You'll be lucky,' she said, 'It's Sunday, and it's not even seven. He's not up yet,' she said. 'Will I get him to phone you?' And then she added, 'I'm telling you now if it's to go for a run, he can't go. We're taking the girls through to Glasgow today. Pollok House and the gardens.'

'No worries, Sheila,' he said, 'Just ask him to phone me anyway.'

'What you been up to anyway Nick?' she asked.

'Oh, this and that,' he said.

'How about you come through to Glasgow with us? Have a day with the girls? I'll even buy you an ice cream.'

Nick walked over to the window and looked out at his little back garden.

'Nick? Are you still there? Nick?'

'I'm still here Sheila. Sorry. Just get Greg to phone me, will you?'

Nick had brushed his teeth and was clearing away his breakfast things when Greg called him back.

'So, what's up man?'

'I was down in London,' he said, 'I had to go down for a quick meeting.'

'With Sam you-know-who?'

'No. But just by chance she ran into me outside King's Cross.'

'Just by chance? I don't think so.'

'No. It wasn't like that. It was. It was just pure chance. She was going to a meeting.'

'Aye. Right.'

'Anyway. It was good to see her. And it was just as a friend. I don't want her messing with my head again.'

'It's not my head I'd like her to mess with.'

'Do you never give it up?'

'So. What's up? You were pretty wound up during the week.'

'I'm still pretty wound up, Greg. I wonder what the hell my life is for. What is my unique contribution to this planet? I've concluded that the planet would be better off without me.'

'Whoa up there. Steady on man.'

'Not really. I'm not sure I'm even important to myself.' He laughed a bitter laugh. 'Changing the subject, have you ever seen a film called *In the Bedroom*? Sissy Spacek and that English actor, you know the one...'

'No I don't...'

'Tom..'

'Cruise? ...'

'I said English.'

'Courtney?'

'No.. Tom .... You know ... He was in *The Full Monty* ... Big guy. Older. In his fifties maybe. You must remember him.'

'It doesn't matter. I've not seen the film.'

'OK. Well I think you should watch it. I watched it recently and it had a big effect on me. It might tell you a lot about how I'm feeling.'

'*In the Bedroom* huh? This sounds like a film I should watch with Sheila. Might give her some ideas.'

'No. It's not that kind of film. Anyway. I just wanted to say, as well... I was thinking in the middle of the night.'

'As you do...'

'Yes. As you do... the film got me thinking. I was thinking about how I've been - passive, very passive, just letting things happen. Remember that night on the train. Remember how I told you how good it felt to grab that annoying little runt who was upsetting everyone, grab him by the throat. It felt good for a reason. I was actually doing something, making something happen, not sitting about waiting for other people to do things. I've been thinking that's what I've been doing wrong since Ruth was killed. Letting other people take control and watching them do it. Waiting around for them to do things and then reacting,' his voice had been getting louder, louder. 'I've been waiting, watching, doing fuck all, just watching while other people did nothing, walked away from it, washed their hands.'

'All right mate, no need to shout... I can hear you... but I'm not sure I know what you mean, where you're going with this.'

'You will.'

'Eh?'

'And another thing. I've started worrying what would happen if I died. Would there be anything of me left? If I knew I was going to die tomorrow, or next week, would I live the rest of my life differently? Do the things I really wanted to do?'

'Yes,' Greg's tone was playful, trying to move the conversation into a different gear. 'And are you intending to die anytime soon?'

'Greg,' Nick said, 'We none of us know the day nor the hour. I'm sure you learned that in your bible class same as me. So I'm telling this to you... in case, well...'

'In case what?'

'In case anything happens to me.'

'OK. This sounds serious. Do I need a pen?'

'No. Not now. Thing is I'm putting some stuff up in the Cloud that I'd like you to take care of if anything does happen to me.'

'Go on then.'

'I'm going to email you a delayed message from my Outlook account with the username and password for a Cloud account. You should get it Monday morning. I don't want you to have it before then. There'll be an audio file up there called 'Nick'. If anything happens to me over the weekend, I want you to listen to it and then use it how you see fit. It might explain some things. But if nothing odd happens, don't open it mate. I'm relying on you. I'll explain later. One way or the other, I'll phone you back in a couple of days. If there's no phone call, no other contact, before Monday, or if you know that something bad has happened to me, you'll know that's' the trigger to download that file and listen to it.'

'This sound very mysterious mate. What's going on?'

'Och, y'know. You waken up in the middle of the night and you realize you're all alone. No-one knows what you've done, why you've done it. I'd ask Dorothy, you know Clare's mother. She's the last relative I have left... but I don't know if she's up to dealing with 'the cloud'... and she's in Wales. So, poor old me. I'd much rather have someone else, someone more reliable, but it turns out the only person that I can really trust is you, you bugger.'

'If you've got something on your mind just spit it out now mate?'

'It's not something for the phone. And we're both going to be busy today, aren't we? Sheila said you're all off through to Glasgow. Kids day out.'

'Sheila's day out more like,' Greg said, 'She's been after me for ages to take the kids to Pollok House. One of them has a project for school they're working on.'

'Great stuff. Well don't let me hold you back. You OK for Wednesday.'

'If anyone can be sure of anything. After all, we none of us know the day... remember?'

'Ha bloody ha. I'll phone you in a couple of days. But in the meantime, remember what I said to you. If anything happens, the explanation'll be in the Cloud.'

* * *

Nick put the kettle back on. He took an A4 page and sketched out a mindmap of what he wanted to say, used it to structure his recording: Ruth's death; the dilemmas he'd wrestled with; digging deeper than the police could, or would... than the prosecution service could... or would; how he knew of Jimmy's guilt and why he couldn't accept the judgment of the court; the overriding rationale for his course of action, the only course of action any father in his situation would take: that the only acceptable ending, the only one that might bring anything worthwhile out of this, was to give Ruth a voice, if people could be made to reflect on what had happened, if lessons could be learned. He finished by saying that he'd post another file if he did get a fuller true account of her death from Jimmy, but if he didn't, this would have to stand as his record.

He uploaded the *mp3* file and headed back out to the pickup. The sun was fully up when he arrived back at the bunker. It was going to be a fine day. He stood outside the door for a moment. He could hear nothing. He'd brought nothing extra with him. He took a deep breath, put the key in the padlock and opened it. Torch in hand, he stepped inside.

* * *

He didn't know, but should've maybe anticipated, that loosening the ropes tying Jimmy had made it easier for him to reach some broken glass on the floor of the bunker, the glass Nick hadn't cleared up after the Tilly lamp smashed. It had been a bit of a feat, but

Jimmy had had plenty time to work at it. He'd used the glass to cut the rope binding his ankles and with greater freedom of movement, he'd been able to hold a piece of glass between his heels, to kneel back towards it and to work away at the bonds that tied his wrists behind his back. After freeing himself, he'd been limbering up, stretching, keeping loose. Whenever Jimmy heard the padlock banging against the metal door, he'd positioned himself behind the door, waiting.

Once Nick was fully in the room, Jimmy jumped him from behind the door, a shard of glass in his hand. Nick heard the movement and stooped a little. It was just enough. If the blow had struck him on the neck as Jimmy had intended it might have been serious, but the glass only damaged the shoulder of his jacket and Jimmy had overreached and overbalanced, such was the effort he put into it. Nick hit up with his elbow and caught the side of Jimmy's face. Jimmy staggered back against the door but, as Nick turned to face him, Jimmy caught him with a kick between the legs. Nick folded over in pain and Jimmy followed with a right-handed uppercut on his chin that sent him sprawling back on to the floor. Jimmy stood for a moment, the open door behind him and Nick dazed on the floor in front. He was tempted to finish Nick off, but it was a risk. Nick was strong, and he was trying to get up again. So Jimmy turned on his heel and ran for his life, along the track past Nick's pickup and onto the road. He heard a car somewhere down the hill so headed in that direction. If there was a road, there'd be other cars, people, escape. But by the time he reached the main road it was Sunday morning quiet: not a car in sight.

Jimmy was running along the road now, but the next engine he heard was behind him. It was Nick's pickup starting up. It'd been facing uphill. Nick would have to turn, then drive down so he still had a minute or two to find somewhere to hide. The road offered no cover. The pickup would catch him up in no time. But there was a small clump of trees at the side of the field opposite, some way in. If he could make it over there, he'd be able to hide, see which direction Nick took, hole up till it was safe to come down and head back to the road. Even if Nick saw him in the field and chased him, there was a farmhouse over to the right, half a mile maybe, a bit more. He could head for there, knock them up. He scrambled over the fence, ripping his jeans on the barbed wire that ran along the top, then sprinted towards the trees.

* * *

When Nick had first tried to stand up, his legs had buckled. His balls were aching and he felt a bit sick. He staggered and had to hold on to the door to stay upright. The biggest risk was if Jimmy got down to the main road. Nick picked up the longest piece of rope left on the bunker floor and the cricket bat. He eased himself into the pickup but had to sit for a minute before he fired it into a five point turn on the narrow road. It was Sunday. He prayed the main road would be empty. Just before the junction, he pulled onto the verge and jumped out. Running down towards the main road, he couldn't see Jimmy anywhere to right or left on the long straight stretches of road, so he decided to work his way back up the hill looking for clues to which direction Jimmy had taken. As he turned, he noticed a strip of denim waving in the breeze on the barbed wire opposite. There seemed to be no cover in those fields save for a clump of trees, twenty or thirty yards into the field. A thoughtful cow was looking at the pickup. It turned and looked at the clump. Then looked back at Nick. Clever cow.

The adrenalin was pumping round his system now, the pain gone. He vaulted the fence and loped towards the trees. A few yards short he stopped and turned suddenly. Just in case. Nothing. No-one was on the road. He turned back and saw a foot hanging down from the tree canopy. The foot disappeared again. Nick moved forward cautiously, peering from side to side. Under the canopy of branches, at the point where he'd seen the foot, he stopped, tempting Jimmy to jump. There was a rustle above and he dived to the side. With nothing to break his fall, Jimmy crashed face down on the ground beside Nick, rather than landing on him as he'd intended. In a flash Nick was straddling Jimmy's back, his arms round his neck, pulling his head up.

'Guess who?' he said.

Jimmy's hands were trapped under his body. He'd been winded by the fall. He couldn't move. Nick jerked his head back again. A strong sharp pull and he'd maybe break his neck. But he couldn't kill him like that, defenceless, cold-blooded. And what would happen to the story then. There'd be no-one left to tell it. Except for the girl. Nick paused for a minute. The girl? Why had he not made more of an effort to find her? Maybe he should've gone back to her? Hired a private detective? It had just been so hard to believe she had been involved in the killing, or the rape, knew anything about it. Well, that was all academic. He was where he was. If this all worked out the way he hoped, he'd maybe go after the girl later.

He took the rope and tied Jimmy's hands and ankles as before, hoisted him up over his shoulders in a fireman's lift and headed back towards the road. He was almost there when he heard a car coming towards them. There was nowhere to hide. It felt like he was in a scene from a black comedy. But this was no comedy. Here he was in the early morning light standing in a field near the road, muddied from the struggle, his face grey like death, a body thrown like a sack over his shoulders. The heads of the two people in the car swiveled to keep him in view as the car slowed then passed by. Even worse, he recognized them. It was Mr and Mrs Campbell, two of his clients. They lived in Drymen, in a bungalow with a large vegetable and fruit garden where he'd done some structural work.

Jimmy started shouting, 'Help, Help, Help!!'

Nick threw him to the ground, where he wriggled about, still shouting.

The car was past them now, but he could see Mrs Campbell looking round at them. Who would they speak to when they got to wherever they were going... probably back home to Drymen? He couldn't take Jimmy back to the bunker now. He might only have an hour, less, maybe minutes before someone arrived, before the police started snooping around. He couldn't go back to Stirling either. It was only a question of time. They'd find things in his house. He had no choice. He'd have to run. And Jimmy would have to come with him.

He dumped Jimmy, wriggling and swearing, in the boot of the pickup. As he shut the tailgate, two collared doves scuttled off from a nearby tree. He reversed back up to the hut. There he tied up Jimmy's arms and legs more securely and lightly covered his mouth. If he choked this time, he choked – so be it. Fuck. He didn't want it to happen, but at least, if it did, he wouldn't have to worry what to do next. Just another unintended death. So much for his careful bloody planning. He'd be judged to have been reckless. That was the word, wasn't it? 'Reckless'. Reckless endangerment. Maybe the Procurator Fiscal would go for culpable homicide, not murder: that would be rich.

This was the endgame now, running for cover. No point in making it easy for people to follow him though. He went inside and picked up the remaining pieces of rope and any other obvious signs he could see of his short occupation. He padlocked the door and threw the key into the undergrowth. Climbing into the back of the pickup, he knelt over Jimmy. 'We're moving house,' he said, 'Just you and me. We're going somewhere you can't escape. And this'll be our final journey. The end of the story you started when you killed my daughter.' He lay the carpet over the trussed-up body. He checked his phone. It was just after eight. Fifteen minutes later, he'd crossed by small roads to the other side of the Forth Valley and was on his way towards Callander. From there he could head on towards the Highlands of Scotland and their wild spaces.

17. Destination

When Greg put down the phone after the early morning call from Nick that Sunday, he didn't have time to think. Alice and Jess jumped on him. Sunday was the one morning in the week when the family had a long lazy breakfast, the girls still in their pyjamas, watching a film or some cartoons together, before dressing up for the eleven o'clock family service that Sheila insisted they attend. But today they weren't going to Church. They were going to Glasgow. Greg calmed the girls down and settled them in front of the TV while Sheila had her shower. When she came back through to the bedroom, she found him sitting on the bed. 'We need to talk about Nick,' he said, looking out of the window at the steep slopes of the Ochils, just emerging into daylight. 'I'm worried he might do something really stupid,' he said. 'The way he was talking...'

'He's been more wound up recently, hasn't he?'

'This morning, he talked about what he wanted me to do in the event of his sudden death. Said he'd woken up in the middle of the night worried about it, needed to get it off his chest. Told me to listen to some kind of audiofile he's put up in the Cloud... he's sent me an e.mail link on delay with the username and password, but I won't get it till Monday. I've to make sure it gets out there somehow, what he's said on it, but only if something happened to him. Said it would explain his side of the story.'

'What story?'

'There's only one story just now as far as he's concerned, isn't there? Ruth. Ruth. And more Ruth. It's the only thing he cares about.'

'So you think he wants to do something risky? And you're his backstop if it doesn't come off?'

'Sure, that's the whole point. It wasn't anything specific, more the overall implication of all this cloak and dagger stuff. I think he could be going to do something stupid.'

'What else did he say?'

'He told me he was down in London on Friday night and Saturday morning.' Greg said. '*For a meeting*, he said, but when I asked him last week what he was doing at the weekend he never mentioned a meeting in London... Anyway it seems that he met that Sam Hill when he was down there, you know, from the telly. I wonder if he's still... you know...' Greg made a couple of crude thrusting movements and Sheila crinkled up her face in distaste. Greg's temper flared. 'OK! OK already!' he shouted, 'I know what a prude you are.' Sheila said nothing. He took a few deep breaths, scratching his head. 'Sorry,' he said, 'Sorry. It's just... you know... Anyway... ' he took a couple more breaths.

'Go on,' Sheila said, 'Go on.'

'So... he said he met her "by accident" – believe that if you like. I think it's all tied together somehow, the phone call, the trip to London, Sam Hill.'

'So... maybe he doesn't want us involved?'

'No. He does. Why else would he tell me about the recording?' Greg stood up and walked round behind Sheila. He put his hands on her shoulders and kneaded them a little till he could feel her begin to relax. 'I think I should go along to Nick's now. Listen to the recording.'

'Mmmm...' Sheila broke away. 'I thought you said it was a time delayed message, with the password..'

'Yes.. that was his Cloud account... but if I got into his computer?'

'Yeah... maybe.. but that'll be a login as well, won't it?'

'Yes but he's obviously forgotten.'

'What?'

'He gave me the login for his computer ages ago. Just in case anything happened to him,' he said.

But he didn't want you to get the message till Monday, did he? And even then, he told you that you were only to use it if something happened to him. It feels a bit creepy. Going into his place when he's not there.'

'The whole thing's a bit creepy, from A to Z,' Greg said. 'But I think I should go.'

'It's still early. I guess you could be at the house if you really think it's the right thing to do. You'll need to be back before ten though. No later. I don't want to disappoint the girls, Alice especially. You know how she's been building up to this. It's all about her school project. Can't let her down.'

Greg kissed Sheila on the cheek and threw on some clothes while she went down to make herself a cup of coffee. He picked up the keys for the Volvo in the hallway and opened the front door, then turned and came back through to Sheila in the kitchen. 'There was something else,' he said, 'It was a bit strange, but then it must have been on his mind, was maybe related in some way. He was talking about a film. Sissy Spacek and Tom somebody. *In the Bedroom*, something like that. Have you heard of it?'

'I've seen it. Years ago. Before I met you!' she laughed.

Greg screwed up his face at her. 'He told me to watch the film. Said it might explain how he was feeling. I joked about the bedroom... couldn't see any connection – turns out it's not that sort of film.'

'No,' Sheila said. 'Anything but. In the film... it's about...' Sheila fiddled with her mug of coffee, as if she couldn't get the words out.

'What is it Sheila?'

'It's the film. I've just seen the connection. It's about what happens in a family when a child is killed... well maybe not a child. It's their son... in his twenties maybe...'

Through the open door they could hear Robin Williams singing *A Friend Like Me.*

'And...?'

'In the film, the killer gets away with it. Is out free. The parents talk... in the intimacy of the bedroom - that's where the title comes from - they decide to take their revenge.'

Greg put down his keys and sat down. Sheila poured him a coffee.

'There's more,' she said. 'The father? In the film?' She looked out of the window, wiped a spill of coffee from the worktop.

Greg waited. 'The father in the film? ...' he prompted eventually.

She hesitated again, swallowed, 'The father gets his best friend to help him. He kills the killer. A revenge killing. He and his friend bury the body in the woods.'

'And so... what? You think he wants me to help kill and bury Ruth's killer?'

'Would you?'

'No. Obviously not. Honestly. All he asked me to do was to go and listen to this Cloud recording... and only if anything's happened to him, that is.'

'You said yourself that the boy who killed Ruth was scum, not fit to live...'

'Those were just words.'

Sheila walked over to the living room door and looked in on the girls. She shut it and came back to sit with Greg. They sat in silence for some time before agreeing that Greg should phone Nick. There was no answer, so he left a message: 'Phone me Nick. Don't do anything stupid. Phone me.'

'I'd better go now,' he said, 'See if I can access what he's left on the computer. I'll come straight back.'

'Make sure you do,' she said, 'And don't do anything stupid.'

Fifteen minutes later, Greg had used the key Nick kept taped under the front window ledge and was standing in Nick's small hallway. He made for the desk, opened up the computer and found the delayed message with the cloud login and password in his e.mail. He downloaded the mp3 file and listened to it in the car as he drove back home. He stopped the car in a layby and tried Nick's phone again. Still no answer. It was just after nine. He phoned Sheila and told her what he'd heard – the capture of Jimmy, the ex-army bunker, Nick's pursuit of the real story of what happened to Ruth...

'We should tell the police, shouldn't we?' she said, 'Hand over the audiofile?'

'You're kidding me, right?'

'What else is there? You're not going to get involved, are you? Nick has nothing to lose. You're different. Your family still need you.'

'Let me at least go out the bunker. See what's there.'

'Don't be crazy Greg,' Sheila screamed, 'What are you going to do if you find.... I don't know... a dead body, Nick deranged, Nick's body. Oh God. This is awful.'

'But maybe it won't be so bad. Maybe he's not done anything, maybe I can help him see reason.'

'Maybe you should just keep out of it. We were supposed to be going to Glasgow, with the girls. We don't need this. We don't need to get involved. Oh God. What should we do?'

'I need to go, love. I need to go. We can't pretend this hasn't happened. And he's given me Sam Hill's number too. Says I've to let her know what he's done, wants her to have the right story, but only if anything happens to him.'

'She's not important. It's the police that matter now. And we can't become accessories after the fact. If the police ask us about him, we'll have to tell them. It's our duty. What if they turn up here?'

'Why would they?'

'They're maybe looking for him already. And if they don't find him at his house they'll come here. You're his best friend.'

'So, don't be here. Take the girls on the train then. Don't answer your mobile. Just get the hell out of the house.'

Sheila said nothing.

'Listen. This is something I have to do. I have to do it. He's my friend. And he's never needed me more. Can you imagine us going to Glasgow and pretending this hadn't happened, that I hadn't heard the recording he left, then finding out later that we could have averted a tragedy in the making?'

'But what can you do, Greg? You're just going to get involved and become part of the tragedy.'

'I can't do anything else. Look I'm going to have to go. Tell the girls I'm really sorry. Get a taxi over to Stirling and take a train through. I'll keep you posted during the day.'

He cut the call, turned on the engine, engaged gear, then slipped back into neutral and switched it off again. After Nick had stopped seeing Sam, Greg'd followed her on twitter, instagram. Now he had her phone number. She was obviously connected to what was going on, else why had he met her in London? Maybe he'd talked over some of his plans with her. He took a moment to prepare himself, a few calming breaths, then called.

'Who's this?' she said.

'My name's Greg Bright,' he said, 'I'm a friend of Nick Innocenti, a very good friend, and I'm afraid he's in deep trouble.'

'Go on,' she said.

'I know Nick saw you recently and it might help to know what he said to you. I hope I can trust you,' he said, 'You see, I think he's gone off the page. Taken the law into his own hands.'

'Get to the point please.'

'Alright then. We, that's my wife and I, we're very worried about what he's done or might do. I thought you might know something. Maybe he said something when he was down in London. You see I think he may have taken the young man who killed his daughter captive. He desperately wants to find out how she died.'

'Took him captive? You mean, like, "kidnapped" or something?'

'He left me a recording, a kind of testament. What did he say to you when he was with you in London? What did he talk about? Please. It's really important.'

'He was a bit incoherent, almost unhinged. He was very unkempt, not just his appearance, but something in him.' She was speaking slowly, as if trying to catch up. Greg liked the intimacy of her voice close in his ear. It was sensual. Some women just have it, he was thinking. 'I put it down to his overnight journey,' she said, 'but it was more than that.' He could almost hear her thinking on the other end of the line. 'Turn that down darling, would you?' she said. Then there was the noise of a door shutting. 'If you think he's at risk you must get the police involved.' Her voice was clearer now, professional, authoritative.

'No, you don't understand. It's not like that. He's needing support. I don't think he cares if he lives or dies, as long as he gets to the bottom of what happened to his daughter. That's what he talks about in this recording he left. He wants people to know exactly what happened and to clear her name. He's desperate... and the police – they might trample all over it, like they did before. Or worse. Maybe them getting involved might precipitate a more violent end than needs to happen.'

'That's a bit dramatic,' she said, 'Violent ends. I could see a lot of sides in Nick, but violence didn't come into it.'

'It is dramatic. The whole thing is dramatic. And you're one person who might be able to stop him doing something really stupid. Could you come up to Scotland? I need your help if I'm going to stop this getting worse. I know it's a lot to ask, but if you care about him, now's the time to show it.'

'Look , eh,' she searched for his name, 'Greg wasn't it? I don't know what influence I can have. We're not in any kind of relationship. He's an adult. Making his own choices. And I've got a full diary. I'm really sorry but...'

'His emotions are, like, totally fried. This could turn into a real tragedy. I don't want to hear that he's topped himself and we could've done something about it. Do you want to hear that?'

She didn't answer.

'Listen. You're our best shot. I'll send you a link to the file. You can listen to it for yourself. See what you think then.' Greg was nervously tapping out an awkward rhythm on the steering wheel. Then he changed the angle of attack. 'And whatever happens, what a fantastic story this is going to be - man whose daughter is killed isn't happy with the justice system. Takes the law into his own hands. And you're at the heart of it. You can't just walk away from a story like that.'

'So...' her tone changed a little... maybe that new angle had worked... maybe she could see herself as the heroine of the story. 'You think you can find him?'

'I think so,' Greg said.

'Then what?'

'That's what I need you for, your help. He'll do anything for you. You could be the only person who can save him from whatever mess he's getting into.'

'OK' she said, 'Send me the file.' She dictated her e.mail address. 'I'll get back to you.'

Greg had a quick look on the council website to double check the location of the bunker. It only took him another fifteen minutes or so to get out there. He walked around it. It looked bomb-proof - concrete walls and roof, no windows he could see. The door was locked but the muddy footprints and disturbed vegetation said that it'd been opened recently. He rattled the door. Shouted out. Knocked it with a stick. No answer. He took a turn round the back. Nothing much to see there. He put his ear to one of the air vents but could hear nothing. Where the hell was he then, if he wasn't here? Greg jumped back into the Volvo and tried Nick's number again. No answer. As he made his way back to Stirling, the fuel warning light lit up, so he stopped off at Sainsburys to fill up. Anne Armitage, a colleague who worked as a receptionist in the council office where Greg was based, was filling up at an adjacent pump.

'Greg,' she said, 'What are you up to?'

'Oh, usual Sunday,' he said, 'We're heading off to Glasgow today I think, with the girls.' He turned away.

'A funny thing,' she said, 'I wouldn't mention it only I know that you know that man, you know, the one whose daughter died a couple of years back. I've seen the two of you out running together. Nick something? It was in all the papers.'

He turned back round. 'Yes,' he said, 'Nick Innocenti.'

'That's him. I maybe shouldn't say, just gossip I suppose, but I met Mrs. Campbell down the road. She was coming in early to Church here in Stirling. You know her. Very tall woman. Head of white hair.' He looked blank. 'Used to work in Roads. She stays out by Fintry. Or is it Drymen? ' Greg still looked blank. 'Well, she couldn't wait to tell me that she'd seen your friend Nick, you know, earlier this morning. He was standing in a field out Kippen way. "Looked like death warmed up," she said. And she thought there was blood on his face. The thing is, and this is the really strange bit of it,' she put the nozzle back on its hook, walked over to Greg and looked round, as if checking no-one else was listening, 'The thing is...' she looked around again, 'It seems he was carrying a man over his shoulder and the man was tied up.' Her eyes widened. 'The man seemed to be struggling and Nick threw him on the ground. And her husband, well, he just drove on. "None of our business," he said. "Best not to get involved." She was shaken up. Had to tell me all about it. I said to her that they really should tell the police. Couldn't just leave it like that. Poor man. What has he not been through? I hope you don't mind me telling you. It's just I remember that you and him were good friends. And then when I saw you there.'

'Thanks,' he said. 'Call the police? Yes of course. So, did they do that?' They were walking into the cash desk to pay.

'Well,' she said, 'Her husband was hurrying her into Church, telling her they were late, but she said they weren't late. I think he sets the church up before the service and she sets up the teas. She will phone I'm sure, but maybe after church. And she's bound to tell others there... she was desperate to tell me.'

He picked up some milk. 'By the way,' he said, 'Do you know what time this was. When they saw him.'

'I don't know. Like I said, it was early for church. Before nine maybe?'

'Thanks,' Greg said. 'Thanks. I'll maybe give him a call. Go round to his house. See what's what.'

* * *

When Greg got back home, Sheila was still there. She was fizzing. 'Don't you dare put the phone down on me again and then not take my calls,' she said, 'And I don't know why you'd think I'd want to go anywhere on the train while all this is going on.' She stamped her foot. 'And I'd no idea where you were! I was scared you'd gone off to that bunker. What might've happened to you there!'

'Let's continue this in the kitchen,' Greg said, 'I'll settle the girls down.'

'I want to watch *Aladdin* again,' Jess said.

'Well I don't,' her sister said.

They agreed on *The Jungle Book*, the 1960s one. They never tired of that.

Greg went over all the details with Sheila - what he'd seen at the bunker, Sam Hill's phone call, Mrs Armitage, Mrs Campbell, Nick not answering his phone.

'So,' Sheila summarized when he'd finished, 'We have a locked bunker which Nick may have been using to imprison the guy he thinks killed Ruth, interrogate him, maybe worse. And he's not answering his phone so we've no idea where he is now. It's like we're in the middle of some terrible thriller Greg, and we don't know the rules, what happens next.'

'Well if you think about it, it looks like this lad might have escaped,' Greg said, 'And Nick's brought him back. That's when he was seen in the field. Nick's not there now and neither is his pickup. He's not answering his phone. We have to assume the police have been told about him being seen in the field, or if they haven't yet, they'll know soon enough. And that he's taken off somewhere.'

'But where? He could go in any direction from there.'

'But we know him. We should be able to make an educated guess at least. Where does he know well? I'm trying to think is there anywhere he's mentioned recently. I'd really like to get to him before the police do. See if there's anything we can do to avoid this tragedy getting any worse.'

'He's been doing a lot of hill walking hasn't he? The Munros? So he knows the roads to the north well.'

'And he loves the islands. Skye. Mull. Yes, Mull. I think he used to go there as a child - the western part, towards Iona. Can we get the map of Mull and have a look? I might remember the name of the place.'

They laid their old road map out on the table. Greg leaned over and pointed at the map. 'If he was going to Mull, he'd take this road up here, look, through Callander, past Loch Lubnaig then up and west here to Crianlarich, or if he was going from out the Kippen road he might go up Loch Lomondside – that's another route to Crianlarich. Maybe shorter. It's after that that the road divides, North to Glencoe and West to Oban past Loch Awe here. Well, he'd take that road if he was going anywhere up west.'

'I know the road Greg. You don't need to tell me.' Sheila said, then she poked him with her finger. 'Didn't that guy Thomas, what was his name? Arnold? Albert? It began with an A I'm sure. You know the guy. Used to live along from Nick. We used to see him in the front garden. He was always talking about moving north. Didn't he do it, move up there eventually? Bought a garage or something, didn't he?'

"I don't remember."

'Yes.. he was always talking about his sweet peas. You must remember him.'

'Yes. The sweet pea man. I remember him. So?' There was irritation in his voice. What was she on about?

'Well Nick might have called in at a garage about there don't you think?' she paused, 'Alistair, wasn't that what he was called, Alistair Thomas. I remember him telling us about it. Do you not remember? Wasn't it Crianlarich? What a good location he was in, lots of good trade in the summer, easier in the winter? You must remember him.'

'So, I still don't follow.'

'Well, can we not phone him just now? See whether Nick went past there this morning, called in?'

'Bit of a long shot isn't it?' then his tone perked up, more optimistic, 'I know,' he said as if he'd just had a great idea, and then slowly, as if he was speaking to a child. 'Why don't we list all the possibilities, all points of the compass, then phone some random people on each route one by one? Or maybe he's gone back to the Abbey Craig woods, to the wee howff where it all started. He's maybe there now and we're wasting time here. Or maybe we should just stick a pin in the fucking map?'

'Don't swear at me Greg,' she said, 'And anyway what's your brilliant suggestion?'

Greg shrugged. Maybe phoning a few people wasn't a bad idea.

'So' Sheila said, 'We could've phoned the garage by now, while I've been listening to you talking rubbish.'

Just at that Greg's phone rang. Sam Hill. He turned his back on Sheila, walked into the hall and pressed answer.

'Greg?'

'That's me,' he whispered.

'Thanks for the file. I'm at London City airport. I'm coming up. My flight gets into Glasgow airport about 12.30.'

'Great...' he took a quick look over his shoulder to make sure Sheila wasn't behind him, 'In fact that's fantastic. Absolutely brilliant.'

'What's the weather like up there? Sorry. Stupid question. I'll bring my rain gear and my walking boots.'

'Actually it's a pretty fine day,' he said enthusiastically, aware that he was sounding like an ass, but unable to keep the excitement out of his voice.

'Can you pick me up?'

'Of course I can. Absolutely. It's great that you're coming,' he said. 'Text me your flight number and I'll wait at arrivals with your name.'

'Never mind my name,' she said, 'I'm sure you'll recognize me.'

Greg knew he shouldn't feel happy. His friend was in deep trouble. It was a terrible tragic situation. But in the middle of it all, he was going to pick up Sam Hill at Glasgow airport and that felt good. Not good exactly. Exciting, that was it. Exciting. And maybe they could save Nick, save him from himself. Sheila was on her phone now. He stole out of the room and went upstairs to change his clothes. When he came back into the kitchen, Sheila got a surprise. 'Where are you going?' she said, 'Looks like you're all dressed up for something. And that aftershave. God you're stinking.'

'That was Sam Hill on the phone.' He couldn't keep the smile off his face. 'She's listened to the audiofile that Nick left. She wants in on the action. Might be a good story for her... in her professional capacity of course.' He paused for effect. 'She asked me to pick her up at the airport.'

Sheila looked amused. 'And of course you'd know what she sounds like in her professional capacity.'

Greg ignored the comment. 'Her flight arrives at 12.30.'

'So,' Sheila snorted, 'Sam Hill's riding to the rescue and you've volunteered to fetch her at the airport. Look at you, all dressed up. You realise,' and she started laughing, 'She'll get one whiff of that aftershave and she'll be on the next flight back to London.'

'That's right Sheila, bring me down, make me feel small. Thanks.' He fastened the buttons on his jacket. 'Well I don't need your advice. Sam'll be a great help. Look at all the experience she has, the contacts.'

'Did she say anything about the police?'

'She's going to contact them but wants to hang fire a bit longer, see if we can turn anything else up - where he's gone, what's happened.'

'Well you may want to know what I found out before you go and pick up wonder woman.'

He said nothing.

'From the garage? Remember? My stupid idea. "Why didn't I phone every garage in Scotland?" you said.'

'Go for it then. You've obviously found something, genius.'

'Too right. Not just something. We've found him. Nick passed through there earlier this morning, stopped at Alistair's garage to fill his tank. Not long since. He said Nick'd looked washed-out, pale, unshaven, dirty – *as if he'd been digging in his garden* was the phrase used. And he'd been alone. No other passengers, at least none that could be seen. And there's more. Nick asked Alistair to check ferry times for him.'

'Which ferry?'

'The Mull ferry,' she was excited now too, 'We don't have to search Scotland. Just Mull.'

'Mull's a big place,' Greg said.

'Something else too, Mr. Huffy. If Alistair said there were no-passengers in his pickup, what does that suggest to you?'

'Oh God.' Greg rolled his lips together several times, 'God. You think he's killed him... the body over his shoulders in the field, remember... and now he's heading out somewhere to hole up?'

'I'm not presuming anything. He could have him hidden in the boot of that pickup of his. Apparently, he tried to buy a car phone charger, but Alistair didn't have one. That explains why he's not answering any calls.'

They pored over the map of Mull. 'Look there.' Sheila pointed, 'I remember that name, Bunessan, on that long finger pointing out to Iona the Ross of Mull. Do you not remember him talking about Bunessan? Is that not where his parents used to take him on holiday when he was a kid? If he's going to hole out somewhere, it might be around there, somewhere he knows. I'll book you on a ferry Greg. Take your charger and get on that road now.'

'You're forgetting. I'm meeting Sam Hill at the airport at 12.30.'

'Oh geez... how long is that going to take? Glasgow airport to Mull?'

'It's quicker from the airport than it is from here. Erskine Bridge. Then up Loch Lomondside. Give me a minute. He fiddled with his phone. Google says it's two and quarter hours from the airport to Oban. We can aim for a ferry after 3, if there are no hold-ups.'

Sheila had been googling ferry times. 'There's a ferry *exactly at* three,' she said, 'So you'll need to make good time. And first you can drop me and the girls in Glasgow. We'll have a nice day at the shops. I might even treat them to their tea at that nice restaurant we used to go to... you know?... the one behind the Centre... And maybe the cinema after that, if there's something suitable. The one thing I don't want is to be here if the police come calling.' She packed him a daysack. Water, some snacks, a fleece blanket, first aid kit, torch, map and compass. Greg wore his walking gear... boots, fleece, rainjacket.

It was going to be some day.

18. Mull

After Nick left the bunker behind, he felt strangely calm. Even in these terrible moments, it was comforting to see the mountainscape coming into view ahead of him in the early morning light as he cut across country towards Callander, the familiar sweep of the mountains of the Highland Boundary Fault, from Ben Lomond in the west to Ben Vorlich in the east. He'd travelled these roads many times before, for work, with Clare and Ruth on holiday, heading for a day in the hills. He could almost pretend that this was just one more such journey... that he hadn't kidnapped Jimmy Stevens, his daughter's killer... that he didn't have him trussed up in the back of the pickup.

And anyway, what did it really matter, what he did or didn't do? The mountains didn't care. They'd still be there long after he was gone. They'd looked down on vicious cruelties much worse than anything he'd done, or would do, on Roman legions battling savage Celts, on Edward of England and his son on their journeys north to hammer the Scots. On Bonnie Prince Charlie laying siege to Stirling Castle. Dead now. They were all dead. And Clare was dead. And Ruth was dead. And soon enough he'd be dead too. There was no big story, no great meaning to life. Just little stories like his, pathetic little stories that didn't mean shit, just one more *petit recit*.

Petits recits. That little phrase of Lyotard had just popped into his head from nowhere. He'd had to write an essay on Lyotard's philosophy when he was a student. He'd rejected his ideas, of course. Naïve and idealistic as he was then, he hadn't understood... couldn't... Lyotard's vision that nothing really mattered, that all we are doing when we make up the 'little stories' we tell ourselves about our lives, our *petits recits*... all we're doing is trying to create meaning, to make sense, where there is none, trying to mask the essential meaninglessness of our brief existence.

Then, a young man with all his life before him, he'd not been able to understand the importance of Lyotard's work. He'd believed that there was a life to live, a life that meant something, a life that meant everything. But now? Now, he understood. Here he was, just another little collection of atoms briefly arranged together into a person, soon to be spun into new trajectories by random crashes with other clusters of atoms, other individuals who'd soon be gone, the earth where they'd find their eternal rest. How else to explain where he was now, what he was doing? His own unimportant little journey had no more meaning than Ruth's, than Jimmy's, than Clare's. He hadn't chosen this, but it didn't matter. Choice was an illusion people made up to pretend to themselves that they had some control, that their lives meant something. But that was just a fairy tale told to children to protect them from the meaningless reality of life. Maybe Jimmy hadn't chosen what happened either. Maybe it hadn't been murder after all. Maybe Jimmy hadn't intended it. And what about the rape? What if....?

Nick had to slam on his brakes hard and pull off the road to avoid a tractor that had appeared suddenly round a bend, a wide load of hay bales on its front forks. One of the bales brushed the front of the pickup and fell onto the road. The tractor stopped. In his rear view mirror, Nick could see the driver climbing down. Lyotard be damned. He needed to pay attention to what was happening now, needed to make good choices now. Imagine what would've happened if the pickup had gone into the field, or stuck in a ditch. Thank God it hadn't. He crunched the gearbox. Round the next bend he crested the hill and coasted down the slope towards Callander.

All he wanted, all he wanted, was to find out the truth of what happened to his daughter. And then to let her story be told. There was nothing wrong with that. It was the right thing to do. There was right and there was wrong. Some things mattered more than others. Life had meaning. And his life had meaning. And Ruth's life had meaning. He wasn't sure where he was going, or what he was going to do, but he knew it would have to be wild and remote, somewhere where the chasers couldn't find him. The last act had begun and there would only be the two of them, no-one else, before the final curtain descended.

Anyway, whatever was going to happen, just travelling somewhere felt better already, just being on a journey. Journeys always carried their own sense of purpose. He started breathing more deeply, feeling his shoulders becoming softer and looser again. Callander was not yet fully awake, the big pickup scarcely breathing as it tiptoed on through. The twists and turns round the Leny Falls slung the human parcel behind him in the flatbed, first one way then the other. When Ruth was a wee girl, she'd felt sick on these twists and turns every time they came this way. They'd had to stop at the car park on Loch Lubnaig to allow her to recover. Maybe the bends would make Jimmy sick. What if he vomited, choked on it? Too bad. Fuck him. There was no way Nick was going to stop the pickup here, not till he got to the straighter section of road by the lochside. And soon enough, there was Loch Lubnaig opening out in front.

Ben Ledi was mirrored on the glass-flat water. The early morning sun splashed bright colours all the way down the mountain and onto its reflection. He pulled off the road into a layby at the edge of the loch, one where he and Ruth and Clare had often stopped to let Ruth have some fresh air after the twisty road. The layby was empty. Thank God it was early Sunday morning. It'd be rammed by the afternoon. Just as he stopped, the fuel warning light came on. He only had a few litres left. No way he'd get very far on that. He lifted the tailgate and looked in. Jimmy was awake. He wasn't sick. And his glaring eyes were all over Nick.

'Enjoying the journey?' Nick asked. 'We're heading north, by the way, that's why the road's been a bit twisty. Sorry about that. I'd take off your gag but I'm going to have to stop to fill up and I don't want anyone to hear you.' Jimmy wriggled impotently and tried to kick his feet on the flatbed. Nick shut the tailgate. He reassured himself that there was no obvious sign that Jimmy was in there, and then wandered down to the water's edge. Not far from the shore there was a large rock. A picture of Clare, sitting on that same rock, laughing, head thrown back in the summer sun, was still hanging on the bedroom wall. What might have happened in his life if Clare had still been here, if she'd been around to look after Ruth, give her the advice she needed as a young woman? Would she still have gone to that horrible little howff on that wet Friday night?

Other people would sit on that rock, maybe today, maybe next year, other photos in other halls. Who sang that? No. It wasn't photos, was it? Another *suitcase* in another hall. *Evita*. Madonna. Strange, the things that came into your mind. He'd taught Ruth how to skiff stones on this Loch, not far from the parking place. He picked up a couple of skiffers and flew them across the surface of the Loch. He got the second one just right. Ten bounces before it sank. He watched the ripples gently making their way out and then the surface calming again. This could've been a great start to the day, if it'd been a different day and not this day. This worst of days.

Nick washed the mud from his hands, splashed his face with the ice-cold water. It came to him then where he should go. Back to *The Wilderness* – that high lonely plateau on the west coast of Mull. When he was a young boy, his family had taken holidays near Bunessan and he'd looked out on it across the water. The name had fascinated him then. It still did. *The Wilderness* at the end of the earth, or 'as near to it as you could get in Scotland', he'd told Sam the weekend they were on Mull, hoping to climb Ben More. It was a place away from everyone, everything but the land and sea, a place where he and Jimmy might find a fitting end of their story. Before setting off, he opened his phone to check ferry times and found the battery dead. He'd forgotten to charge it. And he'd not brought the charger with him. Damn. Well. He didn't need it. He had no-one to phone now.

On a glorious morning like this it was hard to see why more people didn't want to live in Scotland. It was cold, but it'd warm up as the day went on. Up and over Glen Ogle he went, the derelict railway viaduct bisecting the steep hillside to the left, then down the long sweep to Lix Toll, into Glen Dochart and along to Crianlarich. Before the village, he stopped and checked on Jimmy. He looked washed out, listless, resigned. The twisty road, rolling and rocking him right and left in the rear of the car, had knocked the fight out of him. A garage on the other side of the village billed itself as 7 to 11. He pulled in and filled up. As he entered the shop he was surprised to be greeted in familiar tones, a former colleague who'd worked in the same office before getting off the train, out of the rat race, settling for a quieter, rural, life. What was his name? Alistair?

'Nick. Nice to see a familiar face,' the man said. 'Off up to the mountains?'

'Alistair? Is that you? I knew you'd resigned but I didn't know where you ended up.'

'Well. Here I am. Never regretted it.'

Nick didn't want to be drawn into a long conversation. 'Yes, I'm heading North, not sure where... '

'You picked a great day for it. High pressure sitting in and fresh snow on the tops, or so they said this morning. And that's £85.80 please.' He handed Nick the card reader.

'Have you got a timetable for the ferries at Oban? I might head that way... or maybe somewhere else...' Nick handed over his card and pumped in the PIN. 'Oh... a phone charger. I know it's a long shot but there's someone I've got to call and my battery's knacked.'

'Sorry. I don't have any chargers. Which ferry are you thinking about. If it's the Mull one, I don't have any timetables to give out. Just my own.'

'Yes. Maybe Mull.'

Alistair scrabbled about behind the desk while Nick punched his PIN into the card reader. 'Here we are... It's the winter timetable... Sunday... there's not so many on a Sunday. What's the time now?... Oh. You may just catch the 11.00. If not, there's at least two later on... but they're can be busy at this time of year.'

'Thanks,' Nick said, 'I'm not sure. I may stick around Oban. Or maybe head up Fort William way.' He turned away, then turned back... 'Almost forgot. I need to get some snacks too.' He filled his little daysac - a couple of filled rolls, apples, crisps, chocolate, water – paid and left without further conversation.

The road to Oban always took him back to his childhood and the three or four weeks the family spent on Mull each year. There'd been a simplicity to those summer holidays on the island. No television for a start. Getting to know about tides and beaches, watching gulls soaring in the buffeting western winds above Loch Scridain, photographing the rocks with his little compact camera and fiddling about with digital editing software on the big computer when he got home: each year the same but different. Mrs McAllister who lived at the road end always looked out for him. Each year she'd tell him how much he'd grown. Happier days.

Mull was a good place to take Jimmy. Maybe if Jimmy'd lived there, he would've turned out differently. Instead of the rules of the natural world, he'd grown up with the rules of the street, learned how to succeed in that world. Hundreds of years ago, he'd have been a leader. The strength, the courage, the determination he possessed would've been assets. These were things to admire about him. What a pity they hadn't been turned to good ends.

They reached Oban in good time for the ferry. Nick thought about getting a charger for his phone in one of the Oban shops but didn't fancy parking in the busy town centre and going into a shop while Jimmy lay trussed up in the back. Nor did he fancy waiting in the ferry queue, trapped in a line, cars to either side. So he parked on the empty side of the pier, ran in and bought his ticket, then drove South, past the caravan park and on to the single track road beyond. He found a secluded parking spot by a field of young cattle and reversed in at right angles to the road. Across the sound lay the island of Kerrera. It was good to be near the sea. He filled his lungs with the still salty air. A small pleasure boat was chugging its way down the sound, sails furled, heading for wind in the open sea beyond the island. Nick could see someone walking on Kerrera, maybe doing the circuit walk round the island. He and Clare had done that walk, their first summer together. They'd seen feral goats on the hill by the ruined Gylen Castle. They'd made love in a little dell on the deserted far side, under a blue sky. Nick remembered that sky, over Clare's shoulder, as she moved back and forwards above him, her hair falling to the side, seagulls circling above her, cheering them on, their cries like those of a raucous crowd of football fans, and nearer in, the sound of Clare's heavy breathing as she drove them both towards a climax. He remembered her falling on him, exhausted and laughing.

Kerrera would've been a good place to hole up with Jimmy. The south side of the island. He could take a rowing boat round. But where would he get a boat? And people walked there. Stupid idea. No. *The Wilderness* was the right place: just the name was enough. He surveyed the road behind, opened up the tailgate and pulled the tape off Jimmy's face. The smell in the back of the pickup was rank and Jimmy gulped in the air greedily. A cow came over to the fence for a closer look.

'Where are we?' Jimmy said.

'We're up the west coast. We're going on a boat. And I want to give you something to eat just now. Here. Where it's quiet.' Jimmy looked unwell, sick, a bit scared. 'And if you give me any trouble, I'll knock you out and wrap you up so tight I could stuff you up that cow's arse. Understand?'

'Aye. I understand fine, ya cunt. I understand that you're a mad bastard and I'm dizzy as fuck an I'm needin a piss and ma legs are aw stiff and ma shite is stickin tae ma arse. Gonnae let us out fir a wee walkabout.'

'I don't think so.'

'Bastard! Fuckin bastard! Let us go, you cunt,' Jimmy screamed, straining at his ties, his face a raging red.

'No use getting angry. Save your energy for later. You're going to need it.'

'Fuck aye,' Jimmy said, breathing heavily, calming down, 'See when I get free, you're gonnae be a fuckin dead man.'

'Well you're going to need your food, aren't you? if you get a chance to take me on? And you won't be any use to me either, if you're tired out from hunger and thirst, cos we've got some walking to do, you and me. That's why I've got the food here.'

'Aye,' Jimmy said, 'Go on then. Cunt.'

Nick propped him up in the corner of the flatbed and sat beside him, feeding him like a penguin at the zoo, dropping bite size pieces of food into his mouth, only this was no penguin. Maybe a better comparison would be a wild animal, a trussed-up tiger maybe, hidden in the boot of the car. How ridiculous was that? But that's what he was doing. Taking a wild thing onto a ferry and hoping no-one would see, no-one would hear.

'Have you ever been to the isles?' Nick asked.

Jimmy scowled back.

'Never mind. I'm not really that interested. There's only one conversation I want to have with you, and this isn't the place for it. It's the conversation we're going to have where you tell me what really went on that day, the day you killed Ruth.'

'I telt you awready. She fancied me. She wis gagging fir it. She wis desperate for any fuck she could get.'

Nick shook his head. 'I know what you're up to, but you're not going to rile me this time,' he said, 'It's not going to work. I know that's a lie.' He gagged Jimmy again, carefully checked his bonds and laid the carpet over him. This time, before closing the tailgate, he put, two extra ties over the top of the carpet, fixed to the estate car's luggage fixing points – in the boat, Jimmy's body would be immobile as well as silent. He stood a little longer, watching the water in the Sound, listening to the cries of the gulls and the waves lapping on shingle, the occasional grumble from the cattle. Could he just leave Jimmy here in the car? Walk into the water, let it close over his head, do its soothing work, give him peace? It was tempting. He was weary. So weary. So weary. But he still had more to do.

He got back up to the ferry terminal just in time to join the queue of cars that were already driving onto the boat.

* * *

Once on board, Nick left the car with Jimmy in it – staying in would draw suspicion - and climbed up to the top deck. Outside, in the sea breeze, his mood improved, his brain becoming clearer, more focused. He went over the events of the past twenty-four hours. He'd left a trail in Stirling and out at the bunker. He'd left a trail on his route north – the tractor, Alistair in Crianlarich, the Mull ferry. It'd be easy enough for the police to follow him if they wanted to. But he was ahead of them for now. The long months since Ruth died had now led to this, and this felt good. He was past worry. Things were going to happen. It wasn't going to be long before he'd find out how his 'little story', his *petit recit,* was going to end.

Out from the harbour, the water was choppy. Cloud had come in from the west on a fresh breeze. A few other travellers had braved the open air, in their own spaces, chatting, taking photos. He went inside and asked at the shop if they had any phone chargers. None. He bought a cup of tea and, as they passed Lismore, he found a comfortable seat in the forward lounge for 20 minutes of much-needed sleep. The PA system woke him: Bing Bing Bong; 'All car drivers return to their cars.' By the time he'd splashed his face with cold water and regained his seat behind the wheel, the bow doors were creaking open. He was second last on and so second last off. That suited him too. He wasn't in any hurry. Those in front were mostly heading North to Tobermory. He headed West into Glen More and eased off on the pedals, letting the cars ahead of him take away. There had been snow on the hills but down at sea level the road was clear. The freedom of the narrow island road comforted him. He was on his way to *The Wilderness.*

It was a few years since he'd seen Glen More, a bleak and lonely place, even in the sun. The thin ribbon of road follows the contours of the valley. Low above him, three hooded crows were flying, keeping just ahead by gliding effortlessly on an occasional beat of their wings. Grey shapes in a bleak landscape, eerie harbingers of what was to come, they darkened his mood. He slowed down even more, dawdling, letting them fly on without him. He had plenty time. No need to hurry. The nearer he got to the end of his journey, the less he wanted to reach it. He pulled into a passing place to let a bus overtake him, then another close behind it - both buses full, pale faces staring out of the windows, pilgrims from the cities who'd been on the same ferry as him, heading now for Iona.

He saw them on their way then pulled out onto the road again, coasting downhill now, having crested the island's watershed. In the distance a gash of beautiful bright blue appeared in the bleak landscape, disappeared, reappeared and disappeared again as the road twisted and turned - Loch Scridain. The main road runs along the south shore of the loch, to the Iona ferry, but Nick took the smaller road along the north shore, the remote, little used Gribun road. When it headed uphill, away from the lochside, Nick turned off left, keeping with the north coast of the Loch. This was the road that led to *The Wilderness*. Its humps and bumps were testing the suspension of the big pickup, the gearbox too - third gear, second gear, third gear, coast downhill, then back into second.

It was quieter here. Maybe he should stop and check on Jimmy. But it wouldn't be long now before the road would run out altogether, before he'd have to stop. He crept on round the back of Tiroran House, coasting down the hill then creeping away up the far side of its well-kept grounds. Up and over the next rise, Dun I, Iona's little hill, came into sight further out to sea. The more Nick drove on, the more the road deteriorated and the more his spirits lifted. This had been a good choice, this place he remembered from his childhood, this wild free place between the rocky prehistoric summit of Ben More, and the Atlantic stretching out ahead, all the way to America. They passed Tavool, the last inhabited house, and headed on towards the old Burg farmhouse, the last point on the road. Since he'd left the Gribun road, he'd not seen a single soul. As the road climbed up the other side of a bay, a National Trust sign warned drivers that the road to The Burg was impassible. He stopped to read the small print. Those wanting to walk to The Burg farmhouse, it said, or to head along the coast to the fossil tree, would have to do so on foot. The Burg farmhouse itself was closed to visitors.

Nick was determined to take the pickup as far in as he could and drove on up, skirting round several deep holes, listening to the sump scraping on the stone as he inched forward till he came to an impassable hole, stretching right across the road and down precipitous cliffs. He reversed and parked the pickup off the road, behind a small rise, hidden, as far as he could manage it, from any prying eyes on the busy Iona road that ran along the other side of the Loch. It wasn't far to the Burg farmhouse from here, and beyond that, his lonely destination.

There was a stronger, sea breeze here, straight off the Atlantic, all the way from Newfoundland. He opened up the back of the pickup and pulled Jimmy forwards to sit on the tailgate, his feet dangling over, and untied them. Jimmy squinted awkwardly, adjusting his eyes to the daylight. He was shivering. He looked bemused. Just then the sun broke through and shone on them.

'Look around you at this beautiful wild place,' Nick said, 'Agèd stones, grass, reeds, heather, spread thinly on this stony landscape.' He grabbed the back of Jimmy's neck and twisted it to left and right. 'Look!' he said, 'Look, damn you! Look around you! Can you not see the variety of shape, form, colour, the beauty of the changing light, the pure blues, the sparkling silvers, the lush greens, the sparkle of sun on water. Look! Look!'

Jimmy was still blinking. 'I can hardly see, man,' he said. 'My eyes are aw gummed up. An I'm stinkin man, fuckin stinkin.'

'You sound like a wee kid' Nick said, filled with a new energy, 'A wee whiner. But don't worry. You'll see soon enough.' Nick was drunk on it. Elated. He'd taken action and he'd succeeded. They'd made it, made it here, against the odds. 'This wild place,' he said to Jimmy, 'is the kind of place you should've lived your life. You'd probably have had a better life somewhere like this, with the creatures of the wild: the eagles and deer, the seals, the otters. Can you not smell the fresh sea air, the scent of the ocean? God, I'm drunk on it. It's overpowering.'

Jimmy said nothing.

'Well. Maybe not,' Nick said. 'Anyway. We'd better get on our way.' We're going for a walk. He lifted Jimmy's feet up and untied the rope round his ankles. 'And don't even think of trying anything funny out here,' he said. 'Cos I'd catch you for sure... and even if you did get away, you wouldn't last through a night out here with your hands tied. There are no cars, no people, no houses. That's why they call it *The Wilderness.'* He pulled Jimmy onto his feet and pushed him forward, but Jimmy's legs collapsed and he fell to the ground. Nick picked him up. 'It seems your legs aren't working yet,' he said, 'So we'll sit for a minute just to let you get your circulation back into them. Here,' Nick opened a bottle of water and held it to Jimmy's mouth, 'Have some of this water before we set out. I've got something to eat as well, for later.'

Jimmy seemed to be taking Nick's earlier advice. He wasn't struggling. Conserving energy. But his eyes were sharper now. 'Where the fuck are we?' he said.

'You're on the island of Mull, the Burg farm. We're going to walk to the old farmhouse. From there we can head up hill, above the sea cliffs. It's not a big climb. You can do it easy. And once we're up there, the views, man, the views are fantastic. I did it before with my father...' He was talking as if this was a Sunday afternoon stroll with a friend.

'I'm no goin anywhere.' Jimmy said. 'You'll need tae carry us.'

Nick flipped.

He grabbed a handful of Jimmy's hair and pulled his head right back, exposing his throat. He laid a finger across the bobbing Adam's apple. 'Don't fuck with me son. I can just get my knife and cut across here right now if you want.' He jerked Jimmy's head to the right. 'See that. Four hundred feet down there. That's a sheer cliff drop. I could just slit your throat then drop you over there. They'd never find you. Just kill you right now. Is that what you fucking want?'

Jimmy narrowed his eyes. His mouth twisted. 'You havenae goat the bottle,' he said.

'In fact, what the fuck?' Nick said. He tightened his hold on Jimmy's hair, pulled him up onto his toes. 'What the fucking fuck?' he shouted, 'I've had enough of this. I could just do it now, cut all this crap, throw you down, then jump after you. I don't care.'

'Fuck you man!' Jimmy joined in, hysterical now, both of them shouting. 'Fuck you man! Fuck you!'

Nick pulled Jimmy, struggling, onto his feet and dragged and hustled him, stumbling and overstepping, to the edge. He pushed him forward so that his toes teetered over, only his heels still on the ground, his body hanging over the cliff, only held back by Nick's grip on his hair. 'Is this what you want now? Fucking throw you over!! Now! One push and you're gone.' He held Jimmy's waistband and pushed his head even further forwards.

'Dinny dae it mister. Dinny dae it. Fuck, oh fuck, oh fuck...'

'It's me that's reckless now,' Nick shouted, 'Reckless behaviour. Remember that word from your trial? Reckless. They said your actions were *reckless*... not intended... that's why you were never charged with murder, just culpable homicide. Well I'm fucking reckless now. D'you think they'll charge me with culpable homicide? Am I being reckless now? After you fall, will it just have been a mistake, a bit of clowning around gone wrong? What d'you think? You wouldn't be there to tell the story, would you? Any more than Ruth was. I could make it all up, just like you did. I might even get away with it. Fuckin worth it. What d'you think? Fuckin worth a try, ay?'

'Dinny! Dinny! Naw. Fuckin dinny dae it!'

Nick pulled him back from the edge, slapped him hard. 'No more of your crap!' he shouted, 'If you get me angry one more time, I swear I'll do it. Drop you over the edge. So: here's what's happening. We're not going to stop here. I want to get out there, into *The Wilderness* – that's what they call the place we're going. That's where I'm going to get the true story from you, where we'll reach the end of this story. And you're going to walk when I fucking tell you to walk.'

Back at the pickup, Nick took the rope that had shackled Jimmy's ankles and lopped it round Jimmy's neck in a loose knot. He kept the few feet of slack in his hands. 'Now walk,' he said. They walked. And it didn't take them long to reach the Burg farmhouse.

'We'll stop for a rest here,' Nick said, 'Not far to go now.'

There was colour in Jimmy's cheeks, but he looked miserable, defeated. 'This is horrible, man,' he said, 'I've pissed ma pants an shat massel. Walkin's horrible. It's aw sticky oan ma arse man. Just tell us what you're wantin me to say. Anythin. I'll say it, ay?'

'No. You never seem to understand, do you? I told you already: I'm just after the *true* story of what happened to Ruth, not any old story. But instead of the big hard man, all I've got here is a wee laddie, a wee scaredy laddie. Where's the hard man now? Ay? Where's the hard man.' Nick said, 'Man up, man up for God's sake. And try to remember everything that happened when you killed my daughter.'

19. Chase

Sheila didn't take the girls to Glasgow after all. It had felt like running away somehow, when she might be needed at home. At the last moment she'd told Greg to go on by himself. After Greg had left to pick up Sam, she'd taken the girls for a walk along the back road, then helped them make a dolls' picnic back at the house. Just waiting. Waiting for Greg to phone her again. But when the phone rang, it was the landline: that didn't happen very often these days, just official calls, or sales calls.

'Is that Mrs. Bright?'

'Yes, it is. Who's this?'

'My name's Philben, ma'am. Chief Inspector Philben. I'm phoning in connection with an enquiry I'm making into the whereabouts of Mr. Nick Innocenti. I remember that you and your husband are close friends of his, aren't you?'

'Eh,' she hesitated, 'Eh, do you want to speak to my husband?'

'Yourself, or your husband, Mrs. Bright, if you prefer. Is he at home?'

'He's not in, I'm afraid. Not in. He's out in fact.'

'Perhaps you could help me then. Have you or your husband seen Mr. Innocenti this weekend?'

'Eh, this weekend...?'

'Yes Mrs. Bright. This weekend.' Philben coughed away from the phone. 'Excuse me calling like this, but we think he might be in some kind of trouble. We're anxious to locate him urgently. Anything you can tell us would be of help.'

'Well, there was a phone call. Was it yesterday or this morning. Time flies doesn't it?' She was floundering.

'I'd like to pop over to your place just now, Mrs. Bright? Ask a few more questions. If you don't mind that is? I want to see if there are any clues in what he said, clues that might help us locate him safely, Mrs. Bright.' It was a sturdy, slightly ponderous voice; not a trying-to-be-clever voice, but deliberate, she thought, just like the police should be.

'I don't know how I can help you,' she said with a nervous laugh, 'It was my husband who spoke to him really and he's not here.'

'Do you have a mobile number for your husband?'

'No. Well I do, of course, but the thing is the stupid man has gone and left his phone behind. I was trying to get him earlier and he didn't answer, then I realised it was still here.' Greg hadn't left his phone and Sheila wasn't given to lying. And especially to the police. But the lie just came out easily enough.

'Where has he gone?'

'He went to pick up a friend at the airport. He's taking them somewhere.'

'All the same. I'll pop over to see you. And maybe see your husband if he's back. I want to ask a few more questions about Mr. Innocenti.'

Sheila phoned Greg. There was no answer. Lots of places on that road where the signal wasn't very good. She left a message about Philben's call. When she came off the phone, Alice started pestering her again about the cancelled Glasgow trip – why couldn't they go? - Sheila snapped back at her. 'Can't you just keep out the way? Go and play at something in your room.' She saw the look on the girl's face and immediately regretted it. She took her into her arms. 'I'm sorry,' she said, 'I'm just very anxious about Uncle Nick,' she said. 'Your Dad's had to go away to Mull to try to help him. And there's a policeman coming to the house to ask questions – even the police are worried'.

Philben arrived within the hour, accompanied by a uniformed constable, Helen Barnes. Sheila shooed the girls upstairs and showed the two officers into the front room. Philben sat, perched rather awkwardly, while he questioned Sheila more closely. Sheila tried to maintain a naive ignorance. Yes, they were a bit concerned about how Nick had been, especially since Jimmy Stevens had been released. She didn't know where he might have gone. He enjoyed walking at weekends. Maybe the Lake District, maybe the North. She wasn't sure when he would be back – Greg might. Yes, Nick liked to visit. He often he brought the girls a present. They had Ruth's dolls. Of course, he still missed Ruth. Yes, he did talk about her.

Philben closed his notebook and accepted her offer of a cup of tea. When Sheila went through to the kitchen to set the kettle on, Barnes and Philben joined her. While they were chatting, the two girls appeared at the door. 'We're fed up watching the television,' Alice said. 'Yes,' Jess said, 'We want to go to Mull like Daddy… to see Uncle Nick.'

Sheila had started pouring the tea but stopped. For a moment there was silence. Then Philben stood up. 'We won't be needing the tea, Mrs. Bright!" he said, with a mixture of annoyance and triumph. 'I'm sure you can tell us where on Mull your husband has gone?'

'No,' she said, 'No I can't. Honestly. I don't know. I'm sorry. This whole thing is a complete mess. I'm sorry.'

'Well at least you can save us a bit of time. Give us the details of your husband's car… and Mr Innocenti's vehicle, if you know it.'

Sheila wrote out the registration number of their car but feigned ignorance of Nick's, other than that it was a 'big ugly pickup'.

'I expected better of you, Mrs. Bright,' Philben said, as he left, 'Our job would be so much easier if we got the co-operation of the public, I just hope to God this unnecessary delay won't cause us any avoidable problems… or you might end up in trouble yourself.'

* * *

After they left Sheila, Barnes and Philben headed North. They phoned ahead to Mull but the call was diverted to Oban as it was a Sunday and the Mull station wasn't staffed. After a discussion with the officer in Oban it was agreed that transport would be arranged for Philben to get over to the island whenever he arrived and that a local officer would meet him over there. Meantime, enquiries would begin to ascertain whether Nick's pickup had been on a ferry that day and if so, where on the island it'd been seen. Mull is a big island, but not much escapes notice. Five or six phone calls established that the pickup had been seen driving on the Iona road out of Craignure, then on to the Tiroran Road. When Philben arrived at Craignure, they headed straight out that way in the local police Land Rover and found the silver pickup abandoned on the rough road beyond Tavool that led to the National Trust property and the Burg farmhouse. The sun was already going down towards the sea in the west, before Philben, Barnes and the local constable found Greg Bright sitting on a bench outside the farmhouse.

Greg mustered up a smile. 'You fellas didn't need to come all this way just for me,' he said, 'But I'm very glad you did.'

'I believe you're Mr. Bright,' Philben said, 'I recognize you from the photo in your front room. And it looks like you've had a nasty fall,' he added, nodding towards Greg's ankle, which was badly swollen.

'Yeah. Bummer. I think it's broken,' he said.

'Now you'll need to tell us,' he said, 'Where is Mr. Innocenti?

* * *

Greg had had some day. Sam's flight arrived a few minutes early, but he'd already been there to meet her, fizzing with excitement, grabbing her little backpack, hurrying her out of the airport.

They listened again to Nick's Cloud file, together this time, as they drove over the Erskine Bridge and up the A82 to Loch Lomond. Heading up the lochside, she wanted to talk about the recording, but Greg was finding the driving difficult. It wasn't just that he was aware of her beside him, though he was certainly that - the sense of her, her scent, her crossed legs, the tangle of her hair. Nor was it the questions she was asking. The driving was just exceptionally difficult. Sunday afternoon day-trippers from the city were out in their droves as it was a beautifully clear day. They were slowing the road down, halting at unexpected places, stopping to turn into parking spots, then pulling out into the road again, apparently without checking mirrors. Coming into Crianlarich, four bikers passed them, the last one on a bend. Greg had to brake sharply to let him in. His knuckles were white on the steering wheel. He was getting hot and bothered, annoyed with the other drivers, annoyed that he was looking decidedly uncool in front of Sam, annoyed they might miss the ferry.

'You're stressed,' Sam said, 'Let me drive the next part of the road. I'm fully covered for any car.'

It was humiliating for him to admit it, but she was a better driver. Faster, but also more assured. He for his part eased back into the passenger seat. This close to her, he felt like a nervous boy. He rehearsed in his head something clever to say, tried to start conversations then couldn't keep them going. After a few stuttering starts, she put him out his misery. 'Let's just cut the small talk,' she said, 'I'm concentrating on making the ferry on time. When did you say it was?'

'3 o'clock,' he said, 'And you are making good time now. We should get there easily if we don't meet a big holdup... and I've checked our route on Google maps. There's nothing showing just now.'

'Fine,' she said. 'I'll work to that timescale.'

As they drove on in silence. Sam went over and over in her head what Nick had done, what he intended to do, what her options were. The ferry wasn't too busy so they were easily able to get a place. Once on board, she wanted to go up top, get some fresh sea air after the flight and the drive. They chose a spot that offered a little shelter from the breeze. She closed her eyes and threw her hair back.

Sitting across from her, Greg had the opportunity to look at her as much as he wanted. What is it about a woman like this? he wondered. She's got everything and she knows it. Even those cute little lines round her eyes. Everything.

Sam opened her eyes and caught him looking.

'Sorry,' he said with a lame smile, 'Can't help myself. You're the best thing to look at around here.'

Her eyes widened a little. 'Well thank you. I'll take that as a compliment, since we're sailing through some of the most beautiful scenery in the UK.' She shivered. 'I'm getting cold though. Let's go inside and get a cup of tea. It was stupid of me to leave the jacket in the car. I thought this fleece would be warm enough.' Over their tea, Greg became more comfortable talking to her, sharing the discussion he and Sheila had had over the map, how Nick had talked about his childhood holidays, the name Bunessan.

'Yes. I remember. Nick and I had a weekend over here,' Sam said. 'We stayed in Bunessan. Planned to go up Ben More, but the weather was bloody awful. Horizontal wind from the west. It was too dangerous to go up the mountain. He talked about that whole area. It made a big impression on him.'

'So,' Greg said, 'We head for Bunessan and try to see if anyone has seen his pickup?'

'Seems like we don't have any better ideas,' Sam said.

* * *

When they arrived on Mull, Sam assumed the wheel and pushed the Volvo hard on the narrow single track road into Glen More. She didn't encourage Greg's stilted conversation gambits and so they spent most of the journey in silence. Greg was surprised when she pulled into a layby on the south shore of Loch Scridain. He followed her out of the car and they stood looking over to the other side of the loch.

'The reason I stopped,' Sam said, 'I'm just thinking... the walk he was talking about when I was here with him was somewhere over there. He was fascinated by that area. It had a strange name... some sort of desert...'

Greg laughed out loud. 'Desert? In Scotland?'

'Well not desert maybe, but it was a wild area though, bleak. He'd walked there with his Dad, I think. He talked about it a lot. I've got a feeling he's over there. He knows the area, places to hole up. Time's running out. And he's not going to be anywhere busy, we can be sure of that. I think it's worth a shot.'

'It's a long shot,' Greg said, 'But you're the one who was here with him before. If you think it's a possibility, I certainly don't have any better suggestions.'

They got back in the car and she headed it onto the road on the north side of the Loch. Greg downloaded the map of Mull onto his phone.

'It looks as if it's a very small road,' he said, 'And it ends at a National Trust building called *The Burg*. After that, from the look of the map, you're out into real wild country. And you were almost right with your names... the whole area is called *The Wilderness*.'

'That's it! *The Wilderness*! How could I have forgotten? He talked about *The Wilderness*! Is this the right road that we're on? There's a big house down there ... and the road snakes up and round the hill on the other side.'

'Tiroran House,' Greg said. Then there's Tavool... and after that, The Burg.' A few minutes later, they stopped and read the same 'road closed' sign that Nick had seen hours earlier.

'Is this it then?' she said, 'His pickup's not here. We need to head back. Think of some other plan.'

'Do you think he'd let a sign stop him?' Greg said, 'We've come this far. It'd be stupid to give up now. Let me just run up to the top of this hill and see the next stretch of road. It'll only take me a few minutes. I'll run ahead. You can follow me if you want.'

Sam kicked her heels for a few minutes after Greg had set off, then, impatient, followed him. By the time she got to the top of the hill, Greg had already seen the pickup and was on his way back to tell her. They had a quick look inside. A few dirty tools, some old carpet, plastic bags.

'So,' Sam said, 'He has headed out into *The Wilderness* after all. It's quite fitting, don't you think? I just had a feeling.'

'The engine's cold,' Greg said. 'He's a good bit ahead of us. And it'll be getting dark soon. Do we just keep going?'

'For now,' she said.

'Well there's only one way to go from here,' he said, 'Onward and downward – well that's two ways.' He rubbed his nose and tried to assume a more confident air. 'It's still amazingly clear now the clouds have blown over. But it's getting colder. You'll be glad you brought that big winter jacket. I wish I had. I'll need to keep moving to keep warm. Do you think this is wise?'

Sam walked over to the cliff edge. 'This place makes you dizzy,' she said, 'Don't you think? You could get drunk on your senses alone, the sights, the winds, the smells, the sea sprays, the sounds of the birds, the wind on your face, the sheer physicality of it all.'

'We're wasting time,' he said, 'If we're going, let's go.'

They started walking.

'Do you think Jimmy's with him?' Sam said, 'Or is this where he's come to end it all, take his own life?'

'How could he have brought anyone out here? Look at the place. You couldn't even run a barrow along this track. If he's out there, he's on foot.'

'Maybe he won't be very happy to see us. Coming here must've been about running away don't you think? He doesn't want people to find him.'

'No,' Greg said with a new note of authority in his voice, 'I think he set it up to be followed. He wants the story to be heard. And he can't have that unless you're here to see it, to report it. That's why you came isn't it?'

'So why did he leave it so much to chance? If you hadn't phoned that petrol station, if we hadn't guessed that he would come out here... '

Greg remembered his conversation with Sheila about phoning the garage. Sam was right. Nick thought he was covering his tracks. He'd be surprised they were close behind him.

'It wasn't me who phoned,' he said, 'It was my wife Sheila. If it wasn't for her we'd still be back at basecamp.'

'C'mon then Greg,' she said. It was good to hear her use his name. 'Let's hit it.'

She set a good pace then, and he matched her. When the Burg farmhouse came into view in the gloaming, he accelerated into a run and tripped on a stone, screaming out in pain.

She knelt down beside him.

'It's my ankle.' he squealed, 'I think it's broken.'

She pulled up his trouser leg a little and he screamed again.

'I don't know if it's broken,' she said, 'But it's swollen up like a balloon. We'll need to get you some help. I won't be able to get you back on my own.'

'No,' he said. He checked his phone. 'See. I've got a signal. I'll phone emergency. They'll send someone out for me. You've got to carry on. Find him before they do, if you can - wasn't that what we wanted to do? The fact that I'm a total idiot shouldn't stop you. Have you got a signal?'

She checked her phone. 'Yes,' she said.

'So... Make sure you're safe, whatever you do. Use your phone if you need to. Record anything on camera. Remember you've got to look after yourself. You're the one who'll have to tell the story, however it ends. You need to finish the job. Go on!'

Sam helped Greg hop over to the bench in front of the little farmhouse. 'Here,' she said, pulling something out of her bag 'You can wrap this around you.'

'What is it?'

'It's a rainproof, waterproof skirt - a wraparound. I keep it in the bag, but to be honest I've only ever used it to sit on. Wear it round your shoulders. You're already getting a bit of shelter from the wind here, and this'll help you retain heat.'

There was a map of the peninsula in the window of the Burg, alongside the National Trust for Scotland sticker. Sam put on her glasses and studied it. She looked just as good in her glasses. Better, he thought. She took a photo of the map on her phone.

'OK,' she said, 'I'm going to follow the path that's marked. It goes to a place called 'the fossil tree.' The path stops there, but there's a ladder marked on the map, takes you down onto the shore. If I can't see him from there, I'm going to give up. We'll have done as much as we can. It'll be dark soon, and I'm not prepared to take silly risks. If you can get your phone to work, it's maybe time to call in the cavalry, tell them where we are.'

She left Greg then, striking out on a rough narrow track on the grassy plateau above the seashore, heading more northwest now, round the headland, the sea on her left. She could see a couple of boats on the water, lights beginning to go on in the windows of the little houses across the Sound on Iona, the stone of the old Abbey still warm in the fading light. The track she was following took her ever nearer to the steep sea cliffs, into the spray blown up on the wind. She could hear the massive waterfalls that cascaded over high basalt columns ahead. Soon she was at the top of the old iron ladder that was marked on the map. Spray from the waterfalls was being blown upwards on the wind, like a shower of rain falling the wrong way, up into the sky. There was no-one down there, on the shore. But up above her on the hill, as she turned, how had she not seen them before? There were two people on the steep slope, caught in the dusky western light, a few hundred feet, maybe more, above her. They were facing each other, but she couldn't hear what they were saying, only the wind. They were very close, almost leaning against each other, and then they fell together, one on top of the other.

'Nick,' she screamed, and again, louder, and once again, louder still, but he didn't respond, the swirling wind carrying her voice up and away, scattering her words as it scattered the spray from the waterfall.

She started to work her way up towards them over the rough grassy ground.

20. Closure

When they reached The Burg farmhouse, Nick had tied Jimmy's halter loosely to the bench before giving him a drink. They both sat resting on the grass. watching the winter sun dipping towards the cloud bank that sat on the western horizon, both wondering what was to come. Jimmy had settled into a sullen silence as they walked, but, resting now, he found his voice again.

'Hey mister, go an gie us a fag or something, ay?'.... 'Hey, I'm needin something mister. Have you no got any fags?' .... 'I'm talkin tae you mister. Go an answer us, cunt.' .... 'This place is goupin wi sheep shit mister. You're lyin in sheep shit did you know that?' Jimmy gave a wee laugh to himself, 'I bet it's aw sheep shaggers up here. Fuckin sheep shaggers.' .... 'Mister. It's borin here. When are we goin?' ... It was relentless. He wasn't going to shut up.

Nick raised his head. 'You're wanting to go?'

'Dinny use the rope, but. You can just tie my hands, ay? That'll be enough. I'm no gonnae dae nothing funny. I need to see if I can walk right. I'm that cauld.'

Nick stood up, looming over Jimmy. 'You know I didn't really think we were going to get here. And now that we're here, I'm feeling pretty crazy.' he said. 'So crazy... In fact...' - Nick walked away then and looked out to sea. He took a few deep breaths then turned back and pulled Jimmy up to his feet, facing him, close in. 'In fact,' he went on, 'I've realized now that I don't care about my life anymore. My life is over already. And yours will be too, very soon, unless you tell me exactly how my daughter died.'

Jimmy's lip curled into a kind of smile. 'Naw,' he said, 'See... the thing is that that's what's keepin me alive... no tellin you nothin, ya cunt. You've got to get me tae tell you, ay? So I'm no tellin you nothin.'

'I'm well aware,' Nick said, 'that you don't need to tell me anything... and that what you tell me may not be true. But I will know if you're lying, believe me... cos I know every scrap of evidence, every story told at the trial, so I'll know if what you're saying fits in, or not... and as I was already saying, if you carry on lying, one thing is sure... you're a dead man.' Nick stood away from Jimmy and looked up at the sky before returning to his theme. 'If you don't tell the true story of what happened to my daughter, there's only one thing I haven't decided yet.'

The words were still directed at Jimmy, but the conversation Nick was having seemed to be more with himself. 'And that's whether to kill you straight away, or first to give you some grief, like you gave Ruth. And right now, the way I feel is that you deserve to get some grief, some painful grief, before I put you out of your misery. And then? After you're dead. What'll I do then? I'll tell you know cos you won't see it happen. I reckon I'll head straight up to the highest clifftop and jump off. You see I'm that most dangerous of men: I'm a man who doesn't care, who doesn't give a flying fuck what happens to him... not now... not ever.' Nick repositioned his feet, leaned closer in towards Jimmy.

'So,' he said, 'It's your choice now. Your only way out is to tell me what happened the night Ruth died. Your choice. Once I've got it, we'll work out some way, together, to get that story out, so that people know exactly what happened to Ruth. That's all I want. That's all I want.'

For some seconds, they stared at each other.

'OK,' Nick said, 'I'm fed up with this crap. We're moving on.'

'Naw I canny move no more, honest. I know I was crapping it before, when we got oot the car but it's real noo. I canny move.' He was like a toddler now, whining, trying to manipulate a parent. 'The shite. It's stuck to me, aw hard. Feels awfie. It's horrible, man.'

'Of course you can move,' Nick pulled at the knots tying Jimmy Stevens to the bench. He pulled him roughly onto his feet with the rope that circled his neck.

Jimmy went down on one knee. 'My leg, my bastardin leg. It's sore.'

Nick knelt down beside him. He pulled his knife out from inside his pocket, flicked it open and passed it by Jimmy's eyes.

'I sharpened this before I left the house,' he said. 'Just in case.' Then placing the knife inside Jimmy's left nostril, he nicked the inside of his nose, sending a thin stream of blood trickling down into his mouth.

Jimmy started to scream for help and Nick reached out and held his head still then put the tip of the knife inside his right nostril and scraped the lining of the nostril a bit harder, with a cold eye, as if dissecting a dead rat in the lab. Blood began to pour out of the nostril and over Jimmy's lips, onto his chin, down his neck inside his shirt.

'The next thing I'm going to do,' Nick said, 'Is cut your cock in two... make sure you can't ever use it again. How'd you like that son? Just slice it in two and stuff it in your mouth?' He held the knife up in front of Jimmy's eyes, both of them hysterical now. 'It's one of your favourite words, isn't it? *Cunt*. So why don't I just give you one, with this knife?' He brought the knife down between Jimmy's legs. Nick screamed in his face, totally out of control, 'Or would you rather just start fucking walking?'

They walked.

As they humphed and hurdled along the rough path, Jimmy constantly complained, fidgeting, stopping, asking for his bonds to be loosened. Another ten or fifteen minutes took them to the end of the track, where an old iron ladder led down to the shore. Above them was a steep grassy slope. And above the grassy slope were steep cliffs. Ahead of them were the high tumbling waterfalls, blocking the route round the headland. There was no more easy going, no more paths, not even a sheep track. Nick decided to go up, up towards the cliffs. It wasn't easy walking and soon there would be no more walking. They were near the end of this journey and then, finally, there would be no more chances for procrastination, delay, avoidance. Somewhere up there would be the closure Nick was going to find.

It was slow going, though it wasn't much more than a couple of hundred feet over the rough grass and on up the steep slope towards the base of the towering cliffs. Jimmy's hands were still tied and he fell forwards twice. The third time he fell, Nick decided they were high enough and they sat down on a patch of grass, Nick behind and above Jimmy. They could see a small boat swaying from side to side on the sea below, heading for Iona. Further out, they could see the lights of a bigger ferry sailing for an outer island. The white tops of the waves caught what light there was. Seagulls were circling above them. Two windblown clouds were scudding in at speed, eager to deposit their rain on the top of Ben More. All around the stalks of hardy grasses were waving wildly in the air. His phone would've been useless here anyway. Any recording he'd tried to make of Jimmy making a confession would've been drowned out by the noise of the wind. How many things had gone wrong with his rubbish plan? But at least the end was in sight. There was no way back. Something was going to happen. Let it be what it would.

They sat for some time before Nick started talking.

'You still have no realization of what you've done, do you? To take someone's life like you did, a young woman with so much promise, someone who'd done nothing to harm you. There can't be anything worse than to take someone's life. It's the worst thing any human being can do, the very worst thing, so unfair. How does that feel... to be the kind of person who does something like that, who is so black-hearted that he can rape and kill an innocent young girl? How can you live with yourself? So twisted inside... all the time? So twisted? How can you live with the fact that you're someone who could do something like that?'

At first it seemed that Jimmy hadn't heard Nick. Then he nodded, his hand clenching the loosened rope. He stood up, turned round and faced Nick. Nick thought Jimmy was about to mount some last-ditch attack and so he sprang to his feet defensively. But it was Jimmy's words that attacked him, not his body. A stream of angry words.

'Fair.' Jimmy snapped into a different gear. The words were flowing from some rich seam, deep inside him. 'I'll give you fuckin fair, ya cunt,' he said, 'Nothing in this fuckin world isnae fuckin fair. When cunts likesay youse say 'fair' what they really mean is 'fuckin suits me'. Ay? Cunts like youse wi the fancy joabs and the big hooses. Youse get the firm to pay for your fancy cars, pay for your meals, pay for your fuckin drinks while the rest o us huvtae pay for it from oor ain money It's aw aboot the rules that you fuckers make up, ay?.'

Jimmy took a couple of deep breaths. Nick said nothing.

'I'll tell you something else for nothin, you big cunt, when I was at my primary school they telt me I was smert, an I believed them. See when we goat tae the secondary, forget it man. Turns out I'm sitting beside your fuckin daughter in Maths, man, and she's looking at me like I'm a fuckin clown, like I ken nothing, like I'm a fuckin thicko. An it's right enough. I canny dae half the stuff, fuckin balancing equations an aw that crap, so it's aw stitched up. I'll be daein Maths for Thickos while they dae the real Maths, for scientists an engineers an that. Fuck that for a laugh, ay. That's no fair, ay? Cunts like me, we're never gonnae get the good jobs ay, so we have tae make money where we can.'

'Yes,' Nick said, 'This ... '

'Shut up, ya cunt!' It was Jimmy that was raging now, his face red, slavering in his anger, 'You wanted me to talk so you're gettin it, aw of it, so shut the fuck up an listen! It's fuckin fair you want, is it? Well I've no even fuckin started yet. Rich bastards likesay you, it's youse that make the rules, ay? There's rich cunts like you aw ower the shop. Everywhere, ay? No just in fuckin London, Edinburgh. In Stirlin an aw, up the King's Park, in Bridge of fuckin Allan. They've even goat their ain fuckin schools soas their wee fuckin poncey fuckin kids dinny have tae mix wi the likes o me.' Jimmy paused then, drawing breath, speaking more calmly, even authoritatively. 'That's why if you cum oan tae ma patch, then it's ma rules you play by. Evens up the game, ay? That's what's fuckin fair, ya cunt.' Jimmy spat to the side. He seemed to have turned inward, almost as if he was talking to himself. Maybe this was it. Maybe he was ready to tell it like it was.

'Is that what Ruth did, Jimmy?' Nick said, 'Did Ruth come on to your patch? Is that what made it right for you to do what you did?'

'Dinnae kid yoursell man. Your wee Ruth wisnae the innocent wee girl you've goat her as.'

'I don't believe you. That's just... ' Nick said, then backtracked. 'No.' he said, 'Go on. I need to hear what you've got to say. Keep going.'

'Aye,' Jimmy said, 'You do need to hear what I'm sayin. You fuckin do, ya cunt. You need to listen tae me. It's ike I was sayin, she was up for it awright. You can tell. She was a randy wee fucker. She fuckin loved it.'

'I've heard this before,' Nick said, shaking his head 'If these lies are all you've got, all you're giving me, then this is it. There's no point. This is the end.'

It was the moment to put an end to it, but Nick didn't feel ready, or even angry. All he could feel was disappointment and sadness, not the rage he wanted. Was his life any better than the one in front of him, this negative hate-filled young man? There was something in what he said. It wasn't a fair world and why should it be? Life hadn't been fair to Jimmy and life hadn't been fair to him. First his wife was taken from him, then his daughter. How unfair was that? And he wasn't going to find out what happened to Ruth, was he? He never was. The way it turned out, this journey was just about running away. Running away from being found out, found with his captive in that horrible little concrete bunker. Or running away from life? Or was it about more than that? It'd been Jimmy, after all, that had set the whole thing off, bringing the booze and the drugs, set the whole tragedy in motion. And his daughter's death had unleashed a poison that had spread to him. Someone else was going to have to die now to complete the story. Him or Jimmy Stevens, or maybe both of them. But how could he die again? He was already dead. Jimmy had destroyed his life. His life was worthless, had been since Chief Inspector Philben turned up at his door to tell him they'd found Ruth's body. It wasn't about justice. This wasn't justice. Justice was an idea people made up. This was about the end of meaning, or purpose, of value. Lyotard was right after all. We were all just a bundle of atoms, bound together for a wee bit then blown apart. We mean nothing. Our lives mean nothing. The wee stories we tell ourselves mean nothing.

'You're not going to tell me what really happened,' he said, 'So it looks like I'm just going to kill you.'

He took out the knife and willed himself to stab Jimmy, but he couldn't do it; he couldn't do it. Couldn't have done it to a man who was trussed up, like an animal waiting for slaughter, far less to this boy-man. Maybe if he evened things up? He turned Jimmy round. 'I'm going to cut the rope,' he said. 'Give you a chance.'

When it was done, Jimmy was free to move. He crouched down then on his haunches, nursing his fingers, flexing his toes.

'Get up damn you,' Nick roared, 'Get up.' Jimmy pulled himself up slowly, his fingers still tingling and numb.

'You killed her, didn't you, you bastard? Didn't you?' Nick roared, roared so hard he almost jumped in the air with the effort, trying to inspire with his shouting a rage he somehow couldn't now feel. Now that it came to it, this point, this final point, none of it seemed to matter. It all just seemed pathetic, squalid, petty... his life, Jimmy's life. Nick felt his insignificance. This pathetic drama that had started in the horrible little howff almost two years ago and was now near its end. Down the slope and beyond, a big swell had started up and the waves were crashing in against the rocks, throwing their spray up hundreds of feet, up on the wind and onto them. In a little while more, the seas would still be churning and no-one would remember or care what had happened to him, or to Jimmy.

Then Jimmy started speaking. 'I promise you mister,' he said, 'I didnae kill your daughter.' As he spoke, he stretched his arms out to the side as though warming up for a spot of exercise, reached them up to the sky and circled them back down to his sides. He looked away from Nick. 'They wanted to fit me up for giving her the drugs, and maybe that's what did for her, but she wanted it. She shouldnae have had so much o the fuckin ecstasy like, but she begged us for it, like, just like she begged us to fuck her.' He looked straight back at Nick then. 'But it's just the way it goes pal, ay? Like you said yoursell. Life's no fuckin fair, ay no?'

Nick thought of what was between them. It was about Ruth, but it was about justice too, real justice. That meant something. Not the justice of power, of the courts, but real justice - the triumph of good over evil, of what was right over what was wrong, of righteous anger. It was about a principle, a principle that could almost make Ruth's death worthwhile - that people of whatever age and whatever background must take responsibility for their actions. It wasn't enough to pass it off as some accident. Actions have consequences. And one of the consequences here was that Ruth was dead and Nick's life had been emptied of meaning and that this young man in front of him had learned nothing, might do the same thing, again, and again, and again.

But no amount of injustice could justify further injustice, could it? And maybe none of it mattered. None of it. He'd tried to believe there was more to it, but there wasn't... this was it. This guy, Ruth and him ... and yet the only reason he was here was that it did somehow matter. Goodness mattered. Truth mattered. But this - what he was involved in, what this person in front of him had brought him into – this was neither good nor true. It was bad and it was wrong.

Jimmy was flexing his fingers, his toes, rolling his shoulders, recovering feeling.

'We're just little ants under a stone, our pathetic wee lives,' Nick said. 'Behind you.' He pointed out to sea with the knife in his hand. 'Out there is the ocean. Three thousand miles of sea. What are we in that eh? What importance is there in our lives compared to these stones, that ocean, that sky?'

As if on cue, the wind picked up again, a sudden gust, it almost blew them over. Jimmy was standing, listening, flexing his arms.

'Those cliffs above us there,' Nick gestured behind him with the knife, 'were made by lava, layers and layers of it, millions of years ago. Somewhere down below there,' he waved the knife forward, 'there's a tree, fossilized in the lava, as old as the rock. Men like us – what are we eh? What are we in the midst of all this? Little dots in the Universe, struggling for nothing. Fragments. The only thing that gives any value to our lives is when we raise ourselves above it all, when we see some higher truth beyond ourselves, when we try to find out what is the right thing to do, what is right for the future; when we try to make things better not for ourselves but for those to come, for their future, for the planet's future.. And it's the old words that matter, that have always mattered – truth, honesty, goodness. They matter.' He heaved out a long weary sigh. 'They're what matters.'

There was no shelter in this exposed place. Nick had brought no more food with them. It would be a difficult place to last a night, but they weren't going back anyway. They'd never been going back, had they? And whether this was justice, or retribution, or revenge didn't matter. What he was doing didn't feel right or wrong. It just felt inevitable. This was the time for the only kind of closure that mattered.

Nick noticed Jimmy repositioning himself. He was getting ready too - taking careful note of the land above and below, Nick's position, where Nick's eyes were looking. He was going to have a go, one last go. Well. Never mind. Nick was ready for it. Welcomed it. He wanted Jimmy to make the first move.

'I'm giving you one last chance to tell me what really happened,' he said over the noise of the wind and sea 'For your sake. You'll feel better if you confess it all, before you die, cos I've decided now that's what's going to happen. You are going to die. And me too. I'm going to die as well. That's the only way this thing can end. This thing you started: this poison you brought into my life when you raped and killed my daughter. I realize that now.

I've realized it for a while but didn't ever say it, even to myself. There was only ever going to be one ending - I can see that now. But before the end, you have one decision to make. You just have to decide if you want to tell me everything that happened before you die, to confess… or you can decide to go to hell as a liar, as well as a rapist and a murderer.'

Jimmy said nothing.

'Well then,' Nick said, 'What's it to be?'

Jimmy still said nothing.

'OK,' Nick said. 'It's time.'

Nick stepped forward and put the point of the blade into the fleshy part of Jimmy's neck, under his chin, but careful not to break the skin.

'You see I know you killed my daughter… and I know you almost got away with it. Il heard what you said to your wee pal Craigsy in the howff, when the two of you were smoking dope, when you said that you *should have swung* for what you did – you see I was there… and you knew I was there too. You shouted out *Is some cunt out there?* or something like that… do you remember? That's how I'm sure you did it, how I know you had something to say to me. But you haven't got the bottle, have you? You're a pathetic specimen of humanity, evil, greedy, self-centred, angry. No-one will miss you once you're gone, you know that. Not a single person will miss you.'

Jimmy started speaking then, whispering, hoarse, urgent. 'OK, I'll gie you what you want. I'll gie it tae you straight up. Honest, man.' He held his hands up submissively, as if surrendering. 'I ken. It's got to be the right story this time. I ken that. Nae bullshit. Nae mair.'

'I don't know if I want to hear you now,' Nick said wearily, but the hand on the blade relaxed a little.

'No mister, honest. Honest tae God. Would I bullshit you now?' Jimmy lowered his hands. Nick kept the point of the knife under Jimmy's chin to bring his head up, wanted to see the expression on his face as he spoke.

'It was me that started it, like. I wouldnae have done anything, only Sadie had telt us Ruth was up for it, like.' He paused. But there would be no interruptions. 'It wiz aw Sadie's fault. It wiz her telt us Ruth wanted it, wanted me like. Said she'd get her up to the wee hut. I wiz up there like, waitin fir her, ken. I wiz randy as fuck an I'm no kiddin.' He paused to spit out some blood. 'I liked Ruth, like. She wis awright. When Sadie telt us she was after us, I was thinkin fuckin magic, man, so that's why I got in some eccies an aw? Slows it doon ay? Real happy pills they were, strong as fuck. Sadie said we could do a threesome like. And Sadie's got a sweet little fanny. I wis thinkin, you beauty. Her and Ruth. Fuck. You couldnae blame me for that. It's like aw the sweeties in one jar ay? Ruth and Sadie. Fuck. I'm gettin hard the noo just thinkin aboot it. Your Ruth was a bonny girl right enough. Abody fancied her an I'm no kiddin.' Jimmy paused, his eyes flitting right and left. Repositioned his feet a little. 'You want me to go on?' he asked.

'Yes. Just go on,' Nick said, deadpan.

'So. It's like this. After school, Sadie arrives wi Ruth. Ruth wisnae that happy, like, but it wis her first time an that, ay?, so we says she doesnae have to dae nothin, just watch. Then it aw goes crazy man, the cider, the eccies, weez are watching porno on my phone, an then me an Sadie, we're get it on, like. An Ruth could've run away then, like, she could've. We thought she was lovin it, lying back there, watchin us goin at it. Then Sadie falls asleep and the two of us are having a laugh and then me and her, we get aw sexy, like, so I fucks her an aw, real gentle like. Slow. Sweet. An efter it's over, she's like, "I'm goin," an she hikes hersell up. "On you go then," I says. An that's the last I saw of her, ay?'

Jimmy waited for a response, but there was no feedback. Nick was just looking, the knife tight in his hand. Jimmy stumbled another half step up the slope. He was no longer down the slope from Nick but almost level with him.

'I wouldnae've done anythin she didnae want tae, like. But later, when I hears what's happened I kent I was gonnae get the blame for sure, so I pretends I wasnae there mister, so help me god. For myself like, the way I see it, like, I eyeways reckoned she just tripped and fell in the water, like. That's how she drowned, like. Just a tragic accident.'

Nick was disappointed. Here, at the end, it was another anti-climax. Just another lie.

'I don't believe you, I don't believe you,' Nick said, 'You've forgotten about the tissue damage, the bleeding, the bruising. How d'you explain that if it all gentle lovey dovey like you said. You raped and tormented my daughter and then you killed her, that's what happened. Maybe to you it was just casual sex. Maybe you cared so little for her that you didn't even know that she was struggling against you, then just hoping you would stop...' Nick waved the knife around and Jimmy ducked. 'I don't think she even wanted to go there in the first place. I'll bet there was some story you concocted with that other girl to get her there. You knew it was rape alright, but you didn't care. When you saw the state she was in afterwards, you decided you couldn't let her tell on you, tell what'd happened. Easier just to get rid of her, turn her head down into the water for a few minutes then it's all over. Out the way. That's the way it was and you know it... you said it to Craigsy one night in the wee hut... I heard you... I heard you. And I really wanted to hear you say it again, to own it. I wanted you to admit it directly to me.. Above all I wanted you to own it. I even thought at one time that you might show some remorse, some regret. Stupid eh? I'd even have taken it if you'd only said it because you were scared. But right to the last you've shown yourself up as the dishonourable liar you truly are. So now we're in the endgame. And I'm here to deliver the punishment the court should have given you.'

Nick went up on his toes then, stabbed at his face with the knife but checked his movement within an inch of Jimmy's cheek. It happened so quickly that Jimmy hadn't even flinched.

'James Stevens,' Nick said, 'You're a horror story, whose life is based on violence, expediency and lies. You're never going to change, are you? I think people will thank me for getting you off the streets. Permanently.'

'Awright then,' Jimmy said, his voice hoarse and heavy, 'Nothin to lose now, ay? I'm as good as fucked so you're gonnae get the right story now.' A secretive grin flitted across his face. 'But you winnae like it.'

'What is this? One last play? Yet another *right story*?'

Jimmy hesitated, as if trying to find the exact words, then spat them out into Nick's face. 'Your daughter was a wee hoor who gave blowjobs for fags. An she wasnae even a good ride. I wouldnae even have bothered, but it was her that was wantin it.' He smiled a wee smile, off to the side, as if there was some other person present to appreciate his humour. 'I was doin her a favour,' he said.

Nick was paralysed by Jimmy's brazen taunting.

'Is that no enough for you?' Jimmy said, 'Still canny dae it, can you? You've had aw the chances but you've no got the bottle. Soft as fuck, that's you, soft as fuck. Go on. Try it. Try it if you want tae. See if you can. I'm no feart. I can take you anytime. Your knife's no worth nothin. Shitebag.'

'What!' Nick screamed, 'That's it!'

But before Nick could move, Jimmy grabbed his wrists and wrestled with him, trying to pull him down. They pitched against each other for a moment, but Nick was too strong for him, wrestled one arm free and grabbed Jimmy's shirt at the neck, twisting it, holding him tight, his arm like a rod of iron, immoveable, his face too far away, protected by his long reach. Jimmy's flailing arm was ineffective, his other arm was losing power. Nick forced Jimmy up onto his toes, his hand under Jimmy's chin. Jimmy was losing strength. He was trying to tug Nick's hand away, but he couldn't budge it. Nick broke his other hand, the knife hand, free of Jimmy's grasp.

'James Stevens,' he said in a solemn formal voice, pointing the knife towards Jimmy, 'You have been found guilty of the rape and murder of my daughter Ruth Innocenti, and the sentence of this court is that you suffer the same punishment as you doled out to her... the sentence of death... and this knife will deliver that sentence.' Jimmy stretched for the knife in Nick's hand, but although he couldn't reach it, he noticed that Nick's grip on the knife had suddenly slackened. And Nick was looking not at Jimmy, but behind him; there must be something he'd seen that had caught his attention. 'What the hell,' Nick was saying, 'What the hell is she doing here?'

Jimmy didn't hesitate. He grabbed for Nick's wrist, turned it back and with all his body weight behind the blow, he buried the knife up to the hilt in Nick's stomach, just below his sternum. He twisted it in as far as it would go. Nick was sinking to his knees, his eyes still focused somewhere down the hill, when Jimmy began to speak, fluently, as he twisted the knife, twisting and twisting it in deeper, deeper, right up to the hilt, again and again. 'I got you, ya big cunt,' he said, 'You fuckin beauty! You missed your chance an I fuckin got you. kent I'd fuckin get through this.' Jimmy was triumphant now, yelling. 'I kent I'd get ma wee chance. All I needed. A wee chance. Youse are aw soft, cunts likesay you. An I'll tell you somethin else,' Nick was on his knees now and Jimmy had followed him down too, up close in his face, still twisting the knife. 'You're gonnae get the truth now awright, ya cunt. It was like I said already,' he laughed, 'Just like I said. Only the thing is,' he laughed again, 'It wasnae. It was the opposite.' Jimmy pulled Nick's chin up. 'Can you hear me, ya cunt?' he shouted, 'She didnae want tae dae nothin, ay no? She was bleatin away like a wee fuckin sheep - she wanted her ma, she wanted her da. It's no as if there wis anything to bleat about ay? I wis gonnae give her the time o her life. But you're right. That wis Sadie. She got it aw sorted out, got her to come over. Ruth never even kent I wis gonnae be there, like.' Jimmy saw recognition and pain in Nick's eyes. 'She watched Sadie and me getting it on, then when Sadie conks oot, I get all fuckin frisky wi her. When she wouldnae play along, I shuts her the fuck up, then I wis inside her even though I could hardly get my cock intae her wee fanny it was that fuckin tight.' He slapped Nick's face then. 'Listen! Can you still hear me you big bastard?' Jimmy was still holding Nick's chin now, keeping his head up, 'Can you fuckin hear me?' But there was no strength in Nick's body, its weight falling on Jimmy. Pushing back at Nick, Jimmy overbalanced and fell on top of him, their faces up close. 'I fucked your daughter man, I fucked her stupid, right up her tight wee cunt.'

Nick was whispering something, trying to get it out. Jimmy strained to hear it in the wind.

'An eye for an eye ...' Nick was whispering with his fading breath, '... and... the world's... blind.'

Jimmy pushed himself up on his arms then, glaring down at Nick below him.

'Ken what happened after that,' Jimmy said, 'It wis just like you said yoursell. She wisnae much use for anythin else. Says she's gonnae tell her da, tell her teacher, tell the polis. So, I just puts her oot her misery, ay? Just slips her wee heid under the water till she wisnae breathin. Didnae take long. She didnae suffer at aw. Didnae even twitch. It was a mercy, ay?' Jimmy smiled at Nick but there was no response. Nick was gone.

Jimmy pulled at the knife. It didn't come away easily. He had to put his foot on Nick's chest to get it out. He looked down on Nick and kicked his ribs. There was no reaction. 'Fucker,' he shouted, 'Fuckin bastardin fuckin cuntin fucker!' He kicked Nick's chin, once, twice, three times, then he took out his cock and pissed on Nick's body, took a step further up and pissed on his face, waggling his cock so that the hot stream went into the mouth, over the eyes, dribbled down his cheeks and into his ears. He put it away, zipped himself up and turned down the slope towards the sea with the knife in his hand. In the dusk, he could see a light-coloured coat, someone moving away on the grass below, climbing down over the edge of the cliff. He picked up the torch and sprachled down towards the spot, a surge of new life rushing through his veins.

* * *

Sam had panicked when she realized that Nick was the one underneath, when she saw that Jimmy was on top, when she saw the glint of the knife in his hand. She'd hurried back down the slope towards the ladder to get out of sight, but as she tried to get her footing right on the top rung of the ladder, she looked up again and saw Jimmy turning towards her, starting to move down the steep slope. She slid and stepped her way down the ladder and made for the wet rocks that skirted the little bay.

Up above Jimmy was thinking about what'd happened: self defence it was, for sure. And did he not have a story? What a fuckin story! He'd been kidnapped, abused, tortured in the back of the pickup being hurled round half of Scotland, made to walk here in his own piss and shit, then the big cunt had tried to kill him. So, when he got the chance, he'd defended himself and, in the struggle, the knife went in. If he hadnae wanted to die, he shouldnae have taken out the knife. Nae choice. The person at the cliff edge - she'd seen it. Could maybe back him up. He reached the ladder top and could see Sam in the gloaming, already at the bottom of the ladder, moving away across the stony beach below.

'Hey missus,' he shouted, 'Come back. I'll no harm you. I've just freed mysell. Missus!! Hey!!'

He jumped over and slid the length of the ladder, hardly touching a rung, caught up with her quite easily as she tried to scramble away, making only slow progress over the bigger rocks to the south of the bay, slippy with seaweed. He shouted to her again, close up now, and this time she heard his voice. A breaker crashed over the rocks and soaked her feet. She turned towards him, facing him across a large boulder, only a few feet apart now.

'I'm no gonnae harm you missus' Jimmy shouted over the roar of the sea, 'It was him or me, ken: him or me... he was trying to kill us... I didnae mean tae... but in the fight, ken, his knife went intae him... an it was him pulled the knife, mind, no me... it wasnae ma fault... he was gonnae kill me... you saw it, ay? ... you'll back me up, ay?'

She lifted her head and pulled her hair back off her face, projected her voice, her words measured against the wild sea behind. 'You must be Jimmy Stevens, aren't you?'

His eyes flashed surprise and suspicion. He brought up the knife, red with Nick's blood. 'Aye Ahm are. How d'you ken my name, like?'

'Who doesn't know it?' she said, 'Your name's been on the telly. The whole country knows it. You're quite a celebrity!'

Jimmy squared his shoulders. 'How come?'

'Since you were kidnapped, there's been people looking all over for you. Thank God we've found you safe and well. What about him?' her head nodded up towards the cliffs, 'Is he the kidnapper?'

'Aye... An he's deid an aw, the bastard. Self defence it wis. He wis gonnae kill me.

'Come on then,' she slipped and slid closer. 'We'll need to get you back up somewhere safe. Get you checked over. I'll call for a helicopter to come and find us. It'll be too dark for us to go back over that rough terrain.'

She pulled a tissue from her pocket and offered it, palm up, towards Jimmy.

'You'd better give me the knife,' she said, 'I'll keep it in this tissue till the police can examine it. They'll want fingerprint tests... all that kind of stuff.'

He placed the knife on the tissue and she folded the tissue over before storing it in her jacket pocket. 'OK. Let's go,' she said, stretching her arm out to shepherd him ahead of her, while skipping up onto a large boulder, above and behind him, a shot-sized stone in her hand. She raised the stone high above her head and shouted his name.

'Jimmy!'

As he turned round, she crashed the stone into his temple as fast and as hard as she could, the weight of her body fully behind the blow. It threw him down, his limbs at awkward angles. She jumped down after him. Summoning all her strength, she raised the stone again and before he could move out the way caught him for a second time square on the same spot. This time there was a crunching sound. His body twitched, twitched again and lay still. She hit him again on the same spot. There were bits of bone, blood and brain on the stone in her hand. She removed the knife from her pocket then unwrapped it and laid it down beside his outstretched fingers.

She was already rehearsing the conversation with the police as she looked down at his body. 'It was terrible, Inspector. When he realized that I'd seen him killing Nick, he came after me. He had the knife in his hand, but he slipped on the rocks and that gave me one chance to save myself. I hit him as hard as I could and then hit him again, in case he was just stunned.' She smiled: grimaced more like. It would certainly do her ratings no harm. A shiver of cold guilt ran through her, thinking of her ratings, in the middle of this tragedy. How could she? But she owned it. She knew she could make the most of her story. And Jimmy wouldn't be there to tell a different story, any more than Ruth had been. There was some justice in that.

* * *

She threw the stone out to sea and tucked the tissue into her pocket. The roaring tide was on its way in. If it engulfed Jimmy's body, so much the better. She didn't care, sitting, letting the wind tousle her hair, listening to the surf, she let go of her own grey tears. She thought briefly of stripping off, leaving her clothes on the stony beach, letting the cold water run around her body and take her under. But no. That wasn't her.

She climbed wearily back up the rusting ladder, up to where Nick's body lay. Sitting down beside him, she hovered her fingers over his face. There was no breathing, just the wetness of his lips and the wind in his hair. She put her hand to his heart, but there were no beats, no tremors: his body was already turning cold. The only sound was the sound of the waves crashing on the stony shore below. She lifted his head and shuffled over so she could lay it in her lap. She closed his eyes, brushed the hair back off his face, placed the tissue – the tissue she'd used to touch the knife – on his wound and held it there.

'Nick!' she said, 'You stupid man. I should have seen it before, but now I understand fully: this was the only closure you really wanted to find, wasn't it?'

Printed in Great Britain
by Amazon

87774718R00119